GOVERNOR

Governor Trilogy
Book 1

Lesli Richardson

Dear Copper,

Happy Reading!

Lesli Richardson /

Tymbr Dalton

AUTHOR'S NOTE

Florida politics are messy, nasty, sexy, brutal, funny, insane, impossibly complex, and a lot of fun to write about. (Mostly because they're messy, nasty, sexy, brutal, funny, insane, and impossibly complex.)

Since the focus of this trilogy isn't the politics so much as it is the people, I've taken certain liberties and simplified a few things here and there.

The kinky shit, however, is absolutely realistic.

In this series, however, Covid-19 isn't a thing, so it's not mentioned.

DEDICATION

For Hubby, who keeps me going, for believing in me, and for putting up with me when I'm in frantic mega-bitch mode from working on insane deadlines.

For Trish, my bestie and PA, who also helps keep me sane(ish), and who when I first told her about Carter the bastard extraordinaire said I needed to write him ASAP.

To all my readers—thank you for continuing to buy my books, and your patience with me.

And for Sir—He knows why.

Governor
Governor Trilogy Book 1

Copyright © 2018 by Lesli Richardson
First Print Publication: September 2018

www.LesliRichardson.com

CHAPTER ONE

Now

It's hard not to shiver when the AC kicks on as I kneel, naked, on the floor of my new office, the carpet doing little to cushion my knees. My hands remain clasped behind my head, back straight, elbows out.

This is how he's trained me, and what he expects of me.

My knees are spread as wide as I can manage and still keep my heels tucked under my ass.

He circles me, inspecting me as he smiles and tugs on his shirt cuffs, adjusting the lay of the cufflinks. I know he wants to strip off that suit he's wearing and fuck me right here, spread over my new desk, but he's holding himself back.

Waiting.

I keep my gaze fixed straight ahead, even though my hard cock has a will of its own and is probably dribbling a puddle all over the towel Carter thought to put down before ordering me to kneel.

He might be a bastard extraordinaire, but he's also very practical.

He looks pleased with himself, and he has every right to be. He's the only man I kneel for and he damn well knows it.

It's a price I willingly pay to be owned by *Her*.

His wife.

Who is also, as of when we were sworn in at one o'clock this very afternoon, my lieutenant governor for the great state of Florida.

* * *

Carter Wilson, bastard extraordinaire, is eight years older than me, a decorated Army veteran, my best friend, college roommate, one of my two closest confidants, my chief of staff…

And he's the Master and husband of Susannah Evans.

Susa owns me—mind, heart, soul, and body—and has ever since I first met her in college.

Since she owns me, that means I belong to Carter by default. It was the deal I willingly accepted all those years ago.

Susa grew up the daughter of a lawyer, a progressive Republican who pretty much ran the state GOP for decades. Still does, unofficially now. Benchley Evans was a county administrator, then a county commissioner, followed by four terms as a state rep, and two more as a state senator. The only reason he didn't run for the big G or a national office was a massive heart attack that made his wife put her foot down and demand he choose his family over party and politics for once in his damn life.

He also hailed from a family that first made their fortune in citrus and cattle. As freezes and canker and greening took down the citrus industry, and the exploding housing market chipped away at cattle lands, he'd already moved on to land development, jumping in early when acreage was still cheap.

That meant he could easily afford to send his only daughter to any college she chose, for any degree she wanted.

It was my luck—good or bad, you decide—that we ended up in Tampa together, selecting majors and minors that would help us with law degrees.

But she's also smarter than me in many ways. Far more ruthless politically. That's why, when Carter decided we could change our home state in good ways, Susa insisted it should be me who ran for governor on a third-party ticket.

This time.

After eight years—if I win re-election, that is—she'll be perfectly positioned for her own gubernatorial bid.

I'll do my best to get her elected. Once I'm out of office, I'll return to the private sector while still championing a few key causes that are near and dear to my heart.

But what I'll be looking forward to most by then is time out of the public eye.

For at least the next four years, my official residence is the Florida Governor's Mansion in Tallahassee. I can't simply choose to *not* live there, because it'd be a logistics nightmare for my security detail, as well as an unnecessary expense for taxpayers.

Considering two of the key planks in the platform we ran on were better budgeting and smarter spending, I can't do something that would so blatantly fly in the face of those ideals.

I especially can't cite wanting to be with Susa and Carter whenever I choose as the reason.

I still own my house just outside Tampa, next door to Carter and Susa's house and sharing the same backyard fence. But for the most part, I won't be staying there during my term. Besides, there's already a calendar full of official state functions, and many of them will be held at the mansion that is now my home.

My only consolation is that Carter, as my chief of staff, is expected to either be with me or be on call for me twenty-four/seven. No one will suspect anything untoward if he's spotted coming and going at odd hours. Susa's presence, both as Carter's wife and my lieutenant governor, will not raise many eyebrows, unless she regularly shows up at the mansion at an unusually late hour without Carter or staff of her own. One of the trade-offs we'd already talked about and figured into our plans was that by embarking on this path we'd lose privacy.

Carter is more than ready and willing to give me what I need and crave when Susannah is unable to. He's also ready and willing to be a warm body in my bed so I won't feel so alone every night.

Because before the whirlwind that was my campaign to become governor, the three of us shared a bed nearly every night.

* * *

Where I'm kneeling about three feet from the far end of my desk, I can't be seen when Carter answers the knock on my office door after unlocking it and cracking it open to see who it is. He moves aside just enough to allow someone else to step in, and my breath catches, my pulse races.

Her.

"I only have a few minutes," Susa says in her usual clipped, all-business tone.

Carter closes and locks the door behind her and, moving faster than it seems possible for a human to manage, grabs a handful of hair, tipping her head back.

"*What* was that, *pet*?" he softly growls.

She's never allowed to use that tone on Carter and she damn well knows it.

Her entire posture and voice change, needy and soft, even as my own body responds to Carter's tone. "I only have a few minutes, Sir."

I struggle not to smile, not to laugh. With today's craziness, she likely forgot herself.

I only wish I could be there later tonight to watch when Carter reminds her who she belongs to.

He marches her around behind my desk and I allow my gaze to follow them. He bends her forward over the desk, making her put her hands flat on it, and hikes up her skirt. Since she's also wearing three-inch heels, it means her gorgeous ass sticks out nicely.

"Who said you could wear panties today, pet?" I hear the fabric rip and a quiet *meep* from her.

"Sorry, Sir. I thought—"

"You thought *wrong*."

Another violation.

She's going to have fun sitting tomorrow.

She's lucky we already did a sound check one evening last week, before I took office, and we discovered Carter can't spank us in here if someone's in the outer office.

Like Julia, my administrative assistant.

Who, right now, is sitting out there at her desk, along with a trooper from my security detail.

Holding out the offending material, Carter walks over to me with a playful smile on his face. "Do you believe this shit? Looks like a certain pet has forgotten her place."

"I see that, Sir."

He turns from me, stuffing her ruined panties into his left front slacks pocket. I have a feeling they'll probably end up in my mouth later.

Not the first time he's gagged me with her panties.

Not saying I mind it, either.

"Loyalty."

I immediately relax into the position, knees still wide, but my back now rounded, my left hand on my thigh, my right flat on the floor, my gaze focused down.

It's a Carter thing.

It works—that's all that matters. Countless times he's put me into this position during the day behind a locked office door, but with my clothes on. Especially if it's been a rough day and I need a quick reset.

I can think about *Him*, about what we have together.

It's not a one-way street. Carter is loyal to us, always putting us first no matter what. That might sound odd to someone who doesn't know the three of us. There's a lot of bullshit out there about what people "should" or "shouldn't" do.

Carter sets his own path, trims his sails, and we follow.

Loyalty.

When I first idly floated what at the time I thought was a ridiculous proposition—running for governor—it was Carter, and then Susannah, who had my back and were my most vocal and vicious supporters.

Loyalty.

She is my queen, my heart and soul, my sun and my moon, all rolled into one. My muse, my reason for living. I would kill or die for her if it came down to it. I would—and have—embarrassed the hell out of myself just to make her smile.

Loyalty.

All of these things I think of as I slow my breathing and my back muscles loosen, enjoying a break from the more formal *Primed* position.

Primed is always performed naked. Frequently for long stretches of time. The bastard extraordinaire takes great pride in sometimes torturing me while in that position, expecting me to maintain it.

Or expecting me to fail to maintain it, which brings punishment.

Win-win.

But that's life with Carter.

I didn't say I didn't enjoy it.

* * *

In *Loyalty*, I can hear what's going on but, because of where I'm kneeling and with my head bowed, I can't see.

But I can imagine, based on the sounds.

Her low, pained grunts as she struggles to stay quiet probably

6

means he's pinching or maybe even biting the insides of her thighs.

Which are now, most likely, covered with her own juices.

She enjoys life with Carter, too. We wouldn't be here if we didn't. While this is not a place I ever envisioned myself being, now that I'm here I cannot imagine being anywhere else.

I don't even mean this office.

I mean with these two people, and especially with Carter.

Carter at his best is a loving, kind, gentle, compassionate, funny, brilliant, gorgeous, sexy man.

Since I consider myself straight, those last two are pretty damn fine compliments.

Carter at his worst is evil, sadistic, mean, brilliant, gorgeous, and…

Yeah, sexy.

It pains me to admit that.

No, I'm usually *literally* in pain when I admit it.

Not that he would consider any of those descriptors an insult.

And, again, not that I'm complaining, because I'm not. I wouldn't be here if I didn't want to be.

I know I don't have to speak up and remind him of the time. It might not seem like he's watching the clock, but I'm sure he's calculating exactly how much he can cram into what little time the three of us have alone together right now.

Maybe perhaps *literally* cram.

That doesn't even bother me anymore.

After a few minutes of him torturing her, he speaks.

"*Boy.*"

I'm on deck. I smoothly rise to my feet even as they sting, full of pins and needles and protesting they still need a moment to recover.

Carter smiles at me and my cock twitches. "Come here."

His fist is buried in her hair, her cheek is pressed against the desk, and her skirt is now rucked up around her waist. She's gorgeous and mussed, her blue eyes wild with that special kind of energy Carter has a particular way of building in both of us.

That *please fuck me* look.

Our times together have been few and far between lately, first with our grueling campaign schedule, and now with taking office. We went from sleeping together every night to sometimes barely seeing each other for days at a time.

That, above all, has been the most difficult part of all of this, losing that privacy, that time together. Not even sexy time. I mean being able to close our eyes, take a deep breath, and relax with our heads in Carter's lap.

We've all had adjustments to make. Susa and I trust Carter to take care of us, though.

Like right now.

I'm sure whatever Carter has in mind will carry us through until the next rare time the three of us can be alone together.

Because it will have to.

CHAPTER TWO

Then

Looking back on when our paths initially intersected, the first time I met Carter Wilson I was convinced he was a quietly cocky asshole.

I wasn't right.

I wasn't exactly wrong, either. I came to learn that it wasn't a personality flaw so much as it was one of his charms. Not a bug, but a feature.

As the old saying goes, it's not bragging if it's true.

Which was the funny thing. Because with everything that Carter is and does, despite unintentionally coming off a little cocky, he is not a braggart. Definitely not boastful. Sometimes, he'll even tell you things he's done, if you ask him the right way and at the right time. Yet you get the feeling upon his retelling of events that it was no big deal to him, at the time.

Even when it's rightfully a big deal to everyone else.

Especially things that are a big deal to everyone else.

Maybe it was the age difference between us, or my lack of real-world experience at the time that made me read his surety in pretty much everything he did as "cocky," because it wasn't that he was preening and pecking and making himself look like an ass.

If anything, he is a master of blending in and *not* being noticed. Look up *subtlety* in the dictionary and you'll see his face.

Which, again, fit him perfectly once I learned more about him.

My initial read of him was due ninety-nine percent to me and the filter all of my perceptions flowed through at that time rather than the one percent that was truly about him.

I'm not even exaggerating that ratio. Not in the slightest.

We ended up as roommates in campus housing, a "quad pod" in the oldest dorm building, where we shared a room and a bathroom with each other, and a small common kitchen and dining/lounge area with three other rooms, for a total of eight people in that particular space.

Carter was a sophomore at the University of South Florida in Tampa, and so was I, but he was eight years older than me. At first, I didn't know why he'd started his college career late. Considering I thought he was a cocky asshole nearly upon first sight, I wasn't about to delve too deeply into that well, at the time. I figured I'd find out soon enough.

And I did.

It was the Friday before classes were to start. I'd arrived bright and early so I could hopefully beat my unknown roommate there and grab the bed I wanted. Unfortunately, my scholarship wouldn't pay for one of the newer apartment-style dorm rooms, so I was stuck with this. And since my roommate from last year flunked out, and I didn't know anyone else who'd be in the same dorm situation I was, I would get potluck as far as a roommate and pray for someone who wasn't a slovenly asshole.

Later that first afternoon, after we'd both unpacked—well, okay, Carter was completely unpacked and settled within twenty minutes of his arrival a couple of hours after I'd *started* moving in, and there I was *still* struggling and figuring out how to store my shit two hours later.

That's when, with his back turned to me, Carter removed his shirt. Just a simple gesture, nothing unusual about it.

Until I actually *saw* his back.

I think I made a noise or something because he froze, his head partially turned. Not even looking at me but I got the distinct impression he could see me just fine with his peripheral vision.

"Not pretty, is it?"

I swallowed, my throat clicking as I did. "H-how…what happened?"

His back, while well-muscled, was a gnarled mass of pink scars, what looked like cuts and burns. A hellish road map of pain and trauma disappearing under the waistband of his jeans.

"In-country happened." I suspected from his tone of voice he didn't want to clarify, so I let it drop while he continued changing.

That one exchange perfectly sums up Carter. There was an encyclopedia's worth of pain and bravery and downright *literal* heroism behind the story, which he could have easily mined and immediately turned me into a devoted friend for life based on his stories alone.

He didn't.

Again, that pretty much sums up Carter.

* * *

If you look at Carter's side of our shared dorm room later that afternoon, other than the fact that he has sheets and pillows on his bed, and a pair of sneakers neatly sitting on the floor next to his bed, and a well-worn backpack on his desk, you'd be hard-pressed to think he's even brought anything with him.

Here I am, still vainly trying to make all my shit fit in the dresser, bookshelf, desk drawers, and shove the overflow under my bed and into my closet, including the four totes of extra clothes and other crap I thought I'd need. My TV and DVD player sit on top of the dresser, and my desk looks like my school shit has exploded all over it and is making paper and book babies. While I just made my bed with clean sheets, it still resembles a Sunday late-afternoon hotel room checkout following a really bad—or maybe really good—bachelor party.

I silently stew about all this because I consider myself a neat person. I *had* to be, growing up in my mother's house, or there'd be hell to pay.

Last year, my roommate and I were both very tidy. Although this year I have a lot more crap I've brought with me.

I glance Carter's way every time I make one more futile trip over to my closet and back while trying to tame my gargantuan mess into some semblance of order. As Carter lies stretched out on his bed and silently reads his Kindle without even glancing my direction, I can't help but feel…less-than.

Admittedly a feeling I am used to—once again, from growing up in my mother's house—but at the time this is happening, I *literally* don't have the vocabulary to put it all into context or give it neat and tidy labels.

All I know is that this cocky asshole I've barely spoken five words to since his arrival has shown me up without even trying.

Again, Carter isn't even *trying* to show me up in the first place. My logical brain *knows* this.

My emotions, however, are a fucking mess.

I finally end up kicking another of the totes under my bed, along with an overflowing laundry basket holding my clean towels and extra linens.

A soft snort from the man on the other side of the room catches my attention.

I turn. "What?" I snap.

"Nothing, man. Would you like some help?" During my struggle, he's walked back and forth a couple of times, to the bathroom, or out of the room and back again. While he hasn't been obvious about it, I'd spotted him observing my lack of progress ⋅

during those journeys.

It's on the tip of my tongue to shoot him a snarky reply—

Except yeah, I *do* need help. If I get snarky with him, I might not receive that help. Plus, the tone he'd asked it in *wasn't* snarky. He'd sounded genuinely warm.

Not to mention I have a lot of experience holding back my initial, tip-of-my-tongue responses.

Thanks, Mom.

"Thanks," I mutter. "I'd appreciate it."

He shuts off his Kindle and tucks it into the top drawer of the two-drawer nightstand next to his bed. Then he stands and rounds the desk/bookshelf combo we each have and which sit back-to-back between the beds to form a natural divider.

He's wearing jeans and a dark grey Tampa Bay Lightning T-shirt that cling to his leanly muscled torso. He isn't some top-heavy gym rat. Combined with the lines in his face, he looks like a guy who's earned his muscles the hard way, not in a CrossFit class.

Another way in which I feel I don't exactly measure up, even though I'm not in bad shape.

Carter stands there for a moment, hands on his hips, his dark brown eyes taking in everything before he walks over and opens my top dresser drawer.

I've brought two suitcases of clothes—also now stowed under my bed—but brought several garbage bags full, too. And my closet is stuffed.

I'd learned that past spring to literally move everything out of my mother's home if I wanted to keep my shit. I've left more things in a small storage unit I'm renting at a complex close to the campus.

When I lived in the dorm during my freshman year, Mom cleaned out my room for me over Easter break. I was lucky she left some things boxed up in her garage.

But I'll never forgive her for discarding my belongings, items she'd tossed because they had no value to *her*. Many of my books, comic books, mementos, other things.

Or, more correctly, things she'd discarded knowing they *had* value to *me*. Irreplaceable loss which was laser-focused, deliberately designed to hurt me. I wish I was exaggerating, but it's not the first time she's done something like that for that very reason.

I've determined it *will* be the last time. Hence...*this* mess.

"Let's start here, Owen," Carter says. His tone sounds patient, warm, and I quickly shed any indignation or resentment I started with, because he actually *teaches* me how to refold everything.

Without an ounce of condescension.

By the time we finish that part nearly an hour later, with me doing most of the folding after he shows me the best way to tackle each type of garment, I've emptied my remaining totes of clothes, and my closet no longer looks like it's going to explode. The spare towels and linens have also been moved to a tote, leaving my laundry basket empty and ready for use.

"Are you some sort of ninja minimalist organizer?" I ask, only half kidding.

He doesn't smile, but one corner of his mouth turns up in a slight quirk I'd later come to learn indicated how amused Carter feels. "No."

"How'd you learn how to do this?"

"US Army beats it into grunts during basic. Let's remake your rack."

I'm still processing the first sentence and didn't realize what he meant by the second, until he starts stripping the sheets from my bed.

Five minutes later, under Carter's careful tutelage, my "rack" looks as put-together as Carter's does. I almost don't want to sit on it, it's so neat.

"Thank you, Carter." I hold out my hand.

of the room, the car's interior is showroom-neat. It might as well be brand new.

He now wears sunglasses that hide his brown eyes. He shrugs, a gesture I'll soon come to learn is so typically Carter. "The Snot Box was cheap, it runs, I could afford to pay cash for it, and all my shit fits in it." A smile quirks his lips. "And it's so ugly I'm hoping no one ever steals it."

Those are all perfectly valid reason to own a car as disgustingly green as this one. "The Snot Box?"

He points at the hood through the windshield and smiles, as if it's self-explanatory.

Which, actually, it is. "Fair enough," I say. At least he seems to have a sense of humor. "What's your major?"

"I plan to attend Stetson for my law degree. Right now, I'm going poli sci for my major, with a criminal justice minor."

"Well, we've got that in common. I want to attend Stetson, too. Only I'm a criminal justice major with a poli sci minor. How old are you, again?"

"Twenty-eight," he says. "And no, I won't buy alcohol for you while you're underage, sorry."

I try not to feel defensive over that "Not that I was going to ask. I'll be twenty-one in six weeks. I have better things to do than risk my scholarship getting drunk."

He shrugs again, an easy kind of gesture indicating no skin off his nose. "Just wanted to put it out there. Pissed off my roommate last year."

"Why?"

"Because I wouldn't buy him alcohol. Once you hit twenty-one, obviously, it doesn't matter."

"I'm not a drinker." Although I leave out the fact that life with my mother would drive any rational person to take up alcoholism as a professional hobby.

Which is probably why my step-father smokes pot behind her

back on a regular basis.

"Even better. Last roommate was. He got pissed off when I reported him to the RA after warning him I would do exactly that."

"Why'd you do that?"

"Because he and his friends—who were all underaged—wanted to drink in our room. I didn't give a shit if he wanted to break the law and university rules, but I'm not losing *my* scholarship or risking *my* ass with law enforcement for tolerating underaged drinking in *my* room. Fuck that noise."

"Ah. I can respect that."

"Good. So what happened to your roommate from last year?"

"He flunked out."

Carter smirks again. "Leaving you stuck with me. Lucky you."

He *had* helped me out. I decide to give him a chance and keep an open mind. "You say that like you're hard to live with."

He shrugs. "Fair warning, sometimes I have nightmares."

I wasn't sure why he was telling me that. "Um, okay?"

"And, serious warning, do not *ever* sneak up on me and try to scare me. You won't like what happens. In fact, try to make a little noise when coming and going. Even if you think I'm asleep. I would prefer that you do that. I'll never yell at you for waking me up, I promise."

That, at least, didn't sound cocky. It sounded serious. "Can I ask why?"

A dark cloud briefly envelops his features. "I…don't react well to being startled. PTSD. Nearly broke my last roommate's arm when he did it, him thinking he was going to be funny. Even after I'd warned him not to."

I don't know how to react at first. "Oh." Then I remember the view I had of his back. "Is that all related to you being in the military?"

This grim smirk is devoid of humor. "Yeah, you could say that." He falls silent, leaving us to listen to Mumford & Sons'

Babel album.

At least he has great taste in music, and seems to be an honest guy.

I can work with that.

* * *

We stop at a sports bar before we reach the grocery store. It's one of a local chain of restaurants that dot the Tampa Bay area landscape. I've never eaten at this one before, but it's a more PG-rated version of Hooters, with waitresses who are dressed in garments that are actually more substantial than a mere suggestion of clothes, and the only breasts on the menu are poultry.

The hostess seats us at a booth near the back of the restaurant at Carter's request. When the waitress arrives to take our drink orders, I'm still mentally running through my bills and my bank balance to see what I can afford from the menu.

Carter neatly cuts off my thoughts. "I'll have water and sweet tea, please," he says. "And this is all on my check." He circles his fingers at the table, indicating me, too.

"Just water, please," I say, and she leaves to get them. My focus darts across the table, meeting his dark brown gaze. Flecks of other colors make a subtle appearance there, amber and hazel and dark chocolate. "Thanks."

A hint of humor returns to his features. "You haven't had to put up with one of my nightmares yet. I'd like to build some goodwill while I still can."

"You did that by helping me get organized. Sorry again for that. I swear I'm not a slob."

He shrugs. "Some people don't learn the skills. Can't do something you were never taught."

"I'm usually much more organized. I have a lot more room at home."

"And where is home?" His focus returns to the menu in his

hands.

"Orlando. I mean, my mom lives in Orlando. Where are you from?"

"Vermont, originally."

"Why'd you come to Florida for school?"

He doesn't look up from his menu. "No damn snow, for starters. Then there's the James A. Haley Veteran's Hospital right off campus. I wanted a school close to a large VA hospital."

I feel the click in my throat as I swallow, the image of his back flashing through my mind again. "Oh."

He doesn't move his head, but I feel his gaze on me anyway. "Ask, if you want to. Either I'll answer, or I'll tell you I don't want to talk about it. I'm rarely offended by the ask, if it's polite."

"I don't want to be...rude." Everything about Carter so far knocks me off-balance, but he's not doing it deliberately. I realize it's all *me*, on *my* end.

Like I've forgotten how to adult properly.

Then again, he's eight years older than me, so maybe he thinks of me as a kid.

Now his chin tips up and to the side as he studies me. "As long as what I tell you doesn't get spread around, I'll talk about most stuff. Assume anything I tell you is to be kept in confidence, unless I say it in front of others. Even then, assume on the side of privacy."

"When I saw your back earlier, you kind of sounded like you didn't want to talk about it."

"That was before I realized you're not an asshole."

"Thanks, I think."

He smirks. "You're welcome, kid."

I'm not going to ding him for that, because hell, he *is* older than me.

And he *is* paying for my dinner. "How long were you in the Army?"

"Nearly eight years. Enlisted at eighteen. Pissed my father off."

"Why?"

"Because I didn't want to go through ROTC. For starters, the instructor at our high school was a dick. Always discouraged minorities and girls from wanting to join. Fuck that shit. I didn't want anything to do with him and decided to take my chances. I also didn't want to go to college first. Once I was done with my time in, I wanted to be out and *done*. My brothers all did ROTC in college and went in as commissioned officers. My dad retired from the Army after nearly forty years. Two of my four brothers are still in. Two aren't."

"Four brothers?"

"Six brothers, total." The waitress brings our beverages and says she'll be right back to take our orders before she heads over to another table of eight people just seated by the hostess.

"What do your other two brothers do for a living?" I ask once we're alone again.

He sips his iced tea and doesn't meet my gaze for a moment. "Killed in action," he quietly says.

That's Carter to a *T*. Economy of speech, economy of living. I'm left sitting there feeling like shit, but Carter takes pity on me. "You have any siblings?"

I shake my head. "Only child. Well, by my father, I have two much younger half siblings I've never met. They live out in Nevada. Sister and brother. Basically, I'm an only child."

"I take it your parents are divorced?"

"Yeah. Dad lives in Las Vegas with wife number three and the two kids. My mom was wife two. My mom and Austin, my step-father, live in Orlando. They got married when I was ten. I haven't seen Dad since before then."

"Ah."

"Yeah. We don't talk about Dad much at my house, unless it's Mom and Austin inventing descriptive new ways to insult him."

Which is a mild way of putting it. It's actually an Olympic-worthy sporting event in my mother's house, and everyone's expected to actively participate or risk being viewed as giving aid and comfort to the enemy.

"Sorry," Carter says.

I shrug. "It is what it is."

"I heard that." He picks up his glass of tea and holds it out to me. I realize what he wants and grab my glass of water. "To a good year," he says, gently clinking glasses with me.

"To a good year," I echo.

"Cheers."

"Cheers," I reply.

His gaze locks on mine for a long moment. I don't understand why the intensity I suddenly read there does...something to my insides.

Not in a bad way, either.

I'm straight or I'd label it attraction or desire, anything in that realm.

I sip my water and return my attention to the menu.

* * *

When Carter finds out I can't even scramble eggs—and that I survived my freshman year thanks to the meal plan paid for by my scholarship—he decides that's where we're going to start my culinary education.

"Most people can eat breakfast at any time of the day," he says. "If you end up with hungover buddies, you'll be their hero if you can scramble delicious eggs and make French toast." He glances my way. "Or if you want to impress your girl when she sleeps over."

I laugh at that. "You kind of need a girlfriend to make that happen. I haven't had time for a social life, much less a love life. I can't afford to let my grades slip."

"Good. We'll get along great, then." He's leading me through Publix, back to the dairy section to get eggs, milk, cheese. We buy sugar, cinnamon, vanilla extract. Then over to the bakery, to pick up a baguette.

"Is the kitchen equipped?" I ask. I haven't even looked. Last year's room was in this same building but on a different floor. We didn't have a "kitchen," just a communal fridge, sink, microwave, and two-burner induction cooktop tucked into a tight corner of the common room. I was too busy today futzing around organizing my crap to even look in the kitchen.

"No, but I have what we need. Large blue tote in my closet marked *Mess.* I don't mind if you borrow stuff from there as long as you make sure you wash and dry it immediately and put it back the way you found it when you're finished. And don't loan anything to anyone without asking me first."

"Sure. Thank you."

He nods, then pauses. "You *really* ate every meal like that last year?"

"Yeah. Why?"

"What if the dining halls were all closed?"

"I kept some granola bars and beef jerky in my room."

He literally groans. "*Dude.* You *seriously* need to learn how to take care of yourself better than that."

"All right, *Dad*," I grumble.

When he laughs it sounds genuine, warm. Friendly. He hooks an arm around my neck and pulls me close, scrubbing his knuckles over my scalp. Not painfully, but playfully. Affectionately. He releases me before I barely register he did it. I'm six-four, and Carter's got to be maybe only five-ten, but he feels…*larger.*

Not to mention I sense the restrained power in him.

For the first time in my life, I realize what it might feel like to have a big brother, although I never would have wished the emotional hell of my upbringing on anyone else, much less a sibling.

"Come on." He turns the cart around.

"What?"

"We need more stuff. Basics. I'm going to teach you how to eat like a grown-up." While his words chafe a little, again, he's not wrong.

I tuck my hand-basket, which holds a few essentials like shampoo, into the cart. Carter is now grabbing more groceries, like oatmeal, dried fruit, all sorts of stuff I'm trying not to total up in my head.

"I can't afford to spend a lot," I finally admit.

He shrugs. "This one's on me."

I have my pride, but I'm not an idiot. "Can we take it in trade or something?"

There's a playful twinkle in his eye when he cocks his head at me. "How do you mean?"

"I don't know. I can do your laundry for you or something."

He studies me for a moment before nodding. "Deal. Although I'll never turn down a blowjob." He follows that with a wink and starts moving again, so I know he's kidding.

At least...I *think* he's kidding.

He's kidding, right?

Like hell am I going to ask and look like an even bigger doof than I'm sure he already thinks I am.

Of course *he's kidding.*

I'm...pretty sure.

CHAPTER FOUR

The meal plan I have doesn't kick in until Monday. I really don't want to shell out money at a dining hall when Carter has graciously purchased groceries for us.

He has me go first in the checkout line, since I have so few items.

"I always wanted a little brother," he says as he stacks groceries on the conveyor belt.

"You don't?"

"I *am* the little brother. Mom made Dad get snipped after I was born. She'd always wanted at least one girl. After she had me, she told him if he ever wanted to have sex with her again, he *would* get it done."

"Poor woman."

"Yeah, well, she holds her own against all of us, trust me. We're all terrified of her. I mean, in a good way. She had to be tough with Dad off on deployment so often. I'm not giving her grandkids, though."

"Why's that."

"I got snipped a few years ago, while I was stationed in Germany. Kind of had a thing going with someone then, and it helped with logistics."

"Oh." I'm still waiting for the elderly woman in front of me to count out every fricking coupon in the known galaxy to the checkout clerk, who apparently has an infinite well of patience. "What happened with her?"

He isn't looking at me when he answers, but his voice drops in a way that makes me think it's a painful topic he doesn't really want to discuss. "Things didn't work out."

"Sorry."

"Old news." He shrugs. "You?"

"I'm single."

"I meant kids."

"Kind of need a relationship to have kids."

He gives me a "look." Like a big brother might give a little brother, something between "you know what I mean" and "don't be a smart-ass."

"Eventually, yeah, I'd love to be a father. It's always been a dream of mine." I try not to think about all the emotional baggage surrounding that. "I definitely want kids. School comes first, though. Relationship will have to wait, too. I can't lose my scholarship."

"I don't want to lose my scholarships, either," he says. "I could use government money to pay for an apartment, but I'm trying to save as much of that as possible. That's why I went dorm instead of my own apartment. Way cheaper for me. Keeps me on-campus. Not like I'm not used to bunking with a bunch of other guys. Having only one roommate is sort of an upgrade, for me." He snorts. "Hell, having a real bed and air-conditioning is an upgrade from what I was used to."

I hadn't even thought about all of that. "I figured you picked the dorms because you're from Vermont."

"Nah. Everything I own, with the exception of a few boxes stored at Mom and Dad's place, is in the dorm room. Got used to living light. Raised that way, as many times as we moved when I was a kid for Dad's stations."

"Wow." I mean, I don't have a lot of room to talk, but at least I have a storage unit.

I had more stuff before Mom "cleaned" my room for me. She'll likely never admit it was because I pissed her off by not driving home for Easter dinner because I had spent the entire night before on the toilet, shitting my guts out, thanks to bad sushi.

Mom never gives a sick pass, unless it makes her look good to do so, or it's something like ending up in the hospital, or a communicable bug she might catch.

Likewise, I'll never confront her about what she did, because I know she'll deny the motivation. Which means she'll take satisfaction in lying about it and knowing how much it really bothered me after all.

It's far more satisfying for me *not* to confront her about it, denying her the satisfaction of knowing it burrowed under my skin. It's the only weapon I currently have against the narcissist.

I'm getting the feeling Carter and I will likely get along well this year.

"Not to get ahead of myself," I say, "but if things go okay this year, mind me calling dibs on you as a roommate next year?"

He smiles. "Sounds like a plan to me."

The cashier finally rings me out and I pay for my stuff using my debit card. I try to hand Carter a twenty, the only cash I have on me, but he waves me off.

"It's okay. If I couldn't afford it, I wouldn't do it. Another benefit of this is I have very little in expenses. Besides school, I have my cell phone and car insurance."

"That's it?"

"That's it. I'm drawing a disability pension right now, and I have the stipend from my scholarship. VA takes care of my medical. I'm okay."

Back at the dorm I help him carry everything inside, trying to grab the heaviest bags myself since he's the one who bought it all.

All the cold stuff he bought fits neatly in the two small fridges in our room.

Well, *Carter* makes it neatly fit. I suspect if I'd tried putting it away it wouldn't have worked.

"Bring me one of your empty totes," he says.

I do, and the rest of our non-perishables fit in that, with plenty of room for it to sit next to the fridges and still be out of our way.

His voice drops. "Once we get to know the others, then maybe we can store our stuff in the big fridge in the kitchen. I don't want to have to drop into asshole mode our first weekend here because someone ate our shit."

"Sounds like a plan to me."

He toes off his sneakers. "I go for a run most mornings, if you'd like to join me. Let me clarify—I go out every morning. Might be more of a slow stroll than an actual run tomorrow, depending on my pain. I need to scope out the exercise room in this dorm and see if I like it, or if I'll have to go over to the gym. I'll probably do weights or machines some mornings if I can't manage a walk or run. I get bored on a treadmill."

I've been wanting to get into an exercise routine and this sounds perfect. "Thanks. I'd like that." I find myself…I don't want to use the word "clinging," but there really isn't a better word.

I'm already clinging to Carter.

Except I don't have siblings—who I actually know—my parents are worthless, and I really don't have any close friends.

Carter's good with it, right? Has kind of already adopted me as a little brother. That makes it okay.

Doesn't it?

* * *

Carter hits the shower while I'm catching up on Facebook and e-mail. I picked a dorm this year because my scholarship would pay for it, and if I wanted an apartment—or a better dorm room—I'd have to get a job to afford the difference.

I'm not going to risk my grades to do that, and it's my good luck I'm rooming with Carter.

When Carter re-enters the room, he's shirtless, hair damp, has a towel draped over his shoulders, and is wearing loose shorts. I get a look at his back again as he returns to his side of the room. I now see the scars extend under the waistband of his shorts and make a reappearance down the backs of his thighs and calves.

"How long were you in the hospital after it happened?" I ask.

He glances my way. "That's an interesting question to lead with."

"Why?"

He settles on the end of his bed. I'm sitting on the far end of mine. Like this, we can see each other around the bookshelves and desks that usually provide a natural privacy screen between the beds.

"Most people assume there's some sort of story attached to it. Like they want to hear violence porn or something. And the answer is six months. Another two in a rehab facility before I was discharged."

He scrubs the towel over his short brown hair. "I applied to college while I was still going through rehab, started working on that almost as soon as I was transferred from the hospital into the rehab center."

I do the mental math. "Wow. That means you were injured—"

"Less than two years ago, yeah." He smiles. "I don't do well bored. Kind of a family trait."

"Would you still be in the Army if you hadn't been injured?"

He studies me for a long moment. "I don't honestly know. I didn't want to be career like my dad and brothers, but I thought I'd be in a little longer than I was. I had always planned to go to college and be an attorney after I got out."

"What kind of law do you want to practice?"

"Something that pays well." He smirks. "Maybe go into politics, working for campaigns. You?"

"I haven't decided yet. I want to help people. Make a difference." I lean against the bookshelves. "I mean, obviously, I want to be able to support myself. But I don't want to be some ambulance chaser, or trying to get people out of traffic tickets. Maybe go into environmental or civil rights law or something. I don't know."

Carter leans back against the wall, his arms crossed over his chest. "That sounds very specific."

"I'm not fond of my step-father."

He doesn't uncross his arms, but he makes a small gesture with his left hand, indicating for me to continue.

"Austin works for one of those really big-ass law firms. You've probably seen the ads on TV or heard them on the radio. Have their own 1-800 number, offices all over the state, and even up in Georgia and Alabama. Listening to him talk at home, you can tell he doesn't give a shit about the people he's representing. His favorite clients are corporations who basically pay him to keep them legal, or to get them out of jams for the least amount of money possible. That's not the kind of attorney I want to be."

Carter uncrosses his arms and leans forward, watching me, his elbows propped on his knees. "You sound like you should go into politics. Run for office."

"Me? *Phhpt.* I'd suck as a politician." Although he's effortlessly struck a secret dream I know will never come to pass. Can *never* come to pass, because I'm no ass-kisser, I think both major parties suck, and I know for my own reasons that I would be too much of a liability as a politician and refuse to live my life like that.

Yet I can't bring myself to admit to Carter that I know that it's nothing more than a dream.

I get the feeling Carter sees more than the average person, because now he's studying me.

"What?" I mumble.

"I'd vote for you, if you ran for office."

Now I know he's got to be fucking with me. "You just met me. You had to teach me how to fold my dang clothes."

"Doesn't matter. I already trust you. That's a really hard thing to earn from people." He shrugs. "If I see it in you, why wouldn't others?"

* * *

I take my shower, Carter's words running through my head.

Sure, in my fantasies I run for governor and win, and then kick ass making good changes in our state. Protecting our environment, fixing our screwed up public school system, things like that.

But the reality is I don't come from a politically entrenched family, I have no clue how to go about running for public office in the first place, and, *hellooo*, Carter had to teach me how to fold my damn clothes.

Like I'd be able to keep track of campaign finance laws and all that bullshit.

Besides, I'm not exactly some narcissistic, macho asshole who can go grab the highest office in our state by the balls. I'm not built like that. I'm more a behind-the-scenes kind of guy. My ignominious start in the dorm this year notwithstanding, I'm usually a pretty organized kind of guy. Power behind the throne.

That's where I'm most comfortable. Especially since I don't want to trade my personal freedom for public attention.

I helped a friend of mine get elected to student council all four years in high school. He went to college in Colorado, though. But I helped out with student elections here last year. Helped with campaign organization.

I'm great with that kind of stuff, analyzing data and making it make sense, crunching numbers, seeing patterns.

I want to do something…bigger than myself. With bigger meaning.

Make a name for myself away from my mother and her voice in my head slicing through my hopes and dreams and telling me that I'm not smart or persevering enough to make it on my own without her help and her money.

I need to survive college first. That's step one.

Step two? Law school.

Passing the bar exam is step three. A pretty big step, because it's fucking hard to pass.

Carter turns in before I do, so I use my laptop and earbuds to watch Netflix instead of turning on my TV. I don't want to keep the guy awake after how nice he's been.

I also don't know him well enough to risk watching porn tonight. I need to get to know him better before I take those kinds of risks around him.

It's around midnight when I finally shut my laptop off so I can get up to use the bathroom before turning in.

Removing my earbuds, that's when I hear it.

A muffled moan from the other side of the room. It does not sound like a sexy moan, either.

I peek around the end of the bookshelf. Carter lies splayed on his bed, facedown, both hands tightly fisted in the covers and his face buried in his pillow.

He's thrashing a little, and I realize he's having a nightmare.

Torn, I stand there watching, listening, feeling guilty and uneasy. He warned me not to scare him, so I'm afraid to walk over and touch him and shake him out of it.

I also realize he's crying.

Whatever nightmare currently has him in its grasp, I don't want to know the details. It must be miserable to make him sound like that.

I end up taking the coward's way out and fake a loud cough before stepping into the bathroom, where I close the door behind me with the amount of noise I would normally make if we were both awake. I make no attempt to stay quiet as I do what I need to in there.

When I emerge, Carter's sitting on the edge of his bed, near the end, feet on the floor, head in his hands. In the dim light spilling through our shared window, I can see his chest heaving, like he's just run a marathon.

"You all right?" I ask.

"Yeah," he hoarsely says without looking up.

I get settled in bed. On the other side, I hear him stand, a long exhalation of breath, and then more sounds, like he's straightening the covers.

"Thanks," he softly says in the dark. "I appreciate it."

"You're welcome." I wish there was more I could do for him.

Unfortunately, I suspect it's a battle only he can fight.

CHAPTER FIVE

Saturday morning, Carter is up and moving a little after seven. I don't mind the early hour, even on a Saturday, because while I'm not exactly a morning person I've never had trouble shifting my schedule around someone else.

Thanks, Mom.

Yeah, that's sarcasm.

Deep, dark hollows that weren't there yesterday shadow Carter's eyes, and he's moving slowly, with a decided limp that's far more obvious than last night. Since he's wearing shorts I can see the gnarled, twisted scars along the backs of both legs.

I'm not sure how to handle the nightmare topic, so I take the chickenshit's way out and decide not to mention it unless he does.

"Today's going to be a slow amble." Carter practically grunts the words, every syllable pained and grating. He's sitting on the end of his bed, bent over tying his sneakers.

"No worries. I probably need to build my stamina to keep up with you."

He lifts his head and I spot the hint of a smile there, although I don't understand what's so funny.

"I'll probably run your ass into the ground once I'm feeling better."

I'm no macho asshole. "Honestly? You probably will."

His smile widens into something not quite so difficult to look at. When he shoves himself up and off his bed, he makes another pained grunt and I fight the urge to rush over and help him.

If he wanted help I'm sure he'd ask for it.

He braces himself against the counter holding the sink we share and does some stretches. In my space, I do the same, not wanting to hurt myself in case we do pick up the pace. I've already embarrassed myself enough in front of the man. I'd like to at least hold my own in some way.

When he finishes that he cracks his neck. His T-shirt clings to him, and I feel...inadequate next to him. Here's a guy who lives with pain, who's survived horrors I can't even imagine, and he's pushing himself to do more. And he *still* looks like he's in way better shape than I am.

What am I doing? Whining about my mommy issues.

Yeah.

I decide then and there I'm going to hold Carter as my example, someone I'll aspire to emulate.

"Ready?" he asks.

"No cane?"

"Not today. We'll take it easy."

Taking it easy means taking the elevator down instead of the stairs. He sets off at a pretty fast pace and I have to quicken mine to keep up. It doesn't matter that his rolling, loping limp makes him bob back and forth. I'm quickly breathing heavy in just a couple of minutes.

"*This* is a slow amble?" I manage.

He laughs, not sounding the slightest bit out of breath. "No. This is our warm-up."

A few minutes later, his limp has eased a little and, sure enough, he picks up the pace. It's a slow jog that I finally settle into, matching him, eventually finding the right combination of stride and breathing where I feel like I'm not going to keel over.

We keep this up across campus, heading south toward the Sun Dome. There are others out this morning, running, walking, biking, but not a lot of traffic. It's warm and humid—Florida, duh—but not oppressively so.

Yet.

I can already see that, this year, my benchmark for being "in shape" is going to climb if I truly want to keep up with Carter. Last year I got most of my exercise walking back and forth from my dorm to my classes. I didn't want to mess with a bicycle.

Once we hit the Sun Dome, we lap the parking lot before Carter finally slows to a walk, pausing in a shaded, grassy median to do more stretching.

"You okay?" he asks.

I nod, too winded to talk right now, but I take the time to stretch. If this is him on a bad day, when it comes to keeping up with him on a good day...

Well, I'm going to be absolutely fucked.

"You're doing great," he simply says.

I drop onto the grass with the obvious excuse that I want to do more stretching, but frankly, I need the break.

"Try doing this with a forty-pound pack and in full uniform, in Afghanistan, in summer," he says.

When I look, his gaze isn't on me. He's facing west, but his focus is thousands of miles away. Even I can see it.

"How bad was I last night?" he finally asks.

"I only heard you the one time. I'd had my earbuds in, though, so I don't know how long it'd lasted before I noticed. Sorry."

He slowly nods, then turns to me. His gaze pins me in place as he stares into my eyes.

"Stuff I tell you, it stays between *us*, unless I give you the okay to share it. Understand? About my health, or about my time in, or about anything personal like that."

I nod.

"Car bomb." I have to strain to hear him. "We were on foot patrol, away from our Humvees. Our unit took fire and we got penned in. Little town we'd never had trouble in before. Three of our guys were hit. We called for air support while our guys back at the vehicles tried to come in after us, at least give us some cover.

"This little fucking piece of shit car heads toward us, can't even tell what color it is because it's so thick with dust. No doors, no windshield. Driver dives out of it and I yell at everyone to take cover. I threw myself over the three guys we had down and took the brunt of the blast."

"Oh, shit."

He shrugs, that typical Carter *no big deal* shrug. "Lost three guys, seven more wounded, in addition to me and the three already down."

"What about the three guys you protected?"

He shrugs again. "They made it."

"You're a hero." I don't realize I've said it out loud until he smirks.

"I'm just a grunt, kid. Just another nameless grunt. I woke up a week later back in Germany and wishing they'd kept me knocked out longer. I'd already had four surgeries in addition to the emergency field triage the medics did to keep me alive. That was my first step to returning home and civvie life."

After a few more minutes I suspect are completely for my benefit, I can tell he wants to set off again, and we do. He's still limping but his strides are more even now, less of the side-to-side rolling movement than before, and I have an easier time keeping up with him. We return to the dorm and both of us take long slugs from the water fountain in the downstairs lobby before riding the elevator up.

He's not looking at me when he speaks again. "You did good today, kid."

An unexpected flush of satisfaction fills me. "Thanks," I mumble.

"No, I mean it. Dibs on the shower, though." I finally look at him and he's grinning. It takes a few years off his features. "After you get your shower, I'll teach you how to make French toast and scrambled eggs."

He holds his fist out, and I bump with him. "Thanks."

* * *

I notice Carter apparently won't go shirtless around the others in our pod. When I finish my shower, I find he's wearing baggy sweat pants and a T-shirt. While the dorm building is co-ed, the pods are not, and each floor is divided in half by gender. I know I won't remember anyone's names for a while, so for now I think of the other six guys sharing our pod more in terms of features—Tall, Skinny Blonde Geek With Glasses. Short Fat Gamer Dude. Mr. Personality. Probably Wanks In a Sock Guy. Snooty but Hopefully Not Evangelical Christian Bro. Really Cool Muslim Dude.

Labels like that.

Don't judge me. I'm the dude who needed a *literal* fucking military hero to teach me how to fold my goddamned T-shirts and how to scramble eggs, all right? I'm not saying I'm perfect.

I help Carter carry what we need into the kitchen. It seems no one's up and about yet but us. Twenty minutes later, I'm astounded to realize I'm actually making French toast.

Damned good French toast.

He shows me how to slice the bread properly, even though apparently we should've let it get stale first.

By the time we finish with the French toast, I'm almost literally drooling. It's the scrambled eggs that finish me off, however, and convince me that Carter's a damned genius.

These aren't merely scrambled poultry parts shit from a chicken's ass.

These are *heaven*.

Light, fluffy, perfect, not too dry, not too runny. He shows me how to whisk the eggs, adding in just a little milk. How to keep turning and working them in the pan.

No shit, these are *the* best motherfucking scrambled eggs I've ever had in my life, and I helped make them.

Fuck you, Mom.

By the time we're sitting down to eat, four of our roommates have wandered out due to the aroma and are apparently disappointed to discover we only cooked enough for us.

Carter takes pity on them. "I'll leave a grocery list for you today," he says. "If everything is in the common fridge in the morning when we get back from our run, I'll cook everyone breakfast."

Thus starts Sunday Mornings With Carter.

The next morning, I head out with Carter for our run and he's moving a little better than yesterday, limping less than he was. He takes us in a different direction, north across Fletcher Avenue and past a golf course. We're running faster than yesterday, but don't go as far, and I know without Carter saying anything it's because of me and my trouble keeping up with him today.

"You think they went shopping?" I manage to ask on our way back despite the brisk pace.

He flashes me a grin. "I know they did I checked before we left. That's good. Might mean we can use the big fridge after all."

After returning from our run and showering, Carter and I head to the kitchen. This morning we're making French toast and scrambled eggs again, and I don't even fucking care, because at this rate I could eat those eggs and that French toast every damn morning of my life.

The other guys gather around as Carter teaches me how to cook, and I realize he's teaching them as well. He's a natural teacher, a natural leader. Even though at six-four I'm six inches taller than him, he still feels...*bigger*, somehow. I can tell from the way the other guys react to him that they're feeling something similar.

An unusual jolt of jealousy flashes through me. He's *my* roommate, and *I* get dibs on him.

Which is a stupid thing to think, I know.

He's now the de facto quad pod padre, and I tell him as much once we're back in our room after we've finished eating—and the other guys have helped out by cleaning up the kitchen and dishes.

There's that easy shrug again, a hint of a smile in place. "Makes our lives easier," he says, but he doesn't clarify and I don't ask.

It looks like this year is off to a fantastic start for our little group.

If only I knew...

* * *

The dining hall downstairs will be open tonight. From what I've discovered, they have a decent salad bar, so Carter and I opt to go with that after he offers to buy. I spend my post-run Sunday skimming through textbooks and reading lists in preparation for my classes this coming week. When it's time to head downstairs to eat, I poke my head around the corner of our privacy wall.

Carter's stretched out on his bed and reading his Kindle. I now realize there are three pictures on the small bulletin board stuck to the wall over the head of his bed. "Who are they?"

He looks up, over his head. The picture on the left is of three military guys wearing dark sunglasses and dressed in desert camo, all sporting shaggy beards and mustaches. The picture in the middle must be a family shot, due to the seven men—one of whom is a younger Carter—gathered around an older man and woman. The picture on the right looks like an older one, of two much younger men, likely still in their late teens, who both resemble

Carter so strongly I instinctively realize it's his two deceased brothers.

Carter shuts off his Kindle and sits up, tucks it away in his desk, and points to the picture on the left. "Gohber, me, Kenney," he quietly says. "They died that afternoon. We were best buds from basic on." He points to the middle picture. "Us, before Tom and Pete shipped out on their last tour and we lost them. Last picture ever taken of all of us together." The picture on the right. "Tom and Pete," he quietly says. "Tom was two years older than me. Pete was four."

I watch as he stares at the pictures for a long moment. Then he kisses his fingers and reaches out, touches the picture of his brothers, and of his fallen friends.

And here I am, bitching about a narcissistic mother and an absentee father.

I can't begin to comprehend what this man has endured and survived. All I know is I can damn sure try to not make his life any more difficult while we're rooming together.

I stare at the first picture. You can't see Carter's eyes because of the sunglasses, but with the full facial hair and the keffiyeh around his neck he looks even older than he does now. All three men do.

"I'm sorry," I lamely say.

Carter's still looking at the pictures. "Not your fault." He finally turns, but doesn't meet my gaze. "Let's go eat."

I follow him out of our room and wonder what other heartache the man has experienced in his life. Only eight years older than me, and he's already lived a lifetime.

Whereas I'm still feeling like I'm nowhere close to getting my shit together.

I do know that, when I grow up, I want to be like Carter.

CHAPTER SIX

I fall in love with Susannah Joleen Evans the first day we meet, on our first day of classes. Not some love at first sight bullshit because of her looks, either. Although, yes, I think she's beautiful.

That's not what seals my fate.

We share a class, the three of us. Florida Politics & Government. I don't know it at the time, but Susa is working on a mass com major with a poli sci minor, with her eye on a Stetson law degree. Carter and I have two classes together this semester, this one, and Introduction to the Social Sciences.

This one is a Monday-Wednesday-Friday morning class that starts at nine. When Carter and I arrive about twenty minutes before the first class is scheduled to begin on Monday, we practically have our choice of seating. Carter chooses a desk in the back of the room, the desk closest to the far corner. Then he moves his desk so it's positioned against the wall. He even angles it so it's facing out toward the room.

When he spots me watching him, he shrugs. "Don't like sitting with my back to a room or a door. Force of habit."

I don't ask because I more than suspect it has something to do with his time in the Army, the scars covering his back like a topographical map of the Andes, and his nightmares. Friday night's dinner pops into mind, how he specifically requested the booth in back after glancing around the restaurant, and had sat facing the room.

But since I would prefer to sit next to him, I take the desk next to him, to his right and between him and the door. I slide it back against the wall and a little closer to him so we can more easily talk.

She walks in about five minutes later and I notice her immediately. She briefly pauses in the doorway and scans the room, no hesitation in her manner when she heads directly for where Carter and I are sitting. And it's not that there are no other seats—the room's still over half empty.

Yet she offers us a smile as she approaches. "Mind if I sit here?" she points to the desk that would be in front of Carter if he hadn't moved his desk all the way into the corner. Now, that desk is sort of positioned on his left side.

Blue eyes that look like they could flash-freeze you, or form a warm, sunny summer sky. Her longish brown hair is pulled back at the nape of her neck with an elastic band in a casual ponytail. Jeans and a loose blouse can't hide the fact that the watch on her wrist is likely worth more than my car and Carter's put together. Not flashy, but definitely money. Nails not so long they'll slow her typing tip long, graceful fingers, and are perfectly coated in a shimmery teal blue. Subtle makeup on a face that doesn't need it.

Carter shrugs, and something in my heart pulls tight and makes me nod, too. Mostly because Carter's nodded, but also because there's something…confident about her. In a quiet way, though, reminding me a lot of Carter.

"Thanks." Before she unshoulders her backpack she grabs the desk and angles it the way Carter did, parallel to his and backed against the wall.

Maybe it's my imagination, but while Carter watches her it almost seems like a dark cloud flits across his face, shadowing his eyes for the briefest moment. As he glances my way again he quickly schools his features.

She produces a spiral notebook and a tablet from her backpack, along with the course's main textbook. Instead of chatting non-stop with us like I thought she might, she takes out a pen and opens the text, skimming through it.

Carter and I had been discussing what to make for dinner. Since he's offered to teach me how to cook I'm not stupid enough to turn him down. Especially after the weekend's breakfast offerings.

The other guys in our quad pod are now looking at him like he's a god.

We return to our discussion. Carter had been in the middle of describing a Greek dish to me that sounded delicious. My mother never offered to teach me how to cook. Any time I asked to help, she ran me out of the kitchen.

I'm not going to lie and say I wasn't starved for some positive attention, because I was. Even if it means following my older roommate around like a needy puppy.

I'll take it. Not like Carter or I have girlfriends or jobs. We're both full-time students with goals, and the more time I spend with the man, the more I like him. The more I feel...drawn to his calm nature. Like the world could be ending and he wouldn't break a sweat.

I felt like that even before I learned he was a literal hero.

I don't think the woman is paying either of us any attention when she speaks five minutes later. "My dolmades will knock your socks off."

I stare at her. "Pardon?"

Carter's silently watching her again.

She doesn't look our way. "*Dolmades*. That's what you're talking about making, right? And I make a mean tzatziki sauce." She finally glances at me with those incredible blue eyes before her gaze lands on Carter. "You make your moussaka, I'll make the rest and provide the kitchen and the groceries. Tonight?"

I am incapable of letting the growing, tense silence sit for too long and I don't even know why. "You don't even know us. Why do you want to cook with us?"

She finally turns to face us, and her gaze swivels to and settles on me. "I broke up with my boyfriend, Kendall, three weeks ago, before he headed out to France with his family. He's due back this evening. I know the first place he's going to stop is my house. I would appreciate some…backup. I can hit the grocery store near me. They have everything we'll need. I'll buy. I should be able to get you guys out of there by midnight. He won't take much convincing. He's a damn idiot."

I can't pull my attention off her. Next to me, I'm aware of Carter shifting position in his chair.

"You don't have any older brothers who'll take care of this for you?" he asks. "Or your *dad*?"

"*Please*. My dad will ruin his life. I don't want that, I only want him *gone*. He's not dangerous, just annoying as fuck."

"He doesn't have a gun?"

"He hates guns. I'm more dangerous with a ball point pen than he is with a gun. He'd shoot his own damn head off with it."

I realize I'm watching this like a tennis match. Carter settles back in his desk, arms crossed over his chest. "How would your father ruin his life?"

She smirks. "You're not from around here, are you?"

"No."

Her full-on smile melts me. "Susannah Joleen Evans, daughter of State Senator Benchley Evans. Former Hillsborough County commissioner, former state rep, and the spine and brain stem of the Florida GOP. You can call me Susa."

I'm mesmerized. I've heard her father's name before, bandied about between my mother, step-father, and their friends.

As someone that my step-father respects—and sort of fears.

"How old are you?" Carter asks instead of responding with his name.

"Turned nineteen last week."

"You're not living in a dorm?"

"No. Daddy bought me a house in New Tampa. He and Momma live up in Tallahassee full-time, even though they still have the house in Tampa. I wanted to live in a dorm. Really wanted to be on my own, *finally*. Had it all booked and everything. So, of course, Daddy threw a shit-fit and called the university president himself. Next thing I know, a real estate agent is calling me and begging to show me houses, and Daddy's given him a budget to work with. That was Daddy's compromise—my own house, or live at home. And I did *not* want to drive in from Brandon every day."

Holy. Shit.

Carter looks at me and I realize he and I already have some sort of spooky silent communication going on. Spooky in a good way. I perfectly understand that his slightly arched eyebrows are a question. He's waiting on me to say yes or no.

I'm useless in a fight, unless it's exchanging snarky Facebook comments and memes.

I shrug. *It's up to you.*

Carter slowly nods. "Okay. You have yourself a deal." When he shakes with her I feel a little jealous, but now I'm not sure if it's because someone's intruding on my time with Carter...or because I want to shake her hand, too, and Carter got to do it first.

Then she offers me her hand.

Her grip is surprisingly firm and she looks into my eyes when we shake.

I'm...*gone.*

"Carter needs to take the lead," I stupidly say, closing my mouth before I accidentally spill any of his secrets or make myself look like more of an idiot than I already have.

Her focus returns to him, her head cocked, appraising him. "Why's that?"

"I have...experience," he says, smiling.

* * *

We don't get to talk for much longer because the instructor arrives and class starts soon after. Halfway through the class, Susa gets into a discussion with the instructor that basically silences the whole room as she comes back at him with facts and figures I damn sure know aren't in my fucking textbook.

The instructor is maybe in his fifties and crosses his arms over his chest. "And how, exactly, did you come by all this knowledge?"

I can't tell if he's being condescending or genuinely curious, but I do see the way Carter's now watching Susa.

Reappraising her.

A desperate need for them to like each other thrums through me.

"Because Daddy helped write that bill, for starters. He's the 'Evans' in question in the full title." She sits back, a playful smirk on her face, tapping her pen against the desk, her legs crossed and one foot bouncing a little. "And I was standing right there in Gov. Alexander's office when he signed the dang thing. Somewhere, I have the pen he used. He gave it to me."

The instructor's eyes widen. "You're Senator Benchley Evans' *daughter*?"

She lifts her chin a little. "I'm *Susannah* Evans," she says. "And I'm going to make a name for myself, thank you very much."

Somehow, I believe she's absolutely right. I hope I'm there to see her do it in person.

By the end of class there's a couple of things I know for certain—she's nearly two years younger than me, acts older than

Carter, and seems to have a brain that can run circles around both of us and the instructor.

Am I turned on?

Hell, yeah.

I also know she's way out of my class, so to speak.

At the end of class, she holds out her hand for Carter's phone. He passes it to her after unlocking it, and she plugs her name and address into it, then texts her phone from it.

With a playful smile, she returns it. "Can you be there by five? I'll go shopping on the way home. Anything special you need for your moussaka, or can I get what I usually get?"

"Whatever you usually get," he says, studying her.

She gives him a playful smirk. "What are your names? You never introduced yourselves."

"Carter Wilson."

She looks my way. "Owen Taylor."

"Carter. Owen." She's already packed her stuff. "See y'all at five, then. Feel free to bring laptops or textbooks or whatever. I'll be happy to tutor y'all for free in this class." She drops us a wink before she heads out, leaving both of us watching her.

At the same time, Carter and I turn and our gazes meet.

I feel a wall go up in him, just a subtle way he shifts position. "Looks like we have dinner covered," he says.

"Looks like we do." I feel like he's…studying me. I don't get the distinct feeling he's that into Susa, though. Hell, she's ten years younger than him.

Before he can walk out, I reach out and touch his arm, staying him, letting the room empty.

"Are we okay?" I softly ask.

As if it was never there, the wall disappears. "Yeah. Why?"

"I just… Sorry. Nothing." There's me, frantic to be a people pleaser.

Thanks, Mom.

He tips his head, indicating *her*. "I don't want anyone to get hurt tonight. Sorry. My brain was already running through logistics, and I kind of shifted modes without thinking."

Relief fills me. Of course. Military. "Sorry."

He playfully smacks my shoulder. "Don't apologize. It's nice having a friend who can read me the way you seem able to." He pauses and turns back to me. "Never hesitate to be honest with me, Owen. Please. I don't have many friends."

I opt to lighten the mood. "And now you're stuck with an annoying little brother."

He grins, and something about it makes me think he hasn't been used to doing much of that lately. "Yeah, I am. Let's get moving. I'll meet you back at our room later, and we'll leave by four thirty."

"Sounds good." I follow him out with thoughts of Susa's blue eyes floating through my mind and threatening to harden my cock.

This is going to be an interesting semester.

CHAPTER SEVEN

I make it through the rest of my classes and return to our room, beating Carter there. I have enough time to grab a quick shower to rinse off the sweat from walking between buildings. I shave again.

Then I throw on jeans and a button-down short-sleeved shirt. One of my better ones, light blue chambray, sort of serious but not stuffy.

Carter arrives about that time, takes one look at me, and slowly shakes his head as a smirk fills his features.

"What?"

"You know this isn't a date, right? She's using us to get rid of her ex-boyfriend."

"She's using *you*," I say. "I might look big because of my height, but you and I both know *you're* the muscle. I'm the distraction waving at him while you kick his ass."

He drops his backpack on his bed. "Why do you say that?"

"I've never been in a fistfight in my life. Hell, I don't even fight over parking spaces. I can stand there and cross my arms and look tough, but I'm pretty damn useless as a bodyguard."

"Don't put yourself down. You're in good shape. You just need some training, and PT with me every morning will take care of a lot of that." He glances at the time. "I'll grab a shower, too, since it's still early." He shoots me a grin that relaxes me.

He's not upset.

Maybe this is how big brothers rag on little brothers, I don't .

know.

I never had one of either to know, the half-brother I've never met not withstanding.

We're heading to Susa's in my car tonight, and Carter's navigating from his phone. Frankly, I'm kind of glad he asked me to do the driving.

I don't have the fanciest car, but I really didn't want to roll up in the Snot Box and have Susa laugh her ass off at us. No, I don't have great luck with women, but there's something different about Susa.

Yeah she's asked for our help, but I sense how damned strong she is in other ways.

She's lit, not even like a furnace, but more like a nuclear reactor.

I wonder how close and how long I can stay near her before I catch fire and burn.

I don't even think I'd mind all that much, to be honest.

* * *

Susa's house isn't just a *house*. It makes my mother's McMansion look like a fucking abandoned Alaskan latrine. Elandra Marriott Solemar doesn't like to be shown up, but…

Yeah.

She'd be jealous. I can imagine the way her eyes would narrow as she wonders what she has to do to show the person up.

A silver Mercedes S560 four-door sedan sits parked in the driveway. I'm already feeling inadequate rolling up in my three-year-old Subaru. One of the few nice things my mom's done for me, handing down her used car to me and paying for my car insurance and registration, since I earned a full scholarship. That, in addition to a very small monthly stipend from her that's barely enough to cover my cell phone, gas, and a few other expenses, like laundry. The additional living expense allowance from my scholarship takes care of the rest, which is why I'm careful with my money.

Except I pay for my mother's largesse in many painful ways both large and small, trust me.

Last year, I picked up a few extra dollars here and there tutoring students. With my own increased class load this year, I'm not sure if that's going to be an option.

Susa greets us at the front door as we make our way up her walk. She's changed into loose shorts and a USF Bulls T-shirt that hangs off her and hides her form. She's barefoot, so now I can tell she's probably around five-four.

Even dressed like this, she's still beautiful.

"You guys are right on time. Welcome."

It's not exactly sparse, but it looks like she went shopping at IKEA to furnish it to the bare minimum. Yet it still has a homey feel despite that.

I relax immediately, liking the vibe. It's not the slightest bit pretentious.

"You live here by yourself?" Carter asks as we follow her inside, his head craning as he looks around.

"Yep."

"Why didn't your dad want you living in the dorms? Was he worried about your safety?"

She snorts. "Not exactly. More like my privacy. Or, to be more accurate, *his* privacy."

I let Carter do the talking. "Why?"

We reach the kitchen and while they're playing conversational tennis again, I'm swept up by the room. Dark grey granite shot through with threads of black and gold, dark cherry cabinets, stainless steel appliances, and expensive charcoal-colored slate tile floors.

Fuck the rest of the house, this *kitchen* is likely worth more than my mother's house.

"Because I'm Benchley Evans' daughter. There are people who'd pay big bucks to hack into my laptop and see my communications with him. Or see what I might be doing that could be leveraged against him as embarrassing information. Anything they think they can use against me or him."

"Is there?"

She turns and leans against the counter. "My daddy didn't raise an idiot. This is another reason I broke up with Kendall. He's a...liability."

"That's an interesting way to phrase it."

"He likes to party, likes to have a good time. Drinks too much and talks too much. His family's carrying some serious financial debt, too, which I didn't know at first. That all adds up and makes him an additional liability for a number of reasons."

"Is that important to you, that people have money?"

"No. It's not his income bracket that's the problem, it's his debt-to-assets ratio. He's already in debt for running up a credit card he never should have applied for when he was eighteen. Used it to buy a gaming system and stereo for his car. Idiot. Besides, I don't like feeling that maybe one of the reasons he's dating me is because he thinks I'll pay for stuff. I'm a trust-fund baby, not a trust-fund idiot."

"I don't know about Owen, but I'm debt-free."

I realize I'm being brought into the conversation and turn. "I don't have any debts. No money, but no debts."

"That's fine," she says. "I appreciate your honesty, both of you."

"How old are you, again?" I ask.

She wears a smirk that would do Carter proud. "Everyone assumes I'm close to thirty. I just turned nineteen. Some kids had expensive private schools and tutors—I had the halls of our state capitol. I learned at the sides of the best political assholes this state ever hatched or imported, and I plan to show them all up. I'm going to get myself elected governor."

Her tone bears not a hint of braggadocio. She says it in a quiet, calm way, as if listing items she purchased from the grocery store.

I needed milk and eggs.

I bought cereal.

Apples were on sale.

I'm going to get myself elected governor.

I think *this* is the exact moment I know for certain I'm in love with her.

Okay, sure, I will admit I spent a moment wondering if I'd be the First Gentleman of the state, or how that title worked, exactly.

She's watching Carter, as if she senses he might laugh at her audacity. Instead, he meets her statement with a look of sober appraisal.

"I think that's great," he finally says. "You strike me as the kind of person who will do just that."

"Plan is to get my law degree, go into practice for a couple of years, make some connections of my own, then run for state office."

"House or Senate?"

"Haven't decided yet. Depends on poll numbers at the time, who's weakest. Whether I'll need to move somewhere else first to establish residency in the district. The rep and senator in this district were both just elected, and they're pretty strong contenders. Daddy's district is further south of here. But they'll both be term-limited out by the time I'm ready. So will Daddy. Who knows? Depends on their successors."

Carter's standing there, slowly nodding with his arms crossed over his chest. But his gaze is on the floor, like he's turning something over in his mind as he's listening.

"Two terms as governor, then I'm going national," she continues, holding her elegant hand out flat before zooming it up toward the ceiling. "Straight to a US Senate race."

"POTUS?"

"Probably not. I like having my freedom." She playfully smiles. "Maybe a cabinet position, at some point. Depending on which one I'm offered. Regardless, I can score gigs as a talking head on some network. Pull in some major dough that way. Write a book, speaker tour, all of that. Become a respected GOP strategist."

I speak up, feeling like I'm getting left behind, even though I don't have anything close to the concrete plans she's laid out trying to congeal in my brain yet. "I'm going for law, Carter's majoring in politics, you're majoring in communications. We're like our own campaign team."

Their gazes sweep my way, meet along the journey, briefly pausing on each other before landing on me.

I feel like I've goofed up or something. Like now they're humoring me.

Like in that brief pause they shared, they've already nailed down a whole playbook's worth of plans.

"What?" I ask, my cheeks heating.

Then Carter smiles *that* smile, the one that says everything's okay. He pats me on the shoulder. "Let's get cooking, buddy."

* * *

Despite her youth, Susa obviously knows her way around a kitchen. I'm torn between trying to pay attention to what Carter's showing me, and what Susa's doing.

"Where'd you learn to cook?" Carter asks her

"Nana taught me. She wasn't really my grandmother, but she felt like one. She'd worked as a cook for Daddy's family when he was growing up. She got married, raised her kids, then her husband died. She nearly lost her house because he didn't have life insurance and she'd stayed at home to raise their kids. Daddy paid off her house and debts, moved her in with us—as family, not as an employee—and helped her sell her house so she'd have money to live off of. He always introduced her to people as his other mom. She adopted me as another grandchild. We had a cook on weekdays, but Nana took over for Sunday dinners and special occasions. Daddy used to fuss at her to relax and rest, but she loved to teach me about cooking."

Her brow furrows, and she sniffles a little as her voice drops. "I loved her so much. She really was another grandmother to me. She died two years ago, and I still can't believe she's gone."

Intellectually, I know people have close relationships with their family.

I am *not* one of those people. I was raised feeling inferior, and I feel inferior to both Susa and Carter now for myriad reasons, but not of their doing. They're not trying to make me feel like that.

Over the past year, I've read a lot of books and have started working on myself, on my outlook. I know the relationship I have with my mother isn't healthy. Except self-improvement is also one of those "easier said than done" kinds of things, you know?

Carter has lived a lifetime already. Susa acts like she has. As we prepare dinner, I sort of fade to the background and listen to them talk, especially as Carter asks her political questions about his adopted home state. Susa is an amazing font of information.

I feel…useless. In more ways than one.

I mean, if someone wanted to ask me about Mumford & Sons, or Imagine Dragons, I could tell you all sorts of minutiae about them and other bands. I could wax melodic about the works of Neil Gaiman and Hugh Howey.

While I'd been hyper-focused in high school on passing my AP classes to jack up my GPA and make sure I aced my SATs to secure my scholarships, I'm a literal empty vessel when it comes to practical information of nearly any kind.

Hell, I can't even change a damn car tire. I'm lucky I can put gas in the fucking thing.

Yet here stand these two people, discussing legislative issues that I couldn't tell you anything about, even though I was raised in this fucking state.

I *literally* cannot tell you who our lieutenant governor is right now.

The only reason I remember our governor's name is because I didn't vote for the asshole, and it was my first ever election. His administration was embroiled in scandals even before he was sworn in, and it's ground our state legislature to a halt in terms of getting anything passed. Everyone's too busy covering their asses or caught up in committee investigations.

Even a bi-partisan gun safety bill to revise how concealed carry applications and background checks are handled got hijacked by NRA lobbyists and ended up dying before it ever left committee.

These two people before me sound...*passionate* in terms of politics.

I kind of wish I was, too. I want to help people. I want to do good things.

These are the kinds of things I wish I knew.

"Can you teach me all of this?" I ask during a break in the conversation.

She smiles, revealing a cute dimple in her left cheek. "Sure. A lot of it's history. Some of it's insider knowledge. Right place, right time. Like Daddy says, time is never on your side."

"Doesn't feel like it, does it?" I note.

She shrugs, and it's such a Carter-like gesture I think maybe they're perfect for each other despite the ache that settles inside my soul over that thought.

She tips her head at us. "But Nana used to say that you should always take time to make time, or else you'll regret it."

"Which one's right?" I ask.

"Both," Carter quietly says, his gaze resting heavy and sad on me. "I can tell you from experience that it's both."

CHAPTER EIGHT

I have no idea what we're cooking. As the preparations continue, it's obvious Susa and Carter know what the hell they're doing. She's not referring to a cookbook, or to a recipe on her phone, as far as I can tell, and neither is he. They teach me how to brown meat, how to make sauce, how to stuff the...whatever it is we're stuffing.

More than the cooking, they're discussing Florida politics. I'm doing my desperate best to listen and follow along and not get lost. Carter is picking Susa's brain about everything from lawmakers to laws to lobbyists.

She's a virtual encyclopedia of information. I mean, *literally*, she's a political savant, and not only regarding Florida politics. She's quite knowledgeable about national-level issues, too. Beyond the actual facts, she also knows invaluable context and backstory.

Once everything's in the oven and I volunteer to scrub pots while they talk—because, in all honesty, I'm enjoying listening to their discussion and how intense they are about it—it allows me a few minutes to actually focus all my attention on the subject matter.

During a brief lull in the conversation I find my voice. "Did you mean what you said in class earlier?" I ask her.

She turns to me. I see the flecks of sapphire in her light blue eyes and know I'm in love with her, even if I can't say anything. Getting shot down by her would not only be expected, it would likely draw pity from her, and Carter, that might be too much for me to emotionally deal with right now.

"Which part?" she asks.

"About making your own name?"

"Absolutely." She leans against the counter, crossing her arms over her chest before she tips her chin up and firmly meets my gaze. "I'm not just Daddy's DNA. I think he wanted a boy, but he got me. He wants me to take over his position in the state party one day. I have no desire to spend the rest of my life introduced to everyone as Benchley Evans' daughter, Susannah."

It flashes through my mind that I'm seeing the *real* her, the strong, no-bullshit Susannah Evans, a woman the whole world is going to know one day.

This is where it starts. Right here, tonight, in her kitchen. It's big—*huge*. I'm sure of it.

I've never been more certain of anything in my life.

She's a force of nature, and we're witnessing the emergence of the butterfly whose wings create the hurricane.

I want to be swept away by the force of her winds, sucked into her vortex and held captive in the eye of her storm.

When I shift position, my gaze meets Carter's and…for a moment, there's *something* there, but it's like he's dropped into inscrutable mode again. Before I can even ask him about it, he's back to smiling Carter.

"What about tutoring me?" I ask. "I'm going to need it."

She nods. "I'd be happy to." A playful smile quirks her lips. "I'll take it in trade."

"Trade?"

She glances at Carter. "Cooking for me. Or, at least, doing the dishes. I love to cook, hate to clean up. And cooking for one sucks. I'd rather cook for three." She focuses on me again. "How's that sound?"

A chance to spend more time with her? "Sold."

Carter snickers. "Slick negotiator. I've already got him agreeing to do my laundry, and I thought *that* was a victory." They bump fists and share another smile.

My face heats at that, but he didn't say it in a mean way, more playfully.

Still, her smile widens and the dimple makes a reappearance. "I have a washer and dryer. Bring your laundry here. It'll save you time and money. That's one of the sucky things about living here—I'm alone *all* the time. I was looking forward to being able to make friends in the dorm. Get to have a normal life and normal friends, for a change."

Her smile fades. "Except Daddy's right that it'd be hard for me to trust people. I'd never be able to let my guard down there. Not once they know who I am."

"You trusted us," I note.

She cocks her head and smiles at me. "There's just something about you I…trust."

"Ha!" Carter says to me. "See?" Then, to Susa, "I told him the same thing."

"Daddy says I'm an excellent judge of people. I mean, I trusted you, too," she says to Carter. "Sorry, didn't mean that to sound wrong."

"No worries," he says. "I didn't take it that way."

She glances up for a moment, apparently composing her thoughts. "I am Daddy's daughter. I'm driven, I can be cut-throat. But I'm also going to show him I can do this without needing him to plow the way for me." She motions at the house. "I have a trust fund he set up when I was little. It's paying for college and living expenses, and I'm in control of it. He said to consider this house a gift. He bought me a car for graduation.

"But I don't go running to him every time I have a problem and asking him to fix it for me. I'm still mad at him for making me get a house, but on the other hand, I understand *why* he did it. He's trying to make sure I don't end up with a scandal attached to my name before I even have a political career. It'd take one stupid decision by a roommate to put *me* in a newspaper article. I hate that he's right about this, but it was an argument I decided wasn't worth having with him."

She's not merely an old soul, she's ancient, in this way. Seriously, if I couldn't see her face, I would assume she's at least thirty or older. This is a grown woman wearing a hot teenager's body, and I'm totally...gone.

Lost.

It's nearly six thirty when the doorbell rings. Susa and I freeze, she in mid-sentence while discussing an environmental bill that is in danger in the state House, a bill that she actually helped work on during high school.

Carter doesn't skip a beat. He heads out of the kitchen, toward the front door.

Susa and I realize where he's going and we both scurry after him. My throat goes dry because I have no idea what we're getting into.

I do notice as I follow Carter into the front hall that his limp has virtually disappeared, and he's holding himself tall, spine straight.

I don't know how long he can maintain that, but I plan on backing him up however I can. I might not be much use, but I'll try.

I won't leave him alone, that's for sure. Even if he probably doesn't need me.

Carter motions for Susa to step up to the front door and peek out the viewfinder. She does then nods, confirming it's Kendall.

"Here we go," Carter softly says. He points for Susa to move back and stand behind me. With me looming right behind him, he opens the front door.

The guy standing there is somewhere between me and Carter in height, so maybe six feet tall. But he's downright skinny. Compared to him, I'm a damn bodybuilder. I'm feeling pretty cocky about our chances now.

As long as he doesn't, you know, pull a gun and murder us right where we stand.

Carter keeps his left hand on the edge of the door, his right on the doorframe, his body blocking the doorway. "Can I help you?"

The guy frowns at him, then sees Susa standing behind me where she's peeking around me. "Who the hell are these guys?" he asks, obviously directed at her.

Carter snaps his fingers and points at his face with his right hand. "Eyes on *me*, kid. Answer my question." Even Carter's voice has changed, deeper than normal, an easy force behind his words that I realize was probably pretty damn helpful during his time in the military.

I pull myself to my full height, put on what I hope is a dark, threatening scowl as I cross my arms over my chest, and stare down at the guy. I can't guess his age, definitely younger than Carter, maybe my age.

The guy apparently needs a moment to process our presence. Finally, he says, "I want to talk to Susa. *Alone.*"

As *if.*

"She doesn't want to talk to you, Kendall," Carter says, already starting to shut the door. "Good-bye."

"Wait!" The guy actually puts his hand out to prevent Carter from closing the door, and even I know that's a mistake.

Carter's voice drops into a threatening growl. "Back. *Off.* She broke up with you. She's *done.*"

"Susa, please! At least *talk* to me!"

"What part of 'she broke up with you' aren't you grokking, kid?"

"But I love you!" He's still trying to talk over Carter's shoulder and to her.

At that declaration, it takes everything inside me not to climb over Carter and go after the guy myself. I'm reasonably sure I can take him, through sheer body mass and indignant, jealous outrage, if nothing else.

"You're in love with Daddy's money, Kendall," she shoots back with a stinging venom in her tone that makes my heart sing. "If you show up here again, you're going to get hauled off by deputies. Go away. We're *done*."

"That's it, kid," Carter says, closing the door.

The kid sticks his arm inside, and Carter heaves the door shut, trapping the guy's arm and making Kendall yelp in pain.

Carter throws his weight against the door, pinning him there. "Want me to break it, Kendall? All I need to do is yank your hand back. Think I can't do it? I will. Leave, *now*, and you won't need an ER trip." He yanks the door open just long and far enough the guy can jerk his arm free. Then Carter slams it shut so hard I hear the sliders in the living room rattle from the change in air pressure.

Carter flips the deadbolt and presses his eye to the viewfinder. "You have fifteen seconds to get in your car and leave," Carter yells. "You try to fuck with our cars, you're leaving in an ambulance."

He watches, then starts to softly chuckle.

"What?" Susa and I both ask.

"He just tripped running for his car. Nearly knocked himself out against the fender." He remains there, watching for another moment. Then he straightens, nodding, before he turns. "He's gone."

Susa throws herself past me at Carter, giving him a long hug that I'm struggling not to feel jealous over.

"Thank you!" she says.

I really didn't do anything but stand there. Of *course* Carter's earned her gratitude—and her hug.

His gaze catches mine before he returns her hug. "You're welcome. Anytime. My pleasure."

Then she turns and hugs me, too.

I hope she can't feel the way my cock hardened in my jeans. And her hug lasts a too-brief forever, leaving me smelling a sweet floral scent that I realize is her shampoo or something.

She's wearing a broad grin. "I'd be willing to bet he doesn't come back."

"Can he call your phone?" Carter asks.

"I blocked him on my cell, and I don't have a landline. I never answer numbers that aren't in my contacts."

"Good girl," Carter says, and I note the way she blushes even as she gives him another smile.

And that her glance lingers a hair too long on him.

"Dinner smells great," I say more to break my own growing tension than to interrupt their silent exchange.

She awards me with a smile. "And now we can sit down and actually enjoy it."

* * *

The small, four-person dinette set feels even tinier in the large dining room area just off the kitchen.

"We could have eaten at the breakfast counter, I guess," she says, "but this way we can see each other." The table is round, so there's no "head" of the table, but she's put Carter between us, with her on his right, me on his left, and the empty chair between me and her.

At least I'm facing her, meaning I have no trouble stealing long glances at her while she's talking with and focused on Carter.

The food is amazing, and I'm still not sure exactly what I did. I know I couldn't recreate it by myself. I was too distracted listening to their discussion while we cocked.

Which brings me to a question that I know might sound out of left field to them, but one I need answered.

"How did you two cook without recipes?"

They both look at me, then glance at each other before focusing on me again. "I have those recipes memorized," she says. "I've made them, no kidding, over a couple hundred times growing up." She shrugs. "I don't need a recipe."

We both look at Carter, who's now wearing an amused smile. "It might piss you off," he warns both of us.

My gaze narrows. "Why?"

His focus returns to his food. "I have a really good memory." He forks another bite of food into his mouth.

"Like a photographic memory?" I ask.

Another of those totally Carter shrugs. "Not quite eidetic, but close enough."

Fuck me, now Susa's re-evaluating Carter. I see the way her gaze narrows, how she seems to be…calculating.

"Tell me about the Carris-Thompson environmental bill," she says.

His eyes unfocus for the briefest moment. I remember them talking about it earlier, but I couldn't tell you what it was. Our instructor mentioned it in class today. I think.

I'm…pretty sure.

Maybe?

Fuck, I don't know.

Carter starts not only regurgitating everything the instructor said, but some of what Susa had added during their discussion earlier that evening…and apparently the actual text of the bill, which I remember was in our reading material for the class.

"Holy fuck," I mutter when he finally stops.

She points her fork at him. "We need to get *you* elected."

He slowly shakes his head. "Not me." He nods toward me. "Owen is the face. I'd be happy to be the power behind the throne for him." Our gazes lock, and I believe him.

Totally.

Then he looks at Susa. "Or for you."

She studies both of us for a long moment. "Gentlemen," she says. "Not to sound clichéd, but I think this is the beginning of a beautiful friendship."

CHAPTER NINE

I volunteer to wash the dishes. Carter and Susa are still discussing Florida politics, although we've moved on to the state's GOP organization and how dysfunctional it truly is, while the state-level DNC isn't any better. It only takes me a minute to rinse everything and tuck it into the dishwasher while she brings me plastic food containers to pack the leftover in.

"So what would you peg as being the biggest problem both parties share?" Carter asks her. "At the state level."

"Honestly? Rich, white, older men like Daddy. Especially cishet ones. They're trying to court a minority hard-core 'base' that doesn't really exist for either party, guys just like them with money, instead of picking a solid platform to run on. They worry about grabbing national cable news channel sound bites instead of actually doing their damn jobs. Or, on the other end of the extreme, they're too caught up in their political dogma to do their damn jobs. They try to wrap everyone in to everything and, in the end, lose nearly everyone."

Carter leaned against the counter. "Example?"

"State Rep Mitchell Dominguez, three years ago. Democrat incumbent. Lost a state House seat in a deep blue district that should have been his for the taking down in Miami-Dade. He

67

started worrying about what they were doing in DC instead of what they were doing in Miami-Dade. Went national with his platform, when the key issue the citizens in his district were worried about was FDOT wanting to enact eminent domain proceedings on some properties to create new Florida Turnpike on and off ramps, and all the traffic that would bring their region. The GOP guy, new guy, Paul Sanchez, ran unopposed in the primary because no one thought they'd ever unseat Dominguez, and there was a state Senate seat up for grabs, thanks to term limits, that everyone wanted to try for.

"Sanchez was a newbie to the GOP, ran without any local party support. Guy's a *literal* freaking racist. There were first-hand reports of him being buddy-buddy with white nationalists who are, again, *literal* Klansmen. He belongs to this small radical evangelical church who, yet again, *literally* preaches gays are an abomination and should be killed. Massive anti-abortion guy, anti-gay rights. All of that. Fucker *never* should have made it past primaries.

"But few people heard any of that because he kept the focus on that *one* key district issue and hammered Dominguez on his national politics every time the guy turned around. Sanchez controlled the message because Dominguez was sloppy and had a shit-for-brains guy running his comms. Instead of Dominguez looking local and meeting Sanchez there in that battle pit, and saying, oh, by the way, this guy is a flipping *racist*, Dominguez was chasing his own tail at every debate.

"But Sanchez looked good to the locals who were showing up at town hall meetings and saying, 'Hey, I don't want to lose my house or have all that extra traffic in our area.' Sanchez found out who all the FDOT people were behind this, by name, was doing the homework, and calling them out at all these local rallies. He wore out more shoes, knocked on more doors, and made more phone calls.

"So who are these hard-working, middle-class people going to vote for? The guy who's kvetching about what the assholes in Washington are doing, or the guy who shows up and says, 'Hey, you elect me, I'm going to be knocking on Joe Smith's office door in Tallahassee and fighting for you to save your homes.'"

She looks at me, then back to Carter. "You tell me."

Carter had been slowly nodding through all of this as he listened.

"Now, fortunately, someone with half a fucking brain got through to Dominguez," she continues. "He unseated Sanchez two years later, before the asshole could do any real damage to state politics. Didn't hurt Dominguez could leverage the fact that massively pro-life, fifty-year-old Sanchez got his *sixteen*-year-old mistress pregnant and paid for her abortion five years earlier."

"Ouch," I say.

She snorted. "Yeah. Daddy had a personal hand in that ratfuck. I might have asked him how he'd feel if *I'd* been the mistress. He didn't have the info the first time around or he would have used it. *Again*, the GOP couldn't find someone qualified to run in the district to unseat Sanchez in the primary, so Daddy dropped that bomb about four weeks before the general, when it was too late for Sanchez to mount an effective counter-attack ahead of when early voting opened."

The way Carter tips his head tells me that news interests him. "Really?"

"Yeah. Daddy might be staunchly red, but even he couldn't stomach the thought of that guy being tagged GOP for another two years."

"Wait." Carter tips his head back and stares at the ceiling for a moment. "That means you were fifteen when all this happened?"

Holy. Shit.

When I was fifteen, I was focused on passing my high school classes and when Imagine Dragons were dropping their next album.

She smiles. "It's amazing what rich old white guys will talk about when there's a girl in the room who they completely underestimate. Daddy frequently takes me to events instead of Momma, because I'm better at getting him information. Which works out for both of us, because Momma hates going to those things, and she was usually busy with her own work."

"What does she do?" Carter asks.

"Until three years ago, she was a professor of anthropology at FSU. She retired."

"Can I ask a stupid question?" Carter poses.

She smirks, the dimple returning. "Sure."

She's fucking adorable, and I'm *so* fucking screwed.

"When are you running for office?" Carter asks.

She shrugs. "Well, I'm personally not going to screw around with local-level offices. I am going to leverage Daddy's name and contacts, in that respect. I'm independent, not stupid. I know how to play the game. Need to be at least twenty-one to run for state House or Senate. Then, I'm going for the big G. But you have to be at least thirty to run for that, and have to be a registered voter in the state for seven years. That means I have time. Now, all I have to do is get my law degree, make my own rep within the state party, and bring it home. Depending on who's looking strongest when I hit that point, I might run as a lieutenant first. Make deeper connections. I know any GOP candidate will break his own neck trying to kiss Daddy's ass for political brownie points and name me their lieutenant governor."

"Why don't you want to try for smaller local offices first?"

She snorts. "You know how much I can make being a lawyer between now and then? I mean, sure, if it wasn't for Daddy, I'd go that route. Build name recognition and connections. Practice in a populated county where I can run for county commission or school board or something, bring in the poll numbers." She smiles. "And learn the dirt, where the bodies are buried, so I can leverage that when I run."

Wow. She's really thought this out.

I had trouble planning my class schedule last year.

In addition to all of this, she admitted earlier in the evening that she already has a year and a half of college credits completed via dual-enrollment classes she took in high school. So she's actually academically ahead of me and Carter.

I feel like not just a slacker, but like a total loser compared to Susa and her work ethic. She possesses a drive I damn sure don't have at my age, a determination I don't think I'll ever have in my life. I'm not hard-wired that way.

Which is why I know my secret desire to be able to enact greater good through public office is nothing more than a fantasy I'll make myself feel lousy and less-than about every time the thought flits through my mind.

"You must really love the GOP," Carter says. She snorts. "What?"

"I hate the bastards. If it wasn't for Daddy, I wouldn't be in the party in the first place. Not very fond of the DNC, either, to be honest."

"Why not run for office as a third-party candidate?" he asks.

She snorts again. "I'd love to, but that's not going to happen in this state. Maybe some guy could pull it off, but no way could a female candidate make it like that. At least, not in the current political environment. I hate saying that, but there it is. A female candidate needs to be red or blue, needs the weight of the state's party behind her. Especially not for governor. I mean, maybe if she was lieutenant for eight years to a strong third-party male candidate who kicks ass and has good poll numbers? Sure. We're a closed-primary state, so that part would benefit her, at least."

Carter's gaze falls on me. Something about the way his gaze steadily holds mine for a long, quiet moment twists things deep inside me in a good way. The one thing I've learned about Carter in the short amount of time I've known him is that he seems genuine and doesn't need me to try to impress him. I can be myself around him in a way I can't around my mother and step-father or their friends.

He doesn't deliberately make me feel stupid, or in the way.

But I can't identify the expression on his face right now as he's contemplating…something.

"What?" I finally ask.

He glances at her, and their gazes meet. The good kind of twisting inside me is suddenly tinged with green, until they both look at me again.

My face heats under their intense focus.

I'm totally fricking lost—yet again. "*What?*"

Carter seems to do another quick mental calculation. "He's two years older than you. You thinking what I'm thinking?"

"I think so." She smiles at me.

"Okay, *what?*"

"But wait," she says. "You'll be eligible in two years."

Carter shakes his head. "No, not me. I have no desire to run for any office. I'll be happy as chief of staff. That's where the *real* power is, anyway."

"Ahhhh, smart man."

I wonder if they've even heard me. "Uh, hellooo?" I give a little wave. "What are we talking about?"

Carter awards me with another of those smiles I can't process but really like. "Getting you elected governor on a third-party ticket."

"Who, me?"

"Yeah, you."

"Um, I don't even have a law degree yet. Can we *not* put the cart before the horse?" Never mind the fact that no way in hell could I manage to get myself elected.

Susa chews on her right thumbnail as she studies me. "Timing doesn't work out exactly with the election schedule. But that's okay. We shoot for local and lower offices first." She nods. "Yeah, it'd be totally doable that way. Build his rep, his name. Little cushion of time, in case there's a strong candidate we don't want to go up against."

"You guys can quit fucking with me anytime," I mutter.

"We're not fucking with you, "Carter says, his tone completely earnest. "We're *planning*."

"You've got the looks for it," Susa says. "Being a candidate *literally* is ninety percent how you appear to the public. If you don't fuck up in a horrible way, that is. Or they don't catch you fucking a dog, a little boy, or a dead hooker. I *wish* I was kidding about that part."

Her compliment about my looks is totally swamped by my growing fear. "I don't have a law degree yet. You remember that, right?"

She dismisses my objection with an airy wave. "We'll get there. And don't worry, I'll teach you what you need to know." She smiles at me. "We have faith in you."

Later, I'll look back on that moment and realize that's when it was all taken out of my hands.

Believe it or not, I'm totally okay with that.

CHAPTER TEN

It's difficult to believe I've known Carter less than four days. It feels like I've known him for years.

Then, in the space of less than one day, Susa quickly burrows under my skin.

Emotions swirl through me that I don't understand and can't label. Love? Infatuation? Desire? Eagerness?

Premonition?

I don't know. I usually don't like *not* knowing, because, growing up in my mother's home, I've needed to know things like this as a survival tactic.

Except, for the first time in my life, I make a conscious decision to be okay with not knowing and decide to just…let it all happen.

While I'd brought my class materials and my laptop with me, we end up gathered in Susa's living room to talk, with her perched in a comfortable lounger chair and me and Carter on her sofa.

Other than the coffee table, a low table doing double duty as an entertainment center, and a bookcase, it's the only furniture in the large area. The vast, gaping emptiness of the room emphasizes the cozy, close gathering of furniture in front of the TV.

She tucks her feet under her and leans forward a little as she talks, the intensity glowing around her.

I know comparing her to a furnace might get old, but it's the most apt term I can think of. She radiates heat and lights the room.

I would willingly be consumed by her.

Carter has apparently already read through our textbooks and the course syllabus, because he's talking with her about things I know are still a few weeks away, at least.

I finally grab my spiral notebook and a pen to jot stuff down as I listen to them.

Maybe, if nothing else, this'll be one class I won't struggle through.

They spend hours talking, digressing too many times to count into national politics that impact Florida.

I try to absorb as much as I can. Thankfully, they don't mention me running for office again, because I'm not sure how long I can gracefully accept what has to be teasing on their parts.

I'm so lost trying to follow their conversation right now that I'm not even sure if a search and rescue team with GPS could ever find me. Intellectually, I know I'm not a stupid person. But I feel out of my league now.

Way out.

Not-even-playing-the-same-sport *out*.

By the time Carter glances at the time and starts making what are obviously the motions to get us up and moving back to our dorm, I'm utterly in love with Susa.

Worse, I know she'll likely never be able to love someone like me. She deserves someone with drive, ambition.

Someone who doesn't feel lost and clueless.

Someone like Carter.

I've dated a couple of times between high school and now. Yes, I've already lost my virginity, thank you very much. I'm not a total noob when it comes to relationships, even though none of the three girls I slept with ever dug deeply into my heart in a way I could say was "love." It was more a case of we went out, they wanted to do something…and I did.

I was actually relieved when they broke it off with me, because it meant I didn't have to do that dirty work.

When I watch and listen to Carter and Susa, I can perfectly envision them together, a true political power couple if ever there was one.

Except as I pay attention to Carter, I can also see hints that Susa's more into him than he is her.

Or maybe that's just wishful thinking on my part, who knows?

There's no small measure of mixed parts relief and regret washing through me when Carter turns to me and offers a smile as he pats my thigh. "We should think about heading back to the dorm. It's after eleven."

I nod. "Oh, sure. Yeah." This evening spun past me in a flash.

"I had fun tonight, guys," Susa says. When I look, her gaze is fixed on *me*.

Heat races through me and I nod. "Me, too."

"Same time tomorrow, then? We have plenty of leftovers." She smirks so much like Carter I'd wonder if they were related if I didn't know they aren't. "Bring your laundry tomorrow."

"That's right," Carter says to me. "Time for you to start making good on that."

"Sure." I don't mind. It's more time I can spend with Susa. And it means it's money I don't have to spend on the washers at the dorm.

Like *hell* will I complain.

I don't know when the "we" of me and Carter became a threesome, but I can't say I totally mind it, either.

Maybe I'll let Carter drive us in the Snot Box tomorrow.

Hey, I'll take all the chances I can to look as good as I can to Susa.

* * *

"Well, she seems nice," Carter says as I drive us back.

"Yeah."

"And you don't really have to do my laundry if you don't want to."

"No, a deal's a deal." I opt to joke around with him. "Unless you'd rather have the blowjob."

He laughs, an easy, relaxed sound. "That's a hard choice, right there. Don't tempt me too much. It's been a long damn time." But he lets the joke fade into a comfortable silence broken only by my radio playing a local rock station.

We're almost all the way back to the dorm when he speaks again. "What do you want to do for your birthday?"

That's six weeks away. This first week of classes, I'll be lucky if I can remember to take a shower on a daily basis.

Then again, with Susa to look good for, that might not be so difficult after all. "I don't know. I really hadn't thought about it. Why?"

"I'll take you out. My treat. I mean, twenty-one, that's a cool birthday. I'll drive. Get you home safe. Unless you're supposed to go home to see your family or something."

"God, I *hope* not," I mutter. I finally realize my mother has yet to call or text me since I've been in Tampa. I've texted her at least once a day since moving in, knowing if I don't, it'll piss her off.

She's allowed to ignore me, but the converse doesn't apply.

Never has.

"That sounds like a story," he says.

"Just a continuation of what I told you already." I think about his offer to go out. "Okay, yeah, sure. I'd enjoy going out with you. Thanks."

"We can even ask Susa if she wants to come with, if you want."

I bite my tongue not to jump all over that. "Oh, sure. Yeah, that'd be fine."

"Or would you rather celebrate it on a Friday night?"

My birthday's on a Thursday. But come to think of it... "Yeah. Let's do that." I pull into our dorm building's parking lot.

"I'll even take it easy on you the next morning. We'll walk instead of run."

When I look, I spot his smirk. "You're a real pal, big brother."

He grins. "I try."

I can't go to sleep yet. Long after Carter's turned off his lamp and presumably rolled over to go to sleep, I'm perusing information from links in the class syllabus with my earbuds in as I listen to music.

This isn't my only class this year, but I know it is, by far, my favorite.

Even though it's only our first day of classes.

Carter makes it enjoyable—Susa makes it perfection.

It's after midnight when I shut my laptop down. Even with the earbuds in, I hear Carter. He had a nightmare last night, waking me up, but I cleared my throat and he immediately awakened.

Tonight's noises on a scale of one-to-ten sound like an eleven, making last night's maybe a one. Ripples of gooseflesh sweep over me as I listen. It's a low, guttural moan, pained, worse than anything I've heard from him so far.

Sitting up, I remove my ear buds and realize he's also sobbing.

My pulse spikes. This feels...*bad.*

Really bad.

I clear my throat and set my laptop on my desk, but whatever demons have Carter locked in their grasp are pretty damn strong tonight. I get up and walk around the bookshelves. He's on his stomach, the sheet tangled and twisted around his legs. One pillow is on the floor, the other is over his head.

I keep my voice soft, not wanting to startle him. "Carter, it's okay. Wake up."

His whole body tenses as he freezes, seems to catch his breath, then he starts softly sobbing again, more controlled now. In relief that he's awake, or because of his nightmare, I don't know. Yet I can't bear to simply turn away from someone so obviously in pain.

I walk over, grab his pillow from the floor, and sit next to him, holding the pillow in my lap and laying a hand on his back, between his shoulders. He's drenched with sweat.

After a minute, he's calmed himself. I draw my hand back when he rolls onto his side to face me. Even in the dim light, I can see how haggard he looks.

"Thanks," he hoarsely says.

Lamely, I set his pillow on his bed. "You dropped this." I don't feel right simply getting up and leaving without making sure he's okay first.

He sits up, and it puts our faces close, but I don't pull away. "Thank you, Owen. I'm sorry I woke you up."

"I wasn't asleep yet. I was on my laptop. I'm sorry I didn't hear you sooner." I make a mental note to start leaving one earbud out so I can hear him.

He slowly nods and finally meets my gaze. In the dim light, his brown eyes look nearly black, and the haunted expression on his face tugs at me.

This is a man who's been through hell and just relived it.

"You don't have to do my laundry," he finally says. "I have a feeling I'm going to be putting you through hell this year."

"I don't mind." I offer him a smile. "I moved here from Hell. This is like a vacation. And I'll make you a deal in return."

"What kind of deal?"

"I'll do your laundry as long as you promise to ride to Orlando with me any time my presence is requested." I offer him my hand. "Deal?"

He looks at my hand for a long moment before taking it, squeezing, but like he's reluctant to let go for fear that his nightmare might suck him down again. "Deal," he says.

* * *

We walk the next morning. Carter's not limping as badly as our first day out, but I can tell he didn't sleep well, even after the nightmares. We set out early, while it's still relatively cool, and none of our pod mates are up and moving yet.

"Tell me about your mom," he says as we head west along a sidewalk.

"That's a weighty subject." But I talk, mostly because Carter asks me pointed, insightful questions during our walk. By the time we make the turnaround to head back, I realize I've told Carter more about my dysfunctional family—including my father—than I've ever told anyone else.

Ever.

Never before have I ever had anyone I trusted as much as Carter, someone who is utterly beyond the reach of my mother's influence.

I never felt any freedom growing up, even at school. I made the mistake once in ninth grade of confiding to a kid I thought was my friend. I'd talked about wishing I could at least go visit with my father.

Never did I suspect my mother even knew the kid's mother, but within a week I was getting the cold shoulder from Mom. It made me practically frantic trying to figure out what I'd done wrong so I could atone for it.

She let me twist in the wind the better part of two weeks, my step-father no goddamned help whatsoever, before she icily informed me that if I'd rather live with that worthless sonofabitch—because god forbid we use his real fucking name—then I could call him up and have him come get me. Which he probably wouldn't do, because if he wouldn't pay child support, why would he even *want* me?

Which, of course, led to me tearfully begging to stay and apologizing for even saying anything about it to my friend.

Also led me to not trust anyone for years.

Not with stuff like that.

Damn sure not my mother.

Hell, two of the three girls I dated, I never told her about, including the girl last year.

To this day, I'm still not sure which pissed my mother off more, that I'd wanted to go visit my father, or that I dared talk about him to someone else without her permission. Not that it matters, I suppose.

"It sounds like your dad escaped," Carter notes.

"Yeah, but he was no angel, and I say that as an adult looking back. But, no, I don't think he's the monster my mother tried to make him out to be, either."

"It's good you've gained some perspective."

"Especially at my age."

"Do you have any contact with him?"

I shrug. "A little on Facebook. Not openly. Because even though my profile's locked down I wouldn't put it past someone to tell my mother if they saw me interacting with him just to score points with her and my step-father."

"Sounds like a charming woman," he drawls.

"Thing is, she can be. She can come off looking like the world's greatest mother. To the point that it would sometimes make me feel like maybe *I* was crazy. Maybe there *was* something wrong with *me*. Then I'd remember things she said or did and realize, no, it's not me, it's her."

"I take it you don't plan to return to Orlando after you get your law degree?"

"*Hell* no. I think I'll probably stay in Tampa. I still have years to worry about that."

He shrugs. "Never too early to start planning."

I unlock the front door of our building and hold it open for him. "Still wanting to get me elected, huh?" I hope it comes out snarky and teasing.

Yet he pauses, meeting my gaze. "Why can't you believe what we see in you?"

My face heats. Fortunately, I can blame it on the pace of our walk and the heat. "I *just* told you about my mother."

He pats my shoulder. "Let's grab our showers and get some breakfast, buddy."

I follow him inside and wonder not how long I can put up with Carter and his nighttime terrors, but how long he can put up with me and my daytime ones.

CHAPTER ELEVEN

I like to joke—privately, with Carter and Susa—that I am a pet who arrived mostly pre-trained. The first time I make that joke is on that Tuesday afternoon, when Carter and I return to Susa's.

We bring our laundry with us. Carter is the one who suggested we take the Snot Box today, because it's easier to get the baskets in and out of the back hatch, rather than wrangle them into the trunk of my car.

Logic, yo.

But I grab his basket and carry it downstairs for him, stacked on top of mine, despite him offering to carry his own. We've both stripped our beds and it doesn't escape my notice that there are two extra sets of sheets—tightly folded, because even his dirty laundry is stored neater than mine—in Carter's things.

When we reach the Snot Box, he opens the back hatch for me. Once I have the baskets and laundry detergent stowed, then he does something that totally surprises me—he hands me his keys.

"Come on," he says as he heads for the passenger door. "You know the way."

I scurry around after him, opening the door for him. He's still limping more than he was yesterday and it's the least I can do for him. "You serious?"

"Yeah." He grins. "Unless you're too embarrassed to be seen driving the Snot Box?"

I'm feeling a little humbled that he's actually trusting me enough to let me drive his car. "No, I'll drive."

"Thanks, buddy."

I close the door for him and wonder if it's his pain making him hand this off to me. I know he takes a couple of medications, but I don't know what, and of course I haven't pried. That'd be fucking douchey. I saw him taking something not long before we left today and he's definitely moving more stiffly this afternoon than he was this morning.

When I get behind the wheel I realize my legs are longer than his. "I need to adjust the seat and mirrors. Sorry."

"That's fine." Carter settles back in his seat and I notice him wince.

I don't mention it, because he seems to be the kind of guy who doesn't want to be fussed over too much in the light of day. Despite the traffic, we make it to Susa's place about twenty-five minutes later, and I hurry around to the back hatch to grab our stuff before he can.

Susa greets us with a smile and holds the door for me, directing me to the utility room. Even though I wanted to put them in the baskets and carry them, too, Carter's carrying the bottles of soap and fabric softener, because he's stubborn and he's Carter.

"I don't mind if you want to wash my clothes with yours," Carter says.

"That's fine. Makes things easier."

He hesitates in the utility room doorway, leaning against it. "Look, you don't have to do this if you don't want to. I don't *really* expect you to wash my clothes all year."

It's almost like there's a worried tone in his voice. I expect he's concerned about last night, but honestly, it doesn't freak me out. He's the most honest person I've had in my life.

Ever.

I turn, wanting to lighten the mood. "I expect you to teach me how to do it the right way. I'm a well-trained pet. I just need a little fine-tuning in some areas, that's all."

That earns me a hearty laugh and a smile that makes me feel good deep down inside. When he laughs at me, it's never cruel.

That's something I'm not used to, and I think I'm going to come to enjoy it a lot.

"Okay," he finally says, still smiling. "We'll whip you into shape. I just wanted to spare you fingering my briefs, is all."

"Hey, fingering your briefs is a small price to pay to have a wingman to help me face my mother. I'm getting the better end of this deal, trust me."

Once I start the first load and I join them in the kitchen, Susan gives us a formal tour of the house. Now that we're not worried about Kendall showing up out of nowhere, or distracted by cooking and conversation, we can all relax. She doesn't have much in the way of furniture. A desk in one bedroom that looks out on the pool lanai, some boxes stashed in the second guest room—which doesn't have a bed—and a king-sized bed, nightstand, and dresser in the master bedroom, which also looks out on the pool. She has a large flat-screen TV mounted on the wall, but the cable box and DVD player sit on the dresser under it.

She has a hot tub and a large pool on a screened lanai, and the small backyard is surrounded by a tall privacy fence.

I start to think about her skinny-dipping, then immediately shut that thought off when I realize it's threatening to give me a hard-on that I won't be able to easily hide in my shorts.

"Not going to take on a roommate?" Carter asks when we return to the living room.

"Don't need one. Daddy bought me the house, and my trust fund has more than enough in it to keep me going for several years. By then, I'll be earning a living as a lawyer." She smirks. "And if something was to happen, I'll just call Daddy." Her smile fades. "I'm careful with my money. I'm not stupid. I know how lucky I am, and I am not about to squander what I have. He's been teaching me how to manage my money since I was five and started getting an allowance."

We head to the kitchen. I take over heating our dinner while Carter perches on one of the barstools and he and Susa talk more politics. They don't cut me out of the conversation, but honestly, I'm having fun just listening to the two of them. Since I'm only reheating stuff and putting together a salad, I don't really need to focus on what I'm doing like I did last night.

Before we sit down to eat, I transfer the first load of clothes from the washer to the dryer and start a second load. It feels very…domestic. Despite Susa's obvious money, she doesn't come off as pretentious, and neither does her house, despite how much it's obviously worth.

"Can I ask you something?" I say to her as we sit down to eat in the dining room.

"Sure."

"If you're rich, why is this all the furniture you have?"

She smirks. "I'm cheap. I don't need anything else right now. And it's just me. I'll add stuff here and there as time goes on. But the other thing is after law school, I might not even be living here."

"Oh." A sad pang hits me at that thought. "Where would you move?"

"I meant I might not be living here-here, in *this* house. I might buy something else in the Tampa area. Maybe a condo or something without any outside maintenance to worry about. Eventually, I'll need a place of my own up in Tallahassee, I'm sure. A townhouse or something."

Her smile widens, and I don't miss how she glances Carter's way. "Unless we're actually doing what we talked about last night," she adds. "That would definitely give me a reason to stick around this area."

"I was completely serious about that." Carter glances at her. "Get him elected, then get you elected."

My heart nearly seizes at that thought. They've *got* to be fucking with me.

As if they can hear my thoughts, both of them turn and look at me.

"What?" I shove a bite of moussaka into my mouth.

Carter smirks. "He's adorable, isn't he?"

She answers with a winning smile that exposes dimple. "Completely adorable."

My face heats, and now my pulse is racing.

Adorable.

She called me *adorable!*

After dinner, I again volunteer to clean up the kitchen while they talk. I honestly don't mind, because I like listening to them. Once dinner is finished, I hear a buzzer go off on the dryer. I swap loads again and bring the basket of clean clothes into the living room to fold while we talk. Carter talks me through it, and before long, I have a perfectly folded basket of laundry. I still sit there on the floor, caught up in their discussion about gerrymandering of districts and how the current GOP stranglehold is about to be broken once again, thanks to a court ruling that will take effect in two weeks, barring they redraw the districts in less obviously blatant ways.

This has been the best time I've had in…forever.

I don't want it to end.

Don't take any of this wrong—I was happy to help out in the kitchen and by doing Carter's laundry. For the first time in my life, literally, I felt like I belonged.

Like they genuinely enjoyed my presence. When I worked up the nerve to ask questions, Susa was usually the one to clarify and explain things, in a kind and friendly way.

I wasn't made to feel stupid.

Not a hint of condescension in her tone or in Carter's.

What doesn't hit me until much later is that tonight firmly guides me on the journey to what I have now become.

* * *

Susa and Carter seem to enjoy teaching me how to cook. We're there literally every night, and all day Saturday and Sunday, once Sunday Mornings With Carter have wrapped up. We spend that time eating, talking, sometimes quietly studying, or just chilling out watching TV and movies, or enjoying her pool. Two weeks into whatever this is, Carter hands me the keys to the Snot Box Tuesday morning after returning from our shortened and very slow walk. His pain levels today are off-the-charts by my best guess, based on his stiff movements, discernible limp, and pained expression.

"Can you go pick up Susa, please?"

A nervous flutter churns my guts, anxiety and anticipation vying for control. "I thought you were going to drive her today?"

Susa wants to go to IKEA in Ybor City this afternoon after our classes. She asked Carter last night if he'd drive her in the Snot Box, since it can carry more than her car. The plan was for him to pick her up this morning, bring her to campus, and they'd leave after his last class to take her. I was going to stay behind, since they'd need all the room possible in the Snot Box to carry her purchases.

To be honest, I was planning on lying in bed, watching porn, and jerking off, instead of having to do it in the shower like I usually do.

The jerking-off part. *Obviously* I can't watch porn in the shower. I haven't been able to do very much of *that* unless I come back to the dorm between classes or something when Carter's not around.

Although I am considering getting one of those waterproof phone cases so I *can* take my phone into the shower with me.

Except I will give up wanking to porn in a heartbeat to have alone time with Susa.

"I'm hurting too bad," Carter says. "I barely made it through our walk. I probably should have had us hit the workout room instead of a walk. You don't have classes this afternoon, right?"

"Right." I nervously stare at the keys in my hand.

He pats me on the shoulder, then gives me a quick squeeze before releasing me. "You've got this, buddy." I glance at him and spot his playful smile.

"What about you?" I ask.

"What about me?"

"How will you get to Susa's tonight?" We're supposed to have dinner there, of course. It's what we do now. Even if all we do is grab take-out from a dining hall and take it there instead of cooking. Susa loves to shop for and cook for us. When I offer to pay my fair share for groceries, Susa waves me off, and so does Carter.

He shrugs. "I could skip it. It's no big deal." Some nights we drive over separately, depending on when our classes end, and some nights we go over together. It's not uncommon for one of us to leave there earlier than the other, either, depending on what we've got going on, how tired we are, our schoolwork—all of that. Sometimes I'm there later with Susa, sometimes Carter is.

But this... The thought of him skipping tonight altogether feels...*wrong* to me. This magic that we've created in this short amount of time, whatever it is, it's the *three* of us, and I don't want to lose it. I feel like we're actually some weird little family. So what if Susa has the hots for Carter? I don't even care anymore. I'm able to spend time with her, and with him, and it's perfect.

Thus I hand him my keys.

And this feels...

Big. *Huge.*

He cocks his head as he looks at me. "Are you all right?"

"Yeah. I'm more worried about you." His nightmares have been bad the last couple of days. I suspect that's contributing to his increased pain levels. I've had to go over and sit on his bed the past three nights in a row.

Well, I didn't *have* to, but because I'm not a soulless asshole, I do it. I can't help that I worry about him. He doesn't seem to mind me doing it, either. Last night he awakened, but then fell right back to sleep with me sitting next to him.

He trusts me.

I've never had anyone hold that level of trust in me before. I'm not about to ruin it. The three of us are dancing around each other, and it should feel awkward and stumbling and weird, but it doesn't.

It feels finely-tuned, choreographed, and looking effortless for it.

I love it.

"You don't think she'll be weirded out if I show up instead of you?"

"No, I'll text her. I already told her last night that I might need to send you if I was hurting too much to go today. I can't handle wandering through the damn place. I'll be doing good to make it to classes today. You can get the big stuff for her, push the cart, load the car, and more importantly unload it for her at her place. Today, I'd just be standing there and useless. I'll meet you guys later."

Those are all very logical and convenient reasons for me to go along with this. Only I was with them last night, except for when I briefly hit the bathroom right before we left, and I don't remember him saying that to her.

Except...Carter is Carter. I've learned I take Carter at face value, because that's who he is.

My fingers close around his keys in my palm. "Okay. Thanks."

He smiles. "Have fun. Just fill the tank before you bring it back, huh? It's on the driver's side."

"Sure."

He lets me grab my shower first so I can go get Susa. When I pull in her driveway, she's already stepping out the front door and locking it behind her. For a moment, I'm distracted by the fact that she's wearing shorts and sandals. As she starts to walk toward me, I shift it into park and jump out, scurrying around to open the passenger door for her.

That earns me an…odd look.

"What?" I ask.

She smiles—dimple time. "Guys usually don't open the door for me. I like that. Thank you."

"My mom drilled it into me."

I leave off the part explaining that my mom used me as a source of narcissistic supply. Mom loved her friends praising me for how polite I was, even at age ten, and how well-behaved I was.

And that opening doors or holding chairs for her put my attention on *her*. Mom could have given a shit about me, even though I spent my entire life trying to get her to.

I wait until Susa's inside to close the door, making a mental note to always get her door for her.

"I hope Carter's okay," she says when I'm behind the wheel again.

She's seen him in shorts and swim trunks, and heard a brief, extremely condensed version of the story he told me. "Yeah, just a pain cycle." I don't mention his nightmares because unless he tells her, I won't betray his confidence.

"I appreciate you doing this for me today. I'm not messing with your classes, am I?"

"No. We finish about the same time." Like me, Carter has a parking permit. So I drop her off at her first class, then find a parking lot that's closer to her last class than it is mine. I text her the location where to meet me as I'm walking to class.

Not like you can miss the Snot Box. That's one of the pluses about it—conspicuous visibility.

I force myself to concentrate during my classes before I nervously make my way to the car after my second one, just in time to see Susa emerge from the building.

I have the car running, the AC already blowing and cooling the interior, and the passenger door standing open for her when she walks up.

The dimple smile. *Jesus*, it'll be my undoing.

She bounces up on her toes and brushes a kiss against my cheek. "Thank you, Owen."

Then she easily slides into the passenger seat.

Holy hell, now I'm hard.

Fortunately, I wore baggy, comfortable shorts today, and I step behind the door to hide behind it until I can shut it for her.

I've never been to this IKEA before, but she knows the way and easily directs me. Inside it's huge, and we take an escalator to the second floor, where she stops.

"Have you had lunch?"

"No, not ye—"

She's already pulling me along behind her. "I'm an idiot. I didn't even think to see if you were hungry. Come on—my treat."

So the lady buys me lunch. She has one of those IKEA Family account cards on her keychain, which the cashier scans. Apparently it's one of Susa's favorite stores.

I spend the whole lunch watching her, listening to her. Asking her a key question about something in our class to get her talking and then…just listen.

I could do this for the rest of our lives.

With lunch finished, it's time to get started, me pushing a cart for her. I admit that's not totally a gentlemanly thing this time. It means I can follow her and watch her from behind in her shorts.

Which is also another good reason for me to push the cart, to hide my perpetual boner.

When we reach the chair section, she sits in a few, then has me sit in a few.

"Which is your favorite?" she asks.

I think I've misheard her. "*Me?*"

She gently pokes my shoulder. "Yes, you. Which one do you think is most comfortable? You're a lot taller than I am."

"B-but it's your house." I honestly have no clue how to deal with this. No one's ever asked for my opinion on something like this before. I don't want to pick a chair and she hates it and blames me.

I get the head-cock, so much like Carter it's spooky. "Owen, I want *you* to pick," she gently says. "Look, you guys are my best friends. I don't make friends easily, because I've never had friends I could really trust before. I didn't know if someone wanted to be friends with me because of my money, or because their parents wanted an in with my dad, or what. I *really* like you guys. I want you to be comfortable. Please, *you* pick. I'll pick the color, but you pick what's comfortable for *you*."

I nod and turn back to the selections again, trying them out one more time, this time really focusing.

Like Carter, she's a mean-what-she-says kind of person.

I finally settle on one, with a matching hassock. It's comfortable, and the hassock means that regardless of height, someone can sit there and be comfortable. She picks the black leather option and smiles before brushing another kiss against my cheek.

"See? That wasn't so hard, was it?"

"No," I mumble, thinking *yeah*, but something else is *really* hard right now.

She snaps a picture of the tag so we can pick it up later in the warehouse section. Meanwhile, I dutifully follow her around the upstairs area before we head downstairs.

I'm…gone.

Totally *gone.*

In my mind, I pretend we're married and shopping for our house.

I don't give a damn how pathetic that sounds, it's *my* fantasy. Don't shit on it.

Downstairs in the warehouse, we swap. She takes the cart and I grab a trolley. I follow her as she leads the way through the aisles to find the flat-packs for the chair, ottoman, two bookshelves, an entertainment center, and a side table. I'm hoping everything will fit in Carter's car, between the overflowing cart and this.

She pays with a credit card and doesn't even flinch at the total, even though it's hit four digits.

I haven't spent that much except for textbooks and tuition.

Before we can get out of there, though, she stops by the grocery section and grabs several cartons of cinnamon rolls, along with a few other food items.

"I love these," she says with a grin. "I freeze them and eat one at a time, or I'd totally pig out on them."

She's definitely not fat, so whatever she's doing is working.

Frankly, it makes me want to eat cinnamon rolls every day now, even though before today I really didn't have a strong opinion on them one way or another.

I was never allowed to have a strong opinion about *anything* at home. I was expected to agree with my mother.

Or, at least, *not* disagree with her. Last year and, so far, this year, have been spent trying to figure out who the fuck *I* am.

Outside, Susa waits by the carts while I drive the Snot Box around. I have to play Tetris with everything after figuring out how to put the backseats down to make it all fit. Even better, she's laughing as I'm muttering and swearing at the car and trying not to fuck up his headliner or upholstery.

Carter trusted me with his car. Snot green or not, that's *huge*, in my book. I don't want to disappoint him.

It takes me the better part of twenty minutes, but I *finally* get everything crammed in there. I have to tie it all down like crazy because now the back hatch won't close all the way, but I make everything fit and ensure it won't go flying out while I drive us back to her place.

"Oh, I told him we'd gas up before we bring it back," I tell her.

"No problem." We're almost to her house and she waves me past where I'd normally turn. "Keep going. Past I-75." There are several gas stations there, but first she directs me to Home Depot.

"What do you need here?"

She stays me with a hand and a smile. "I'll be right back. Just wait here with the stuff." Before I can move, she's out of the car.

So I do as ordered, even though it's killing me she didn't wait for me to get her door for her. One of us has to stay with the car anyway, because anyone could just walk up and swipe something, since the hatch is ajar.

I'm watching and waiting for her return, and make sure I jump out to open the door for her when she returns.

Once we're both back inside, she hands me…a house key.

"Here."

I start to reach for it until I realize what it is. "What?"

"I want you both to have a key."

"Why?"

"Because I trust you guys. Besides, no one else has a key. Not even Daddy and Momma. That way, if you want to come over and I'm not home, you can get in. I'll give you an alarm code."

She's still holding it out to me. I finally extend my hand and let her set it in my palm.

"Thank you." Those two words feel totally insignificant and insufficient, though.

She pats me on my thigh. "How else are we going to be able to continue your cooking lessons? This way, like if I need to go up to Tallahassee for the weekend or something, you guys can still come over. Laundry, cooking, the pool—whatever. I want you guys to feel comfortable there."

You guys.

Not just Carter.

Not just me.

The *two* of us, a matched set, apparently.

I'm not complaining, I'm merely noting it.

"Thank you." I have to unbuckle my seat belt again to put the key in my pocket, but I manage it. Next stop—we're off to fill the gas tank. She hands me her card and tells me the zip code to plug in.

Then we're on our way back to her house. Meanwhile, she's texted someone a few times. I assume with Carter, but I don't ask because besides being none of my business, maybe it's better I don't know.

You know, in case it it's *not* Carter.

And in case it's someone who will blow my fantasies out of the water.

CHAPTER TWELVE

Upon our return to Susa's house, she checks another key and has me check mine to make sure it works before I can do anything else. Then I start the arduous process of unloading the Snot Box. All of her purchases are going in the living room, for now. Except for the food, of course.

Once everything is inside, that's when I suddenly lose my brain. "Do you want me to assemble stuff for you?" I ask before I have a chance to really think that through.

Part of me is praying *Please, yes*. I would kill for an opportunity to look like a hero to her.

Another part of me is screaming *You fucking dumbass!* Because I am *not* mechanically inclined.

As in, at *all*.

She smiles. Full dimple. "That would be awesome, thank you."

Oh, fuckballs.

I start with the ottoman and chair first. She brings me a utility knife so I can open the boxes, and an IKEA toolkit.

I hope I don't end up nervous sweating my way through my T-shirt at this rate. But, somehow, I manage to get the chair and ottoman put together without embarrassing myself too badly.

Then I have her tell me where she wants it and I move it for her, across from the chair that's already there, off the other end of the couch, and I sit.

Turns out it's pretty damn comfy.

"Do you like it?" she asks, sounding unusually bashful, for her.

"It's great, thanks."

"That's *your* chair." She smiles. "I want you to always feel welcome here."

Every ounce of strength and will I have in my body diverts to trying not to cry as I choke up. "Thank you," I finally say when I can speak without sounding like an idiot.

No one's ever tried to make me feel welcome before.

Except Carter. And now Susa. Oh, she knows some of what I survived during my childhood, but I glossed over the worst of it. Carter knows more than she does simply because I spend more time with him and we talk during our morning exercise routine, which Carter calls PT. I guess that's physical training, from his Army days, although some days it feels like physical torture. To be honest, during our talks it's mostly Carter asking me stuff. It seems like every time I ask him something, he manages to turn it around and focus on me again before I even realize he's done it.

Man's going to be a fucking amazing attorney. I can see it already.

Speaking of our morning PT, it's getting easier for me to keep up with him during the faster paces, and I'm noticing my legs are looking firmer. Haven't dropped much in the way of weight, but I'm not really overweight, mostly sort of soft.

Especially when compared to the toned, hard planes and angles of Carter's body.

About that time, I hear Susa's front door open, and Carter walks in.

The way Susa's face lights up at hearing his arrival shoves away all the good feelings I'd spent the afternoon building up.

She meets him at the end of the entry hallway. "I have

something for you." She goes to her purse, grabs the other key, and proudly presents it to him.

He looks at me, our gazes locking for a long moment before he speaks. "Thank you. I wasn't expecting this. You gave Owen one, right?"

"Of course. Already gave it to him." Dimple. "Let me set alarm codes for you and show you guys how to work it."

Most of the good feelings wash back in as I'm still processing Carter's question to her. Carter actually thought of *me* first.

I don't have the words to express what that does to me. That there's someone who is literally putting me first. The sad thing is, I can't remember another time in my life that happened. I never felt like my mother put me first.

Ever.

Oh, I'm sure if someone asked her that she'd take great umbrage at the suggestion that she didn't put her child first. Which is why I'm not stupid enough to say it to her.

Yet it's the truth. Not once can I think of a time that my best interests, my needs, my *anything* came first in my mother's life. I've always been an afterthought.

And yet, Carter put *me* first.

Right at that moment, I'd walk across hot coals for Carter, if he asked it of me.

I pull myself out of the chair to follow them back down the hallway, to the alarm keypad. She has us pick our codes, programs them into the unit, then has us test them.

Carter turns to me with a smile and produces my keys. I fish his out of my pocket and we swap, then thread our new keys onto our key rings.

"So what'd you get at IKEA?" Carter asks.

"Oh! Let me show you. Owen just put together his chair."

Something about the way she says it...

Yeah, I'm a fucking dumbass goner, all right.

How rotten was my childhood that this little bit of positive attention from them consumes my every spare waking moment? At least, that's what it feels like.

No, seriously. That was *not* a rhetorical question. How fucking rotten was my childhood?

I'm doing my best not to appear like some needy tool, but I think I'm beyond that point now. They still seem to want to be around me, even though I feel like I'm clingy, and I worry that they'll get sick of me soon.

All of this remains unsaid. I am not a fucking ass. I do have a few ounces of common sense, and too many damn years' experience at keeping my mouth shut.

Carter settles on the couch as I tackle assembling the next item, one of the bookshelves. There's two of them, so I hope I can figure out the first one, damn near look like a genius for the next one, and maybe have my shit together by that point so that I don't flub assembling the side table or the entertainment center.

Meanwhile, Susa is chatting with Carter and I'm struggling not to let my attention drift from the task at hand. I could sit and listen to them talk for hours.

We were supposed to cook dinner together tonight, but now I'm assembling this. "I'll get dinner started," she says.

"I can finish this after." I start to stand, but she leans over and kisses the top of my head.

"No, I've got it. We still have plenty of leftovers."

"Want some help?" Carter asks her.

"Guys, seriously, I appreciate the help today. Let me do this for you."

"Owen gets all the credit," Carter says as he meets my gaze. "I just loaned him the car."

"Yes, but I appreciate that, too."

She goes to make dinner for us while I'm struggling over the instructions for the bookcase. It's not making sense, looking at the pieces in front of me when compared to the diagrams on the instruction sheet.

That's when Carter softly gets my attention. "*Psst.*"

I look up.

He points at the piece currently frustrating me and motions for me to flip it over.

I do. Suddenly, the instructions match.

D'oh.

But Carter smiles and settles back to respond to a comment from Susa.

I mouth a silent, "*Thank you.*"

He drops me a wink.

I am reasonably certain, just from having known Carter over the past several weeks, that he most likely would have had everything assembled by now. That he's letting me have this moment, and even giving me a secret assist, warms my heart.

He's trying to help me look good for Susa.

It's tempting to burst into happy tears at this altruistic display from him, but somehow I nut-up and make it through the assembly process. Yes, I know he's in pain today, I can see it in his expression and how he was limping when he walked. Still, it feels like he's centering me in this, and I'm grateful.

The first bookshelf finally goes together, and the second one in half the time, now that I know what I'm doing.

The side table, though.

Ugh.

It's got a sliding drawer mechanism, and now I'm lost again. Carter leans over and plucks the instruction sheet from my hand when he notices my confusion, skims through it, then returns it to me. All while he's holding a conversation with Susa in the kitchen. From her vantage, she can't see what's going on between me and Carter.

Carter taps my shoulder and points at items, helping me orient them and, in a few minutes, it all starts to make sense.

I give him a relieved thumbs-up.

His hand settles on my right shoulder for a moment, giving me a reassuring squeeze before he sits back again. When I glance at him, he's wearing that Carter smirk I know means he's amused.

If I could have a big brother, I'd want him to be Carter.

He drops me another wink and I wink back. I feel like this is our secret, and a huge-ass gift from him.

I'll gladly take it.

*   *   *

Dinner interrupts me. When Susa calls for us to come to the table, I stand, but I realize Carter is sitting on the edge of the sofa and hasn't stood yet.

I pause and give him the arched eyebrow, a silent question.

He tips his head to call me over and holds his hands out to me, wiggling his fingers.

He must really be hurting to need the help. I've had to do this a couple of times during our morning workouts, when he's sat down at a rest break and has trouble standing on his own again.

Carter responds with a silent, *"Thank you,"* and squeezes my hands before releasing me.

I wait to follow him into the dining room. I'm worried about him—I can't help it. He looks after me, I look after him. That's how this works. It's not even any formal kind of arrangement. It's simply the way things shook out between us.

Susa turns as we make our way into the dining room. A scowl fills her features as she obviously spots Carter's limp. "Are you all right?"

"Had better days. I'll be fine. I hope you guys don't mind if I go home early, though."

Part of me minds, because I'm worried about him falling asleep and having a nightmare and me not being there to help him.

Part of me wonders how much he's really hurting, or how much maybe he's trying to toss me a bone and give me alone time with Susa.

I opt to take him at face value. "Will you be okay driving home?"

"I'll manage."

"I don't mind driving," Susa offers. I start to protest when she adds, "I can drive Owen's car, and he can drive you. I'm sure he won't mind bringing me back home."

My mouth snaps shut on any protest I might have had.

Sounds like a damn good plan to me.

I nod, not even trusting myself to not babble at this point.

Except Carter's tired smile tells me a deeper story than he obviously wants to get into with Susa—and makes me realize he's not faking his pain. "I'll be okay to drive," he insists. "But would you mind if I duck out after dinner and not help with the dishes?"

"I'll take care of the dishes," I offer. "Don't worry about it."

"Thanks, buddy."

We've settled in our usual spots at the table, what have been our spots ever since that first night—Carter in the middle, and Susa and I facing each other.

This feels natural to me now. This feels so right that I have no words to express it.

This feels like what I always hoped peace would feel like.

Had my mother's home felt even a fraction as warm and welcoming as this while I was growing up, I might not be able to appreciate this gentle, easy relationship the three of us now have. To me, this is a fragile perfection I'll do anything to protect.

Anything.

Like watching the way Susa's gorgeous blue eyes light up when she listens to Carter speak.

Like ignoring the way an adorable pink blush creeps up her throat and across her cheeks over Carter's smile.

Like knowing that Susa's as much in love with Carter as I am with her, and not even caring anymore. Settling for being a satellite in her orbit via Carter is enough for me.

After dinner, Carter says his good-byes and slowly limps toward the door. I offer to help him out to his car, but he waves off both me and Susa.

She sees him out and locks the door behind him, returning to join me in the kitchen. Now that I know my way around it, I don't need to ask her where things go. I've already started washing the items that don't go in the dishwasher when she hugs me from behind.

"Thank you for today."

I'm glad that I'm standing in front of the sink, because it allows me to conceal my suddenly raging hard-on from her. "You're very welcome. I didn't do much."

"Yes, you did. And thank you for how you take care of Carter."

Now I'm the one blushing. "I don't know what you mean," I mumble, surprised she's noticed anything. Then again, she is pretty damn observant.

"I think you do. I see you watching him. I also saw you help him up off the couch."

My face feels aflame now. "He's my friend."

"He's more than that." She releases me and moves to lean against the counter, where she can see my face. "You guys are like brothers."

I nod. "I never had a big brother. That's what it feels like, though. He said he always wanted a little brother." I hope this isn't going to turn weird. That she doesn't start to ask me a bunch of questions about him, or, worse, ask me how to gain his affection.

Susa does none of those things. "You realize we're serious when we talk about getting you elected, right?"

Now I pause. "I get that you guys are serious, but I think you have way too much faith in me."

"Do you want to change this state? Do good for people?"

Stalemate.

I nod. "Yeah."

"Do you want to be governor?"

"But I can't—"

"Do you *want* to be governor?" she quietly asks again.

Swallowing hard, I force myself to nod.

"Do you trust us?"

"Of course."

She awards me with a beautiful smile—full dimple. "Then that's all you have to do. Just want it, and trust us. Well, and do what we tell you to do, of course."

I snort. "I seem to be getting pretty good at that."

She playfully pokes me in the shoulder. "Then the rest will be easy."

* * *

It's almost ten o'clock when I finish assembling the entertainment center and get it positioned for her. It's the last piece, and I feel a strange and unfamiliar sense of accomplishment over it.

Susa's already moved the low table that had been holding her Blu-ray player, cable box, and other electronic items.

But I need to leave this sweet bubble that's my escape from the real world and return to the dorm. I'm worried about Carter, even though he's a grown-ass man.

Even though I treasure this time alone with Susa.

"Would it be okay if I leave early and head back to check on Carter?" I ask.

She cocks her head as she looks at me. "You don't need my permission, Owen. I think it's great you're looking after him."

But part of me was seeking exactly that—her permission.

Maybe that's not the best word, though.

Her *approval* is closer, I suppose.

I'm so used to hunting and pecking through my life to find even a smidge of approval from my mother that I forget other people don't feel a need to extract every ounce of control that they can from me.

A very large part of me wants to serve Susa, not because she demands my full attention and focus, but because she doesn't.

I want to take care of her, do things for her, even if she only considers me her friend.

I want to be that quiet presence in her life, someone she can count on.

Hell, there are things I wish she'd do to me that I can never speak of, because I wouldn't dare risk alienating her.

Like I'll never admit I've jerked off a few times to the thought of being naked when I wash dishes for her, of her spanking me for an infraction, real or imagined.

Being bent over the end of her bed or, maybe, stretched out over her lap. The feel of her hand smacking my flesh until it's hot and red.

None of this I can admit. As much as I'm coming to love Carter, I can't admit it to him, either.

He wouldn't understand, I'm sure. He said it himself, he came from an Army family. The secret things I fantasize about don't have a place in the world Carter inhabits.

Hell, I don't even understand it. I'm still trying to sort out my mommy issues.

Which sounds really gross when I say it like that, I know. Hence why I'm still trying to sort it all out.

I say my good-byes and head home. When I unlock our room door only thirty minutes later, I'm careful to let myself in quietly. I know he said to make noise, but I want to see how much noise I need to make first without needlessly startling him.

The room is dark, but I'm used to that. There's just enough

light filtering in from the window that I can make my way to my side of the room.

Carter's haggard voice drifts from the darkness. "I'm awake."

I snap on the small light that stays clipped to the head of my bed and walk around the end of the divider. "Are you all right?"

He's stretched out on top of the covers. "Nightmare."

"Look, I was going to read for a while. I can just as easily do it over here with you. Let me change clothes and brush my teeth and sit up with you, okay?"

I'm not sure if he'll try to push me away or not, but I'm relieved when he nods. He's slept like shit the past few nights. He *needs* a good night's sleep.

Five minutes later, I'm sitting up next to him, along the edge of the bed. Carter's lying on his side and facing the wall, his back against me, because it's not like there's a lot of room.

"Thanks," he whispers.

I pat his shoulder and start reading, listening to how his breathing quickly evens out, grows slower, deeper.

Easy.

In less than five minutes, I'm certain he's asleep.

But I meant it. I'm not ready to fall asleep yet. I sit there reading for another hour and hope that, for tonight, at least, maybe he can get some decent rest. After I finally ease my way out of his bed and return to my own, I sit up reading for another twenty minutes to listen in case he has a nightmare.

Fuck it, I'll sleep in bed with him if it means a chance for him to get some sleep and get a handle on his pain.

When I don't hear the telltale sounds of a nightmare, I turn off my Kindle and the nightlight and listen in the darkness for a while longer before I finally allow myself to drift into dreams of serving Susa and earning the dimple smile from her.

CHAPTER THIRTEEN

There is a memory from my childhood indelibly etched in my brain. I was ten or eleven years old, and my mother and brand-new step-father, Austin, decided they would take me to a Saturday afternoon barbecue at the home of one of Austin's co-workers. It was supposed to be a fairly important gathering, even though families were included. Something about two of the senior named partners expected to be in attendance, the possibility of new junior partners being identified from the day's attendees—all the usual bullshit office politics.

Before we even left the house that morning, I received a long, stern lecture from my mother about not getting dirty, not making noise, not being rude, not being whiny, not running around, and definitely not to touch *anything*—all the warnings about actions on my part that would, no doubt, get me into serious-shit trouble with her on the back end of the afternoon, should I not heed her warnings.

I was no stranger to this lecture, so it left me feeling as it always did—like a failure, like I was dirt, like I wasn't good enough.

Like maybe if I tried harder *this* time, I would make Mom proud of me.

She doled out praise like she had to cut off a finger to generate it: rarely, with a lot of fuss about how hard *she* had life, and that I was lucky to have been expelled from *her* particular womb to start with.

The implication always being that if I failed to show sufficient gratitude for my good fortune, it would not bode well for me with her.

I spent that afternoon in a state of abject terror, afraid to go play with the other kids, despite them inviting me to join them, out of fear of what my mom would say. Too afraid to ask her if I could go play because I was scared I'd interrupt her and embarrass her.

Afraid to do much more than nervously smile and nod my head when introduced to adults, limiting my vocabulary to *yes please, no thank you, and it's very nice to meet you sir,* or *ma'am.*

Or offering to refill Mom and Austin's beverages and fetch them food.

That meant by the time the day ended, I was reasonably certain the other kids hated me, or at least thought I was a stuck-up, brown-nosing jerk, and the adults thought I was a darling child.

On our way home, my mother appeared to be in a good mood. She cheerfully chatted with Austin about how well things went, basically ignoring my presence in the backseat. Finally, she glanced back at me.

"You didn't embarrass us today. You can stay up an extra hour tonight and watch TV."

I was so stunned I nearly forgot to thank her. Fortunately, I stammered it out and sat there basking in the glow.

Yeah, I *know.* Tell me about it.

I mean, I know *now.* I look back on that poor kid and cringe, feel…angry on his behalf.

I don't even know what made her that way. She never spoke ill of her parents, and she was a completely different person around her older sister than she was with me as my mother.

As I grew older, the warnings and consequences changed.

More pointed warnings, although they did decrease in frequency.

The consequences, however…

I learned the hard way not to grow too attached to things. Those things were what she went after first. It was a lesson I had failed to heed, mistakenly thinking once I was over eighteen that she wouldn't pull that bullshit any longer.

As I grew older, it took less effort on her part to keep me in line, because she knew she had me by the wallet.

She never beat me, never…I guess I can't say she didn't mistreat me, because she certainly did. My childhood was definitely abusive, when I look back with a harsh and honest eye.

But she never denied me food, always made sure I had nice clothes to wear, and that I always had everything I needed for school, be it supplies or tutoring or anything like that.

Appearances to keep up, you know. She couldn't be seen having a son outfitted in anything less than top-end clothes or accessories.

Then again, those all played into her story that she was a stellar mother. To deny me any of those things would have reflected badly on her. Especially when she used to tell any- and everyone what a shiftless deadbeat my biological father was. How hard she'd had to work to support me when he cheated on her and left us. Before she met Austin, of course.

Looking back, it kills me that I literally felt ecstatic whenever I received the slightest recognition from her for exceeding her expectations. It drove me to sadly insane lengths to try to earn her praise.

Potential opportunities to earn her praise were frequently dangled tantalizingly close, directly ahead of me, carrot and stick.

She was Lucy, I was Charlie Brown, and the football was her love.

I let her tee it up time and again, even when I *knew* she'd yank it away from me. It wasn't until high school when I started to really pay attention to other kids and their parents and realized that what I endured wasn't normal.

I checked out self-help and psychology books from the public library across the street from my high school and kept them stashed in my school locker. I wasn't in a psychology class where I could explain them away.

Talking to the guidance counselor, a woman who I knew was married to one of the attorneys in Austin's firm, was absolutely out of the question.

At best, I wouldn't be believed.

At worst, she might tell my mother—or might mention something to her husband, who'd mention it to Austin, who'd *definitely* tell my mother—and then my life would become an utter living hell of worse magnitudes than I already endured.

By the time I reached high school, I'd hit a manageable cruise level with my mother. I could tell when she was looking for something to nail me on for no good reason, and I would simply give up and wait her out, all while doing the usual things that normally won my way back into what passed for her good graces.

Now the clock is ticking, until I graduate from college, law school, and pass the bar so I can be out and on my own. For now, I'm no longer under her thumb and available for her to take daily potshots at where there is no proof.

She can't text stuff like that to me.

She can't be bothered to call me, usually.

It's no fucking wonder I love college.

It's also no fucking wonder I find myself loving Carter and Susa.

* * *

A little over four weeks into the semester, on a Thursday

morning while I'm waiting for Carter to finish in the shower so I can take mine, I receive a text message that intrudes on what is becoming an increasingly perfect, cherished bubble.

A text that chills my soul.

Saturday afternoon, 5pm. Dinner at the house. Business casual. No shorts or sneakers. +1 if you want.

In total disbelief, I stare at my phone for a long moment. This is *literally* the first time since the semester started that Mom's texted me first and not as a reply to a text I sent her.

It's only the fifth text she's sent me total.

Son of a fucking bitch.

Oh, right.

That would be *me*.

I guess I'm wearing a look, because when Carter steps out of the bathroom and glances my way, he stops and backs up, studying my expression.

"What's wrong?"

There's no use sugar-coating it. "You know how I said I'd trade doing your laundry to go visit my mom with me?"

"Yeah?"

"I might need to throw in that blowjob after all."

He steps closer and frowns in confusion. "What?"

I show him the text on my phone.

He's good at cloaking his emotions, but I'm watching his eyes when I see the mask drop into place.

I expect a lot of responses, but not the one he gives me. "Does business casual mean a tie?"

I shrug. "I'm going to wear one, but you wouldn't be expected to."

A slow smile curves his lips. "This will be fun."

Fear trills through my gut. That looks like a predator wanting to play. "You don't have to go if you don't want to."

The smile disappears and he reaches out, his hand settling on my shoulder. "Buddy, I'm not letting you go alone."

Sudden terror rolls through me. I try to make my next comment sound like a joke. "Don't suppose you'd mind me hanging out with you during break, would you? Before we come back to the dorms?"

He squeezes my shoulder. "Absolutely, we can hang together." The smile returns. "Maybe Susa will let us stay with her for a few weeks."

I don't even want to hope for something like that, because that would be utter perfection, and I'm too used to hoping for something and having it yanked away.

Like my mother's love and approval.

Carter releases my shoulder and starts to head for his side of the room. "I suppose telling her you already have plans wouldn't help?"

"You mean, help like..." I was going to use an analogy of tossing a hand grenade into a dynamite plant before my brain kicks in and realizes how utterly tactless that would be in light of what Carter's survived.

I guess I'm quiet too long. Carter returns and stands in front of me. "Owen, I'm going with you." His voice sounds quietly firm, but with a gentle touch that makes me long to beg his parents to adopt me. "End of discussion."

My deep breath is too close to hitching from the tears I didn't realize lay just below the surface. "How does she fucking rip me up like this? *Why* do I care what she thinks about me?" I flash into anger—at myself, at her, at my father for leaving me with her and not taking me with him, I don't know. "Why am I so weak I can't break out of this cycle with her?"

"You're *not* weak. She's a narcissist. It's what they excel at. At least you don't have to worry about her paying for school, right?"

"No, but my auto insurance and registration. Plus she gives me a small allowance that's enough to pay my cell bill and stuff. I really can't afford to lose that."

He slowly nods, his expression slightly guarded now. "But that's all?"

"Yeah. I mean, if I *literally* spent nothing else, the stipend from my scholarship would cover those. Barely. If Susa wants to keep letting me do laundry there, I could squeak by."

He pats my shoulder. "Go ahead and get your shower. I'll let Susa know about Saturday."

I hate that I feel like a little boy all over again, being told what to do. Except this is Carter, and I don't mind it when he does it. Because Carter has never tried to get anything out of me before. Carter is...Carter.

Carter has accepted me unconditionally, and I don't know if I'll ever have the words to tell him how much his friendship means to me, or how desperately I don't want to lose him—or Susa—from my life.

Before I step into the shower, I text Mom my reply, the only one I can send.

Yes, ma'am.

CHAPTER FOURTEEN

Thus begins the countdown until our trip to Hell.

We don't usually eat lunch together every day. Today, however, Carter makes a point of texting me before my first class of the morning ends to lock in a time and dining hall.

We grab salads and move outside, under the shade of an oak tree, to eat in private. It's muggy and warm, but with the breeze it makes sitting in the shade comfortable. We're both dressed in shorts and we can relax and not worry about people overhearing us. Sitting on the grass, close together and facing each other, it's like the world fades away.

I need this Carter fix right now more than I care to admit. His calm, soothing influence. I could barely function during my morning classes, my mind constantly wandering to that text message I'd received.

I don't know what it means, other than impending mental and emotional torture for me.

I also don't know what it means that being around Carter calms me, grounds me, but right now, I'm not stupid enough to push him away.

"Why do you think she wants you there?" he eventually asks.

"Probably something to do with Austin's work. That's usually the only time she trots me out now, since I'm pre-law. I stopped being the adorably polite kid that earned praise for her from her friends around age twelve, when I had a growth spurt and grew taller than her."

"You're kidding?"

I know what he means and I shake my head. "I wish I was." I can't bear the weight of his brown gaze, so I study my salad. "What's it like?" I quietly ask.

"What's what like, buddy?"

"Growing up in a normal family?"

His snort makes me look up. He's smiling. "When I find out, I'll tell you."

"What do you mean?"

"I mean, I didn't really have a choice about my life. It was expected that I'd enlist in the Army. I'm kind of the black sheep for not taking ROTC in high school and in college and then going in as an officer. Like they think I didn't try as hard as they thought I should."

"Yeah, but your parents *love* you. They'd love you unconditionally, wouldn't they?"

A cloud skitters through his features, gone almost before it appears. "I guess. Not very liberal people, though. I mean, not racist or homophobic, but not…progressive."

"You didn't have to earn their love, though."

"True. So what does your mom do for a living?"

"You mean besides being a professional social climber? She's a real estate agent."

"Same thing, isn't it?" He smirks, making me laugh.

"Tell me about it. Chamber of Commerce, Rotary, all the trappings and bullshit. Her and Austin both. Rubbing elbows with local politicians, but not enough juice for state or federal level pols to take an interest in them. Austin's a junior partner, not a senior partner. He pulls in some respectable billable hours, but he's no rock star moving much higher in the firm than he currently is, and Mom knows that. Even if he managed to snag a high-profile case, he's about as photogenic as a pile of dog crap, and nearly as entertaining."

"Sounds like a charmer," Carter snarks.

A comfortable quiet settles between us for a few minutes.

"Do you think she's going to try to play match-maker for you?" Carter asks. It's an…odd question, I suppose, but then again, based on what I've told Carter about my mom, it's not an unexpected one.

"Doubtful. She'd be afraid of me embarrassing her. Probably why she told me I could bring someone. She assumes I'd bring a girlfriend, if I'm seeing anyone."

"Someone who she wants to decide if they're suitable for you or not?"

"Exactly. Wouldn't be the first time." He snorts, making me look up. "What?"

He's wearing an evil grin. "We can tell them I'm your boyfriend."

For a moment, part of me is sorely tempted to do just that. I'd get disowned, which would both solve a lot of my problems, as well as create new ones.

Carter levels a steady gaze my way, one eyebrow arched. "You're not saying nooo."

"I'm…thinking."

"So that's a yes?"

Honestly? As appealing as it is, it's not worth the long-term trouble for the short-term satisfaction.

"No," I grumble. "As tempting as it is, though. If it was my final year and I had a job, I'd say sure, and enjoy the hell out of the fireworks."

He's wearing a playful smile. "You sure? We could go in there, you playing my dutiful pet, and I could really get some rumors buzzing with those people."

I laugh so hard I choke on a sip of water and he has to whack me on the back. "Part of me would love to see the look of shock on her face when you kiss me right there in front of everyone."

He waggles his eyebrows at me. "Oooh, *baby*."

This is one of the reasons I love Carter, because he makes me laugh. "Unless you *really* want to adopt me as a little brother and pay my expenses for me, I probably shouldn't poke that bear quite yet." I sigh, because part of me would *really* love to see the look on Mom's face as Carter kisses me, right there in front of Austin's coworkers and her snooty friends, and I grab his ass and grind against him, just for the shock value.

I'd *totally* let him kiss me for this cause. It'd be the first action I'd had in a while, fake or not.

"Besides," I add, "you might not even want to be roommates with me after we escape her clutches."

We eat in silence for a few minutes before Carter speaks again. "I have a condition about Saturday." He's no longer smiling, and a little fear fills me.

"What condition?"

"When I say we leave, we leave. Period. I don't want any arguments from you when I do, either. I'm not going to let her torture you. I'll make sure I blame it all on me, come up with a socially acceptable excuse that will work, but you will *not* argue with me. Understand?"

"Yes, sir." I don't mean to say that, but it slips out automatically, a trained response to this kind of sober warning from someone older than me.

He reaches over and squeezes my hand. "You don't have to call me 'sir'." He grins. "But don't get me too used to that. I kinda like it."

As always, Carter leaves me laughing and yet again thankful for a friend like him.

* * *

"I'll go with you, if you want," Susa offers that night when we arrive at her place for dinner and laundry. But since the plus-one is just that, it would mean Carter needs to stay behind. I don't dare bring two people with me without asking my mother first, and I want to call her about as much as I want to strip naked and streak through the middle of rush-hour traffic.

Fuck that, I'd *rather* strip naked and streak through traffic.

Honestly? I *need* Carter. You have no idea how relieved I am to be facing this with my friend by my side. A true hero.

A guy my mom can't boss around.

I'm almost hoping she tries to do that, just to see what happens, even if it means repercussions for me on the other end of things.

It'd be worth it.

Carter speaks up before I can. "It's better if I go," he says. "She sounds like someone who likes to push people around."

A dark gleam appears in Susa's blue eyes that makes me rock hard. "I'd like to see her try to push *me* around," she mutters.

Susa's eyes are a gorgeous shade of warm aqua blue that are nothing like my mother's icy blue orbs.

"Down, sweetie," Carter says. "While I'd pay good money to watch that smackdown, it's better if I go with him. I can get him out of there early." He suddenly frowns as pats his pockets, like he's missing something. "Oh, crap. Looks like I've forgotten my medication, and if I don't take it, I have seizures. We really need to leave, Owen. I'm so sorry. I'm an idiot, and I've spoiled this evening for you. I mean, I know how much you were looking forward to seeing your parents."

Susa giggles. "I believe you."

"I think Mom will, too," I volunteer. I don't want to let on to Susa how downright terrified I am of my mother, but at this point, that's kind of moot. "I *really* appreciate you going with me." I turn back to her. "Sorry we're bailing on you Saturday."

"It's fine, guys. Really. I'm going to study. And Daddy's got a few events coming up soon that I'll be driving up to Tallahassee for, so it's cool."

I believe her. There's no double-edged "tone" in her voice to give me a hint that she's being passive-aggressive.

There's never anything in her voice but honesty. Both of them.

"What's wrong, Owen?" Carter asks.

I take a deep breath. "You guys are going to think I'm a doof."

"Try us," Susa says.

They're both staring at me, waiting.

"You guys are my best friends," I quietly admit. "I've never had friends I'm as close to as you two."

Susa gets up, walks over to the couch, and sits in my lap before I can even process what she's doing. "I'll let you in on a little secret, Owen," she says as she drapes her arms around me.

"Yeah?" My pulse explodes. I'm not sure what to do with this, or with her sitting on my lap. I hope I'm not required to stand for a few minutes because my boner will be struggling for freedom for a while.

"You guys are my best friends, too." She plays with my hair. Not the first time she's done that, and I love it when she does. "I trust both of you, and that's something I haven't had in a long time. It's like I can see the three of us together, years from now, just like this."

"Until some guy sweeps you away from us," Carter adds.

I'm looking right at her and know from the way she's staring at him that her next words are for him, and him alone.

"No one will ever take me away from you."

The silence settles around us for a moment, then she looks at me and kisses me on the forehead. "No one's ever taking me away from you guys. I promise." She smiles and plays with my hair again. "God help any woman who thinks she'll take you guys away from me, either."

I know she means those words for Carter, but I'll take what I can get and feel grateful for it.

* * *

Saturday seems to drag. We start the morning with a run at a blistering pace that I know has to be killing Carter, but also forces me to focus on the impacts of my feet against the pavement and not face-planting into an oncoming car.

Although the thought of seeing dear ole Mom right now is inducing enough anxiety in me that I kind of want to face-plant into a car.

It'd be a lot more fun.

Probably a lot less painful.

But the pace of the run forces me to pull my focus inward. In other words—mission accomplished. I'm not thinking about my mother or our impending drive to Orlando later that afternoon.

Or the hell that awaits me there.

Not until we return to the dorm and Carter sends me into the shower first. I stand there under the water with my face pressed against the cool tile and crying like I was ten again and terrified to so much as breathe too loudly for fear of drawing my mother's attention and accompanying wrath.

And wishing I knew how to get her to love me.

How to make her just.

Fucking.

Love me.

Simultaneously, I'm hating myself for still wanting and needing that, even now. Hoping that particular need doesn't poison the well of every goddamned relationship in my life, including my ones with Carter and Susa. I'd deserve it if they ended up together and froze me out because I'm too needy, too clingy.

Because I'm too much work.

Which were things Mom used to snipe at me about when we

were alone at home, and all I wanted was a little of her fucking time.

I was too much work.

I was too needy and clingy.

I needed to learn to be independent, make something of myself on my own.

That she couldn't carry me throughout my life.

That if I was going to be a man, I'd need to learn to act like one.

That if I wasn't careful, I'd end up worthless, like my father.

Or, maybe Carter and Susa will end up freezing me out because the things scrambling through my deeper brain are too strange and out there for them to deal with once the details eventually bleed through and take over.

Which is another reason why I know their talk about getting me elected is a joke, even if they don't know it. Guys like me don't get elected.

Not if they're smart.

Because guys like me, they can either be happy *not* being elected…or get themselves elected, attract attention from everyone, and risk being outed and totally humiliated—or else they shove themselves deep in a miserable closet. Because if they don't, their lives until that very public downfall are filled with fear and self-loathing, waiting for the inevitable disclosure.

It's a hell of a choice, because they can't be both.

Either/or.

I would love to be governor. I'd love to be elected and help my state.

I would *not* love that closet, or living with the constant fear, and I couldn't bear a public downfall.

At some point in this journey, if Carter and Susa stay with me long enough, I'll have to talk them out of their insane plans to get me elected. Susa is the politician, and I'm smart enough to know that. I'll be happy working my ass off helping her reach her goals. She will do great things, and only an idiot wouldn't see that.

I am a lot of things, but an idiot isn't one of them. I have the test scores to prove that much.

I'm also not strong enough to handle today alone, and it's the first time I've ever had someone in my corner to help me through it.

I don't know if I can ever find the words to tell Carter how much this means to me, or how much I appreciate him doing this.

Let's hope it's not the last time he wants anything to do with me.

CHAPTER FIFTEEN

I spend the rest of the morning trying to study, trying to keep my mind anywhere but on tonight. I've ironed my shirt and slacks, as has Carter.

Carter offers to drive us over in my car and let me take over when we're close to my mom's house.

I gratefully accept that offer.

We head downstairs to leave for Orlando around two. I've been obsessively checking a traffic app so we won't get caught in Disney snarls that will make us late and guarantee my mother's ire. We can always cruise around Orlando to kill some time and deliver us to her doorstep exactly on time.

Carter wears slacks, a long-sleeved dress shirt with cufflinks, a tie, and has brought a blazer, which he carries over his arm. His loafers are shined to perfection and the creases in his slacks are perfect.

He *looks* like an attorney. I know I'm dressed to an acceptable level to placate my mother, but next to Carter I feel like a slob, even though I shaved and I fussed with my tie for so damn long that Carter finally walked over, lightly swatted my hands away, and retied it for me.

Part of me is glad Susa isn't going with us, because seeing Carter dressed like this will only make her fall harder for him.

Hell, I'm straight and I think the guy looks hot—broad shoulders tapering to a V above his narrow hips. But he's not muscle-bound like some of the guys we encounter in the exercise room from time to time. He looks like he could easily work his way through one of those TV ninja course competitions, svelte and lithe and barely breaking a sweat as he did. Restrained power contained by the corporate wrapper he now wears as naturally and effortlessly as he wore the desert camo and keffiyeh in that picture on his bulletin board. If I didn't know his history and hadn't seen his scars or how badly pain hits him on some days, I'd think he was still a warrior.

As we reach my car, I hit the key fob and open the driver's door for him without thinking. It's kind of become our thing now, and I don't mind doing it. He seems to enjoy it, as does Susa.

Yes, I'm a people pleaser. I *get* it. This has become like a drug to me, and little things such as this give me hits. Or doing the dishes, the laundry—anything like that.

I don't fucking *care*. I make no apologies for it, because it's a survival tactic, and it's not hurting anyone. Not like he's leading me around in public on a leash or something.

He hands me his blazer to stow with mine in the backseat before taking a minute to adjust the seat, the mirrors, all of that. He's wearing his dark sunglasses today, and when he looks over at me, I know I'm seeing both a preview of the attorney he's going to be one day soon, as well as echoes of the Army veteran.

With the AC cooling my car's interior, he softly ticks off a few points on his fingers. "I want you to let big brother be in charge today. Do *not* try to manage my relationship with your mother, because I'm an adult and can handle her. Do *not* stress over what I say to her, or what she says to me. If I say we leave, we *leave*. If at *any* time you feel overwhelmed, do *not* hesitate to come find me and tap the side of my foot with yours, even if I'm talking to someone."

"We don't need a code word or something?" I'm not even

joking at this point.

"No, because if you just need a few minutes to pull yourself together and I break out the medicine excuse then, the evening's over. The medicine excuse is my nuclear option."

"I can't believe you're actually going with me."

He cuffs the back of my neck, something he's done several times before, either playfully or while we're talking, but it's one of those things I can't begin to explain how good it makes me feel. Probably due to being starved for even innocent physical contact.

"Owen." He waits until I focus on his eyes. "Big brothers don't let little brothers handle shit like this alone. She's *not* scaring me off. She's *not* going to make me hate you, or quit being friends with you, or think less of you. The *only* thing I want you to worry about today is *you*. Do *not* stress about *me*. Got it?"

"Yes, sir." It wants to slip out, and this time I don't apologize for it.

He squeezes the back of my neck before he releases me and reaches for his seatbelt. But he's smiling.

"I'm telling you, I like the sound of that. Haven't been called 'sir' since I was in the Army."

"I'll call you whatever you want me to. Thank you for doing this today."

He shrugs and starts to back out of the parking space. "Got to take care of my little bro."

* * *

We switch places at the gas station a couple of miles from their house, where we top off the tank. Mom and Austin live in a ritzy gated community east of downtown, where a low-end house probably costs over $500k. When Mom divorced Dad, we were living in an older but nice house in the College Park area, northwest of downtown Orlando. I had friends there, loved going out to play with them after school, before Mom would come home from work. Our tree-lined neighborhood felt *real*, like generations of love and laughter had filtered right down to the roots. We had fun fishing in Lake Ivanhoe, even though we never kept what we caught, the few times we did catch something.

Once my parents divorced, and Mom met and married Austin, we moved. I was given zero input or advanced warning. I came home from school one day to find a moving truck parked in the driveway and that movers had already emptied my room.

Worse, some of my stuff was tossed in the garbage, older toys I hadn't played with in a while, but wasn't ready to relinquish yet.

That was my first hard lesson learned about not getting attached to things. I didn't even have time to say good-bye to my friends in the neighborhood. It was a shocking flashback to how I'd come home from school one day to learn that Dad had moved out. I hadn't been allowed to say good-bye to him in person, although Mom did allow a phone call every so often. It wasn't until later I learned she'd used me as a pawn in the divorce, and had wielded their prenup against him with vicious efficiency.

The new house and neighborhood felt sterile and stiff but seemed to thrill my mother, allowing me to see a happy side to her I both envied and resented, because nothing I'd ever done in my life up until that point had ever elicited that kind of reaction from her. The neighborhood was newer, only built a few years earlier, so there were no large, shady trees anywhere in sight.

We were now living with Austin, too, who moved in. I found out then that they'd gotten married the weekend before at a small private ceremony at a local country club, surrounded by friends, while I was at a weekend day camp.

I had to attend a new school. My mother drove me the next morning and enrolled me, and I found out that she'd already withdrawn me from my old school the day before and didn't bother to tell me. There I was, in the middle of a school year, staring down the barrel of a roomful of kids I'd never seen before in my life.

Another valuable lesson, to not get too attached to anyone.

To keep my mouth shut, nod, smile, and not draw attention to myself.

To work hard behind the scenes and make others look good, eschewing any credit for myself, and people would probably like me. Or, at least, not hate me.

Long, golden late-afternoon shadows paint the high-end housing development in rosy colors that conceal the truth about the virtual hell I grew up in. Like an emotional *Silence of the Lambs* reveal kind of moment, except my mother constructs her person-suit out of slices she rips from my soul on a regular basis.

I've done my best to deny her any new yardage, but…

Here we are.

Pulling up to their house in the cul-de-sac means reliving a lot of painful memories that I tend to shove to the background and ignore most of the time. Hence why I love being away at college.

Also why I don't return on weekends when I easily could.

There are already over a dozen cars filling their driveway and parked along the street. I park three houses down and before I shut off the car, Carter turns to me.

"Deep breaths, buddy."

I nod.

"Remember—no matter what she says or does, I'm not getting scared off. You're *not* alone. Okay?"

If I try to speak right now, I'm afraid I might puke, so I settle for nodding.

My stomach is a tight, painful knot I'm not sure can accept food. I long for the quiet, peaceful dorm room, or Susa's living room.

I don't want to be here.

I don't belong here.

I've never felt wanted here, or that this was ever my "home."

I shut off the car and start to reach for my door handle, but he stops me. "What's our code for when you feel overwhelmed?"

I swallow hard and take another deep breath. "I find you and tap the side of your foot with mine."

"Right. Promise?"

"Yes, sir." And I mean it.

I get out and hurry around to his side to open his door and help him out, both because I know he's kind of stiff right now, and because this is part of Carter's plan that he ran through when we switched off at the gas station.

In case anyone's watching, they'll see him having trouble moving. Injured combat vet is a label he'll happily leverage against Mom today. While I'm terrified, I'd be lying if I denied there's a tiny part deep inside me who wants to see Carter take her down a peg or two, regardless of the emotional and financial fallout I'll deal with later.

We pull our blazers on and make our way up their front walk. I'm kicking myself in the ass now that I didn't drop Carter off and go park, but I also realize how badly I need his steady presence right now.

When I reach out to ring the bell, he cocks his head. "You can't just walk in?"

I snort. "No."

"Fair enough."

Maybe Carter's family has an open-door policy, but if I did that, even though technically I still live here and have a key to the front door, I would never hear the end of it if I did.

Mom opens the door, her brilliant, award-winning smile faltering just a notch when she realizes it's me, followed by the faintest scowl of confusion to see a man with me, before the wattage brightens once more. It's like watching a light bulb dim slightly during a brown-out before it pops to life again.

"Hello, Owen. You're right on time. And who is this?"

My mouth feels like shit-flavored cotton. "Mom, I'd like to introduce you to Carter Wilson. He's my roommate, and he's also pre-law. Carter, this is my mother, Elandra Marriott Solemar."

I'm always to include her maiden name. If I don't, I'll catch holy hell for it. I hate that it's my middle name. For the rest of my life, I'm inextricably tied to her by my name.

Now that she knows who he is, his relation to me, anger briefly flares in her eyes and I struggle to remember everything Carter told me about not interfering.

For his part, Carter turns on the charm in a way I've never seen him do before.

"Mrs. Solemar, it's so very nice to finally meet you. Owen's told me so much about you."

Damn. He's *good.* I can see her anger evaporate as she shifts into preening mode.

He's held out his hand, and while I know she's expecting him to shake with her, he actually kisses the back of hers while giving her a slight bow.

I can see it's obviously derailed Mom's usual comfortable responses. Hell, she even blushes a little. I stomp back my jealousy that Carter was able to make her smile like that when I would have killed for that kind of reaction from her about...

Well, anything.

"It's very nice to meet you, too, Carter." She notes our blazers. "If you want, you can leave your blazers in Owen's room, on his bed. Owen, will you please show your friend around and introduce him?" She turns without waiting for a response.

I'm dismissed.

I turn to Carter and find him wearing a playful smile. Then he drops me a conspiratorial wink and I take a deep breath.

"First barrier—passed," I mutter, earning me a chuckle from Carter as he falls into step behind me.

CHAPTER SIXTEEN

Apparently, Mom's positive first impression of Carter means she won't make me suffer much more than she normally does for bringing him. After I find Austin and introduce Carter, I find myself slipping into my usual patterns—checking to see if anything needs refilling, making sure the garbage cans aren't over-full, and in general doing whatever I can to make myself invisible and of use so I don't grab Mom's attention.

Which only works for a few minutes. I suspect Austin is brown-nosing for a bump from junior to senior partner, hence this shindig. He drags me into a clutch of people to introduce me as his "son" and proudly boast how I'm going into law, just like him.

I don't correct him on either point.

He's not my father, and I'd rather be a panhandler than practice the kind of law he does.

When one of the women in that group eyes Carter, a weird frisson of jealousy unexpectedly rolls through me. She's got to be at least my mother's age, if not older.

"And you are?" she asks him with incredibly creepy interest.

He kisses her hand, too, which makes the old bat giggle like a schoolgirl. "Carter Wilson. I'm very pleased to meet you. I'm Owen's roommate, and, it so happens, we're both in pre-law."

"Really? You look like you're older than Owen."

"I am. I'm twenty-eight."

I can see scorn building in her eyes. "Why did you start college

131

so late?"

"I spent eight years in the Army, before my unexpected discharge."

"Unexpected?" Austin asks.

I buckle up and hold on for the ride, barely suppressing the evil giggle threatening to burp free.

"Injured in the line of duty. Purple Heart."

Which barely even scratches the surface of the story, but now the entire clutch's collective attention is fixed on him.

I don't understand how Carter manages to tell the story in such a way that he's both self-effacing and makes himself look like the hero he truly is. I can't even put my finger on how he manages it, but it leaves me listening to the retelling of events just as raptly as the rest of his audience, despite already knowing the story.

"What rank were you?" one man asks.

"Sergeant. E-5." Which is more than even I knew, because somehow, I'd never thought to ask that.

Apparently, a couple of the men now want to relive their own glory days and start peppering Carter with questions about his service, where he'd been stationed, where he went through basic, and telling him stories of their time in the military, and asking about the kind of law he's thinking about practicing.

I sort of…fade out.

Not that I'm complaining about that, because I'm not.

Unfortunately, it leaves me open to Mom catching my eye from across the room, and from the subtle tip of her head, I know I'm being summoned.

Ignoring her isn't an option.

I ease myself out of the circle and make my way over to her, where she starts to introduce me to people whose names I'll never remember and don't even care to. I nod dutifully. Before my mother can truly get cranked up, Carter appears at my side, and I never even noticed him moving across the room.

The wounded combat vet steals my mother's thunder yet again as the group's interest lands on Carter and he entertains them. He's charming, funny, engaging, self-effacing—he's a natural.

I'm shocked the man doesn't want to go into politics, because he'd be amazing at it.

Maybe Susa and I can change his mind.

* * *

I try to hang in there, I really do. I make it through dessert, which in and of itself is a miracle. Mom's taken some pretty hard jabs at me tonight.

Making up for lost time, I suppose.

I laugh them all off because she set up every barb to look like she's "just kidding" and delivered them in front of witnesses. So despite how much I'm hurting inside, I have to smile and laugh them off like I don't think she's serious, like I think she's *just kidding*.

Two words I fucking hate.

Inside, it feels like I'm going through one of those death by a thousand cuts kind of tortures.

Why can't she just fucking *love* me?

I have to stand there like the dutiful son, pretending this isn't ripping me apart even more because I know it's just an act.

It's not real.

Nothing about tonight with her has been real.

Reality is all the times I asked for some of her time, whether for homework or to go do something with me, and I was told how busy she was and how I didn't appreciate how hard she worked. How I should be more grateful she spent so much time working, because it helped pay for all the nice things she gave me, and the nice house we lived in. Always emphasizing how my father never helped out at all.

Reality is being one of the "orphaned" kids at school events where everyone else's parents showed up, like science fairs and school plays.

But she was busy.

Every fucking year. Every fucking time. Because of her money, and later because of Austin's money and the prestige of his law firm, and the fact that he made generous donations to the PTO, teachers would hold phone conferences instead of in-person parent-teacher meetings.

Reality is my mother couldn't have recognized a single damn one of my teachers if they'd walked up and smacked her in the face.

Reality is I can't count the number of times Mom had either one of her assistants or one of Austin's take me to or pick me up from events. She was too busy.

Always too busy.

Reality was once I was older, she set me up with my own Uber account and had me use that, until I was old enough to drive myself.

And now she wants me to stand here with a smile on my face and pretend she's Mother of the Year.

Worse?

I'll let her.

Worse still?

I'll enable her, agree with her, smiling and nodding my head like the good little puppet I've been all my life.

For a few minutes, between dinner and dessert, I escape to my old bathroom and lock myself in, struggling not to cry because she'll recognize it, know that I've been crying.

Worse, so will Carter. I know he will. I don't want to cry around my mother, but I refuse to cry in front of Carter. Not after everything he's survived and endured.

Maybe he can kick my ass even after all he's been through, but in this one way I want to try to measure up.

To endure.

But it's so fucking hard.

The evening is more tolerable for Carter's presence, and for the way he keeps running interference, but he can't stop every instance. Then he's across the room, engaged in conversation with one of the senior partners who could talk the paint off a wall, when Mom traps me by hooking her arm through mine.

Old, ingrained reactions kick in, the familiar, sour taste in my mouth, the tense pain congealing in my stomach. All these are no strangers to me. My gaze drops to the floor and I struggle to remain in place as my body tenses.

If I pull away from her, the way every instinct I have is screaming for me to, I'll pay later.

I'll pay in ways I probably can't imagine for daring to embarrass her by doing it.

Carter's not here, and I can't bring myself to look around for him, knowing Mom will somehow sense that. She doesn't care if I'm paying attention to her, but she will definitely care if it's obvious that I'm *not*.

Mom's droning on about some fundraiser she's leading, and I hope to god she's not thinking about trying to enlist me to help her with it. The last thing I need is more stress on me. At least I have the excuse of my classwork I can use.

"I'm sorry to interrupt, Mrs. Solemar, but I think I left my meds out in Owen's car, and I'm overdue to take them. Owen, if you'll give me your keys, I'll go get them."

It takes me a second to realize Carter is standing right there beside me now.

Even better, my mother's released my arm. I force myself to look at Carter as I fish my keys out of my pocket. The expression on his face is asking—no, *telling* me.

I slide my foot over and tap his before I hand my keys to him.

Every ounce of will I have goes to not bursting into relieved tears when he gives me the most sly and subtle of Carter smirks and a slight nod.

He understands. "Thanks," he says to me, then focuses on Mom. "I'm so sorry to interrupt."

"Oh, not at all, Carter."

I shift to fill the space he just vacated and turn to one of the women Mom is talking to and ask her a question about her daughter. I remember the woman mentioning her over dinner. But even better, it takes me out of arm-holding range of my mom.

When Carter returns, I know we're escaping even before he opens his mouth. I read the gleam in his eyes as he meets my gaze. "Man, I am *really* sorry. I think I left my meds sitting on the counter back in our room. I can't find them. I could have sworn I'd put them in my pocket."

"Oh, we really need to get you back, then," I say. "How overdue are you?"

"An hour."

"Yikes."

Carter speaks to my mother. "Ma'am, I am *so* sorry about this. I feel like such an idiot." He glances my way. "I mean, I *could* drive home and take them and come back to get you, if you'd rather? I'll pay for the gas—"

"Don't be silly," Mom says. "It's quite all right, Carter." Of *course* she says that—she's got several witnesses who would have thought she was a monster if she'd insisted that a disabled war vet drive all the way to Tampa and back just so I could stay behind.

"But I feel so bad about this." I spot the gleam in Carter's eyes. "I know Owen was looking forward to tonight. He was so excited when he received your text the other morning."

"We're just very glad you were able to come with him this evening, Carter," Mom says.

Carter is pitch-perfect. "I truly appreciate your hospitality, Mrs. Solemar. I had a wonderful evening. It was great to get out of the dorm tonight. We're usually busy studying and don't get out that often. Especially with as badly as I'm usually hurting. Owen's so nice, he hangs out with me, brings me food from the dining hall, runs errands for me—he really takes care of me."

I honestly can't tell if Mom's cheesed off or not, and I really don't care. I feel like I'm on the verge of a panic attack.

"You're welcome back any time, Carter," she says. "It was a pleasure to meet you."

We make our good-byes and I grab our blazers from a room that is called mine but damn sure never felt like it. All night, Carter's been acting progressively stiffer, pained. Now he's holding my arm as I slowly walk us back to my car.

He keeps his voice low. "You okay?"

"Yeah. Thank you."

"It's all right."

I help him into the passenger seat. "Stop just outside the development." His tone is firm, but kind.

My reply is automatic. "Yes, sir."

I do manage to not cry until after we've switched places. Carter pats me on the thigh and lets me cry, pretends I'm not. He turns the music on and drives.

It's relief and stress and...

And the realization that this man has done more for me in this short amount of time than my own mother has in *years*.

Has *cared* more about me.

By the time we return to the dorm and I collapse, I'm exhausted. I know that I'll sleep well tonight, at least.

Not exactly an easy sleep, but sleep nonetheless.

Sleep in a place that feels more like home in just a few weeks than any house I've ever lived in.

Sleeping under the same roof as a man who's quickly come to feel more like family than anyone I'm actually related to.

CHAPTER SEVENTEEN

Carter exchanges texts with my mother the next day. She responds with an eloquent, warm-sounding series of messages that would normally indicate someone was perfectly fine with what happened and not to worry about it. She also repeats her statement that he's welcome back any time.

It means, to me, that Mom wants to get her hooks into Carter in some fashion because her guests must have said a lot of positive things about him after we left.

Part of me simmers in anger that she can text with him like that and pretty much ignore me.

Not anger at Carter—anger at *her*.

Meanwhile, Mom returns to not replying to my daily texts.

Status quo—resumed. I guess I shouldn't complain, because at this point her "attention" to me would probably all be negative, or at the very least unpleasant. I also know I shouldn't let it get to me because it's all part and parcel of her being a narcissist, but I'd be lying if I said it doesn't sting.

Carter starts to bring up my birthday again. The question of whether or not to include Susa in my birthday celebration is rendered moot when she opts to head to Tallahassee that weekend to attend a weekend conference with her father. Some sort of political thing. It's a valuable opportunity for her to network and make connections of her own. It's the kind of event she lives for and thrives on. While she asked if I minded if she went and missed the actual celebration, I would never ask her to miss something like that just for my birthday. Plus, she'll actually be with us on my birthday, which is fine.

Besides, it'll give Carter and I time alone together to just be guys, and I know that's healthy, even if I have no clue what it entails. While I'll miss Susa's presence, I'm also eager to do this, to have this rite of passage.

Susa gives us free range of her house for the weekend. She's promised to return early enough Sunday for us all to cook dinner together, and for her to teach me how to make *spanakopita*, a Greek spinach and cheese pie dish that I love.

This birthday is, no shit, the best one *ever*. What they've done for me is damn sure better than what my own mother did, which is to not even bother to text or call me, or send me a card on my actual birthday. Although an extra twenty-five dollars appears in my weekly allowance—and I make sure to thank her for that as soon as I see the deposit alert on my phone.

As opposed to when I emerge from my shower on Thursday morning after our run, I find Carter has left a birthday card on my pillow with a fifty-dollar Panera gift card inside.

He knows I love the place but I won't eat there very often because of my finances.

He's already left for his morning classes, which means I can sit there on my bed and not worry about feeling embarrassed as I sniffle back tears over the sentiment he wrote in the otherwise funny card.

Thank you for your friendship, and for putting up with me, little bro. This has been an amazing year so far, and I can't wait to see what the future holds for both of us. Looking forward to helping you celebrate many more orbits around the sun. — Love, C.

Susa gives me her card that evening when we go over for dinner. There's a fifty-dollar VISA gift card tucked inside a cute card with several dogs on the front making a joke about bones and overindulgence.

She also wrote a note inside.

To my sweet "pet," thank you for your laughter and your friendship. Thank you for everything you do for me, and if I fail to say it enough, I'm sorry, because I do appreciate everything you do. Thank you for being you, and thank you for being in my life.
Luv, Susa
XOXOXO

Again, I feel myself blinking back tears even as I laugh. Then she hugs me from behind and Carter hugs me from the front, enveloping me in their affection. She picked up the "pet" joke after I first made it and runs with it.

Maybe another guy might be offended, but I relish it. I like doing things for her, things that don't cost me money but pay me back a thousandfold just from her dimple smiles, her hugs.

Her laughter.

Her friendship.

A guy could get used to having family like this. Obviously, I've been starved for simple affection, and any inanimate tool could figure that out.

It's that the "joke" hits pretty damn close to home to my secret fantasies, so I cherish and revel in every bit of it. This is one case where the joke is on me *and* is more than welcome. Because I can hide the truth within it.

She's also bought me a Publix cake, marbled with buttercream frosting, my favorite. Together with Carter, we cook what's become one of my favorite meals, her homemade lasagna.

We eat dinner on the couch, watching my favorite movie, *Batman*, the 1989 version with Michael Keaton.

Best.

Birthday.

Ever.

I wish I was kidding, but I'm not. These two people have put together the most amazing evening I could have ever asked for.

"Thank you for this," I tell them as the end credits roll. "Tonight was amazing."

Susa sits in my lap to hug me, lingering with her head against my shoulder. "You're worth it, Owen. You're family." She smiles at me and I know I'm lost to her. Whatever she wants from me, I'll always give it to her.

Even if it means I'm settling for doing her dishes and helping her with IKEA runs and watching while she's probably imagining if she should hyphenate her last name to Carter's or not. Not that Carter's showing that kind of interest in or attention to her, but I know it's not me she really wants.

I don't care. Susa's emotional scraps are a hell of a lot more than my mother ever gives me. I'll accept them gracefully and without hesitation, and give thanks for them.

Carter had carried my plate and his to the kitchen. He returns, leaning over the back of the couch and throwing his arms around both of us from behind.

"Group hug!" He kisses me on the cheek, then Susa, and makes both of us laugh in the process.

"You guys *are* my family," I softly admit, hoping they don't think I'm dopey.

"Of course we are," Susa says. "We *are* a family. We take care of each other and look out for each other."

"And we love each other," Carter says. He's still holding both of us, and I'm in no hurry for the hug to end because it's keeping

Susa right there, snuggled tightly against me. "Because I do love you guys."

"I love you guys, too," I say.

"Me, three," Susa adds.

This feels like perfection. I wonder what's going to slam into us in the future to destroy this fragile bubble. It can't last forever, can it? I'll treasure it for as long as it endures and worry what to do about my shattered heart in the aftermath when that dreaded day eventually arrives.

Now, on Friday night, I'm putting myself in Carter's capable hands and letting him show me a good time. I've never done anything like this before. I never tried to sneak alcohol when I was in my teens, because there was no way I could do something like that without my mother figuring it out.

Ahead of her wrath, I always feel like the terrified ten-year-old. Anything I did that she didn't approve of always ended the same way, with her comparing me to my father and asking me if I want to be "useless" like him.

Friday afternoon after our classes, we pack bags for the weekend—and since we need to do laundry anyway, we grab that—and head over to Susa's in the Snot Box. She'd packed a bag so she could leave from campus as soon as classes ended, meaning, unfortunately, we won't run into her.

Susa still hasn't invested in a guest bed. I'm happy giving Carter the bedroom and taking the couch for myself. Susa told us to feel free to use her bed, and Carter's said he doesn't mind sharing her king-sized bed with me if I don't.

Then again, if he gets me drunk enough, I might not even care. Besides, how would it be any different than me sitting up with him in his bed when he's had nightmares, or the three times I've actually fallen asleep there next to him?

Actually, maybe it would be better if we shared the bed, because I won't hear him if he has a nightmare and I'm in another room.

Honestly, I'm looking forward to this experience. I trust Carter and know he won't let anything bad happen to me. This is a rite of passage I desperately want. I spent so many years under Mom's thumb and never doing anything that I can't wait to see what happens.

I never got to be normal.

Once we moved, I never had "close" friends. Even the guy I could call my best friend in high school, the one I helped win the student council election, we really didn't do anything together like kids usually do.

I wasn't allowed to.

I learned not to ask. If someone asked my mom for me, especially in front of witnesses, of course she'd usually agree to it.

I'd also pay like hell for it later.

But if *I* asked her?

Even in front of people the answer was nearly always a no. Unless it had something to do with academics that would help me earn a scholarship so she didn't have to pay for my college tuition.

There was more than a small measure of fear running through me, the hell she'd drag me through and the repayment she'd extract, if she had to shell out a penny of her own money because I wasn't "smart" enough or didn't work hard enough to earn a scholarship.

We both grab showers at Susa's and change there. Carter tells me to dress in khakis or jeans and a casual button-up. He's wearing khakis, so I match him. I don't know where we're going tonight and, honestly, I don't care. He's in charge, and I'm happy to follow along like a good pet.

"I'm pleasantly surprised," he says as he drives us in the Snot Box.

"About what?"

His sunglasses hide his eyes, but the smirk is there. "I figured you'd be asking me a million questions about our plans."

"Hey, I'm the birthday boy, and you said tonight is all on you. I'm not going to question you."

"Good boy."

He's smirking, but something about the tone of voice he says it in plucks a few hidden strings deep inside me.

I suppress a shiver.

A good shiver.

I know he's kidding around, because he's Carter. Ever since the pet joke became a *thing* with the three of us, he's said stuff like that.

I can't help that every time he does it hits home inside me, hard, and I'm damn sure not asking him to stop.

Especially because I *like* it.

CHAPTER EIGHTEEN

Our first stop is a nice steakhouse in the Hyde Park neighborhood, west of downtown Tampa. Valet parking, the whole nine yards.

Granted, I've eaten in plenty of fine establishments in my life with my mother and Austin. Places where you can't even walk in the door without a tie. I know which fork to use, how to keep my elbows off the table, all of that. But as Carter hands his keys to the valet and joins me, then places a hand in the small of my back to guide me forward…

Something about this feels…*different.*

Not a *bad* different, either.

This kind of feels like a *date.*

We're seated in a booth along the wall. Once the hostess leaves us with our menus, Carter smiles at me from across the table. "Trust me?"

"Of course I do."

He holds out his hand, and I realize he wants my menu. I hand it to him and sit back, realizing the evening is truly out of my control.

I…*really* like that. Because unlike with my mother, where I rarely liked or agreed with what she wanted to do but was required to go along with it anyway, I know Carter won't fuck with me. It's a weird, strange, new thing for me to accept, that there are decent people out there, and one of them is now my best friend.

When our waitress arrives, she wears a chipper smile. "And how are we doing tonight, gentlemen?"

"We have a birthday boy," Carter says, indicating me. "We'll both have water. I'll have sweet iced tea, and he'll have a rum and Coke."

Okay, we're starting this right out of the gate, I guess. I've already got my ID out and ready to show her.

"Thank you." She examines it, smiles as she returns it, and notes our drink orders. "I'll be right back with those and to take your appetizer order."

Carter has already closed his menu. "This is our first stop of the night. I have a little surprise after dinner."

"I'm sure I'll enjoy it."

He grins. "I hope so."

She brings our drinks and Carter orders us stuffed mushrooms as a starter, and places our food orders, too. Apparently he's either paid attention to me or is a really great guesser, because he orders exactly what I would have ordered anyway—filet mignon, rare, salad with Italian dressing, and a baked potato with butter and sour cream. Not that we've been out for steak like this at a restaurant before, but Susa did buy us some one day and we grilled them on her lanai on a brand-new grill she'd purchased just for the occasion.

One afternoon we'd been discussing food, and the best meals we'd ever eaten at restaurants. I'd mentioned filet was my favorite cut, and what I usually ordered when going out somewhere with my mom and Austin. Because a very strange quirk is that Mom and Austin didn't mind spending money on food. It was one of the few things my mother would refrain from criticizing me about.

A little suspiciously—in a good way—Susa sprang the steaks and new grill on us two days later.

For once, it's freeing to have good suspicions instead of bad ones, and it's yet another way these two people make me feel like they care about me.

Once we're alone again, Carter holds up his glass of tea in a toast, and I pick up my rum and Coke.

"To friendship, to brotherhood, and to forever," he quietly says.

Another of those pleasant shivers rolls through me. "To friendship, to brotherhood, and to forever," I echo before we gently clink glasses.

He's watching me even as he takes a swallow of his tea. I literally have never had so much as a sip of wine, because it was never offered to me by Mom or Austin, and I never dared ask. I can smell the rum in the drink and take a tentative sip with the tiny straw in it.

It's nearly eye-watering, but I like it.

Carter slyly smiles. "My pet's growing up."

That almost makes me laugh-snort Coke out my nose.

"Go easy on the alcohol here, or you'll be too sloshed to enjoy part two. You can have one more of those here, if you want one. You *will* be getting more alcohol later."

I'm wondering if he's planning on taking me to a strip club or something, because he knows I've never been to one of those, either.

I don't ask. Why ruin the surprise? Carter's obviously taken great joy planning tonight for me.

That's good enough for me.

When I was growing up, if I was lucky, I was asked where I wanted to go for dinner for my birthday. Other birthdays, Mom decided we were going out and where we were going out, and I acted happy for it regardless.

Because not acting appreciative, even if I'd hated the restaurant, would have definitely been extracted from me later in far less enjoyable ways.

I learned early on how to pick my battles and which ones weren't worth fighting.

Most of them weren't worth fighting.

Yet another reason I made damn sure I earned a scholarship, and why I plan on keeping my grades up so I don't blow it.

Maybe it's the fact that I ate a light lunch early in the afternoon to save plenty of room for dinner, or maybe it's because I'm a lightweight when it comes to drinking, but I feel the rum hitting me about twenty minutes later. We've already finished our appetizer and are working on our salads. I'm on my second rum and Coke, with a glass of sweet tea on standby for when I finish that.

It feels like my face is suddenly hot, flushed, and I guess I laugh or something because Carter smiles as he tips his head and studies me. "Someone's got a buzz."

Now I definitely laugh. "Yeah, guess I do."

"Do me a favor, buddy, okay?"

"Sure."

The humor disappears from his features. "Promise me you'll never drink and drive. Not even a couple of beers. Not until you're more experienced and know exactly how much you can handle. I know I can have one beer and I'll be okay. But I never drive after more than that. If you ever get into a situation where you've had more than one, promise me you'll call me, any time of the day or night. Understand?"

I nod. "Yes, sir."

His sober masks shatters into a playful grin. "How about we make it a rule you call me that, huh? I *really* like it."

I hold up my drink in a salute. "Anything you say, *sir*."

* * * *

Best.

Steak.

Ever.

I don't know what the hell they did to it differently than any other filet I've ever eaten in my life, but that was one fucking great steak.

For dessert I get a heavenly and gigantic piece of chocolate cake with vanilla ice cream. The staff brings it out with a candle in it and singing their version of a birthday song.

I'm still slightly buzzed when we leave there and head to part two of the evening.

"Where to now?" I ask. "Strippers?"

He laughs. "You'll see."

I'm simultaneously disappointed and intrigued to discover our destination is a boutique craft beer tap room and brewery not far from the steakhouse. Carter gets us a table and goes up to the bar to place our orders, taking my ID with him. He returns with two glasses of ice water.

"I know I'm a little tipsy, but that's the clearest looking beer I've ever seen."

He grins as he returns my ID. "They're coming. Hold your horses."

A few minutes later, a waitress brings us our orders. Carter gets a smallish glass of something very pale and amber in color.

I get three planks set in front of me, each with four small glasses set in cutouts, arranged from darkest to lightest in color on each one. The waitress quickly explains what each one is, including leaving us with a small whiteboard with each choice listed.

"Holy crap," I mutter as she leaves us. "That's a lot."

He grins. "Figured we might as well start testing and training your palate now." He picks up his glass, sniffs it before sipping, and smiles. "Want a sip?"

"Sure." It's a little on the bitter side, but not like black-coffee bitter. "What is that?"

"It's an IPA brewed over in Ybor."

I stare at the twelve glasses before me. "How do I start doing this?"

"Well…" He picks up the little whiteboard and points at the first option, the darkest one on the first plank. "That's a coffee and chocolate porter. It'll taste a little heavy, probably a little bitter, but sip it slowly and see if you can taste the notes in it."

I pick it up and do what he did, sniffing the contents first before hesitantly sipping. It is bitter, but not unpleasantly so. I can taste hints of a molasses kind of undertone, and coffee and chocolate. "That's good."

"Don't drink it all at once. Try the others."

We work down each flight, as he tells me they're called, Carter explaining all the choices to me. What really hits me hard—and maybe I was feeling even more emotional than usual because of the alcohol—was that at no time did he come off as condescending, or make me feel stupid.

In fact, I note this. "Sorry I'm so stupid about—"

"Hey, *no*." I look up at his firm tone. "I don't *ever* want to hear you use that word about yourself."

I blink back tears. I heard that word multiple times a week—if not a day—growing up. Usually with Mom chiding me, "Don't be stupid." Sometimes with her outright calling me stupid.

"You're new to this," he adds. "Don't ever say that about yourself. You're a smart guy."

"I've never had alcohol before. I said that, right?"

He smiled. "Yeah, you did. But I didn't mean alcohol. I meant you're new to having people who love you."

Okay, now I *am* crying. He hands me a napkin and sits back to let me pull myself together. "Sorry," I mutter.

"Stop apologizing, buddy. We're here to have fun tonight, okay? I want this to be a night you'll remember forever."

"It already is."

And that's the truth.

* * *

Two of the choices are *really* damned good, and Carter even takes a little sip of each. Then he orders two sixty-four ounce growlers of those to take home with us later.

But we're not done yet.

He orders me a glass of each, larger than the glass he'd had.

"Enjoy."

I'm definitely drunk now, and giggle a little. "Wow. Planning on taking me home and having your way with me, sir?" I waggle my eyebrows at him. "Because you probably *totally* could at this point."

He rests his elbow on the table, props his chin in his palm, and smiles. "Don't give me ideas, buddy. Or are you offering me that blowjob instead of laundry option?"

I hold up the first glass, a dark amber barleywine. "Another couple of these, I might just bend over and let you fuck me, if you promise to give me a reacharound."

"Oooh, *baby.*" He blows me a kiss. "Lucky for you I believe in informed consent, and a drunk can't consent."

I struggle not to blow beer out of my nose as I laugh. I love that we can joke around like this without it getting weird.

Then again, I am *really* fucking drunk now.

And I'm *loving* it.

This has truly been the most perfect birthday of my life, one where I don't feel resentful or like I'm a disappointment.

I know I'll cherish this night—as much as I can remember of it—for the rest of my life.

* * *

I barely remember the drive back to Susa's. I do remember I kind of lean on Carter to make my way outside the tap room, the world spinning a little. I squint as we approach the Snot Box.

"I love you, sir, but your car is butt-ugly."

He chuckles. "Yeah, it is. But we'll never lose where we parked it."

"This is true."

Fortunately, I don't throw up in his car. I'm not that drunk, I guess. We make it to Susa's and he makes me wait in the Snot Box while he goes inside first, turns off the alarm, and puts the two growler jugs in the fridge. Then he comes out for me and helps me out of the car. I don't want to lean on him too much and hurt him, but I over compensate and almost fall over the other way.

"What are you doing?" he asks. "You're going to fall."

"You're so nice to me, sir, and I don't want to hurt you!"

He snorts. At least, I think it's a snort. "You're drunk, Owen. I've *got* you. Lean on me, buddy." He gets me inside and heads straight for Susa's room.

"Oooh! Looks like I'm going to bed with you after all!"

Now he definitely laughs. "That's right, Owen. You're going to sleep with another man tonight."

"Haha! Does that make me a metrosexual, sir?"

He sits me on the edge of her bed as he laughs again. "I don't think that word means what you think it means, buddy." He kneels in front of me to help me get my shoes and socks off. I stare down at him, his hunched shoulders, and for a moment I wish our positions were reversed.

I wish it was me kneeling, for him or Susa, at this point I don't even care.

Then he sits back and smiles. "You need help with your shirt and pants? Or are you too drunk?"

I try to get my shirt unbuttoned and give up after the first one. He helps me out, unbuttoning it down to the fourth button and then pulling it up and over my head for me, followed by my undershirt.

I flop back. "Might as well strip me, sir."

He laughs again, shaking his head as he reaches down and unfastens my belt and slacks. I sort of flop around a little so he can get them down and off me, then I lay there in my briefs, unsure what I'm supposed to do next.

"You want to sleep like that?" he asks. "Because I gotta say, that doesn't look comfortable."

"I'm stuck, sir."

He helps me sit up and gets me turned and situated on the bed. He strips down to his boxers and turns on the TV, then turns off the lights. He grabs his laptop and sits up next to me.

I roll over onto my side and look up at him. "Thank you for tonight, sir."

His gaze settles on me, and it feels like something's passed between us.

Or maybe I'm just *really* fucking drunk. Still, I trust Carter, especially after the way he took care of me at my mom's house.

He reaches over and runs a hand through my hair, ruffling it playfully, a smile on his face that almost looks…sad. "You're very welcome, boy. Happy birthday." He's looking at something on the screen.

"What are those?"

"Hmm?"

I squint, trying to see, and point, but everything's blurry.

"Oh, it was a link on Facebook. You know how much I love Doctor Who."

"Yeah?" It's something we share, although he knows more about the show than I do.

"They're rings with Gallifreyan writing on them."

Okay, the more I look, and squint, the more I can see that's what they are, a dark blue with the round, ornate scrollwork etched in grey. "Those are cool."

"Yeah." I don't understand the wistful, almost sad expression he's suddenly wearing, so I decide to try to cheer him up.

"Do you want to talk?" I ask.

"Sure." He sets his laptop aside. "What do you want to talk about?"

I shrug. I'm at a loss now. "I've never done this before."

"Done what?"

"Sleep with a guy."

I think he's humoring me. "You haven't, huh? Seems like you've fallen asleep in my bed a couple of times already."

"Oh." I think about that. "Yeah, I guess I have. Sorry."

"No, I didn't mind at all. I sleep better with you there."

That makes me feel good in unexpected ways. "Then if you need me to, you ask me. I'm happy to."

"I will." He studies me. "So what do you want to talk about?"

"I don't know. What do guys usually talk about?"

"Well, we could talk about fantasies."

"Fantasies?"

"Yeah." He smiles. "What gets your rocks off? We've never really talked about that."

My inhibitions are gone. I want to live in this exact moment forever. "You'll laugh."

"No, I swear I won't." He holds his hand up. "I'll share if you share."

Maybe it's because of the alcohol, I don't know. I've *literally* never talked to anyone about this before. "I want to...take care of someone, you know?"

"Take care of them how?"

"Be of service to them." My face heats, but I don't even care anymore. "Like be their slave. Not do disgusting things, but... Like when you took my shoes off for me. Like..." I don't know how to explain it.

"Like how you take care of me and Susa?"

"Yeah!" I nod. "Exactly! The chores, be...available to her."

"Available how?"

"You know." More heat floods my cheeks. "Sexually. Be under her control."

"Her Mistress to your slave?"

"Yeah." He's not laughing at me, so I stumble forward through this. "Being put over her lap and spanked if I displease her."

Carter leans in. "Being made to kneel for her to please her?"

My cock is now rock-hard and twitches at that mental image. That's actually one of my hottest fantasies. "Yeah. Stuff like that."

"Discipline and service, then. What about bondage?"

"Like ropes?"

"Maybe. Or being made to wear her cuffs and collar like her good boy."

"Oh, *yeah…*" I reach down and squeeze my cock through my briefs.

"Must be making you horny," he says as he grabs his laptop.

"Yeah."

He pulls up a browser window and calls up a website, quickly browsing to what he wants, then showing me.

It's a porn site, of course. But this particular video…

Holy shit!

It's literally something out of one of my darkest fantasies. He full-screens it so I can see it more easily. A woman in a corset and short skirt is sitting in a chair while a naked guy kneels on the floor in front of her.

He's wearing a leather collar, leather wrist and ankle cuffs…

And nothing else.

He's giving her a foot rub, and she's holding what looks like a rattan cane in her hand, resting across her lap. Pretty soon, she starts making him kneel in different positions, occasionally smacking him with the cane if he does something wrong.

Without considering the ramifications, I shove my briefs down and start stroking my cock. Everything else fades away—even Carter's presence right there on the other side of the bed—as I drop into the fantasy.

In my mind it's Susa, not the woman on the video. And it's me rubbing her feet and performing the different poses per her orders, basking in the sweet smile she's wearing, absorbing her praise like she's the sun and I'm a plant desperate for its true shine and heat after years spent in a greenhouse under grow-lights.

That video ends too damn fast, but he calls up another one. This is two guys, one dressed in jeans and a tight black T-shirt. The other guy wears a jock, leather cuffs on his wrists and ankles, and a collar. Except he's bent over a bench and hooked to it with clips. The man on top starts spanking him with a paddle, and now I'm…gone.

I want it all—all of that.

Carter's voice pierces through the haze. "I bet you'd be a good boy for me, wouldn't you?" It's the same tone of voice he used on me that night at Mom's, when we returned to the car and he told me to stop outside the gate.

"Yes, sir."

He strokes my hair. "I could teach you positions. Let you serve me. Teach Susa how to be a good Domme for you. Would you like that?"

I nod, my gaze fixed on the screen. The Top has laid the paddle across the other guy's back, walks around to his head, unzips, and starts face-fucking him. "Yes, sir."

Carter's hand grips my hair firmly, his voice rasping in my ear. "Then show me how much you'd like it, *boy*. *Come* for me. *Now*."

I do. It's the most powerful orgasm I've ever experienced, like my balls are going to turn themselves inside out.

Sweet oblivion quickly takes me under.

CHAPTER NINETEEN

I wake up the next morning in bed beside Carter.

Okay, that's not exactly...accurate.

I wake up draped *over* Carter, with my head on his chest. He's already awake. He's got one arm hooked around my shoulders, and is scrolling through e-mails on his phone with his free hand.

I also feel like an elephant stampeded through my brain and that pain is more than enough to drive away any feelings of mortification I might have about the position I find myself in when I awaken.

Although I'm not exactly complaining about the way it felt to discover that I was snuggled against someone, before my brain engaged and I realized who that someone was. Unfortunately, with my head throbbing, I'm also not exactly in the best frame of mind to unpack and examine any of that right now.

I slowly sit up, groaning as I do. "What the hell?"

"Welcome to adulthood," Carter says, sounding all too amused. "Hangovers 101."

"Duuuude. This is *not* fun."

"No, the fun part was last night. Especially after we got back here."

Some mental images flash through my head, and I groan again.

Holy.

Shit.

Never in my life have I ever wanted anyone to find out about my fantasies.

Especially Susa. It's bad enough this happened in her bed. At least she wasn't here last night.

I also hope I haven't borked my friendship with Carter beyond repair. "Look, I'm really sorry for whatever I did."

"Why? I'm not sorry. You had honest fun for the first time in your life. Dude, I was in the military. You think I've never seen guys jerk off before? Or wasn't one of them? Or getting drunk? Or jerking off after getting drunk? Last night was nothing, buddy. We're good." He smiles. "But I do want to talk today."

My stomach feels scrambled, and not only because of my hangover. "Talk?"

"Yeah. I suspect you're feeling pretty miserable inside for some reasons that you don't need to be. Since Susa's not here, let's talk. Okay? Between us. I have some valuable real-world experience that tracks pretty closely to what we, eh, discussed last night."

I'm not sure I remember everything we discussed last night. There are snippets in my brain, but some of it's…fuzzy. "I think I need coffee first." I look down at my stomach. "I'm not…" I swallow hard. Unless I imagined things last night, Carter must have cleaned me up.

Carter's out of bed now. "Yes, I cleaned you up after you passed out. I didn't want to accidentally get spooged." He looks entirely too amused at the mortified sound I make over that matter-of-fact statement. "Buddy, you're adorable. I'll go start the coffee. You go wash your face. You'll feel better."

He heads out of the room. He's wearing boxer shorts.

Last night…

There are bits and pieces of memories swirling around, some

clearer than others. I *think* I remember everything clearly up until the car ride to Susa's.

I remember us talking a little. Something about Doctor Who rings.

The porn.

I shiver as I remember the sound of his voice in my ear, firm and commanding, as I jerked off.

I remember experiencing pleasure so intense I literally passed out.

Fuck.

I climb out of bed and head to the bathroom and use it, wash my hands, my face. I shuck my underwear and pull on a pair of sleeping shorts from my overnight bag before I make my way out to the kitchen.

Carter's already set out a bottle of ibuprofen and a glass of water for me on the counter.

"Thanks."

"You're welcome...*boy.*"

I freeze, gooseflesh rippling my skin.

"How does that make you feel?" he asks in a conversational tone.

"How does what?"

"That. When I call you boy like that. *Boy.*"

I think I whimper as my eyes drop shut. Part of me wants to slither to the floor, onto my knees, so I can kneel before him.

I can only nod.

When Carter speaks again, it startles me a little because he's standing right behind me now, his quiet voice in my left ear.

"What if I tell you we can make most of your fantasies come true for you, *boy*? What if I tell you I was once exactly in the position you're in? What if I tell you not only am I okay with you calling me *Sir*, capital *S*, but I'd like to help you explore those fantasies?"

It's hard to breathe, and not because of the hangover.

Because it feels like I'm perched upon the precipice, hanging from the apex of something *huge* and I'm terrified to let go and fall into Carter's waiting arms.

I'm also terrified to *not* let go.

"What's the...what's the catch?"

"There is no catch. You decide you want to stop doing it, we stop."

My hands are shaking too badly to open the bottle of ibuprofen. So badly, in fact, that it sounds like I'm playing maracas until Carter's hands close around mine, he takes the bottle from me, opens it, and shakes three tablets into my palm. Then he closes the bottle, sets it down, and leans against the counter, right next to me. I sense him looking me in the eyes—rather he's trying to, because I won't meet his gaze yet.

I *can't* look at him yet. I swallow the tablets and chase them with water. I have to hold the glass with both hands.

I'm still trying to process that not only is he not going to use what I did last night against me...he wants to help me do...*more*?

"Slow breaths, buddy. You're going to hyperventilate."

I realize only after he says it that, yes, I'm gasping for air. I have to lean forward, my hands braced on the counter, eyes closed. I think I'm close to a panic attack. I've had a couple in my life, during the summer between my junior and senior years in high school, before I was certain I'd landed my scholarship. I never told anyone about them, afraid that would bring more of Mom's wrath upon me for being "weak."

Because I also worried it would provide an additional easy target for her to wound me.

Carter's hand settles between my shoulder blades. "Owen, you're a submissive. I've had a feeling you were ever since we met. I've *been* where you are. I *know* what you want, what you *need*. I also know how terrifying it is admitting it. Please, let me help you."

Part of me wants to say yes right now.

Part of me wishes he was Susa.

The two parts of me are at war, but kinda on the same…side, I guess?

"I'm so confused."

"I know, buddy." Everything about Carter right now seems gentle and tender, like I'm a frightened horse he's trying to calm. I get that. The rational part of my brain that excelled on my SAT scores and had the stratospheric GPA in high school *understands* this.

The part of me I've always kept locked tightly away and been terrified to show to anyone else is screaming to be acknowledged and finally set free.

So to speak.

I'm crying and don't even realize it until I hear the sound of paper towel ripping and he dabs my cheeks with it. The other hand doesn't leave my back.

"Owen, there's *nothing* wrong with you. Not a damn thing. Some people are dominant in all areas of their life. Some are dominant in nearly every other part of their lives, and being submissive for a little while is a mental and emotional vacation for them. Some people are submissive more often. Some are what are called Alpha submissives. And some people are switches."

I struggle to absorb his words. "What are you?"

"Started out submissive, situationally. Became switchy. Now, I'm a Dominant. And that happens, too. People evolve. Start out one thing and realize later they're something else. Or they're one thing in one situation, and another thing in others. There's no right or wrong."

Oooooh, yes, there is. Especially in my mother's house.

"Do your parents or family…know?" I ask.

Now he snorts. "*Hell*, no. That all happened in Germany, when

I was in the Army." A soft sigh escapes him. "We can talk about all that, too. Most of it. Some of it's still too difficult for me to talk about. Too...raw."

I think about what he'd said about a situation not working out. "The woman you got the vasectomy for?" I force myself to look him in the face, even though I can't quite bring myself to look him in the eyes yet. So I focus on his lips. Morning stubble shadows his cheeks, as it does mine.

He nods. "Yeah. This is one of those times I'm going to ask you not to repeat what we talk about, and I'll give you the same courtesy. Not even with Susa. Okay?"

I suck in a shaky breath. Carter's presence in my life, from day one, has been nothing but...good.

My anti-Mom.

"Yes, Sir."

There's a ray of joy so sweet and pure in the look he gives me that it makes something inside me respond, beg for more, like part of him is calling out to me.

I'm still perched on that precipice and looking down on both sides.

Do I return to what I know? A miserably closeted life where I'm too afraid to confide in anyone and I hide the real me?

Or do I allow Carter to coax me down and trust him to catch me?

My life has been spent in fear, in useless attempts to make my mother happy, all so she'll love me.

All so she'll *want* me.

Carter wants me, who I am and the way that I am.

I force myself to look him in the eyes. "This is between us?"

He nods. "Unless you want us to bring Susa in."

Tendrils of fear threaten to strangle me again. "What if she wouldn't be okay with that?"

He shrugs. "If I don't think she will, we won't tell her. But I'm pretty sure she will."

"You do?"

"I do." His gaze holds mine and I feel calm trying to creep in. "We can talk today, if you want to," he says. "Or we can do more. At the very least, let me make you some French toast and get some food and water in you. You'll feel better."

"I thought submissives were supposed to do all that."

He's dead serious when he lays his other hand on my shoulder and squeezes. "Every good Dominant knows their first responsibility is to take care of their submissive."

CHAPTER TWENTY

While Carter cooks breakfast, he makes me sit at the counter and drink another glass of water before he'll let me have coffee.

"I don't want you to get dehydrated," he says. "One of the best things you can do after a night like last night is drink water."

I do as I'm told. There's part of me that knows this is just a temporary bubble of perfection, but I don't want to escape it. I want it to continue.

Not the hangover—the rest of it.

This.

Whatever *this* is.

"I hope you had fun last night," he adds.

"I had a *lot* of fun last night. That meal was amazing. I'd like to go back to the tap house. I think maybe one of those flights would have been okay. Possibly two."

"Yeah, the two full pours, on top of three flights, and two rum and Cokes, really knocked you for a loop." Carter smiles. "Hey, good news is, now you have a baseline."

"Yeah. Oh, wait. We have more of those two I really liked, don't we?"

"Yep. Maybe later we can *moderately* indulge," he says. "Have some with dinner."

"Agreed. With the moderation, I mean."

He doesn't look up when he speaks again. "Or, we can finish them both off tonight, before Susa gets back tomorrow, and see what happens."

The air has taken on a sudden density it didn't possess before. I don't know what the right answer is.

I don't know what he wants to hear.

I know what *I* want to say, and it terrifies me at a visceral level I didn't even know existed within me before now.

Because I want to say yes.

I want to not just say yes, but *fuck* yes.

He glances at me, his brown gaze full of intense mystery.

"We could," I say. "What do you want to do?"

When Carter meets my gaze, I force myself not to look down, not look away.

"Honestly?" Not trusting my voice, I nod. "I want us both to stay sober while I show you what I think you need today. That way, you can tell me if I'm right or not. We can get drunk together later." He focuses on cooking again.

Together...

Carter is a study in contradictions. You'd think a guy with his history, his experiences, would be hard in mind and personality. Kick-ass, taking shit from no one. The Carter I've come to know is multi-faceted and full of mysteries whose depths I now realize I have yet to plumb. There is so much I don't know about him.

He has a gentle, tender side that I suspect only Susa and I get to see.

"Okay."

He doesn't look up from the stove. "Okay, *what?*" It's not snippy in tone, more matter of fact, and I realize what he's looking for.

"Okay, Sir," I say.

He smiles. "My *very* good boy."

That feeling deep inside my gut tightens again, in a good way. In a way that I want to continue feeling.

* * *

Breakfast is, of course, delicious. Because, of course, it's fricking Carter cooking it.

The other guys in the quad pod were disappointed when we told them we weren't going to be there Sunday morning, but we told them they were welcomed to continue the Sunday Mornings With Carter tradition in our absence.

Seriously, if they can't cook French toast and scrambled eggs on their own by now, they're hopeless and deserve to starve.

I want Carter to myself tomorrow morning.

Especially now.

I am feeling reasonably better by the time we finish eating. Enough so that I offer to take care of the cleanup. Washing dishes actually makes me feel better because I don't mind doing it. I've enjoyed some of the best conversations of my life during our times together while cooking and then following dinner, listening to Susa and Carter talking about politics or anything else while I stand at the sink.

Carter lounges against the counter and sips another cup of coffee as I wash dishes. "Let's discuss some boundaries," he says.

"Boundaries?"

"Limits." He turns to me. "Hard limits, soft limits. For both of us."

"Like what?"

"Like what we do can't interfere with school. We both have to keep our grades up."

I nod. "Okay. That's easy."

"No pictures. I mean, nothing compromising. That also goes both ways."

"Agreed." But I don't understand how I could take a

compromising picture of him if I'm the one who's…whatever it is that I am.

"We'll have different modes. Vanilla mode versus the rest of the time. Your default mode will be boy to my Sir."

I need a moment to digest that and Carter doesn't rush me. "How do I know the difference?"

"If one of us needs to flip into vanilla mode, we use the other's name."

"I feel like I'm missing something. That sounds too easy."

"It doesn't have to be difficult."

We spend so much time around Susa, I suspect that vanilla mode will end up being our default soon enough.

"Okay."

"Yes, *Sir*," he corrects.

Two emotions simultaneously vie for superiority—need and rebellion.

Need wins out.

Easily. "Yes, Sir," I repeat.

"Good boy." He reaches over and doesn't just ruffle my hair. It's like he's massaging my scalp, and it feels so good that my hands still and my eyes drop closed, my head bowing as he does it.

"See?" he softly asks. "This isn't all about pain and beatings. Not unless you want it to be."

I might literally kill anyone who tried to interrupt us right now. Contentment flows through me as I breathe, basking in…this.

Whatever *this* is.

His hand slowly slides down the back of my head and closes around the nape of my neck, resting there. "Finish the dishes, boy," he quietly says. "Then come meet me in the living room." It's not his usual tone of voice. It bears the edge and firmness of that night when leaving Mom's, but it's also tender.

"Yes, Sir."

I can't suppress my disappointed moan when he releases my

neck and leaves the kitchen.

I have to shake myself out of the spell and hurry to finish, to get the dishwasher going and to wash and dry the items that don't go in it. It takes me less than ten minutes, and I scurry out after Carter.

He's still wearing his boxers and nothing else, and watching TV from where he's lounging on the end of the couch. When I emerge from the kitchen, he points at the floor in front of him, and despite knowing I'll be blocking his view of the TV, that's where I stand, right next to the end of the coffee table.

He looks up at me. "Beyond what we've talked about, here are my rules to start with." He ticks them off on his fingers as he lists them. "Full honesty, even if you feel embarrassed. You follow my orders when I give them, or you flip into vanilla mode and explain why you can't, as the situation warrants. You will not date anyone. From this moment on, I handle your mother. Thoughts?"

"I'm not dating anyone, so that's easy. But how are you supposed to handle my mother?"

"It means you bring everything to me."

"I'm supposed to text her every day."

"Is that her rule, or something you started doing because she expected it?"

I think about it. "The second." He arches an eyebrow at me and I realize what I've done. "The second, Sir."

I'm rewarded with a playful smirk. "Good boy. Does she reply every day?"

He knows this, but I answer anyway. "No, Sir. She usually doesn't."

"What happens if you don't text her every day?"

"I honestly don't know, Sir. I know she'll make life hell for me."

"How?"

"She would probably withhold my allowance."

He slowly nods. "So that's the only hold she has on you?"

"It's a pretty damn big one, Sir. I'd have to get a job."

"What if it wasn't an issue?"

I'm not sure what he means. "I don't understand."

"What if there was a way to eliminate that concern from the equation?"

I laugh. "Like, you mean hitting the lottery?"

He remains strangely serious. "Don't worry about the specifics. If money wasn't an issue, and that worry was removed, would you still text her every day?"

My smile fades. "Carter, I'm not going to ask you or Susa to support me. I feel bad enough you two won't let me chip in for groceries more often." I've resorted to leaving twenties stashed in Carter's belongings, or somewhere in Susa's house, as I can afford it. Then when I'm asked if it's my money, I just shrug and neither confirm nor deny.

Who says I won't make a great attorney?

"That wasn't my point, *boy*. Answer my question without over-thinking it."

Part of me rebels at engaging in useless what-if rhetoric. Because I am beholden to my mother, to keeping her favor until I graduate from law school and start working, so that I'm not utterly fucked.

"Yes, Sir, if it wasn't for the money issue, I wouldn't worry about texting her every day." I add a caveat. "I mean, and if I can bum a place to stay during breaks if I need to, off you or Susa, when I can't stay in a dorm."

He leans forward and sets his mug on the coffee table. "Unless you decide to end this arrangement between us, you are always guaranteed a place to stay." He meets my gaze. "Even then, if you end this, as long as we're still friends you don't ever have to worry about being homeless, I promise."

I blink back the sudden prickle of tears in my eyes over that statement. I know he means it. Carter never engages in idle bravado. "Thank you, Sir."

"You don't have to thank me for being your friend, boy. I hope we get to be much more than that, and for the rest of our lives." He doesn't clarify that remark and continues. "You need to understand that part of what I'm going to do is break you down in the ways you need to be broken."

I try not to react, but a frisson of fear sweeps through me.

He tilts his head as he studies me. "What's wrong?"

It's spooky how he can read me. "That doesn't sound...good, Sir."

"It's designed to instill your trust in me."

"My mother has broken me all my life, and I damn sure don't trust her."

"Maybe 'break' isn't the right word to use," Carter says. "I'm sorry. I didn't mean to scare you. This won't be an easy process, though. I'm not approaching this as a game. I can promise that, on the other side, you'll understand better what I'm trying to say, and you'll thank me for it."

"Because you've done this?"

He sighs. "That, and because I know what *not* to do."

CHAPTER TWENTY-ONE

So here I stand this Saturday morning, my hangover mostly not bothering me now that I've had ibuprofen, water, and breakfast, with my best friend and roommate looking up at me from where he's sitting on our other friend's couch.

Then Carter quietly says one word that makes a record screech painfully echo through my fuzzy, aching brain.

"*Strip.*"

I blink, thinking I misheard him, or that he's going to smile and laugh and say something like, *You should have seen the look on your face!*

But none of that happens. He sits, motionless, waiting.

"Sir?"

I can't read his expression. "Was I not clear?"

"I..." I swallow hard. "What does that have to do with what we're doing?"

"Because most of what we're doing, when we have appropriate privacy, will be done with you naked. So you'd better get used to it now. Don't make me repeat myself, *boy*."

I'm...torn. I mean, sure, in high school I dressed out for PE and we had showers, or in our room at the dorm, but this is...

Deliberately baring myself to someone. Hell, I barely let the three girls I slept with see me naked.

Carter sits back, his fingers laced behind his head, waiting.

I don't even know what *to* say.

I do not want to say *fuck this shit* and turn and walk away. Hell, last night I jerked off while lying in bed next to him. The fact that I was drunk is besides the point—I trust him. Not like he hasn't seen me naked already.

With my cheeks flaming hot, I push my shorts down and step out of them. When I straighten, my instinct is to stand there with my hands covering myself.

Carter doesn't move. "Hands at your sides, boy." His tone remains calm, softly firm.

I didn't think it was possible to blush this hard and not pass out from a stroke or something. Somehow, I make myself obey and stand there in front of him.

His gaze is focused on mine. "You aren't the first guy I've seen naked, Owen." His tone still sounds gentle, friendly. "You're going to be amazed how quickly you'll get used to being naked, and how weird it'll feel when you aren't."

"You said my name. Does that mean we're...done?"

He smiles. "No. It means if you want to ask me why I'm stripping you, go ahead."

I take a deep breath. "Why, Sir?"

"The goal is for you to learn to focus only on what I tell you to, regardless of distractions. To focus on *me*. Whether you're kneeling in front of me when we're alone, like we are now, or we're in the middle of a crowded store and I need your attention. I want you able to tune out everything except what I tell you to focus on, which usually means me. It also means forcing you to get rid of feeling self-conscious, and this is the easiest way to do that. That also means conditioning you in a variety of ways. Besides, I can't spank you if you've got clothes on. I mean, I *can*, but it's a lot more fun without them in the way. Questions?"

Yeah, a fuck-ton of them, but I shake my head and hope many of them will be answered along the way.

"Another rule is that I now control your orgasms."

"*What?*"

He hasn't moved, still sitting there with his hands laced behind his head, but he arches that eyebrow at me again.

"What, Sir?" I repeat.

"It's about control. This isn't some fraternity pledge-week game. This is long-term, and I'll teach you self-discipline, self-confidence, and show you that you can do anything you put your mind to. You'll learn to push yourself harder than you ever have before, and take pride in your accomplishments. I'll reward you, I'll punish you, sometimes both at the same time. What do you have to lose? But riddle me this—think about all that you stand to gain, hmm?"

Okay, so most of my fantasies feature Susa taking control of me like this.

I nod, unable to say it.

"Are you agreeing to that term, to me controlling your orgasms?"

I nod.

Carter forces the issue. "*Say* it, boy."

"Yes, Sir."

"No. Say, 'I want you to have control of my orgasms, Sir.'"

"You're a bastard." That pops out before I can stop it.

Except Carter laughs. "Not the worst I've been called, boy. Not the worst you'll call me, either. And not the first time I've been called that. I'm *absolutely* a bastard, and I'll proudly admit it." His expression hardens. "Now, *say* it, or say my name and put an end to this. Your choice."

Part of me wants to say his name and end this madness right now.

A bigger part of me is dragging the rest of me over the edge of the precipice, toward him, wanting this.

Wanting *all* of it, because for the first time in my life it's something *I* want, and it's within my grasp.

Not just wanting it—*needing* it.

"I want you to have control of my orgasms, Sir." I whisper the words, because that's all the volume I can manage.

Carter's face transforms into a beaming smile that makes my pulse surge. "Such a *good* boy for me," he softly says as he rises from the couch to stand in front of me.

Internal programming is thrown into complete chaos as my soul, body, and brain all struggle for control.

Then he reaches out and grabs my cock, squeezing it. It startles me and I flinch, but his other hand cups the back of my neck and traps me there even as my cock hardens in his hand. He pulls my head forward, so our foreheads are touching.

"Good boys get rewards," he says as he quickly strokes me. "You may come."

I...I don't even know what's going on. My body is merrily following along, my cock aching in that glorious way that tells me I'll be coming *really* fast. That it's someone else's hand on my cock besides mine is a strange sensation, but Carter obviously knows his way around a cock. I'm not exactly lubed, but I'm leaking pre-cum and he smears that around with his hand.

When my cock explodes only moments later, I reflexively reach out and grab him for balance, holding on and trying not to fall over from the intensity of my climax. The sudden lubrication allows his hand to quickly slick back and forth, using more pressure, almost too intense to bear now. I think he's going to stop, but he continues, and the hand around the back of my neck tightens to keep me in place.

I'm helpless, gasping, and incredibly feel myself getting hard again.

That's when his grip on my cock eases as he continues to

slowly stroke me. His hands are slightly rougher than mine, hints of old calluses haunting his, where mine are smooth and soft. It's a deliciously different sensation.

"Good boy," he whispers.

I've never gotten hard again so quickly before. I also realize my hips are rocking back and forth in time to his motions, my body actively participating in whatever *this* is even though my brain is still stuck in *what the fuck?* mode.

I can't exactly say I want him to stop, because I don't. When my eyes drop closed, one finger painfully digs into the back of my neck.

"Eyes *open*," he firmly orders without raising his voice. "Eyes on *me*." When I immediately comply and find myself staring into his brown gaze, he smiles again. "*Good* boy," he coos.

My grip tightens on his body and I whimper, helpless, as his hand skillfully pulls me close to the edge…

And keeps me there, reading my body and not getting me over.

I'm sooo fucking close, too, and even when I try fucking his hand harder, he compensates, leaving me frustratingly horny.

"Please," I finally whisper, reduced to begging and no longer too proud to admit it. "Please make me come."

One eyebrow arches.

"Please make me come, *Sir*."

Another smile. "Good boy." And he does, this time needing to drape an arm around me and lower me to the floor because my knees give out from the force of my orgasm.

We sit there with me cradled against him, my eyes closed, my head resting against his chest. We're both covered in spooge now and he doesn't apparently care.

I guess I shouldn't, either.

I don't know when my tears started, but at some point I realize Carter's rocking my body, his arms around me, his chin rubbing against the top of my head.

"That's it," he whispers. "Let it all out. You're not alone anymore, boy—I've got you. You're mine, and I'm not letting you fall. I'll *always* catch you, I promise."

* * *

I don't know how long we sit there, but by the time I finally come back to myself, everything's sort of dried out and crusty, and I'm feeling more than a little self-conscious.

I'm also wondering if Carter expects me to reciprocate.

I'm...well, I'm straight, and I'm not sure how I feel about that possibility.

I guess maybe I should have asked a few more questions before we actually started this, but I trusted him.

Pausing, I think for a moment. No, that's *trust*, present-tense. I *still* trust him, as weird as that might sound.

Believe me, I *know* it sounds weird.

I feel...wrung out. More than just physically, but emotionally.

He's still holding me, and I'm sure sitting on a tile floor isn't good for his pain, but he's not making any moves like he's uncomfortable.

"Better?" he asks, back to his usual voice.

"Are we still..." I don't even know how to ask. "Sir, or Carter?"

"We're always Sir and boy by default, unless one of us specifically flips it back."

"Okay." I think about it for a moment. "I mean, yes, Sir."

"Do you want to talk about this now or later?"

Now is as good as any time. "Now?"

A chuckle. "Is that a question or a response, boy?"

"A response, Sir?"

Another laugh. "So, here's the thing," he says. "To answer what I'm sure is your first question, no, I'm not going to demand or even ask you to reciprocate. If you ever want to volunteer, I'd likely say yes, depending on the circumstances. But if I'm going to control your orgasms, I'd be a pretty shitty Sir if I didn't give you relief from time to time. While orgasm control turns me on, long-term chastity does not. I'll also be using orgasms as rewards."

"Are you gay?"

"No."

Okay, so this doesn't really make sense to me, but maybe that's his…point? I don't know.

I lie there, not wanting to move yet. I finally force myself to ask the next question. "Why did I start crying?"

"That's not uncommon, especially after someone's first scene. Cathartic emotional release." He rubs his chin in my hair. "You're starved for affection, for positive reinforcement."

He's not wrong, even if I don't understand any of this.

"Do you need me to move yet, Sir?"

"No, I'm okay, boy. If I need you to move, I'll say so."

I draw in a deep, shuddering breath. Even the few times I'd been with girls, there was always something…missing. I didn't know at the time if it was something lacking within me or more to do with them. My very first time, during my senior year of high school, she hadn't been a virgin and she'd said she enjoyed it with me, yet that experience left me feeling empty later, emotionally speaking.

So had my other two times.

Also, I guess it's pretty telling I only had one time with each of them. The girl I briefly dated last year broke things off with me shortly after the first time we slept together. Said it was her, not me.

Maybe I wasn't dominant enough for them.

This, however, feels like what I wish those times had felt like despite the way I feel…scrambled. Now, it's like there's a firm anchor keeping me in the moment, gently weighing me down, attached to the present.

"Have you…taken charge of guys before like this, Sir?"

"Have I topped men? Yes. Men and women."

A comfortable quiet descends upon us. I've never felt a need to fill the silence with Carter the way I do with my mother.

Ever.

Everything has always felt easy between us, and with Susa, too. Even this is quickly becoming easy. I don't feel a need to cover myself like I did before.

My brain is…the only way to describe it is *quiet*.

For the first time in my adult life, there aren't a million thoughts running through my mind, including a list of my own shortcomings that I'm beating myself up over.

"We'll keep doing this, Sir?" I quietly ask when I realize that.

"Yes. Unless you decide you want me to stop doing this, and specifically tell me we're not doing this any longer, we *are* going to keep doing this."

After a long, slow breath, I nod. "I want to keep doing this, Sir."

His chin rubs against the top of my head. "Good boy. So do I."

CHAPTER TWENTY-TWO

Instead of cleaning us up, Carter has an alternate suggestion. About fifteen minutes later, he has me help him up from the floor and we head out to the pool. He shoves his shorts down and jumps in the deep end.

I follow. When I break the surface, he's already swimming toward the shallow end, smooth strokes cutting through the water. I'm not a pretty swimmer. I always feel like a manic Labrador retriever splashing around compared to Carter's neat, strong, disciplined strokes.

I follow him to the shallow end, where he lounges against the stairs. They're wide, divided by a metal handrail, and he takes up one side.

"We'll patrol the living room in a little bit," he says with a smirk. "Clean up the splash zone."

"Am I still allowed to ask questions, Sir?"

"Always. Unless I've specifically ordered you to remain silent."

"How often will we do…this?"

"Do what? Orgasm play?"

"I mean everything. *This*."

"We're doing it now." He tips his head back and looks at the sky through the screened pool cage. It's a sunny day and the water's perfectly warm, but there's literally a cloud situated over us right now. Carter's face is bathed in a study of soft shadows contrasted with rippled light reflected off the pool's surface.

Much like the man himself.

"I'm going to introduce rituals and protocols to our relationship," he says. "A few at a time. Rules. I won't set you up for failure by dumping a bunch of stuff on you all at once and then have you beating yourself up over it."

"Protocols?"

"Calling me 'Sir', for starters." He lifts his head and meets my gaze. "In fact, even in front of Susa, I want you to call me 'Sir'."

Terror fills me. "But—"

"I've decided we are going to bring her in."

My eyes widen. "*What*?"

"That's your biggest fantasy, isn't it? Of her dominating you?"

I swallow hard. He's right, but still... "She hasn't asked to be part of this. You don't even know she'll want to be part of this."

Worse, what if she doesn't want to be friends with us anymore?

"She will."

"You can't guarantee that."

"I know she will," he repeats.

"How?"

"You haven't noticed that she's naturally an in-charge kind of person?"

"I mean, yeah, I have, but—"

"Then what's the problem, *boy*?"

My mouth snaps shut as the delicious quiet in my brain is once again shattered by all the noise and fears usually bouncing around in there.

"She's our friend," Carter continues. "I will never do anything to put that friendship at risk. But there is something you need to know."

Terror roils my gut. I think, here it is, the ugly truth. Some secret pact between them, maybe? Simultaneously I need to know, and yet I don't want to hear whatever it is he's going to say.

Maybe he senses my inner turmoil, because he continues. "I suspect Susa has a strong submissive streak she might want to explore, under the right circumstances. It makes sense, because she sees me as safe, as a friend and an authority figure. She trusts me. Like you trust me. She needs downtime, too. All that intensity wears a person out."

Never mind I'm convinced she's in love with Carter, which would be why she would react well to him, but I don't say that. "What are you going to do?" I'm actually terrified to know.

"Nothing like *this*. I'll approach her about you when I feel the time is right and introduce her to dominating you. Let's be honest—you're well past more than halfway there already. She lets you do the dishes all the time. You help her with her laundry and other chores. Easing her into a formal dynamic with you will be easy. I'll put it out there to her if she wants to try the submissive end of things that I'd be open to exploring that with her."

A mixture of longing and dread fills me. Absolutely, I would love my deepest fantasies to come true.

Except how would I feel seeing Susa kneeling for Carter?

Not that she's kneeling—that she's kneeling for someone else.

Someone who's not me.

Then again, I try to picture her kneeling in front of me, *for* me, and that doesn't feel right no matter how I try to frame it.

"You *will* hand this over to me, boy," he quietly says, the firm tone returning. "This is out of your control, regardless. You *only* deal with the things I tell you to deal with. Your schoolwork, for starters. That's above everything else. You'll continue PT with me every morning as we have been, unless you're sick or injured." He smiles. "Like this morning. Laundry is your chore, which will now include putting mine away for me. I expect you to learn how and where I like my things kept in our room. Understand?"

"Yes, Sir," I numbly say. I'm still trying to process that he's going to tell Susa my secret. "I guess this gets me out of running for office, huh?"

Carter looks genuinely confused. I didn't think that was possible. "Why?" he asks.

"I mean…*this.*"

He laughs. "If you think you're the first or last person to run for public office with a skeleton in your closet, think again. You're definitely not the first subbie."

"What if this gets out?"

He stares me dead in the eye. "It won't, I promise. I would *never* do something like that to you."

I settle in on the other side of the steps, where I take a few minutes to chew over everything he's said. "So I don't get to date?"

That slight shadow passes over his eyes again, like it did that first day we met Susa. "No. Why? Is that a problem?"

"I…" I take a deep breath. Not like I've had anyone I wanted to date.

Except Susa.

"No, Sir," I quietly say.

"Don't worry, I'm not going to be dating either. Between school and this, it'll take up all my time. You won't be lonely."

When I think about what he did to me a little bit ago in the living room, my cock twitches, even in the water.

The way it felt waking up next to him this morning, before I processed it was him.

No, I won't be lonely, or lacking for attention, I suppose.

"We're going to start with training you to basically be my valet," he says. "You're going to start showering with me—"

"Wait, what?"

"What?"

I stare at him. "*Showering* together?"

"Is this a problem, boy? I've seen you naked. I jerked you off a little while ago. I warned you you'll be spending a lot of time naked. You're naked in here, with me, right now."

True, true, true, and, of course, true.

He's still staring at me. "Is this a problem, boy?" he repeats.

"No, Sir." My voice sounds tiny to me, but even as I answer, I realize this doesn't feel like any of the countless times Mom's upbraided me for something.

This doesn't feel...*wrong*.

Weird and strange and new, yes.

The *rightness* it's imbued with can't be denied.

He studies me for a moment before he speaks again. "You'll open doors for me, the way you already have. I'm going to teach you positions I want you to kneel in. We're also going to start with some domestic discipline this weekend. How and where we do that will vary depending on the circumstances. I can't spank you in our dorm room if anyone else is around, because they'll hear it, so I'll develop alternatives."

Thoughts of that simultaneously terrify and thrill me.

"There will be times I make you cry," he continues. "Sometimes on purpose, sometimes incidentally. While you are in kneeling in position, I don't care if snot's rolling down your face, you don't break position unless I've given you permission to do so. Not to blow your nose, not to wipe your tears. Understand?"

It makes me uncomfortable, but maybe that's the whole point, so I nod. "Yes, Sir. What about during breaks?"

"Breaks?"

"What if we're not together?"

He looks genuinely confused. "Why wouldn't we be together?"

Maybe I'm not making myself clear. "I mean, during semester breaks. When we won't be in the dorms."

He turns a little, facing me. "You're going to be with *me*," he says, sounding matter-of-fact. "You let *me* worry about where we'll stay during our breaks. One of the trade-offs of this dynamic is that while you obey me and do what I tell you, I promise to take care of you in all ways. Including where we live. I told you, you will always have a place to live with me."

The good kind of fear, for once, trills through me. "What if I can't afford it?"

He reaches out and catches my chin, hints of a smile curling his lips. "Are you questioning my ability to take care of you, *boy*?"

"No, Sir." I've answered before I even think about it. "I trust you."

"Good." He releases my chin and tips his head back again, but the sun's out now, so he closes his eyes. "I own you, I control you, and I *will* take care of you."

* * *

After a while, we head inside, grabbing towels from the pool bath on our way in. Carter has me check the living room and make sure I clean up my cum where it dripped.

It was…a *lot*. And, fortunately, it was over the tile and not the area rug.

Once that's cleaned up, he has me start a load of laundry and then orders me to join him in Susa's master bathroom.

He smiles and indicates the shower with his hand, and I climb in.

Nerves fill me, but I'm determined I'm going to see this through. Maybe it won't make sense to someone else, I don't know.

Here's the thing—yes, this is weird, and sudden, and nothing I expected to happen. But if I have a choice to step off the crazy-making hamster wheel that is life with my mother?

Absofuckinglutely I'll give Carter a shot. I'm no worse off than I was before if I end up stopping this.

Maybe I have a lot to gain.

Actually, there's no maybe about it. I have everything to gain, including finally getting a chance to do something that *I* want to do to be happy in my life, with people who make me feel more like I'm family and loved than my own family ever did. I never imagined my deepest, darkest fantasies would coalesce like this, but I'll take it.

One of the things I know I need to do to be a functional adult is follow my own path and do the things that make me happy, that sing to my soul.

This is one of those things.

I've never intimately showered with someone before. In these close quarters, I can't help but get a good look at the scars on Carter's body.

He drizzles body wash on a washcloth and hands it to me before he turns to face the wall. "Start up on my shoulders, work your way down."

I've literally never done this with another person before. I tentatively reach out to do it, and he chuckles.

"You can use more pressure than that, boy."

I do. "I don't want to hurt you."

"Trust me, this doesn't hurt. I will tell you if something hurts in a bad way."

It's impossible for me to identify what feelings are rolling through me right now. I'm completely without a frame of reference.

"Why this, Sir?" I ask as I work my way lower.

"First tell me about when your parents divorced."

My hand slows, stills. "Why?"

"Because I asked. Don't stop what you're doing."

I take a deep breath and resume scrubbing his back. "I don't remember everything. It was ugly. I remember them screaming at each other a lot before Dad moved out. I didn't get to see much of him before he moved to Nevada for work."

"What about before?"

"What do you mean?"

"What was life like before? All the way down, boy. Ass, and back of my legs."

I swallow hard but I scrub lower. "Life with Mom was always tense. She was in charge at home. They bickered and fought all the time. I suspect Dad started cheating a couple of years before she caught him. But at least when Dad was home, he'd take me out and do stuff with me some evenings and on the weekends. We'd leave Mom at home, or she was working or something, and go fishing, or see movies. Stuff she didn't want any part of."

The scars are even worse down the backs of his thighs and calves. I know now from talks we've had that the scarring along his back is mostly from burns, where flaming fuel got under his tactical vest. Shrapnel from the blast mostly hit him lower, along his ass and legs, below the vest. Although a couple of larger pieces did pierce through his vest, one of which punctured a lung. The back of his upper right arm took some shrapnel, past where the vest covered him, and the back of his upper left arm received some burns, because he'd landed on his left side on top of the three downed men he was trying to protect, shielding them with his body.

It worked, though. Even though the blast killed others, the three he covered survived.

At a great personal cost to Carter, and one he says he'd pay again in a heartbeat, because they were men under his command.

That's the essence of Carter.

My mother would bitch and feel resentful if she so much as got a hangnail while shopping for a present for me on Amazon. I've heard parents say they'd die for their kids. I honestly doubt my mother is one of them.

But this man before me wears the proof of his selflessness in his flesh.

This is one of the many reasons I know I can open myself to him and trust him, even though it might sound crazy to anyone who doesn't know the man as well as I do.

"Why *this*," Carter says as he turns to take the washcloth from me before indicating for me to turn around so he can wash my back, "is because I suspect you have no clue how to process intimacy or be intimate with someone, not even with yourself."

My eyes close as he scrubs my back for me. It's an indescribably good sensation.

"And," he continues, "if I manage to achieve nothing else with our time together besides instilling self-confidence in you and teaching you how to open yourself to someone in a healthy way at various levels of intimacy, then I'll be happy and consider it a success."

He places a hand on my left shoulder, holding on as he leans over and scrubs me lower. "Because even if you were dating right now, you'd be miserable. It's no coincidence you have a shitty relationship with your mom and you haven't really ever had a girlfriend for any length of time."

Meanwhile, as he's scrubbing my back, my cock…

Yeah.

I'm hard again.

Before I can even process it, Carter spins me around, pins my back against the wall with his left forearm over my throat, and his right hand once again grips my cock. He's not choking off my air, but from this position I know it's because he's choosing to let me breathe.

The intensity in his expression as he strokes me terrifies and thrills me at the same time. "Hold on to my arm," he orders, moving the left one a little and indicating he means that one.

I reach up and wrap my fingers around the arm across my throat as his right hand strokes my cock again. I'm sensitive, but I'm also hornier than hell, and the slight edge to the pleasure only makes me that much harder.

"You need to learn to ask for what you want from me, boy.

You can't deny yourself because you assume you can't have it. *Tell* me what you want."

Twenty-four hours ago, had you told me I'd be begging my roommate to jerk me off in the shower, I'd have laughed at you.

Now?

"Please make me come, Sir. I want to come."

His triumphant smile makes me throb. "*Hold* it, boy. Do *not* come yet."

The command has exactly the opposite effect, and I'm afraid I'm going to disobey him. "I...I—"

His hand slows, stills, leaving me whimpering and my hips rocking. "Good boys learn how to control themselves. There will be times I spend hours edging you and not letting you come, and if you come without permission, you'll be punished. I'm not cruel enough or sadistic enough to do that to you today, though. I meant it when I said I won't set you up to fail." He smiles. "Not at first, and only when you realize it's for fun."

He squeezes my cock, long, almost painfully but letting up just short of that. My breath raggedly saws in and out of my lungs as I stare into his eyes.

What the *hell* have I gotten myself into?

And why the hell didn't I figure this out about myself sooner?

And please, *please* let this last. Everything he's said so far strikes deep and true in my soul. If he's playing me, fucking with me, it's going to destroy me.

Because I really, *really* want this.

That's why I struggle to comply. I chew on my lower lip and focus on him, on his brown gaze, and try to take my mind off the way his fingers circle the head of my cock and take slow strokes.

There's no noise other than the shower running and my own breath as I struggle not to tip over the edge despite how he's working my cock.

A few moments later, Carter's gaze narrows even as a smile

fills his face. "Good boy," he whispers "*Come* for me." As he says this, his hand speeds up and my body complies.

I force myself to keep my eyes open, focused on him and his, as the orgasm slams into me. It's intense nearly to the point of pain. My balls throb as he strokes my cock, and he finally stills his hand only when I'm gasping and struggling to remain in place and not pull away from him.

"Eyes on me, boy," Carter says as he releases my cock. I don't understand what he's doing at first, until I realize he's jerking off.

In his left eye is a darker fleck of chocolate brown mixed in with the lighter hints of amber, gold, hazel. They're mostly brown, and intense, expressive.

His breathing grows loud, harsh, and I spot the moment he tips over the edge, even though I can't see what he's doing down there because I'm pinned in place. The lines around the outer edges of his eyes grow a little softer, the inner corners of his eyebrows lifting a tiny bit, and then he moans.

Considering he's just given me three, I don't think I should begrudge him this one. Especially since he's done all the damn work.

Once he finishes, he needs a minute to regain his senses. He takes a deep breath before releasing me.

It surprises me most of all when I realize I don't want to let go of his arm, at first.

I *liked* being pinned to the wall.

"We need to go shopping," he says as he steps back and rinses his hand in the spray. "When we finish our shower."

"Shopping, Sir?" That already feels natural, calling him that. I don't know what kind of shopping, though, because Susa left us plenty to eat.

He smiles. "Don't worry, boy. This one's all on me."

CHAPTER TWENTY-THREE

When we finish our shower, Carter has me dry him off before myself, and orders me to get dressed and go commando under my shorts.

Definitely *not* something I'm used to doing, but I suspect I'll be getting used to it soon enough.

He follows suit.

Ten minutes later, we're in the Snot Box with him driving. I'm a confusing mix of horrified and intrigued when our first stop is an adult toy "superstore" at the corner of Nebraska and Fletcher. I've driven past it a couple of times en route to other destinations, but I've never worked up the nerve to stop there. I've never been inside any "adult store" before.

Guess Carter's going to pop my cherry in this way, too.

I'm too nervous to speak. Before I can open my door and get out, Carter stops me. "If I'm driving, I don't expect you to get the car door for me, unless I specifically say so. I might change that at some future time. I expect you to open and hold other doors for me, though, including the passenger door of a car if I'm not driving. Then you walk with me, on my right side whenever possible, and a step behind. If I turn, I expect you to adjust accordingly. If I step on you, it's your fault. Understand?"

"Yes, Sir."

He grins. "Nervous?"

"Very much, Sir."

"You do *not* speak unless I directly address you and ask you a question," he says. "And you don't worry about prices. If we're going to do this the right way, I need some training aids."

He opens his door and I scramble to get out and follow him. I hold the store's door open for him and in we go.

My brain knew what to expect, but I find myself trying not to gawk. There's a section of sexy clothes, a section of DVDs, another, smaller one of books. When the clerk behind the counter greets us, Carter responds and waves I offer what I hope isn't a sick-looking smile and continue after him.

We seem to be the only customers right now. We pass through a bachelorette party and novelties section, finally reaching what is apparently our destination.

Adult toys.

He navigates us to a display of leashes and collars, quickly selects a heavy black leather collar with matching wrist and ankle cuffs, and hands them to me to hold as he moves on. Right next to that section is a selection of gags and blindfolds. He chooses a bit gag and a black leather blindfold.

My cheeks are once again aflame, but I say nothing as he adds them.

Next, we reach the butt plug section. He selects a couple, including a vibrating one with a remote control, drops them into my arms, and moves on. I swallow hard, trying not to stare at them and also struggling not to get hard, since I'm freeballing it right now.

I guess there are cock rings in my future, too, because three different ones are added to the growing pile. Then he locates the implements section. It's smaller than I imagined, and there isn't a very large selection. Plus, many of them look relatively cheap.

From Carter's scowl, I can tell he's not impressed either, but he still picks out three different paddles, and away we head to the check-out counter.

On the way, he stops and picks up lube, condoms, and a couple of other items that he carries, so I don't see what they are.

Then we reach the counter.

Without a word, I put everything on the counter and step back.

"Did you find everything you need?" the clerk asks. She's a cute and bubbly blonde, probably mid-twenties, maybe a little older than me. She wears a short-sleeved collared pullover shirt with the store's logo on it and a pair of jeans, which is not what I'd expect, under the circumstances.

"Sure did," Carter says, as charming as ever. "My boy and I are going to have some fun."

I bite back the urge to amend that statement, because I can tell from the knowing smile she gives Carter that she now assumes we're gay and I'm his boyfriend.

I suppose if I'm not dating it doesn't matter if people wrongly assume that about us. Especially a clerk I will hopefully never see again in my life.

If I'm lucky.

After he pays, he takes the bag and hands it to me to carry. We head out and I hold the door for him. When we reach the car, Carter actually opens my door for me, and he's wearing a pleased smile.

"You did great," he says.

Okay, as embarrassed as I felt being in there, I have to admit something about his praise helps offset it more than a little.

Our next stop is a feed store a short distance away. I don't even know why we're here…until Carter winds his way through the store and we end up in the tack section.

Carter's eyes light up as he inspects their selection of riding crops, and he picks three different ones. He also grabs several double-ended snap clips, a couple of panic snaps, and off we go to pay.

From there we drive to a large pet store. A six-foot-long leather leash, a long choke-chain collar for a dog, and a token for a pet tag add to the growing list of purchases. Then we stop by the engraving machine at the front of the store. Carter's wearing an evil smile as he programs in what he wants the blue, dog bone-shaped tag to say, and we watch it engrave the words:

ɔoy

Property of Sir

Followed by his cell number.

Our last stop is a home improvement store, where he buys a hundred feet of rope, among other things.

Including a two-pack of the smallest padlocks they sell, real ones, not the stupid ones like for luggage, and a small pair of bolt cutters.

I say nothing. I can tell some of the things he's added to the cart, like wooden dowels about three feet long, will likely be used on me. Not sure about the two-foot length of plastic irrigation pipe, though.

Not sure I want to know why he added kneepads, either, which he picked up in the tile flooring section.

It's a little past noon when we return to Susa's.

"Unload the car, please, boy," Carter says before going inside. "Everything in the living room, for now."

I follow orders. After I have the car emptied he uses his key fob to lock it from the front door, then locks us in.

"Strip," he orders. "If we're alone like this, here or at the dorm, you strip inside the front door." He hesitates. "Obviously, at the dorm, I mean inside *our* room, not the quad pod."

Once again, I comply. I mean, it's moot to argue about this.

I return to the living room where he's already getting things ready. He unpackages everything, combining all the wrappers and detritus into one of the bags, which he ties shut and hands to me.

"Put that inside a plain garbage bag and put it out in the garage, in the trash bin. And you're allowed to speak again."

"Yes, Sir." I return to the living room after accomplishing that to find him using the bolt cutters to remove the rings from the chain collar. He crooks a finger at me to lean in, and I do.

He drapes it around my neck and checks the length. Apparently happy with it as-is, he nods and threads the tag onto the split ring that came with it, adds it to the collar, and then uses one of the padlocks to lock it around my neck.

I'm not sure what to think of this. It'll hang under my shirt, so I'll be able to hide it.

I have a feeling I won't have a say when I'm allowed to take it off.

He hands me one of the padlock keys, but before he lets go of it, he looks me in the eyes. "This goes on your keyring, but you are *not* allowed to use it for yourself unless it's an emergency, or I've given you permission to use it. Emergency means medical reasons, or airport security, or something like that. You *will* be punished for disobeying me about this. Understand?"

"Y-yes, Sir."

He releases the key and I thread it onto my keyring, next to Susa's house key.

That seems like a fitting place to put it.

He adds one to his keyring. There are two more keys, and three more locks, and they were all keyed alike. I don't know what he's going to do with them since he sets them aside, for now.

"To answer your obvious question, no, you won't normally be wearing the tag on that collar. I'll have to order a more appropriate one. That tag will go on your play collar."

"Play collar, Sir?"

"The leather one. But you will be wearing that collar normally. *Mine*."

My cock twitches at the possessive tone in his voice. I have a feeling if Mom showed up and tried to assert authority over me right this minute, Carter would stand and get in her face and say exactly that word in that way.

Mine.

He quickly buckles the leather collar on me, and the wrist and ankle cuffs. He checks the fit of the bit gag and the blindfold and has me kneel in front of him.

"You can talk around the gag," he assures me. "I'm well-versed in gagspeak."

I nod. I'm blind and mute. My ears listen for any sound I can make out.

Startled at the feel of his hand coming to rest on the top of my head, I'm quickly soothed as he once again rubs my scalp as he did earlier. He also presses on the side of my head, making me lean so my head rests against his thigh.

"Just sit there for a minute, boy," he whispers. "This is *all* you have to do, is kneel, breathe, and wait on me to tell you what to do next."

Something about the way he's rubbing my head, combined with being blindfolded, and I soon find myself slipping into that quiet mental space I occupied earlier.

My mind completely empties as I focus on breathing, the warmth of his thigh against my face, the way his hand strokes my head.

I feel like I'm the center of his universe right now.

He feels like the center of mine.

I'm starting to get it.

Around us, the AC kicks on, I hear a neighbor somewhere behind Susa's house crank a lawnmower, but these things can't penetrate the rapidly expanding velvet bubble in my mind.

I can see the two of us, alone, with no distractions.

No one pulling his attention from me.

His hand stills but remains on my head. "How's my boy?"

I take a deep, satisfying breath. "Good, Sir," I mumble around the gag.

"Excellent. Another five minutes, then we'll try something else."

I...strangely find I don't want to move. "Only five?"

He chuckles, his fingers moving against my scalp again. "How about ten?"

I sigh, contented, wishing this sweet mental silence would never end. "Thank you, Sir."

CHAPTER TWENTY-FOUR

Carter removes my blindfold so I can switch out the laundry, then has me return to the living room and kneel in front of where he's sitting on the couch.

He was right about one thing—I'm not thinking about being naked anymore.

"The four main positions I will expect you to know for now are *Primed*, *Loyalty*, *Devotion*, and *At Ease*. At Ease is basically what you're doing now, knees together, except with your palms down and flat on top of your thighs." I move my hands into the correct position and am awarded with a smile. "Very good."

I feel a surge of pride roll through me.

"Primed is sitting up, back straight, knees as wide apart as you can manage, with your hands behind your head, fingers laced together, elbows out to the sides."

I sit up and he makes a couple of minor tweaks to my position. I'm aware that this exposes me to him completely, but we're beyond that point, I suppose.

Well beyond it.

Like, it's twenty miles in the rearview mirror kind of beyond it.

Carter sits back, smiling. "Excellent, boy. Stay like that. Remember, when I put you in a position, I expect you to maintain it."

It only takes a few minutes for me to realize this won't be as easy as I first thought it would. At least, this particular position won't.

His smile widens. "Yeah, we'll need to build your stamina. Not as easy as it looks, is it? You may speak."

"No, Sir. It's not." But there's already something inside me wanting to try to do better, to improve how long I can maintain it.

To earn his praise and make him smile.

Loyalty is easier, my head bowed, knees not quite so far apart, my left hand flat on my thigh, my right hand flat on the floor.

"It's called that because it resembles swearing an oath," Carter explains.

Devotion is performed with my knees together, a full formal bow, my hands flat on the floor in front of me, forehead touching the floor, back rounded. When I assume that position, I hear him move, then his hand rests on my head.

"Every night before bed," he quietly says, "you will perform this at the side of my bed for me and hold it until I release you. Understand?"

The name of the pose is self-explanatory, as is this ritual. "Yes, Sir."

He rubs my head and peace fills me.

"Primed."

I sit up and assume the position. Carter circles me, stopping behind me.

"How'd you feel when you saw what I bought today, boy?"

"Curious, Sir. And a little scared."

I flinch when his voice next comes by my right ear. "Why scared?"

"All the rope. The riding crops."

"Not the butt plugs?" He sounds very amused.

"Those too, Sir." But dark and secret shadows inside me

stretched their wings and smiled with fanged teeth barely kept hidden when I thought about what Carter would probably do to me with those.

Or what Susa might do to me.

He returns to the couch and spends the next half hour or so putting me through the various positions. I think my favorite is Loyalty, mostly because of the name and the feelings it invokes in me.

By the time he allows me to stand again, my knees are killing me.

Now the kneepads make sense.

I hope.

He smiles. "Yes, the kneepads are for you doing this. For when I decide you need a long session on the floor. Want you to appreciate how difficult these can be first, though. Go ahead and check the laundry, please."

I do, and what was in the dryer is ready to come out. I move a load from the washer to the dryer and bring in the dry clothes to fold them.

When I do, I find him braiding rope onto one of the panic snaps. Fascinated, I watch. I've never seen that done before, the way he's splicing the end of the rope into itself.

He watches me watching him and smiles. "Ironically, I learned this in Boy Scouts."

When he's finished, he's created a piece of rope that's approximately forty feet long and has panic snaps braided onto both ends. He neatly coils and stows the remainder of the rope in a plastic shopping bag.

"I'll cut that into shorter sections later," he says.

"Can I ask a stupid question, Sir?"

He smiles and picks up a small metal ring, one of two he's also purchased. He threads the ring onto the rope and then loops the end of the rope around the coffee table leg, hooking the panic snap to the ring before pulling the rope taut.

Ah.

Carter hooks the other panic snap to my right ankle cuff. It's amazing that I've grown accustomed to wearing the cuffs so quickly. I stupidly stand there, staring at my foot.

"Of course you may ask, boy."

"Why?"

Carter smirks. "Since we'll be limited in some things we can do, I'm going to improvise. Everything I do to you has a greater purpose. Teaching patience, self-control, obedience. Willful disobedience when necessary. Protecting the property. Sometimes, just for sadistic funsies and fucking with you, but not until later, when you've learned this side of me better and know what's play and what's serious."

He unclips the rope from my ankle and the table. "Trust. Routines. I will start small and build you up. This is for our dorm room." He coils the rope. "It's long enough to give you full movement inside our room and the bathroom. You'll wear it at night, and when you're in the room when I'm not there. Just like with your collar, you're not allowed to remove it without permission, only for pre-determined reasons and emergencies. I will take it off you every morning."

"What if someone sees it?"

"We'll keep our room door closed and locked," he says, handing the rope to me. "When you're not using it, stow it in one of the totes under your bed. For now, go put it with our things."

"Yes, Sir." I do that, then return to finish folding our laundry. When that's completed and I've put it away, I return to the living room, where Carter's watching TV on the couch, to find out what he wants me to do next.

"Lunch, boy?"

"Yes, Sir."

He pats his lap. "Spanking first." He hasn't changed out of his shirt and shorts.

I'm still trying to sort all this out in my mind, but I find myself walking over and climbing into position over his lap once my brain's processed the command.

Carter's hands settle on my ass and the back of my neck, his fingers there curling around my collar. "All right, boy. I'll take this one a little easy on you. This'll be fast, then you can make us lunch."

I have no conscious memory of ever being spanked as a child. My mother had far more effective and painful ways of punishing me without laying a hand on me, punishments that wounded me far deeper.

A spanking would have at least been some attention she'd paid to me. Physical contact.

As Carter gives me my first ever spanking, I feel not only his hand striking my flesh, but that blissful quiet returning to my brain. Part of my brain is still processing pain, stinging heat blooming in my ass cheeks, even the fact that I've started crying again.

The other part of my brain feels like it's dropped into that sweet, dark, velvety safe space once more, and everything in that world is peaceful perfection.

When I finally come back to myself, I'm still facedown over Carter's lap, sort of. He's leaned over, mostly lying on the couch now with one arm draped over my back, basically stretched out next to me.

"I think you're right about something, Sir."

"What's that, boy?"

"I don't know how to process intimacy, and I have no idea how to have a relationship with someone."

Carter strokes my hair. "It's okay, boy. We'll work on things together."

* * *

During the rest of the afternoon, I remain naked except for the cuffs, leather collar, and chain collar. Carter sheds his shirt but keeps his shorts on. He has me put down a towel to sit on the couch with him, but...

Yeah. He was absolutely right about the fact that being naked feels comfortable now. I'm no longer feeling self-conscious about it.

Some studying was done, mostly by Carter. He tried to help me by quizzing me on material, but I'm not sure any of it stuck. My brain is swirling with a mix of things new and old, the realization that many—okay, *most*—of my fantasies will actually come true, and not only is my best friend not horrified at me over them, he's going to be the primary person to help me realize them, and more.

My...Dominant.

After recognizing my brain is *done* for the day, Carter takes pity on me and has me start dinner, and that's when the drinking starts. Late that evening, we're both deep in the bag and have almost completely emptied the two growlers Carter bought the evening before.

I also now sport several marks across my ass from the riding crops, the dowel, and the piece of irrigation pipe—which packs a wicked punch.

After eating dinner on the couch and cleaning up the dishes, I'm back on the couch again. This time, Carter has me lie with my head in his lap as we watch TV, and he strokes my hair in that delicious way that sends my brain spinning off again, even without the help of the alcohol.

I feel...

I feel *cherished.*

Like a cherished pet, but still, cherished.

I'll take it, soak up every ounce of it, because literally for the first time in my life I feel *wanted.*

I cannot begin to express how addictive that sensation is.

Carter has me keep the cuffs and collar on when we go to bed, and he changes into boxers. I kneel at the side of the bed in Devotion as he'd told me to earlier, and I earn a good boy and a head rub for remembering and not needing to be reminded, even as drunk as I am.

"Up. In bed."

I'm not exactly sure on what side of the bed I'm supposed to sleep, but he opens his arms to me to snuggle against his side.

Of course I go, and yeah, I completely own that it makes me needy and clingy. But lying there with him and knowing nothing is expected of me is…

It's something I don't want to lose. I also realize once we're back at the dorm I won't have this anymore, because of the size of our bunks, and that makes me sad.

"What if Susa freaks out, Sir?" I ask in the darkness.

He nuzzles the top of my head. "She won't. That's not a worry you need to have. Sir will take care of that."

Maybe Susa will want to snuggle in bed with her pet from time to time.

I can only hope.

* * *

At some point in the night, I awaken to realize we've rolled apart in our sleep. I'm lying on my right side, and I can't feel Carter.

When I hear the noise again, what must have awakened me in the first place, I immediately pinpoint the source—Carter.

He's having a nightmare, and it sounds bad.

Without thinking, I roll over and seek him out in the darkness, drawing him into my arms. "Sir, it's okay. Wake up. I'm right here. It's just a nightmare."

I feel him start awake, his body tensing before silent sobs leave him trembling in my arms.

The only thing I know to do is what I do, and that's drape a leg over his, my left arm around him, and slide my right arm under his pillow so I'm cradling his body against mine.

I feel his hand slide up my left arm to my elbow, where he wraps his fingers around my upper forearm.

His breathing is already starting to slow and ease when he turns his head to face me, pressed against my chest.

I'm wide awake now and stone-cold sober, but Carter almost immediately slips back into sleep.

Okay, then.

I still haven't asked him about his nightmares, about what images haunt him. Absolutely, I will do this for him. Also turns out he's completely right about something else.

As I lie there cuddling with him, his hair soft against my face, I don't feel the slightest bit self-conscious that I'm naked.

I'd also be lying if I said having this kind of contact with another human being isn't a little soothing to my soul, too.

CHAPTER TWENTY-FIVE

Sunday morning I awaken early, still lying on my side with Carter sound asleep in my arms. I don't move, afraid I'll wake him.

Susa is due back later this afternoon. She told Carter she'd text him when she left Tallahassee, so we'd have a timeframe.

Part of me can't wait to see her.

Part of me feels…terrified.

I don't know when Carter will talk to her about all of *this*, but I know I'll exist in an emotionally painful limbo until it finally breaks open.

Carter eventually stirs in my arms, a long, deep inhale my first clue he's awake.

"Good morning, boy." Carter's usually smooth, mellow voice is always deeper first thing in the morning, with gravelly undertones until he's been awake for a while.

"Good morning, Sir."

Before I can process it, he's flipped me over, onto my back. He straddles me, easily pinning my wrists over my head with his left hand. I'm sporting morning wood—kind of can't help it—and my cock lays straight and rigid against my abs. I can see the front of Carter's boxers are slightly tented, too. Now, being pinned down like this, my cock begins to throb and twitch.

We've both looked at my cock, and then our gaze meets.

"*Please*, Sir," I whisper without even stopping to think about the ramifications.

Who says I'm not an easily trainable pet?

A slow, nearly evil smile spreads across his features. It's filled with satisfaction, mirth, mayhem.

"Ask me *properly*, boy."

"Please make me come, Sir."

"Hmm. Not quite needy enough. Let's see how you can beg."

I don't know what he needs from me, but there's now a quickly growing puddle of pre-cum on my abs. "I'm horny, Sir. *Please*, may I have an orgasm? Will you please give me an orgasm? May I please come?" I'm not sure exactly what combination he's looking for this morning, but I'll keep asking until I hit upon the right phrase.

I'm not too proud to beg for this. Not when, for the first time in my life, it feels like something worth begging for.

Carter's gaze narrows. Yes, he's an extraordinary bastard, all right. I can see this is fun, to him.

Actually...it's kind of fun for me, too. I mean, in a needy, desperate sort of way. The thought of saying his name and stopping this, or disobeying him and jerking myself off without permission, doesn't even cross my mind.

"Who's going to be my good boy today?"

"Me, Sir."

"We need to study."

"Yes, Sir."

"Another day off from PT," he says. "We'll start up again tomorrow. You'll wear your leather cuffs and collar until we know Susa's on her way. Chain collar stays on. I'll take the tag off for you and put it on the leather collar. You'll stay naked until then, too. Once I give you permission to get dressed, you may wear shorts and a T-shirt, no underwear. Until further notice, no underwear without permission. Wearing underwear without permission will result in punishment, and I don't mean like yesterday, either. I'm talking *real* punishment you absolutely will *not* enjoy."

"Yes, Sir." I'm practically squirming under him now, eager to please him because I'm desperate to earn this orgasm.

"I want these sheets washed. And her towels, after we've showered, and her bed remade perfectly."

"Yes, Sir."

He leans in so close I almost think he's going to kiss me.

It shocks me to realize I won't mind if he does. I can feel my cock rubbing against his abs as he stares down into my eyes.

"Repeat after me—I am Sir's boy, his cherished pet, and I belong to him."

I stare into his eyes. "I am Sir's boy, his cherished pet, and I belong to him."

"Again."

"I am Sir's boy, his cherished pet, and I belong to him."

He sits up a little, even while pinning my wrists over my head with his left hand. With his right, he scoops the puddle of pre-cum onto his fingers and wraps them around my cock. "Again."

"I-I am Sir's boy, his cherished pet, and I belong to him."

"Do *not* stop. Keep repeating it until you come. You may come. Eyes open and on me. Whenever I give you an orgasm, unless you're blindfolded or in a position where you can't see me, your eyes are always open and on *me*." He begins slowly stroking me.

With the warm, strong heat of his hand engulfing my cock, I struggle to keep my eyes open and talk at the same time. "I am Sir's boy, his cherished pet, and I belong to him. I...I am Sir's boy, his cherished pet, and I belong to him. I am Sir's boy..."

The rational part of my brain recognizes operant conditioning and positive reinforcement when it sees it.

But the rational part of my brain is also happy to sit back and enjoy the hell out of this. I start rocking my hips in time with Carter's hand, my gaze locked on his as I repeat his mantra over and over until, not even a couple of minutes later, I'm exploding with sweet, blessed pleasure rolling through me.

Far better than any orgasm I've ever given myself.

"Good boy," he coos, smiling.

My eyes drop closed while I try to catch my breath. He's still pinning my wrists down and I make no move to get free.

I don't want to.

I feel him lean in and he presses a tender kiss right in the middle of my forehead. "My *very* good boy," he whispers.

Honestly? I can*not* remember the last time my mother ever kissed me.

Carter holds me as I cry.

* * *

We shower together before breakfast, because now Carter's been spooged, although he doesn't seem to mind. The chain collar stays on me even in the shower, but he's swapped the tag out, attaching the tag's split ring to the D-ring on the front of the leather collar.

Before we finish our shower, Carter has me bend over and brace myself against the wall. While I suspect what's coming next, I still flinch when I feel his lubed, gloved finger press for entrance.

"Breathe through it, boy. Think how easy this'll make annual exams at the doctor," he teases.

The truth is, I've played with myself like this before, in the shower. I don't own any toys, because I never had the privacy when living at home.

Thank *god* I never had anything like that at home. I can only imagine the torture my mother would have put me through if she'd discovered them.

The smallest butt plug Carter bought, which wasn't the smallest one they sold, slides inside me after only a few minutes of prep.

"Can I ask why, Sir?" once he lightly smacks my ass and

allows me to stand.

"Sure." He doesn't say anything else as he strips off the glove and leans out of the shower to toss it into the garbage can.

I realize I need to ask properly. "Why the butt plug, Sir?"

He turns and smiles. "Because it amuses me, for starters. There will be other things in your future that you should be prepared for." He arches an eyebrow. "If Susa ever orders you to bend over so she can fuck you with a strap-on, I'd better never hear a report from her that you didn't obey her."

I swallow hard. "Yes, Sir," I whisper.

I can't lie and say the thought isn't hotter than hell, or something I haven't already fantasized about countless times, because my cock is once again hard. It's sort of a natural lie detector.

While I can tell Carter's is sort of stiff, he doesn't rub one out this morning. I suspect he's a grower, not a shower, but I haven't actually seen him fully hard yet. Yesterday morning, he had me pinned against the wall and I couldn't look.

Not that I *need* to know. I'm just...you know, curious.

After our shower, I'm back in my leather collar and cuffs to cook breakfast. We haven't heard from Susa yet, but we don't want to be surprised. As sadistic as Carter claims to be, that's not how he wants to spring the news on her about what's going on.

Definitely not how I want her to find out, either.

I'm still terrified him telling her might mean an end to our friendship with her, but I trust Carter. If he says it won't...then it won't.

This is the point in the story where if a friend were confiding all this to me, I'd stop them, ask them what the fucking *hell* they think they're doing, and tell them they're a fucking idiot, plus insane, to boot. Anyone I told this to would likely say that to me.

Not that I *have* anyone to tell this to.

Except...they haven't seen Carter's scars. They haven't

listened to him in the grip of a nightmare.

They don't know Carter.

I do.

For the first time in my life, I feel a greater sense of purpose than I ever have before, and I know this is a path I want to walk.

Have to walk.

Need to walk.

Sitting with the butt plug in takes a little getting used to, but fortunately we're eating on the sofa again—me sitting on a towel, of course—so it's soft.

Yay.

After breakfast and cleaning up, Carter receives a text from Susa that she's on her way and will probably arrive in less than three hours. We have to study today, but first Carter wants me to practice my positions for a few minutes.

I kneel on the floor in front of the couch, where I was yesterday.

The velvety, dark calm returns to my brain while I do, and I savor it.

Carter notices, smiling at me from his place on the couch as I move from Devotion into Primed. "Subspace already, boy?"

"Is that what it's called, Sir?"

"That's what it's called. By the way, can't remember if I told you this or not, but Primed is always done naked. I might put you in the other positions while you're clothed when we're alone and only have a few minutes, but Primed is always naked."

"Yes, Sir."

He cocks his head. "Don't want to ask me why?"

"Does it matter, Sir?"

His gaze narrows and hints of a smile curve his lips. "You're really learning fast, aren't you, boy?"

"I hope so, Sir."

"Primed is for *me*. You're completely open to me, exposed,

vulnerable, ready. It means you trust me, you're submitting to me in any way I choose, and you understand you're under my control."

"Yes, Sir."

He leans forward and rubs my head. "Good boy. Go take out the butt plug, wash and dry it, and put it with your things, along with the leather cuffs and collar. Day collar stays on. Same T-shirt and shorts you wore yesterday. Everything else can go in the car, except for our computers and books and stuff. Make sure her bed is made like I've taught you. Then patrol the house, go through and empty all the garbage cans into a garbage bag, and put it in the bin in the garage. Make sure we haven't overlooked anything. There should be no trace of what we've been doing, except for my marks on your flesh and your day collar."

"Yes, Sir." I go to do as I'm told and realize that my life has not only shifted completely off its foundation since Friday night...

It's now sitting atop a far more stable one.

* * *

I manage to get some studying done. Not a lot, but Carter and his nearly perfect memory would put anyone to shame, so I try not to feel badly about that.

The rest of me feels...

Amazing.

Nervous as hell awaiting Susa's return, though.

She's texted both of us that she's less than twenty minutes away and is stopping for gas. Carter puts me on the floor in Loyalty one last time, right in front of the couch, where he can sit there with his hand on my bowed head.

"I want you to address Susa as 'ma'am' from now on, boy. Understand?"

More fear fills me, but I tamp it back. "Yes, Sir."

"And you follow my lead."

Now, I *know*. This talk will happen *tonight*, and it terrifies the fuck out of me.

"*Devotion*."

Without thinking, I bring my knees together and roll my back, breathing out, clearing my mind as I bow.

His hand remains on my head, moving with me.

When Carter next speaks, his voice sounds deeper, stronger, and he grips my hair firmly, in control. "Do you trust me, boy?"

"Yes, Sir."

"Do you *really* want to be owned by me?"

I swallow hard. "Yes, Sir." In less than forty-eight hours, I've hard-shifted completely to the position that the thought of *not* being owned by Carter terrifies me.

He makes a soft, pained *oomph* as he gets off the couch and lowers himself to the floor. He presses his face against the right side of my head, his lips by my ear.

"I swear to you I will *never* let you fall, boy. If I am alive, I *will* catch you. *Always*. No matter what we do, no matter what happens, *never* forget that."

I struggle not to cry, *again*, especially so close to Susa's return. Before Carter, I was a master at masking my emotions.

Now? I'm an emotional wreck. "Yes, Sir. Thank you."

He nuzzles the side of my head for a moment. "My very good boy. You've made me so proud this weekend." He ruffles my hair again and sits back. "Help me up, please."

I break position and stand. Carter holds his hands up to me. As I grip them, our eyes meet, and something deep inside my soul goes blissfully quiet for the first time...ever.

I instinctively know this man will be in my life for the rest of my life.

Turns out I'm good with that.

CHAPTER TWENTY-SIX

I'm standing at the front door, waiting, watching through the viewfinder for Susa's arrival.

"She's here, Sir," I call out when she pulls into the driveway.

"Go on, boy. I'll be right there."

Despite my nerves I'm nearly vibrating with anticipation to see her again. I hurry out so I can open her driver's door for her, basking in the playful smile she gives me when I do.

"Welcome home, Ma'am."

Carter didn't specify it had to be a capital-*M* Ma'am, but it is, in my mind.

"Thank you," she says. I offer her my hand to help her out. She's wearing a black pencil skirt and a grey blouse, and her brown hair is down, straight, flowing around her shoulders. She's wearing light makeup, and I suspect she was at a brunch this morning. Like Carter, she already looks like an attorney. If I didn't know how old she is, I would think she was already graduated and in practice.

Once she steps out of the car, I open the back door to grab her overnight bag and laptop case from the backseat. I turn to find her wearing a playful smile and I know I'm blushing, but I can't help it.

She's barefoot and holding a pair of pumps in her hand. It's not uncommon for her to drive barefoot when she's wearing dressy shoes. In the house, she's nearly always barefoot.

She rises up on her toes to kiss my cheek. "Thank you for carrying my things inside. You can put them on my bed."

"Yes, Ma'am."

I turn and see Carter smiling from where he's stepped just outside the front door. As I hurry past him, he whispers, "Good boy," to me.

I set her things on the end of her bed, and when I emerge, Carter's shutting the door behind her.

"So how was your birthday celebration?" she asks me.

"Good. A little over-imbibing, but Carter took good care of me."

She wears a playful smile. "I'm sure he did."

"I washed your sheets and remade the bed, Ma'am. And the towels. Everything's clean."

"Aw, thank you, sweetie. You didn't have to do that."

Yes, I did, because Carter told me to. Although I didn't need Carter's order to do it—I would have done it anyway. "You're welcome, Ma'am."

"Are y'all hungry?" she asks.

Carter smiles. "Worked up an appetite this morning," he says.

"Let me go change clothes, and we'll get started on dinner. It'll take us a little while to put it together.

A few minutes later, she returns. She's scrubbed her makeup off, pulled her hair up in a messy bun, and wears the oversized USF Bulls T-shirt over shorts. She looks absolutely adorable.

"God, I'm glad to be home. When I wasn't at the conference with Daddy, Momma was all over me worrying about me."

"Worrying how?" Carter asks.

"Just being a typical mo—" She sucks on her lower lip as her blue gaze falls on me. "Sorry," she softly says. "I didn't mean to…"

I save her. "Hey, I know my mother's the exception, not the rule. It doesn't bother me. I like hearing about your and Carter's families."

She walks over to me and hugs me, long and hard, and I savor it. Over her shoulder, I watch Carter. He's leaning against the kitchen counter, his arms crossed over his chest, and he's wearing that playful smirk of his.

"It's so good to be home," she mutters against my shoulder. "I missed you guys."

"We missed you, too," I say.

She releases me and steps over to Carter, hugging him.

What surprises me is that I can't identify the source of the green ripple of jealousy that winds through me.

Is it jealousy that she's hugging him? Or that he's hugging her?

Before, I would have said the first.

Now?

I'm not sure.

It unsettles me. Not enough to make me want to stop what Carter and I have started, but I know it'll end up being a topic of conversation between us at some point in the future.

* * *

This is apparently another of those meals that Susa doesn't need a recipe to make. She shows me how to layer the dough in the baking dish, supervises me making the spinach and cheese filling, and once it's all assembled and in the oven, she reaches up and ruffles my hair.

"Good job, you."

I freeze for a moment, because the way she did it reminds me of Carter.

Only…I get hard.

I mean, *really* hard. Instantaneously hard.

And I'm freeballing it. I hope she doesn't notice.

"Thank you, Ma'am."

She cocks her head at me, then looks at Carter, her gaze narrowing a little, like she's putting something together in her mind.

Carter takes the opportunity and runs with it. "We'd like to talk to you about something."

Oh, shit.

Well, that's one way to kill my boner.

"About what?" she asks.

He's been sitting at the counter, on one of the barstools. Now he climbs down, moving a little slowly and stiffly from his pain, and walks over to us.

"So, Owen and I have been doing some talking this weekend," he starts.

I pray I don't end up having a panic attack.

"About what?" she asks.

"A lot of things. But primarily, about the future, and our relationship to each other." He stands next to me as his hand settles on my right shoulder and squeezes, reassuring me. "Long story short, Owen likes to be of service. He's happiest when he's taking care of people. Like you and me."

Her eyes are focused on mine now. I know my cheeks are hot, red, and I'm struggling not to hyperventilate, but I can't speak.

"Like bringing in my things?" But she says it slowly, like she's already ten steps beyond our current point in the conversation and trying not to rush ahead of Carter in case she's wrong.

"Yes. Like doing the dishes, helping cook dinner. Laundry."

"He's a submissive."

She doesn't ask it—she *says* it.

I guess it shouldn't shock me that she knows that, but I swallow hard anyway.

Carter squeezes my shoulder again. "Yes. And he'd like to

formally serve me and you. Doing things like that for us."

Her focus shifts to Carter for a long moment, nearly too long. Like they're the ones now having a silent conversation and I'm not privy to it.

I'm not sure how that makes me feel.

She turns back to me, staring up at me for an almost uncomfortably long time. Her next question shocks me so much it takes me a moment to answer. "What are your hard limits?"

I glance over to Carter, who gives my shoulder another squeeze.

"I-I…" I take a deep breath. "I have to put schoolwork first," I finally say. "No compromising pictures. I don't date." She glances at Carter again, another brief, silent conversation, then back to me. But she doesn't interrupt me, so I continue. "I'm to help you with things around the house, like I do now."

When I don't continue, she focuses on Carter.

This time when he squeezes my shoulder, it's firm, more a command. "Tell her the rest, boy," he softly orders.

Now I can't look her in the eyes. I stare at her feet, at her toenails, which are neatly painted the same shade of dark fuchsia as her fingernails. "Sir controls my orgasms."

Carter takes over, another shoulder squeeze silencing me. "He needs a lovingly firm hand. He wants to serve. Absolutely no emotional or mental humiliation. I'm using domestic discipline with him, and rituals, protocols. He's to call you Ma'am, and to call me Sir. No one can learn about this, meaning absolutely no compromising pictures."

A hand gently grips my chin—*Hers*. She tips my head up, forcing me to look her in the eyes. "Are you happy with this?" she softly asks.

"Yes, Ma'am. I didn't know how much I needed it."

"He's not allowed to lie," Carter adds.

"Safewords?" she asks.

"Our real names," Carter says. "He's to follow orders, or flip into vanilla mode to explain why."

She stares at me for so long I do what I didn't want to do. The prickle of tears stings my eyes as her face blurs.

But she pulls me in for a hug, holding me as I cry.

I feel Carter's arms wrap around both of us, from the side. "And there was a lot of *that* this weekend," he sadly says. "That bitch has totally fucked our boy's head. I want to teach him what healthy love and relationships feel like." His hand strokes my hair. "We can do this. I've promised him that as long as he wants to do this, I'll take care of him."

"Okay," she simply says after a long moment, her hand gently rubbing my back as she holds me. "Then we'll do it together." She ends the hug but cups my face with her hands. "You'll be our good boy, won't you?"

Now I'm seriously crying as I nod. "Yes, Ma'am. I want to be your good boy."

Carter steps away to grab me a piece of paper towel, but she takes it from him and wipes my face.

She wears a kind smile. "I think we'll be doing a lot of talking tonight, won't we?"

Overcome with emotion, I nod as I go in for another hug and she holds me.

She ruffles my hair. "Sweetie, it's going to take a lot more than you wanting to be our obedient pet to send me running. Trust me, the stories I've heard about politicians and their secrets? This is *tame*."

* * *

Carter shows her my chain collar, and she smiles as she runs her fingers over it. "I like it."

Carter has me take my shirt off but leave my shorts on, which relieves me. Carter and Susa are doing most of the talking, but I'm the prime topic of conversation instead of politics. I'm still battling bouts of tears and feeling pretty damn angry at myself over that.

Finally, Carter holds my face the way Susa did and waits until I focus on him. "You're in decompression mode," Carter tells me. "You've *literally* survived a lifetime of abuse. Honestly? I'd be more worried about you if you *weren't* crying and acting emotional right now."

I'm not sure if he's trying to humor me, but I opt to go with the default—Carter doesn't bullshit me.

We continue cooking dinner, Susa showing me how to make meatballs, Carter closely watching me. When we're down to waiting for the food to finish cooking, Susa leads me out to the living room, where she sits on the sofa where Carter had been sitting earlier.

"Go ahead and kneel for me," she says.

I glance at Carter, who stands next to where she's sitting, his arms once again crossed over his chest.

He nods.

I sink to my knees in front of her. This is…

It's better than a fantasy come to life.

This is *real*.

She's real.

"*At Ease*," she softly says.

I assume the position as Carter tells her about it. She puts me through the rest of the positions, ending with me in Devotion, and I feel subspace pulling my mind down into its comforting depths.

While I kneel there, I feel a hand on my head.

It's not Carter's.

"I read a lot," Susa says. "A *lot*. Including romance books, which I love, because it's pure escapism for me. I've read BDSM fiction that would curl your hair. Carter's right, though, sweetie. You have some pretty deep emotional wounds. Is this what you want to do?"

"Yes, Ma'am," I say.

She strokes my hair again. "Okay. I already told you both that no one's taking me away from you two, and I haven't been dating, either, so add me to that pledge. I've had more fun with you both since we've met than I ever have."

"You hear that, boy?" Carter sounds amused. "You can say it."

I sigh. "Yes, you told me so, Sir."

"Told him what?" Susa asks.

"That you'd be okay with this," Carter says. "He was worried you wouldn't want to be friends anymore."

"Oh, sweetie." She pets my head. "It'd take a lot more than this to make me walk away from you two. I don't think you're capable of doing anything that bad, either." She continues stroking my head, and it feels like pure heaven. "What kind of play am I allowed to do with him?"

I draw in an eager, shuddering breath.

"Whatever you want, within our hard limits," Carter says. "With the caveat that nothing you do can expose him to being discovered by someone else. He will always be able to safeword for something outside his hard limits, or something that disobeys an order, rule, or protocol I've given him."

"Fair enough," she says. "And he's not allowed to text that bitch anymore?"

Panic flares in me. I realize I haven't texted my mom since Friday.

Carter's hand appears in the middle of my back, keeping me in place, as if he read my mind and realized I was about to sit up.

"*Stay*, boy," he firmly orders. "I'll give you that one, because I think you just remembered you haven't texted your mom this weekend."

Shit!

Carter's talking to Susa. "He's still going to be texting her, but I'm going to step back the frequency. I promised him he's staying with me during semester breaks."

"Well, that's easy to deal with," she says. "You'll both stay here, with me."

"What will your parents say?" he asks.

She snorts. "Not a damn thing, because it's none of their business. This is *my* house. It's in *my* name. I'm an adult. They know you're friends of mine. If they didn't trust me to make sound decisions, then they shouldn't have given me my own house, a trust fund, and taught me how to manage my money, now, should they?"

He snickers. "You are a unique woman, Susa."

"I try." Her hand is still on my head, her fingers playing with my hair.

"Except you don't have guest beds," Carter notes.

"Well, not like I can't go shopping." The feel of her fingers in my hair has driven me even deeper into that sweet mental vacation. "When can he sit up?"

"With permission."

"Can I give him permission?"

He must have nodded, because Susa pats my head. "Sit up, sweetie. *At Ease.*"

Carter's hand disappears, as does Susa's. I sit up and move into the position.

She's smiling. "Neither of you will go homeless as long as I'm around," she says. "So if the bitch cuts you off, you let *me* handle her, huh?"

Carter clears his throat, but he's wearing that smirk.

Susa sighs and playfully rolls her eyes. "Oh, *fine*. Let the sadist have *all* the fun."

CHAPTER TWENTY-SEVEN

I spend the next several days in a daze. Carter takes things easy on me with Susa now in the know and participating somewhat during our evenings together. I don't have to be naked at Susa's, but I do have to go shirtless. Carter tells me being naked in front of her is an eventual goal, so I'll need to mentally work myself up to it.

I get the feeling Susa and Carter have conversations about this without me around, because he doesn't seem to want to push the issue too hard. Maybe she isn't comfortable with me being naked, I don't know.

It doesn't really matter, I suppose. I do what I'm told.

I trust Sir, and Susa, by default.

We haven't done any domestic discipline in front of Susa, either. Or sexual…stuff. That happens in our room at the dorm, for now, but is also something Carter's told me will eventually happen in front of her.

Maybe even with her taking part, if she chooses to.

He doesn't tell her everything, though, only things she needs to know about me, about what he's doing with me. I've been warned this is a marathon and not a sprint.

I quickly grow used to being on my tether in our room. He

develops a ritual about this, too. Carter takes it off me in the morning. I go to his bed—if I haven't fallen asleep next to him in it—and kneel in Devotion to wake and greet him. Then he has me lay my head on the bed and scratches my scalp for a moment while I breathe and center myself. All the while, Carter softly talks to me, tells me what a good boy I am for him.

I feel calmer than I have in years, and that's not an exaggeration.

Carter has me text Mom every other day now. She hasn't replied to any of them, but he's had a couple of text conversations with her, the contents of which he hasn't volunteered to me.

I haven't asked.

Maybe he's blamed it on him and our studying, I don't know.

If he wants me to know, he'll tell me.

Right now, his pattern is that, during our morning shower, he jerks me off.

I've even gotten better about speaking up and asking for it. He's warned me that he will be transitioning us to a different schedule, but he outright admitted when I asked that, yes, it is positive reinforcement.

He wants to reprogram my emotions.

Yeah, like *hell* do I want him to stop.

He only jerked off in front of me one time, on Wednesday morning, with me pinned against the wall by the neck like he did that morning at Susa's. He took care of me first, then himself. If he's getting relief at other times, when I'm not in our room, he hasn't said.

I haven't asked.

Yet.

I'm not ready to take that step at this time. I'm too busy trying to learn who I really am, figuring out this new phase of my life. No, he hasn't pressed me about it, hasn't asked me if I want to. He's kept his word, even though he has to be aware that, at this point, if he did ask me, of course I'd most likely say yes.

There's not much I wouldn't say yes to now, if he asked it of me.

By Friday, I crave our morning ritual. I'm eager for us to work out, either a run or the exercise room, and get to the shower.

I'm eager to get out of bed.

I'm...*eager*.

Which is the thought that shocks me so much as it hits me during our post-run shower Friday morning that Carter notices and frowns.

"What's wrong, Owen?"

I blink, shocked he used my real name. He calls me *buddy* around people in public, if anyone can hear, and *boy* when we're alone or with Susa. "Huh?"

"You just had a look. What's wrong?"

"Nothing, Sir."

"Owen, that wasn't a nothing look. *Tell* me." He crosses his arms over his chest and stands there, waiting.

I'm not even sure how to say it. "I guess I had a revelation, Sir."

He gives me "the look." It doesn't have a label, but everyone has one of their own.

The quit-screwing-around-and-tell-me look.

"I realized that, this week, I've been *eager* to get out of bed. Genuinely eager. Not just looking forward to something, like I used to look forward to spending time with Susa."

One corner of his mouth quirks up in a smile. "You're enjoying this, then?"

"Yes, Sir."

"Even the tether?"

My face heats, but I nod. "Yes, Sir." I don't know how to explain that, in a way, the tether is quickly becoming a comfort.

I'm allowed to take it off if I need a shower, or to go out into the quad pod, but once I'm locked inside our room and naked, I immediately put it on, along with my leather cuffs and collar. If I'll only be in our room for a short time, such as a few minutes between classes, I'm even allowed to put on only the right ankle cuff, with the tether hooked to it, and stay dressed.

It reminds me of what I'm doing with Carter. That even when he's not physically with me, he's still in control and taking care of me.

I've also noticed I'm blushing less frequently now when answering his probing questions. He told me that uncomfortably personal discussions would get easier, and he's right. They're still uncomfortable, but I'm not always mumbling my way through them like I used to.

"Excellent. Wait here." He steps out of the shower and returns a moment later with lube, a glove…

And the vibrating butt plug.

Oh, shit.

He looks at me as he pulls the glove on. "Turn."

I do, bracing my hands against the wall and assuming the position I know he wants me in. Every morning, another part of our routine is he plays with my ass, even if only briefly, usually right before he jerks me off.

Operant conditioning, FTW.

#Idontcareifitsweirdbecauseitworks

He's also been working with me with the butt plugs at night, putting one in when we return from Susa's and then allowing me to take it out before we go to bed. I've worked up to this one, but he hasn't turned it on yet while I wear it.

I wonder if I'll be allowed to come this morning after all.

My cock jerks and twitches as his fingers lube me. Yeah, I'd be lying if I said I didn't enjoy this part, too. I've become intimately acquainted with how good it feels to have him playing with me like that. He's already warned me he plans to add prostate milking to our future play, between semesters, when we'll have more privacy at Susa's.

I looked it up.

Yeeeeeaaah. Honestly? I can't wait. There is something so freeing about not having any control over this, and it's a sweet irony I'm clinging to and hoping never ends.

I suck in a sharp breath as he starts fucking the toy into me. Then comes the uncomfortable, pinching burn before the widest part passes through and it's seated inside me. I hear him strip off the glove and he leans out to toss it in the garbage can.

Before I really have a chance to get used to it, he turns me to face him and pins me to the wall, his left forearm over my throat.

"You may come, boy." But in his right hand is the controller.

I can't completely contain my shocked yelp as it bursts to life inside me, my hard cock immediately jerking as the toy throbs against my sweet spot.

Aching pleasure rolls through my balls and I'm exploding before I can barely even process it. I struggle to keep my eyes open, on him.

Carter wears a gleefully sadistic smile if I ever saw one.

The toy shuts off.

"Excellent," he says, releasing me. "That's exactly what I wanted to see happen. Good boy."

I'm slumped against the wall and gasping for breath. "Holy shit," I mutter.

He laughs and sets the controller outside the shower. "That stays in. Take lube with you. If you need to use the bathroom, take it out, do your thing, then put it back in. You may return here for lunch and take it out. And take a quick shower, if you feel you need one. Wash it, dry it, and put it away."

"Yes, Sir. Thank you, Sir."

His gaze narrows even as his grin turns predatory. "Oh, you thank me *now*, boy."

Yikes.

*   *   *

We walk to class together. This is our Florida Politics & Government class that we share with Susa.

Walking with the toy inside me is a little uncomfortable at first, and Carter slows his pace to give me time to get used to it.

He has also allowed me briefs today, thankfully, and I didn't even have to ask for them.

I'm not sure if that should worry me or not.

Susa's already there when we arrive, and has moved our desks into their usual positions. We always sit in the same place we ended up in that first morning, and we arrive early enough to get the seats we want.

There are only two other students there besides us, and they're sitting close to the front of the classroom.

There's something different about Susa's smile this morning. I don't know how to describe it. Almost...

Oh, shit.

She's wearing a Carter smile if I ever saw one.

"Good morning, Ma'am," I quietly say, and she offers me her hand to kiss. Obviously, I can't drop to my knees in front of her in public, so Carter came up with this alternate greeting.

"Good morning, boy."

I turn to put my things down as Carter leans in to hug her and kiss her cheek, the way he always does. When I've settled in my desk—which takes me a moment to get comfortable—I realize Susa's eagerly watching me.

While her right hand is in her lap, it looks like she's holding something.

Oh, fu—

I somehow manage to remain silent when the toy hums to life inside me. Not the intense, pounding throb of in the shower, but it hardens my cock and—

It shuts off.

I'm looking Susa in her blue eyes and the way they're now narrowed at the outer edges tells me everything I need to know.

She's in charge.

I stare at her for a long moment before my gaze shifts to Carter.

He's sitting back in his desk and, yes, wearing *that* smirk. He glances Susa's direction before cutting back to me, his meaning clear.

You okay with this?

Then he arches an eyebrow in silent query.

For a long moment I hold his gaze, knowing he's awaiting my next indication if this is a go or no-go.

This is my chance to shake my head and I know he'll take the controller back and not do anything with it.

Or…

I nod, once.

He leans in, indicating for me to lean in, too.

"Good boy," he whispers in my ear, reaching up to ruffle my hair.

I look at Susa, who while her hand is still in her lap, lets me see that, yes, she does now, in fact, have the controller.

I'd kill to keep receiving the pleased smile she gives me, and the silent *good boy* she mouths before sitting back and opening her text book to glance through today's lesson one last time.

CHAPTER TWENTY-EIGHT

I receive two more jolts from the vibrator, on that same gentle humming setting, before the instructor arrives to start class.

Nothing during class, though.

During class, Susa, and Carter, are all business, focused on the instructor.

I do my best and hope they'll go over their notes with me later. I know they said nothing we did would interfere with our schoolwork, but since they can tutor me in this class—hell, Susa should be *teaching* this class—I'm sure this won't be the norm.

At least, I'm hoping it won't be the norm, because I'll never be able to focus if it is. Hopefully, it's simply a step toward the next phase of whatever *this* is between the three of us.

I'd be lying if I said a huge part of me wasn't looking forward to the future, because I am.

At the end of class I stand, but Carter stays me with a look while the room empties, leaving the three of us. Without a word, he motions for me to follow him.

Susa falls in behind us.

He leads us down the hallway to a stairwell at the far end of that floor, one that's open for general use but which receives little foot traffic when the elevators and a larger stairwell in the center of the building are far more accessible and convenient for most people.

Once the door to the stairwell closes behind us and Carter verifies we're alone in there, he takes my backpack from me and sets it on the floor with his, then pins me against the wall with his left forearm across my neck.

Operant conditioning is a bitch. My cock has hardened, between this and the toy inside me.

"Ask her," Carter softly orders.

My hands hold his arm, the way I always do in the shower when we do this. Susa stands there wearing an evil grin and holding up the controller. I'm simultaneously horrified and turned on beyond measure.

"*Please*, Ma'am," I hear myself whisper.

"Eyes on *her*, boy," Carter says, his gaze never leaving me. Carter covers my mouth with his right hand. "Give it to him."

Susa makes sure I can see her thumb the controller.

Thank god Carter's hand is covering my mouth. The toy explodes to life inside me as it did earlier in the shower, and I have no choice but to climax right there. I come almost immediately, whimpering as my cock jerks and throbs and spills in my briefs while I desperately struggle to stay upright.

Thank god the bastard gave me briefs.

Note to self—underwear might mean a blessing or a curse.

Or, in this case, both.

After a moment, she shuts the toy off, leaving me gasping and trembling where Carter holds me in place.

Her smile now looks sweetly angelic. Carter uncovers my mouth but keeps me pinned against the wall.

"What do you say, boy?" Carter whispers.

"Thank you, Ma'am."

She leans in and nuzzles her nose against mine, pausing before pressing a kiss to the tip of it. "You're very welcome. You're my *very* good boy."

My heart gallops even harder at that, and it takes every ounce of energy I have not to burst into happy tears.

Carter releases me, pulling me in for a long, strong hug while Susa hugs me from behind. Finally, Carter pats me on the back and ends the embrace. "Good boy," he says. "Go clean up in the bathroom and get to your next class."

Susa starts to hand the controller back to Carter, but he smiles. "No, you hold on to that." His gaze meets mine. "You'll need it tonight when we come over for dinner."

Oh…

I swallow hard, both dreading and eagerly anticipating tonight.

* * *

I somehow manage to make it through the rest of my classes without fucking things up too terribly. Thank god I didn't have any tests today.

When Carter arrives at our room after his last class, he lets himself in and is pleased to see me naked and tethered. He walks over to me, where I'm sitting on my bed studying, and ruffles my hair.

"Good boy. Let's get ready to go. Shorts and T-shirt. Commando."

I don't know if that means I can relax a little, or if it means I'll be stripped and played with once we reach Susa's.

I guess it doesn't matter either way. The ice has definitely been broken, Susa's on-board with this, and…

I guess there really isn't an "and" to add to that.

This is *it*.

I'm still terrified. I'm worried I'll disappoint her, or him, or…something.

This being a functional adult shit is hard.

Really hard.

I've put the toy in my backpack, per Carter's orders.

Along with my leather cuffs, collar, the leash, and a couple of other items he specifies before we leave.

And, of course, our laundry.

We ride over to Susa's together with Carter driving the Snot Box. I'm glad we're not driving separately today. I feel...

I don't have words to describe it.

On the way there, Carter breaks the quiet. "Are you all right, boy?"

"Yes, Sir. Nervous."

"You should be nervous. I'd worry if you weren't. That's a normal reaction."

"Then I'm all sorts of normal, Sir."

He chuckles. "Hopefully not *too* normal." He glances at me, a smile on his face, but I can't see his eyes because of his sunglasses.

"I suppose not."

"Also, I want to give you advance notice. Not this weekend, but sometime next week, there will likely be a couple of days where I ask you to go home early so Susa and I can speak alone. I hope that's okay."

My pulse rabbits, because old habits die hard. "Speak alone about what, Sir?"

"About you, and this. I need to know she has your best interests at heart. I mean, I'm sure she does, but I want some time to discuss things with her, things you and I have talked about. And I need to have some heart-to-heart conversations with her, too. Nothing bad. Is that all right?"

"I don't understand the question, Sir."

We roll up to a red light and Carter looks at me after we come to a stop. "Owen, I'm asking if you're okay with me having some alone time with her. Talking with her about things we've talked about, among other things."

"You're *asking* me, Sir?"

"Carter and Owen time. Yes, I'm asking you."

I think about it. "As long as she promises to keep things private, then yes, Sir."

He smirks when I use the title, but I can't help it. It feels normal, *natural* to call him that now.

I *prefer* calling him that, even after such a short time. I'd be lying if I said it didn't, and I'm not allowed to lie.

Besides, if I always tell the truth, I never have to worry about contradicting myself.

Upon our arrival at Susa's we let ourselves in, as we normally do now, and find her in the kitchen. Tonight is lasagna, the leftovers of which will feed us for most of the weekend.

Usually, Susa manages to hug Carter first. I'm not sure if she does it intentionally or not, but I've never minded it. Not really. Because she frequently hugs me a little longer. Besides, I always let Carter walk ahead of me, especially now, so of course she reaches him first.

Today, she bypasses Carter and comes straight to me for my hug. "How are you?" She asks after she releases me.

She looks a little...worried?

"Good, Ma'am. Why?"

"Are we...okay?"

That genuinely confuses me. "Of course. Why?"

"After this morning."

Why do I feel like I'm missing something? Confused, I turn to Carter.

The bastard's smirking. "He's fine, Susa. He enjoyed himself. I can see we need to work on your sadistic side."

She sticks her tongue out at him, making him laugh and amusing the hell out of me.

Also, it eases the tension in me. We're okay. We're *alllll* okay.

"Shirt off, boy," Carter says as Susa hugs him.

I resist the urge to glare at him and instead set my things down and comply. Of course I blush as I do it. Susa's seen me in a bathing suit before, and that didn't bother me.

This is different, though.

"You know," Carter says to Susa, "he *actually* called me a bastard last weekend." Except he sounds amused, not upset. "Can you believe that?"

"A bastard, huh?" She also looks amused and smirks at him. "Well, he's *not* wrong, Carter."

His smile widens. "I didn't say he was wrong. I just asked if you can believe it."

"You're a bastard extraordinaire. *Sir*," I add with more than a little snark.

I must not have a very strong sense of self-preservation.

But that also amuses him, making him laugh. "I think my boy just gave me a nickname."

"The bastard extraordinaire." Susa firmly nods. "I like it. Suits you. If you're going to be a bastard, be an extraordinary one."

I have to admit, Carter's easy, rolling laugh eases things deep inside me that I didn't know had grown tense. I like that I can make him laugh like that, even if partially at my own expense. It softens the lines in his face and takes some of the wear and tear off his features.

I don't think I've ever made my mother laugh like that. Laugh at me in mean ways, sure, plenty of times.

But nothing like this.

Through Carter's nightmares, I've heard hints of the horrors the man keeps stored in his memory and in his flesh. If I can balance those sounds with *this* one?

Yeah, I'll do it.

He smiles and playfully swats me on the shoulder. "Go get our laundry started, please."

"Yes, Sir."

Carter's laugh might inspire me to try to move mountains, but it's Susa's smile that seals my fate. Her sweet smile, those blue eyes crinkled at the edges—knowing I've made her smile means everything to me.

I don't ever want to stop doing this if I can make her smile.

* * *

Once the lasagna's in the oven, and our laundry's in the washer, Susa wants to do more.

The bastard extraordinaire, of course, allows it.

That's how I find myself kneeling in front of the couch in At Ease—with my shorts still on, fortunately—to talk with her.

She's sitting at the end of the couch, Carter at the other end and watching us, one leg crossed over the other as he lounges against the back, his hands laced together on top of his head. Deceptively relaxed, because from the tilt of his head I know he's watching, listening, and ready to interject himself if he feels he needs to. He might fool Susa, but he's not fooling me.

It comforts me greatly to know he's paying attention.

"I want to talk about this morning," she says, and my face heats. "For starters, are you *really* okay with what happened?"

"Yes, Ma'am."

"That won't be the norm," she says, and I'm simultaneously relieved and disappointed.

"Why not?" Carter snarks. "I thought it was a hoot and a half."

"You're a sadist," she shoots back.

"Duh."

I can't help smiling and I glance at Carter, who drops me a wink.

Susa focuses on me again. "Would you want to do more with me?"

The smile freezes on my face as my throat goes dry. "More?"

"More."

I'm almost afraid to ask, but she doesn't speak, and neither does Carter.

"More how, Ma'am?"

"Well, for starters, would you be comfortable being fully naked around here? And wearing your cuffs and collar?"

No. Nononono. Nope. Nooooo.

That's what's running through my mind.

What do my lips say?

"Yes, Ma'am."

"Good boy," Carter says, but he's not smiling now. He looks serious. Now I'm certain he's paying attention to every breath I take, every syllable Susa utters.

Everything.

Susa leans forward, reaches out, and cups my cheek. Her touch is soft, warm, and I know I'm not supposed to break position, but I nuzzle her hand with my face anyway.

"Do you want to be a good boy for me?" she asks.

"Yes, Ma'am." My eyes fall closed as I soak in her touch.

She's *touching* me.

She's not disgusted by me, or by what I want.

"How long have you wanted to do this?"

"I don't know, Ma'am. A few years." I discovered it on the Internet, and, fortunately, Mom is a complete technical idiot. It was one way I could hide things from her. In retrospect, I suppose it's why things didn't work for me with my girlfriends.

They weren't…this.

Her.

Her thumb strokes my cheek. "I'm not sure I'm going to be very good at this. At least, not at first."

"That's all right, Ma'am. I'm sure you'll do fine."

"I'll be taking some things slow. Are you okay with Carter showing me stuff?"

My pulse races. "Yes, Ma'am."

"And will you be okay with me watching him do things to

you?"

More heat fills my face. I wonder what *things* she means, because that could mean a lot of *things.*

Including shower time. "Yes, Ma'am."

"Go ahead and get naked, boy." When she withdraws her hand, I start to lean forward, to try to maintain contact with her hand.

"*Boy,*" Carter says, his tone not quite sharp, but enough to jolt me out of Susa's spell.

My eyes open and I realize what I'd been doing. "Yes, Ma'am." I see Carter nod at me, encouraging me, and I stand.

I can't keep my eyes open, though, so I close my eyes as I push my shorts down and take them off, folding them by feel. She takes them from me.

"Eyes open, boy," Carter says, but his tone has shifted back to the gentler range.

Has it only been a week since we started this? It feels like a lot longer. I can barely remember how lonely and bleak my life felt before Carter entered it, and now...*this.*

I open my eyes to see Carter now sitting forward and watching me with an intensity that almost makes me uncomfortable.

He tips his head toward Susa, and I know what he wants.

I force myself to focus on her.

I'm also forcing my hands to remain at my sides and not cover myself.

She sits back, watching me. "How do you feel right now, boy?"

"Nervous, Ma'am."

"Why?"

"Because I don't want to disappoint you, or Sir."

"Don't be stupid, you could never—"

"*Devotion,* boy. *Now,*" Carter orders as he stands. Automatically, I once again drop to my knees and assume the position, my head and hands against the floor. "*Susa,* a word." I hear Carter stride out of the living room. "*Now.*"

I flinch at his tone—beyond any kind of firm he's ever used on me. I hear her stand and hurry after him, the soft sound of her bare feet padding across the tile, and the way the ambient sounds in the room change as she moves through it.

With my heart racing, I kneel there, straining to listen. But I hear a door close, followed by the muffled sound of Carter's voice.

At war within me, the urge to follow and defend her. Not that I think Carter would lay a hand on her, but I just…

I don't know what happened, what I missed.

My pulse pounds in my ears as I struggle to hear any hint of what's going on.

Just as I'm about to break position and go after them a few minutes later, I hear a door open from down the hall, followed by the sounds of them returning.

I know it's Carter's hand that settles between my shoulders. He actually kneels beside me on the floor. I hear him, the soft grunt of pain as he settles, feel a gentle wash of warmth from how close to me he now sits.

"Good boy," he softly says. "Thank you for obeying me."

This feels…

I don't know. Like *something* happened.

"Am I in trouble, Sir?" I whisper, not sure if I'm even allowed to speak right now.

"No, you didn't do anything wrong, boy. You were perfect." His words warm me even as he now strokes my head, slowly rubbing my scalp in that sweet, addictive way he has.

Like he knows how to short-circuit my brain and shut it down.

In a few minutes, I feel myself sinking deep into subspace, relaxing, the sweet hum filling my brain.

Quiet. Everything's quiet.

"At Ease."

I slowly roll up into the position. Carter's sitting on the floor next to me, and he looks…

I don't know. I can't read his expression. The wall is there but it feels different, somehow. Not like he's trying to shut me out, more like he doesn't want me to worry about him.

Susa sits on the couch where she was, and likewise, I can't read her expression, either.

Then she smiles at me and crooks her finger.

I go.

She has me put my head in her lap and pulls my arms around her, then folds herself over me and hugs me, her face buried in my hair.

"Such a good boy," she softly says. "My *very* good boy."

Boom. Subspace completely re-achieved. I no longer care what happened, because she's tightly holding me and whispering to me that I'm *Her* good boy, and that I'm *Hers*, and...

Honestly?

The world can end right fucking now and I'd be a happy camper.

I'm *Hers*.

And I'm *Her* good boy.

CHAPTER TWENTY-NINE

Susa wants to be the one to put my cuffs and collar on me, and Carter allows it.

Thus, a new ritual is born. When she's there and I'm to wear them, I'm to bring them to her to put on me.

I'm good with that.

Unfortunately, I'm also sort of embarrassed that I'm...

Well, hard.

Like, *really* fucking hard. That's despite already coming twice today. It wasn't quite so mortifying that morning after class, because Mr. Happy Bone was concealed inside my briefs and shorts.

I can't hide from her what effects all this has on me now.

Worse?

I'm kind of leaving a trail. Or, would be, if I wasn't kneeling on a towel, where Carter's put me in Primed and is keeping me there while he and Susa have a very animated discussion about one of her father's votes that week.

Carter's like a conversational mongoose tonight, coming at her from different angles, flipping perspectives to play devil's advocate, and generally tying her in knots in a way I'm not used to seeing her or him.

I don't know why tonight is different, why he's doing this now. Usually he takes a more methodical approach to their debates, and Susa's normally unflappable no matter what arguments or tactics he engages in.

I listen and ignore the twinges in my back and the way my knees are protesting.

"His vote basically is a budget cut for education, Susa, and don't try to argue otherwise. *Loyalty*. I mean, really? Cutting STEM program funding like that in the name of charter schools? A sneaky side-run?"

It took a moment for the command to percolate through my brain. I breathe a sigh of relief and drop into the more relaxed position, which also allows me to reposition my feet.

"Good boy," Carter immediately says. He stands and walks over to me, resting his hand on my head. "That was a trick, yes. Excellent listening, boy." He ruffles my hair. "Five minutes like this, and then I'll let you up and you can relax. Susa needs to catch you up on the class today. I'm sure you weren't able to pay attention very well."

I can't see his face but he sounds amused.

"Thank you, Sir."

One more head-pat before he returns to the couch.

When he releases me from Loyalty, Susa has me grab my notes, my textbook, and my towel.

"Right here," she points at the floor in front of her, against the sofa.

I sit where she tells me, between her legs, my back pressed against the sofa. Then she drapes her legs over my shoulders and I realize maybe I'll need a make-up session for my make-up session.

Carter laughs. "Susa, that's just cruel."

She reaches down and ruffles my hair. "Dinner will be ready in ten minutes. This is his reward for being such a good boy."

"Ahhh. Very smart."

"I have my moments." She quizzes me on a few things, which I stammer my way through. When the timer on her phone goes off, she pats my head. "Let's go eat."

Once we finish with dinner, and after I have the kitchen cleaned up, I return to the living room. This time, she sits in the same place, only turned sideways, legs stretched out on the couch.

Then she pats the space right there, her meaning obvious.

Swallowing hard, and unable to miss Carter's evil grin, I lie down on my back where she indicates, snuggled against her with her legs on either side of me. My head rests against her chest, and she holds her notebook in front of me, where she can read it to me.

This isn't much easier than before. I spend the first ten minutes or so reveling in the fact that she's snuggling with me like this.

Sure we've all snuggled together on the couch before for movie nights, but we were all clothed and there definitely wasn't such a blatantly sexual overtone to the situation as there is right now.

My legs are draped across Carter's lap, and he's propped his feet on the coffee table. His laptop sets on a padded lap desk on his thighs, and his elbows rest on my shins.

"Owen?"

My attention snaps back to Susa. "Yes, Ma'am?"

"If you let him come now," Carter warns without looking away from his laptop, "he'll fall asleep almost immediately because of his full tummy. That means he won't get any more studying done tonight."

I feel her breath against my left shoulder. "He's not getting much studying done *now*," Susa notes.

"You can always order him to put shorts on."

"But I like the view."

I realize while they're discussing me like I'm not even here, they're talking about me in such playful, affectionate tones that it…fascinates me.

That's when it hits me.

She likes the view!

Carter saves whatever he's working on and finally looks at us. "He's holding an *A* average across the board," he notes. "If he gets anything less than an *A* in this class, I will hold *you* responsible and take it out of *your* ass, sweetie." He's looking at her when he says that.

"I'll get an *A*," I insist.

She sets her notebook aside, on the coffee table. "You're tense," she says to me. "You need to relax. We need to get you through this nervous phase so you can focus."

Her hand closes around my cock, which makes me flinch. A startled gasp escapes me.

Yeah, that's *not* going to help me focus.

She pulls me back against her. "Relax, *boy*," she says as her hand slowly strokes me. "Let's take care of this."

"Reward should usually *follow* the action," Carter drawls. "Not precede it." He's set his laptop on the coffee table and turns to watch us. His hands close around my shins, pinning me in place. "Eyes on her, *boy*."

I tip my head back a little and find myself looking up into her blue gaze. I know she's mentioned previous boyfriends before, but I never asked for details. Apparently she is not unfamiliar with a cock. Maybe her technique isn't as skilled as Carter's, but then again, he's got one of his own he's had plenty of time to practice on.

I'm not sure if I'm allowed to come or not, because she hasn't said so. But if she keeps that up, permission isn't going to be the issue.

"Is he allowed to come?" Carter asks, as if reading my mind.

"Oh, yeah. You can come."

It doesn't take me long to comply. I try to keep my eyes open as long as I can before they finally fall closed as the force of my climax carries me away. This is a fantasy come true, *Her* sweet warmth pressed against me as her hand grants me pleasure.

As I lie there trying to catch my breath, Carter clears his throat.

My eyes pop open. "Thank you, Ma'am," I say.

She smiles down at me. "You're very welcome, boy. Let's clean up, you can put shorts on, and then we'll show Carter you are perfectly capable of studying some more."

Of course I will. I'll do anything she asks of me.

Carter smirks. "That's it. Spoil the boy, why don't you?" Again, it's amusement that tinges his tone.

Susa once again sticks her tongue out at him, and a sharp edge appears in his gaze.

"Keep that up, *pet*, and you might find yourself in cuffs."

She tosses him a smirk of her own before untangling herself from me and heading to the kitchen to wash her hands.

I'm somehow managing to sit up. Carter releases my legs, and I look to him to make sure this is okay.

He reaches over and ruffles my hair. "You heard her, boy. Clean up, and put on shorts. I can see I'll have to be the mean Dom to her good Domme."

I manage to stand without falling over. "You're not mean, Sir."

"Oh, you haven't seen me mean, yet, boy. Maybe one day, when I think you can handle it."

If I haven't seen mean yet, I'm not sure if I want to.

Right now, I need to get cleaned up so I can study, because *absolutely* I want to prove Susa right.

But I stop and turn before I've even taken a couple of steps. "Sir, does this mean I belong to Her now?"

"I'm still at the top of the food-chain, if that's your question, boy. Unless you don't want me there."

Fear flashes through me, and I shove it away. "I still want you there, Sir."

He nods. "Good, because that's where I want to be."

I head to the bathroom to clean up, my brain struggling to

process this latest development.

Make no mistake about it, I'm loving it.

I'm just...processing.

*   *   *

Yes, I did study, thank you very much. By late Saturday, Susa's given me my first spanking with Carter closely supervising and critiquing her technique. It becomes easier to relax when naked around her, too.

Might be because the two of them gave me three orgasms before lunch, leaving me literally drained.

As Carter warned me, I am growing accustomed to this, finding it easier to focus only on him—or Her, as warranted.

While I do a lot of studying this weekend, there is also a lot of talking—and a lot of cathartic crying on my part that I know, somehow, I need to get over. By the time late Sunday afternoon rolls around, I'm exhausted and feel like I'm about to drop.

Carter studies me. "I think I need to take you back to the dorm," he says. "Would you mind if I ran you home and came back here?"

I'm at that nearly numb point, but unlike earlier points in my life, this numbness isn't because I'm in so much emotional pain that I'm trying to protect myself from it.

This time, it feels like I've scrubbed myself raw in good ways, sloughing off dead flesh so that tender, fresh skin is now exposed and needs time to acclimate.

This is the good kind of numb.

"That's fine, Sir." I don't even know what time it is.

I get dressed and Susa hugs me, long and hard. "See you tomorrow morning, boy," she says, kissing my cheek.

"Yes, Ma'am."

I sit slumped in the passenger seat as he drives me home in my car. We'd taken mine today, and I don't care if Carter drives me or not. The two of us switch vehicles back and forth so often now that we each have keys for the other's car on our own key rings.

I think he's going to just let me out when we arrive, but he parks and won't let me carry my own stuff. He accompanies me upstairs and once we're safely locked behind our door, he sits with me on my bed and holds me for a minute.

"Why am I so exhausted?" I ask.

"Because this is hard work you're doing. And I'm *really* damn proud of you for doing it, too."

Hell, I'm too tired to even perk up over that praise. "Thank you, Sir."

He kisses the top of my head. He does that more often, and I don't mind in the least. He's affectionate with me, and I know he's right that I've got "skin hunger" from going so many years without.

"Okay, boy. I want you to spend the rest of the evening relaxing, napping, watching TV, whatever. Chill out. Complete free time. You can snack if you want to, but I'll bring you dinner in a few hours."

"Thank you, Sir."

He makes me look him in the eyes. He does this sometimes, forcing me to meet his gaze and not letting me go until I have. More conditioning, more acclimating me to intimacy.

Not allowing me to escape the hard work.

I love him for it, too. Maybe this is why we were destined to meet, so I can become a better person with him, and with Susa, in my life.

We sit there like that for at least a minute. "You don't even have to put on the tether today, if you don't want to. Or your cuffs and collar. Not until tonight."

I nod. "Yes, Sir. Thank you."

He drops one more kiss on the top of my head before he heads out again. I still strip, because as Carter warned me, it feels weird to be dressed now when I'm behind closed doors. Plus, bonus, it saves on laundry.

As I lie there and channel surf, despite my exhaustion I can't get comfortable. Something's…missing.

Finally, after about fifteen minutes, I dig the tether out of the storage tub and connect it to the leg of my bed. I don the leather collar, cuffs, and attach the tether to my right ankle.

Peace settles over me, and I find myself quickly dozing off, the TV softly playing on, unwatched.

CHAPTER THIRTY

The addition of Susa to what Carter and I have only makes it better. I start to relax even as I'm learning new things, and Carter adds more protocols and rituals to our daily routine. I lay out his clothes for him. When we're together, I wait for permission from him—or Susa, if Carter's not there—to eat. I end up sleeping in his bed more often than not now because of his nightmares. It's a tight fit, but to be honest, I've found I sleep better like that, too.

When Carter suggests maybe removing the tether requirement except for at night, I unexpectedly burst into tears that he comforts me through before quietly telling me the rule can stay in place.

I know it's weird, but I like it. I like the tangible connection to Carter, and Susa, by extension.

The day collar hasn't been off for more than a few hours here and there. He checks the lock every day, though, and bought a small bottle of 3-in-1 oil to make sure the lock doesn't freeze up from going through a shower or two every day.

Nearly two weeks after the revised new world order has taken effect with Susa added to the mix, another impact jars my bubble of contentment, courtesy of Carter.

Keep in mind that, while I've conversed some with my father via Facebook Messenger, I haven't seen the man in over ten years.

Since after the divorce, since he moved to Las Vegas.

Since he got a new family.

I also have no contact with any family on his side. His parents died when I was little. He has a couple of brothers and sisters, and I apparently have cousins aplenty, some of whom even live in Florida, but fuck if I know any of them.

Thanks, Mom.

Dad's first marriage lasted less than a year and they had no kids. Then he met Mom and, a few years later, they had me.

Then they imploded in a way that made the Hindenburg disaster look like a dry fart.

Hi, haha, your first family was fucked up—*mulligan!* Hit your save point and respawn, motherfucker.

Oh, your oldest son? Don't worry about him. We gave him a—*checks note just handed in*—wait, sorry. Our bad. Your ex is a totally vengeful narcissist. Honestly? It's too late for him, now. Save yourself while you can.

Because of course there are plenty of *why didn't he take me with him* thoughts to spare in my cranium.

Why didn't he fight harder for me?

Logically, I know that he was probably overwhelmed by Mom and the force of...*her.* God knows I've been overwhelmed by her my whole damn life. Countless times. To the point it's usually easier to just give in and knuckle under.

Before I met Carter, that is.

That's why it shocks the hell out of me when Carter makes the announcement that Thursday evening that we are, in fact, flying to Las Vegas.

That not only are we flying out, we're leaving tomorrow, Friday, right after class.

And, oh, yeah, they've already purchased my ticket.

I'd been sitting on the floor in front of Susa's couch, leaning against it, my head resting against Susa's leg while I read a textbook. I'm sure if I could see myself that I'd probably laugh at how goddamned ridiculous a sight I must be—naked, collared, sitting there with Susa playing with my hair while she reads like I'm a poodle or something.

But it's become my favorite place to sit.

I blink, confused over Carter's announcement. "What did you say?"

"It's your little brother's birthday this weekend, and they're having a party. You've been invited. I told your dad you'd be there."

"Wait...*what?*"

Not a hint of teasing in his expression. "What words confused you, boy?"

"The whole goddamned sentence." I close my book. "For starters, how do you even know about Danny's birthday? I didn't even know that."

"I looked up your father on Facebook a few weeks back, friended him, and I've been talking to him."

I honestly don't have a response for that. For *any* of it. I feel a little...betrayed.

Susa shifts position, draping her legs over my shoulders, which effectively traps me against the couch because she knows damn well I never want to move when she sits like that.

"It's a gift from *me,*" she says. "I want you to spend the time with him." She starts stroking my hair again. "You should get to know your little brother and sister."

I'm still staring at Carter. "I thought you said *we're* flying out."

"We are. All three of us. We'll share a hotel room. I'm renting the car. We'll drive you over to your dad's place and pick you up. Your little brother and sister are really eager to meet you."

I wonder when they concocted this plan. They've had plenty of time to do it, I suppose. Besides the Sunday nearly two weeks ago, where I ended up sleeping five hours straight until Carter returned with my dinner and had to wake me up, they've had a few evenings together. Either Carter drives to Susa's separately, or he drives me home and returns, or I leave Carter there and Susa brings him home.

"Your dad really wants to see you," Carter says. "He was afraid to ask you to come visit before because of your mom. He didn't want to cause you trouble with her. I assured him that's no longer an issue."

Technically not true, but my allowance has continued to appear on schedule, so I'm going to keep listening to Carter.

"I-I can't afford this."

"I *can*," Susa says, leaning in to rest her chin on top of my head. "This is happening. Period. We didn't want to tell you until tonight because we didn't want you working yourself into a frantic panic."

"When we get back to the dorm tonight," Carter says, "we'll pack."

And…that's that.

I'm too stunned to really ask questions.

When we leave later that evening, we're riding in the Snot Box. Carter drove tonight.

I finally ask him. "Why did you do that?"

"Do what?"

"Contact my father?"

"Because I wanted to see what kind of man he was before letting him back into your life. You already have one completely toxic parent. You don't need another one."

"Before…*letting* him back into my life?"

"Yes." His matter-of-fact tone would be borderline maddening if this wasn't Carter and I wasn't used to it.

And, oh, I wasn't collared to the man.

"You didn't think I might want input into this?"

"Yes, but I knew you'd come up with a thousand anxiety-based excuses that all can be boiled down to 'Owen doesn't want to piss off Mom.' Your sister and brother are young. They have a right to get to know you, and you them. Your dad admits he's not perfect, but says he didn't want to make life harder for you with her."

I'm still...stunned.

"How did you explain your involvement in my life to him?"

"The truth—I'm your roommate, your best friend, and I've adopted you as my little brother. I'm almost eight years older than you, and have a much better perspective on this whole thing than you do. Oh, and that I despise your mother and how she treats you."

He grins.

Literally grins.

Carter doesn't grin very often.

Speechless, I sit back and do what I've become accustomed to doing since this started, and that means doing exactly what Carter tells me to do.

* * *

Carter has to unlock my collar and remove it before we pass through the TSA checkpoint because he doesn't want to hold up the line having me manually checked. He relocks it around my neck when we reach the other side.

His Achilles' heel shows up as our plane pulls away from the gate in Tampa and taxis to the runway. I've flown a couple of times, and Susa's apparently got frequent flyer miles.

Carter, however, appears legit terrified.

I've vacillated between hating them and loving them ever since the revelation last night, but this is a new and unexpected wrinkle.

In everything else Carter does, he is completely unflappable.

Until now.

I'm sitting in the middle, with Carter on the aisle and Susa at the window. She's already donned a sleep mask and one of those

U-shaped travel pillows is around her neck. If it wasn't for her hand settling on my thigh, I'd think she was already asleep.

He doesn't speak much during the flight, doesn't settle in to read, the way I do, or sleep, like Susa. He orders a soda water to drink and then basically sits there with his hands wrapped around his armrests.

He is terrified, even though he's trying to hide it.

Ironically, that makes me feel better. *This* Carter I know how to deal with, because I'm the one who's spent months helping him through nightmares.

That's why, only thirty minutes into our flight, I pry his right hand off his armrest and put it on my left thigh, patting the top of his hand before I focus on my Kindle again.

He gives my thigh a little squeeze and leaves his hand right there.

If I can be a comfort to him, all the better.

Once we reach Las Vegas, Carter takes over renting the car, because he's older than we are. Which is a weird thing to think about, because Susa acts older than me.

I default to taking the backseat after holding the passenger door for Susa. When the three of us are together and Carter's driving, that's our standard permutation. If I'm driving, Carter rides shotgun. Our first stop after the airport is a mystery, until we pull into the parking lot of a steakhouse.

"What are we doing here?"

"I don't know," Carter snarks. "I thought maybe spa treatments, pedicures. What do you *think*, boy? Dinner."

"I...I can't afford this."

Carter turns, a stern look on his face. "Boy, *stop*. I'm paying—"

Susa clears her throat.

Carter rolls his eyes. "*Susa's* paying for dinner tonight."

A laugh chuffs free from me at the interplay between them. She can get away with bratty behavior like that with Carter, stuff I would never try. I've even heard her call him Sir a few times in a non-sarcastic way, like what I'm doing is rubbing off on her, but I've never seen Carter take her in hand like he does me.

I'm not privy to what goes on between them alone, however. Part of me suspects maybe she's trying things first-hand to make her a better Top.

I've been told I can ask Carter any questions I want, but he might decline to answer if it's going to violate anything she's asked him not to talk about.

That means I haven't and won't ask. I'd rather not know.

They've both volunteered a few things to me over the past couple of weeks, stuff they've discussed. That's good enough.

I trust.

That's what's most important, something Carter's emphasized to me over and over again, that I need to learn to trust. If I can't, I'm going to have a miserable damn life.

We head inside. While I've seen pictures of my dad on Facebook, when he walks in with his wife, Katie, and my brother and sister, it still jars me a little. My last memory of hugging him before saying good-bye and not realizing it'd be the last time I ever saw him is still etched in my head. He had a full head of brown hair and my green eyes.

The green eyes are the same, but his hair is shorter now and mostly silver. He's sixty-two, a couple of years older than Mom.

Katie is thirty-two. Which is something I knew, because it's always been one of Mom's prime points to blast him over.

Danny is going to turn five tomorrow and he looks nearly identical to me as I did at that age. Susie—who primly insists on being called Susan—is six going on sixty, apparently, and has my dad's green eyes but her mom's black hair.

It's ironic that I have two "Sues" in my life who both act way older than their calendar age, I suppose.

Katie warmly hugs me and quickly shows she's the anti-Mom, thank goodness. My dad and I awkwardly hug for a long moment.

I'm shocked that I find myself struggling to hold back tears when they prickle in my eyes. Susa takes over talking and asking questions while Carter rests a hand between my shoulder blades for a moment, hanging back with me while the hostess seats everyone else.

"Deep breaths, boy," he whispers. "You've got this."

Now that I'm here…

Fuck you, Mom.

I *want* to be here, and I'll be damned if I'll let my fear spoil this precious gift I've been given.

CHAPTER THIRTY-ONE

In our dinner conversation, we stay away from the past, mostly. Dad asks me about school, about what the three of us are studying, and I ask the two kids about stuff.

They are cool kids.

I have a little brother and sister.

I'm still trying to wrap my head around that. Before now, they weren't *real*, as stupid as that sounds.

Katie and Dad don't live far from the steakhouse, and we follow them home. It's a modest home in what feels like a middle-income neighborhood. It's not even as nice as the house I remember us living in before the divorce, but inside is clean and feels homey.

Like there's real love being nurtured within its walls.

Danny and Susan show me around while Dad, Katie, Carter, and Susa sit in the living room to chat. I join them a short time later after stopping by the bathroom to pull myself together again.

Once Katie's put the children to bed, I guess that's when Dad feels he can finally open up.

He removes his glasses and sets them aside. "I owe you an apology, son. I'm sorry I left you behind."

I don't even realize I'm crying until Susa's up and reaching for a box of tissues Katie hands her, and Carter switches places to put me between him and Susa on the couch.

"I'm not going to say this is none of my business," Carter says as I cry on his shoulder, "because Owen's my best friend. This is *absolutely* my business. But that woman is damned toxic."

"I know." Dad glances at Katie before looking at me again. "I cheated on your mother. I'm not proud of that, and it's a story Katie's already heard. What I thought was drive and determination on Elandra's part was way more darker and disturbing than I ever bargained. She pushed me away and punished me every chance she got for me so much as having an opinion that differed from hers."

I would normally call that a cop-out, except I was raised by the woman and I know *exactly* what he's talking about.

"After a while," he continues, "no matter how I tried to approach her to go to counseling, or to work with me...I gave up. Yes, I handled it wrong. If I could take it all back, I would. I would have taken you and left her and not given her ammunition to use against me. Unfortunately, our prenup had an infidelity clause in it, and I was stupid."

"She would have been vicious even if you hadn't cheated," Carter says.

"Yeah, but she couldn't have wielded the prenup against me the way she did. I didn't have the money to fight her. I could barely afford the child support every month."

That gets my attention. "Wait...what?"

"What?" Dad asks.

"Child support?"

"Yeah. Over double what the state mandates. That's another reason I had to move for work. I was making nearly double out here. It was the only way I could afford the payments. I knew if I was so much as a minute late with one, she would have dragged me into court with a contempt motion."

Rage burns within me. "She told me you never paid any

support. That you made a couple of payments, told her you couldn't afford it, so she 'let you off the hook' because she could afford to take care of me."

He's better at hiding his emotions than I am, but he slowly shakes his head. "Every month until you turned eighteen. Did you ever receive any of the cards I sent you for your birthday, or holidays? Or any of the phone messages I left when I'd call to talk to you?"

I'm...I'm *trembling*, I'm so enraged. I've never felt like this in my entire life, and it scares me.

If Mom was standing in front of me right now, I'm not sure I could stop myself from wrapping my hands around her throat and strangling her.

That fucking terrifies me.

"Why don't the three of us step outside," Carter quietly says, standing and gently tugging on my arm to get me to stand, too.

I want to call her and scream at her right now, which might be why Carter reaches down and fishes my phone out of the back pocket of my jeans and tosses it to Susa before we follow Dad outside.

It's still hot, but since it's after dark I can feel cooler air trying to work its way in. It's not muggy like Florida, but as I stare up at the sky, at an unfamiliar vista of stars not usually visible with Tampa's light pollution, I struggle against the urge to throw my head back and scream until my throat is raw.

Carter's never left my side, keeping a hand on my shoulder, or along the small of my back, or even holding my arm.

Dad steps over and I realize he's crying now. He's left his glasses inside and stares at me with a weight and weariness I recognize all too well. "I'm so sorry. I'm sorry I left you behind. I thought maybe she would treat you kinder if I wasn't around."

"She didn't," Carter says, but he's totally focused on me.

"She lied to me about everything," I flatly say. "Everything.

She said you couldn't be bothered to pay attention to me, and I was lucky she took such good care of me. Once she heard about you getting remarried, she said that was proof you had shiny-object syndrome, and that you'd likely be cheating on her before long."

"That's what abusers do," Carter says. I'm not so out of it that I miss he's using what I think of as his "Sir" voice, but his tone is soft, gentle. "They isolate their victims, groom them, make them dependent upon them, and turn everything around so the victim blames themselves without question."

"I don't even know my cousins," I finally choke out. "My aunts and uncles."

"They want to get to know you," Dad says. "I told them you were coming out to visit. A couple will be here tomorrow, but there are still a bunch in Florida who want you to contact them. My older brother, Dan, still lives in Tampa, with his wife, Judy."

That's right, I'd forgotten about Uncle Dan. That's likely why Dad named his son after him. They don't have kids, not for lack of trying on their part, based on what I gleaned from our dinner conversation.

"He'd like it if you give him a call," Dad says. "If you want to," he quickly adds.

Carter pats my shoulder. "He will, when we get back to Tampa. We'll arrange to have them come to Susa's."

I'm still struggling through my rage, through a turbulent rush of emotions smacking me all at once.

The truth that my mother was far more cruel to me than I'd ever dreamed possible.

No, there's no fucking way I can ever stay under her roof again. And if she does cut me off...

Well, there's Carter and Susa. They've promised to take care of me, to help me out.

I turn to Dad and hug him. "I'm sorry I didn't reach out to you often or do this sooner. I just...I was *scared* of her."

"I know, son. It's okay. I'm so sorry I left you with her. I thought I was doing the best thing for you."

"I know."

"I miss going fishing with you. I don't know if you saw it, but I still have that one picture of us, it's hanging there in the living room, along with a couple of others. They're the only ones I was able to take. I mean, I have some smaller pictures, but not a lot."

It's that soft comment that finishes me. The three of us end up sitting right there on the ground, Carter behind me and me in the middle as I sob in my dad's arms.

When I moved out before the start of this school year, one of the things I made sure I took were pictures of me and Dad that were hidden away in storage totes in closets or tucked into photo albums. I suspected if I didn't that I might never again be able to get them.

Right now, I'm glad I did.

There's only one picture of me hanging on my mother's walls, and it's my high school graduation picture, and she and Austin are in it.

If it wasn't for that picture, the casual observer in her home would assume I never existed.

* * *

We finally leave their place about ten o'clock local time. The hotel room is a suite with a king-sized bed and a sleeper sofa, but Carter tells me we're all sleeping in the bed.

I'm too wrung out to argue. I don't even think about it when he takes me into the shower and bathes me, then hands me sleeping shorts to wear and curls up with me in the middle. Susa grabs a quick shower and joins us, wearing a T-shirt and panties, I'm assuming, but I'm too busy crying to feel the slightest bit sexy or nervous or anything else.

I feel…gutted.

Raw.

Wounded in even deeper ways than I ever realized before. Like an abscess I thought was cleaned out is far deeper than previously known, exposing a much greater vein of infection just getting started.

"Let it out, Owen," Susa gently says where she's pressed along my back with her arm around me. "You can't hold on to this."

"And don't do anything rash," Carter cautions. "Let's get you through the weekend, get home to Tampa, and decompress from this. We have finals coming up soon. You're not going back to her house, so it doesn't matter right now."

I know he's right, but it's so tempting to grab my phone and upload every damned last one of the pictures I took—or Susa or Carter took for me—from dinner onto Facebook and tag my mother in every last one of them.

In the short span of time I've known her, Katie is already a far better mom to me than my own mother. There's nothing fake or pretentious about her. Her house isn't perfect.

Her kids have slightly messy rooms that show evidence of life and love.

Their refrigerator is covered with photos and schoolwork and things they've drawn. She works part-time and volunteers at their school. Danny's just started pre-K.

They have a beloved pet cat.

As I fall asleep securely nestled between the two people who know me best in the entire world, I wonder to myself if Katie would be okay with me calling her Mom.

CHAPTER THIRTY-TWO

I feel worse than the morning of the hangover when I awaken Saturday. In sleep, I've rolled toward Susa and find Carter is spooned along my back, while Susa has cuddled tightly against me.

My brain takes a few moments to process this.

That Carter's arm is around me, and Susa's body is pressed against me.

My eyes snap open when this finally hits me, along with the fact that despite how much my brain and heart hurt right now, I'm sporting epic morning wood. Normally, Carter and I go run, and that kills my boner, until we hit the shower.

I can't get out of bed without waking both of them, either.

Sure, Susa's become quite adept at jerking me off during play, but this is…different.

"No, you don't need to think about moving," Carter rasps from behind me, his arm tightening around my waist.

His hand dips lower, under the waistband of my shorts, and wraps around my erection. He doesn't start stroking me, just holding me.

Still not helping.

I struggle to remain still and not fuck his hand even as he softly chuckles in my ear.

Susa draws in a deep breath and opens her eyes. "Mmm. Morning."

I don't know if Carter's intent was to distract me, but it's working.

"No run this morning, obviously," Carter says to Susa. "But I think boy deserves a reward for last night."

"Oooh, nice. What kind of reward?" Her hand also snakes under my waistband, over Carter's, lower, now cupping my balls.

Carter shifts position so I can roll onto my back. Now they're both smiling down at me.

This doesn't feel fair to them. "Do...do you want me to do something for you?" I'm terrified to ask that, terrified they'll both say yes, but it's the good kind of terror. I'm not sure how I'll respond if they take me up on it.

They exchange a look. "You don't need to worry about that right now, boy." He squeezes my cock, making me moan. "Shorts off."

Neither of them release me as I manage to shove them down and shimmy out of them.

"Good boys earn rewards," Carter says as he slowly starts stroking me. Susa plays with my sac, and within a couple of minutes they have me nearly out of my mind with need. I beg, plead for permission to come, and am ordered to put my hands behind my head and keep them there.

Their hands change places, Susa stroking my cock while Carter plays with my balls, and they do that several times as I'm reduced to a literal puddle.

Finally, Carter sighs. "What do you think, pet?" He's called her that a few times. It seems to be his pet name for her, and why would I begrudge that?

"I don't know. He has been *really* good."

"True." His hand is now the one on my cock.

She props herself up on her other elbow and leans in, her lips just above mine. "Who's our good boy?"

"Me, Ma'am. I'm your good boy!"

"That's right," Carter says. "You have been a *very* good boy.

Would you like Ma'am to kiss you while I make you come?"

"Yes, please, Sir!" I'm not even sure if it was penetrating through to my brain what I was agreeing to. He could have just as easily asked if I wanted to be fisted in the middle of the casino downstairs and I might have said yes by that point.

Susa sweetly smiles at me and slants her mouth over mine. Her tongue traces the seam of my lips and makes me open my mouth, now a full-on sultry, sexy kiss that makes me moan.

"Come, boy," Carter firmly orders as he starts jerking my cock.

I'm actually glad she was kissing me, because I'm sure it muffled the sound of my cries as I explode in their hands. I'm not even sure what's going on as Carter orders me onto my hands and knees and Susa climbs up to the head of the bed, spreading her legs.

Turns out she wasn't wearing panties after all.

Carter fists my hair and guides me up, between her thighs. I'm struggling to mentally process this when her hands cup my face and tangle in my hair. "Good boys get other kinds of rewards, too," she says.

Carter's hand disappears, but he grabs my collar and twists, taking up the slack. He's not choking me but if I tried to pull away, I'd be feeling it.

It's obvious what they want me to do.

Fuck *yeah*, I want to do it.

I dive between her legs and pray I'm halfway decent, because this is something I've never done before. She's bare except for a small, well-trimmed landing strip. I bury my face there and inhale her sweet, musky scent, taste her, listen to her and Carter telling me what a good boy I am and what to do.

When she comes, she's grinding against my mouth and Carter's whispering what a good boy I am in my ear. I can feel Carter's erection rubbing against me through his shorts, but he holds me in place and orders me to do it again.

And again.

Turns out three is the magic number. That's when Susa finally gasps with another sweet cry.

"Carter," she says.

Carter eases back on the collar but tugs, making me sit up.

My face is covered with her juices, and I feel dazed, blissful, subspacey...

And I'm once again as hard as a rock.

Carter grins. "There's our good boy." He ruffles my hair. "Go get in the shower. I'll be right there. Close the door so we don't steam up the whole room, please."

"Yes, Sir." I do, after using the toilet.

He joins me a couple of minutes later. I hear him using the toilet first, then he steps into the shower with me, immediately pinning me against the wall and jerking me off with a wide smile on his face.

I thought maybe he'd take care of himself, too, but he doesn't. When he turns so I can scrub his back, I notice he's not hard anymore, but that's not my problem, I guess.

I'm Sir's good boy, and I'm slowly but surely learning to only worry about the things he tells me to.

Life feels better that way. Over the past couple of weeks, I've felt less anxious in most ways. Before all this, I'd be more than halfway to an ulcer this close to finals.

Now? No big deal. I mean, yes, I'm studying hard, but Carter and Susa constantly reassure me I know the material and that they are accurate outside barometers of how well I'm doing.

I've *got* this.

Even better, I've got *them*.

* * *

After Susa takes her shower, we head downstairs and have breakfast.

"Are you sure you don't want to come to the party?" I ask. Dad and Katie invited them to join us.

"We'll come by later," Carter assures me. "I think you need some time with them. Cake's going to be served at two. We'll join you then and hang around with you and them until after dinner."

"What are you guys going to do today?"

"I haven't been to Vegas before," Carter says. "We're going to look around before lunch."

"I want to go shopping," Susa says.

Carter laughs and meets my gaze in the rearview mirror. "On second thought, maybe I'll stay there with you and let her take the car. Save me, boy."

I wasn't expecting to laugh like that, but it was so atypically Carter that it's hysterical.

From his smile, I can tell he's pleased.

"No, you don't get to run out on me," Susa says. "Someone's got to help me shop. I might need a new suitcase to carry everything in, too."

"Oh, lord," Carter mutters, but that, too, sounds playful.

I feel…light.

Like a weight has lifted from my shoulders.

I feel…

Happy.

I thought I was starting to learn what happiness is from my time spent with them, but this feels like even a level beyond that. Like I've unlocked some bonus level or something.

Not for the first time, I wonder if this is what normal people feel like on a daily basis.

They drop me off and say quick hellos and good-byes to Dad and Katie and the kids. Once Carter and Susa leave, I follow my dad and Katie to the kitchen and—what else—offer to help out.

"So how long have they been dating?" Katie asks.

"Oh, they aren't. We're all—" My mouth snaps shut, realizing this is the first time I've confronted this scenario. Of describing...*us*.

"She's sort of adopted us," I say, going into a very quick version of her story, and Carter's. "We'll be staying with her during breaks."

"That'll piss your mom off," Dad says, and he's not wrong.

"I really don't care if it does."

That's the first time I've ever been able to say that, completely mean it, and not feel gut-wrenchingly terrified when I do.

*   *   *

I have a great time on Saturday. I meet family I never knew, Dad's and Katie's. I especially enjoy Susan warming up and proudly introducing me as her "big brother" to people.

I wonder if this is how Carter feels. If so, I can understand now why he took such a keen interest in me early on when he heard about my background.

Susa and Carter join us for cake, and have actually brought a present for Danny that's wrapped and everything, and is from the three of us—even though I had no clue she was going to do that, but I feel even more grateful to her because of it.

Saturday night, we return to the hotel after dinner and I lie there and get debriefed by Carter and Susa. More tears, but I'm feeling far less volatile than I was yesterday.

I've earned the double reward of being able to come again, and then take care of Susa, like I did that morning.

I sleep like the dead, and if Carter has a nightmare, it's not loud enough to awaken me.

On the fight back to Tampa Sunday afternoon, I'm sitting on the aisle, Carter's in the middle this time, and Susa again occupies the window seat. Ever since we took off, he's kept one hand on Susa's thigh. Sometime her hand covers his, sometimes not, but it's like he's scared to let go.

I awakened feeling...off. Part of me wants to simply blow it off as my emotions wildly swinging out of control, but I don't understand the vague unease filling me, like there's a whole subtext I'm missing.

I don't know what happened between Carter and Susa before they returned to Dad's house yesterday after dropping me off.

Or maybe I'm just letting insecurity and anxiety and Katie's innocent question get the best of me.

That's the most likely scenario.

Thanks, Mom.

Even though it feels like I've known Carter for my whole life, one thing I've learned for certain in the short time we've been together is that he's *not* someone to mince words or hold back truths.

If he's got a problem with you, he'll tell you. Maybe he's a bastard extraordinaire sometimes, but he's an honest one.

Except...my mind spins a thousand nervous fantasies. I know they've talked about Susa maybe trying things with Carter, so she can see how they feel.

Did they play? Did he top her?

I think about the unexpected next step I was introduced to and wonder about *that*. Nothing Carter and Susa have said would preclude *them* from taking things to new level. And Katie even thought they were dating. Hell, I know Susa is in love with Carter.

Did they have sex?

Did she enjoy it?

Did *he* enjoy it?

That last thought stops me in my tracks as I ponder the implications of why I care so much about that.

I'm not sure if I feel more jealous over the possibility of him enjoying it or her enjoying it, and that...confuses me. Confuses me in the same way that earning praise from Carter makes me feel good and confuses me.

Lots of things about this whole situation confuse me, but the thought of giving either of them up fills me with a deeper anxiety and fear than the ones currently dancing the hokey-pokey through my mind.

I'll take the confusion, because at least it's a peaceful confusion. I know it doesn't make sense, but it's the best way to describe it.

I've never known such a deep peace as when I'm on my knees in front of Susa.

Yeah, okay, or in front of Carter.

I don't understand *why* it feels so calming, but I crave it, like a drug. I get now why smokers can't quit, if the hit they receive is anything like the one I get kneeling with my head bowed.

Or getting my ass spanked.

Believe me, that one surprised the hell out of me, too.

The more confident Susa grows during our play, the more I enjoy it, and the deeper I go.

The deeper I go, the less inhibited I feel, because Carter's never given me any reason to think he'll ever betray me, or her.

I don't mind him supervising our play or showing her how to do things. In a way, I suppose it's a comfort that he wants to make sure she doesn't harm me.

I never thought I'd see myself in this position—any of the positions, actually—but now that it's part of my life I never want it to end.

It's what I never knew I needed, and it fills that void inside me perfectly.

Susa.

I don't know why serving Carter when the two of us are alone also fills me with…

Contentment.

Sexually, I respond to Susa during our play. That excites me in ways I never dreamed.

On the flip side of it, the demands Carter places on me away from Susa...they also excite me in different ways.

To earn his praise.

To hear those two damn words.

Good boy.

Not just good boy, but *my* good boy.

To let out a long-held breath and relax into his touch when he scratches my head as I kneel in front of him.

Learning positions for him.

I might swear at him sometimes, and not want to do what he tells me to do, and bite back screams of pain over what he's doing to me, but I *am* consenting to it. All of it.

Because when I watch Susa watching him, the excitement in her eyes, her rewarding me for being her good boy...

It's all worth it.

Every bit of it.

Carter was right about me not looking up shit online, though. Because too much of it's porn. The sites he's directed me to have been helpful, even if I still seek answers within myself.

The emotional math isn't complicated—one narcissistic parent, one absent parent (thanks, Mom) and throw in a nasty divorce. A woman who wasn't happy unless she was making me suffer.

A woman I've never been able to please in my life.

A woman I can never remember telling me "good boy" one single time. It's no wonder I'm addicted to Susa and Carter's positive reinforcement.

We hit turbulence, and suddenly, my hand is tightly engulfed by Carter's. When I look, he's facing straight ahead, his eyes squeezed closed. His hand on Susa's thigh hasn't moved, though, even though her hand now rests over his. She seems to be asleep, or nearly so, even though it's difficult to tell with her sleep mask on. Then again, she's an experienced flier.

Whatever happened this weekend away from my ken can wait.

If anything happened. There's a very good chance nothing happened other than shopping.

I squeeze back, letting Carter know I'm there and not going anywhere.

I see him silently mouth, *Thank you.*

I will not ask him about it now. If there is anything that happened and he wants to tell me, he will. If he doesn't, fair enough.

Considering what he's been through, he probably doesn't have good memories to associate with flying. I don't want to add to his stress by being a needy pet on top of that. This is one small way I can serve him.

And considering how much I gained this weekend by him and Susa pushing me to go, actually taking me, and being there with me to support me…

Well, I know he's my friend. Both of them are. They love me. That's all that matters.

His grip eases about twenty minutes after the last bump, but he doesn't let go, and I make no move to free my hand. In fact, he strokes the back of my hand with his thumb. We finally land at Tampa without dying, and it's not until we're on the ground that he releases me and takes a deep breath.

"Sorry that wasn't very 'masterly' of me," he softly snarks.

But I reach out and stay him with my hand. "*Carter,*" I say.

He looks at me.

"Considering how much you support me, if you think I'm not going to support you when you need me, think again."

He reaches out and squeezes my hand. "Thank you, Owen."

"You're welcome, *Sir.*"

He smiles. "My good boy."

Susa clears her throat, and he rolls his eyes. "Fine. *Our* good boy. Happy?"

She grins, making me chuckle. "Yep."

CHAPTER THIRTY-THREE

We stop to eat dinner on the way back to Susa's. But we're only at Susa's long enough to unload her things—including the new suitcase full of stuff she purchased in Las Vegas—and hug her good-bye. I want to help her unpack, but Carter and Susa insist that's not necessary tonight.

We return to the dorm room and without thinking, I immediately strip and retrieve the tether from its storage tote and set it up, donning my cuffs and collar.

I didn't realize how much I'd missed wearing them this weekend, but I did.

When I turn, I realize Carter's been watching me this whole time, leaning against the wall and with his arms crossed over his chest.

An inscrutable expression darkens his gaze.

"What's wrong, Sir?"

He slowly shakes his head. "Not a damn thing, boy." His voice sounds…hoarse, though. Choked up.

Emotional?

He disappears into the bathroom, though, so I can't ask him about it.

When it's time for bed, I go over to Carter's bed and drop into

Devotion. He touches the top of my head.

"Come here, boy." When I sit up, he's patting the bed.

I climb in and he spoons against me, on our sides. "Thank you, boy," he says.

"You don't have to thank me, Sir. Besides, you're the one I should be thanking. You and Susa, both, for taking me this weekend." And I have to admit sleeping like this isn't the worst thing ever. It's kind of nice sharing a bed with someone. Even with Carter.

Although sharing one with Susa this weekend was even better, having both of them there with me.

Not feeling alone.

* * *

Our PT resumes the next morning. Carter sets a blistering pace, which surprises the hell out of me because I know he was moving pretty damn slowly when he got up.

He's also not very talkative this morning. I do my best to keep up, which has been getting incrementally easier every week. Not saying I'm in nearly as good of shape as he is, but I'm not embarrassing myself, so that's something.

Our morning shower—joy for me, and for him—and then on to class.

Commando, no toy.

Yay.

It means I can focus on the lesson.

It's after class where my world unexpectedly tilts sideways.

Once we're alone in the room, Carter isn't looking at me as he grabs his backpack. "You're going to spend the night at Susa's," he says.

"Sir?" I'm certain I've misheard him.

Now he looks at me. "You heard me. She'll pick you up from the dorm after your last class and you'll go with her. Go back to the dorm as soon as your last class ends, pack, and text her so she can get you. Make sure I receive a good report from her. Be my good boy."

I turn to Susa, who's wearing a playful smile. "When did this get decided?"

"We talked about it over the weekend."

"Where was I?"

"At your dad's." She reaches up and ruffles my hair. "Unless you don't want to spend the night with me."

I turn to ask Carter about this, but he's already gone, and it honestly takes me a moment to process that.

That he's *left*.

My heart races, and not in a good way. Part of me wants to chase him down and ask him what the *hell*?

I even take a step toward the door, except Susa reaches out and catches my arm. "*Owen*."

I turn.

"Is this okay? Or do you need to safeword?"

"What about Carter?"

"This is you and me tonight."

"But…what about Carter?" I feel stupid asking that again, like I'm stuck in a loop.

"Either tell me this is okay, or safeword."

The stupid thing is, just a few weeks ago, I would have immediately said yes and dove headfirst into this.

But…

What about Carter?

I know he said there would be tests from time to time, shaking me out of my usual headspace.

Maybe after last weekend this is one of those times?

I finally nod. "It's okay, Ma'am."

"Walk with me, please."

Which completely rules out what I was going to do…which is

chase Carter down and ask him what's going on.

Maybe that's her point.

Usually, Carter and I walk together from this class and part ways to go to our respective buildings for our next classes.

It feels…weird, not in a bad way, walking with Susa.

We finally stop at a juncture in the sidewalk where I can veer off toward my own building.

Carter is nowhere to be seen.

Susa crooks a finger at me to lean in, and when I do, she brushes a kiss across my lips. "Be my good boy today," she says. "Text me once you're packed and ready to go."

"Yes, Ma'am."

She walks off and I stand there watching her until she rounds a corner.

If Carter's point was to throw me out of my routine, well, mission accomplished.

But I'm not sure I like what this feels like.

When I reach my class I sit in the back, instead of closer to the front where I usually do, so I can hide what I'm doing.

I text Carter.

Is everything okay, Sir?

He texts me back a few minutes later.

Everything's fine, boy. :)

But this doesn't *feel* fine.

On the other hand, I guess I'm not the best person to decide what feels fine or not after how I was raised.

Maybe that's Carter's point.

Maybe this will be fine and tomorrow we'll resume our usual routine, and Carter will point to this as an example that change, the unexpected, doesn't automatically equate with something *bad* happening.

I have two options—safeword, or go with this.

I try one more time, just to make sure.

Carter, please tell me we're okay?

I hold my phone in my hand until he responds a minute or so later.

Owen, I promise you, we're fine. :)

I know that I have to take Carter at his word. None of this works if I don't trust him.

Despite swearing I'll leave this alone, I'm compelled to ask.

What about tonight, Sir? Your nightmares?

The thought of him going through them alone rips at me. It takes him another minute to reply.

I'll be fine, boy. I want you to be my good boy, obey Ma'am, and have fun tonight. Understand? :)

Carter is not a huge user of emojis. When he does use them, I know he means it.

I respond the only way I can.

Yes, Sir. Thank you.

I sit back, take a deep breath, and try to process this so I can focus on my class.

It's also the moment I realize that I will do anything to *not* fuck up things with Carter. Even if it means I don't have a girlfriend, or date, or that I spend the rest of my life like this. Because, emotionally, my relationship with Carter has been more satisfying than any relationship I've ever had before, and Susa comes a close second to that.

*   *   *

As ordered, I return to our room and quickly pack, then text Susa that I'm ready. Carter isn't there, either, and I struggle with confused emotions over that. I'm also torn between wanting to put on the tether while I wait, or rush downstairs to wait for her.

Turns out she gives me an ETA of five minutes, so I grab my stuff and head downstairs. I emerge from the building just as her car turns in to the dorm parking lot.

I drop my stuff in the backseat and she leans in for a hello kiss after I buckle my seat belt.

"How's my boy?" she asks.

I don't know if the heat filling my cheeks is excitement or fear. "Good, Ma'am."

"Let's go home. We're going to study, eat leftovers, and then play after dinner. Okay?"

"Yes, Ma'am."

She's driving, because she's made no attempt to swap places with me. I've driven her car a couple of times, and it terrifies me every time. Her car is only a few months old and worth way more than mine.

It feels weird to pull into her driveway and not see the Snot Box sitting there. I was almost hoping this was a mindfuck and Carter would be waiting for us here.

A few weeks ago, I would have killed to have this alone time with her.

What the actual *fuck* is wrong with me that I'm struggling because I'm alone with her and Carter is absent?

Inside the front door, I stop, toe off my shoes, and start stripping. Ironically, I'm so nervous that I don't need to feel self-conscious about an eager erection—I'm soft.

I retrieve my cuffs and collar from my bag and find her in the kitchen so she can put them on me.

This feels…different. Not necessarily *bad* different—I *hope*—but I'm not used to this.

"Tell me what you're thinking, boy," she says after I'm suitably attired.

I shrug. "I wasn't expecting this."

"Kind of the bastard extraordinaire's point." She smiles, and it eases every concern I had back to a dull, manageable anxiety instead of the manic, gnawing, borderline ache of fear growing inside me.

"I'm still worried about his nightmares," I add.

She nods. "He texted me screenshots. If he didn't feel he could handle it, he would have said so. I also might have put my own condition on tonight."

"Condition?"

"Yeah. That if he wakes up with a really bad nightmare, he's to call us, and I'll send you to the dorm."

I'm not sure if he'd do that, because Carter is a master of looking after others before himself, but it does ease a few more worries inside me. "Thank you, Ma'am."

"Of course. I don't want him having nightmares."

We settle in to study, but I have to ask one more thing. "Are we going to do…*this* a lot?"

"This?"

"Me and you alone?"

She shrugs. "I think he wants to see how we'll do."

"He's not going to leave us, is he?"

"Owen, look at me."

I do.

"Carter isn't going anywhere. I am not going anywhere. Are you going somewhere?"

I shake my head.

"Good. Then we're all on the same page. This is Carter wanting to safely test things out. A sort of load test."

"Load test?"

"To make sure everyone's on the same page and really happy with how things are. Please, just relax and go with the flow, all right?"

"Yes, Ma'am."

I mean, I'll try, but that's a hell of a lot harder than it sounds. Believe me, I know.

* * *

We study, we eat dinner, and then...

Play.

Susa catches my hand and leads me to her bedroom. The new suitcase is sitting on the floor near the bed, and she leads me over to it.

When she unzips it and opens it...

Oh, boy.

I hear the *click* in my throat when I swallow.

"Yes, there's a reason I didn't want you helping me unpack last night." She's wearing a smile as she leans in and pulls out a clear acrylic paddle. "We didn't just go shopping for something for Danny's birthday. There's a reason it's called Sin City, and not just because of the gambling.

The suitcase—a large rolling one—is full of...

Oh, boy.

"Did you rob a sex store?"

"No, but there are a couple of specialty shops in Las Vegas that sell good quality implements and other BDSM paraphernalia." She points at the bed. "Bend over the end of the bed, *boy*."

The hard edge in her tone hardens my cock as I comply.

She grabs my wrists and pulls them behind me, and I hear her apply a snap clip.

"You questioned Sir this morning," she says with that same darker edge in her voice. "Made him basically repeat himself to you. In the future, unless you didn't actually understand what was said, do not question his decisions, or mine. That's twenty strokes. I want you to count them."

The good kind of fear rolls through me, much like what I felt when Carter and I first started this. "Yes, Ma'am."

She wastes no time, and it's not a fun little playful smack, either. It's a hard, stinging swat across my left ass cheek that brings tears to my eyes. "One, Ma'am."

By the time she's delivered number twenty, I'm legit crying.

I don't know why, either. I mean, as in, I have no clue. It's not the pain, it's something else, and I can't identify it.

She puts the paddle down and her cool hands soothe my flesh. "There's my good boy, all better," she coos. "Everything's forgiven and all better."

I'm...*gone*. Totally, utterly, completely *gone*. She kneels behind me and kisses my flesh, soothing it with her mouth, up and down. My hard-on had disappeared during the spanking, but now it's back with a vengeance.

She stops and I hear her move away for a moment. When she returns, she blindfolds me. I hear the rustle of clothes and feel the mattress dip in front of me.

Her fingers plunge into my hair and she lifts my head. "Get busy, *boy*," she orders.

She pulls my face into her pussy and I...

I can't tell you how long I lie there. It could have been fifteen minutes or fifteen hours, quite honestly. I'm too intent on making her moan and getting her over. I lose track after the third one, and I listen as she directs me, tells me things to do, and I revel in the pleasured moans I receive in response.

This is…

Fuck me, this is Heaven. My ignored cock is rubbing against the bed and I don't even care if I never get off again, because I'm making Susa make noises that have me flying like nothing else ever has before.

It takes her jerking on my ear to finally stop me. I lie there with my cheek pressed against the inside of her left thigh. Her scent fills my lungs and her taste fills my mouth, covers my lips, my chin. There's probably a wet spot on the bed now.

Fingers tangle in my hair and she starts massaging my scalp, just like…

Just like Carter.

I struggle not to think about him, not to worry about him, but he might as well be right here with us anyway, and it almost feels wrong that he's not despite me loving the fact that I have Susa to myself for tonight.

I remember the evening he gave me the hidden hints for assembling the IKEA furniture. Is this another way of him trying to help me out?

I guess I shouldn't question it.

She finally sits up and unclips my wrists. "Blindfold stays on," she says, but her fingers catch my collar and she guides me up the bed and has me lie on my back, where my freshly beaten ass reminds me of what I've already been through.

She takes my hand and puts it on my cock, then settles in next to me, spooned alongside me, my head nestled in the crook of her left arm. "Take your time and play with yourself," she softly whispers in my ear. "Don't make yourself come."

It's even hotter not being able to see, trusting her. Her right hand caresses my body, plays with my nipples, slides down and cradles my sac. I feel her swipe a finger along the head of my cock, over the slit, and it makes me shiver with pleasure.

I hear a soft noise. "You taste good, boy."

I have to slow my strokes even more because that nearly makes me come. "Thank you, Ma'am. So do you."

She tasted me!

Her hand closes over mine. "Stop," she whispers.

I do.

We lie there for several minutes while she's apparently waiting for me to cool down a little.

"What if I want to suck your cock, boy. Are you okay with that?"

I try to speak, clear my throat when a squeak comes out, and try again. "I belong to Ma'am," I manage. "Whatever you want to do within my hard limits and with Sir's permission."

Wait…does she *have* permission from Sir to do that?

"Good boy." Apparently she does, because she untangles herself from me, sits up, and then she pulls my hand away from my cock. "Oh, wait."

She gets up and I remain where I am. I can hear her, track her progress in the room. She returns and lifts my hands over my head. I hear an unfamiliar clink, like chain, confirmed when I feel it as she attaches it to my wrist cuffs with two snap clips.

"There," she says, sounding satisfied.

Apparently, she has modified her headboard to include a new pet restraint system.

She pushes my legs apart and I feel her breath first. It washes over my cock, making it eagerly twitch.

"Oh, almost forgot."

She grabs my cock, then I feel her stretching something and putting it over my cock and balls.

One of the cockrings Sir bought from the adult store a few weeks ago. This one kind of lifts and separates everything.

It also makes me throb in a nearly painful way.

"Don't come yet, boy," she says.

My world unhinges. I lie there, helpless, struggling to obey as she does things to me with her mouth that I didn't know could be done to another human. I'm literally in tears begging to be allowed to come when she chuckles.

"Good boy. You can come."

I do, almost immediately. Second most powerful orgasm I've ever had, next to the night of my birthday celebration where I blacked out.

Although alcohol might have contributed to the blackout. Still, it doesn't take away from how hot that was.

The butt plug orgasms are now third place.

She turns the TV on and snuggles in next to me, but doesn't unclip my wrists or remove the blindfold. I lie there next to her, listening, inhaling her scent with every breath. She's always touching me, too, either her leg against mine, or a hand, or something. I don't feel alone or ignored.

I feel like I'm waiting for whatever it is that she wants to do next.

Being blindfolded for this long forces me to focus on her and makes me lose track of time. I'm getting hard again from her increased touches and explorations when she shifts position in bed. I feel her straddle me.

"You can come, boy." She takes the cockring off me and engulfs me with her mouth at the same time she lowers her pussy onto my face.

Don't have to ask me twice.

I'm a fast learner and use some of the things she's taught me tonight to get her over a couple of times before she finishes me. I'm humping up into her mouth, eager, this whole thing even hotter because I'm her immobilized plaything.

I'm her toy.

I'm Hers.

This time, she rolls off me and unclips my wrists, then removes the blindfold. She'd turned off the lights at some point and it's only the TV for light now. I blink, the world coming into focus and her smile lighting my soul.

"Let's clean up and go to sleep, boy." She leans in and kisses me, full-on the way she did in Las Vegas, with tongue and everything.

A few minutes later, we're falling asleep tangled together. She's put on a long T-shirt I think might actually be Carter's, but I'm naked and in cuffs and collar.

I can't help it that, as I fall asleep with her snuggled in my arms, I'm worried about Carter.

CHAPTER THIRTY-FOUR

It's the smell of coffee brewing Tuesday morning that awakens me. When I roll over in the darkened bedroom, I gravitate toward the heat source I feel next to me.

What makes my eyes pop open is the fact that it's a very Carter-shaped body I just rolled against, and he's dressed. Well, half-dressed. He's wearing shorts.

"Good morning, boy." He hasn't been awake for long himself, because his voice sounds gravelly, thick.

I sit up. "What time it is?"

"Just after six." He reaches up and catches my collar, pulling me back down into his arms. "No PT today, if you were wondering. I overdid it yesterday."

I'm wide awake now. "When did you get here, Sir?" I never heard him arrive.

"A while ago. You going to settle in and snuggle, or do I need to spank you?"

I settle in, and he quickly drifts back to sleep.

I realize I have no idea what Susa's normal weekday morning routine is like. I know she's not a morning person, but she's very disciplined.

She's also not in bed with us.

And now I'm wide awake.

When the bedroom door quietly opens a while later, Susa appears. She's already showered and dressed, and she smiles when she sees Carter's asleep. She leans in and kisses me good morning, then whispers in my ear.

"See you later. Give him a kiss for me."

And she's gone.

I do all I can do, and that is close my eyes and doze while waiting for Carter's alarm to go off on his phone a little after seven.

He stretches, reaches for it, and shuts it off. "Motherfucker," he mutters, which is his usual first word of the morning, or something similar, on weekdays. "Pet leave?"

"Yes, Sir."

He stares at me for a long moment. "She punished you, huh?"

When the hell *are they having these conversations?* "Yes, Sir. I'm sorry. I wasn't trying to question you, I just…" I sigh. "I mean, I was, but only because I was worried there was a problem."

"Boy, I promise you, if I ever have a problem, I will *tell* you. I might mindfuck you for my sadistic amusement, but I'll never play passive-aggressive games with you when it comes to our relationship. *Ever.* I won't let Susa do that, either. I need you to trust me."

"I'm sorry, Sir."

"It's okay." He groans as he sits up. "Coffee, please. Bring it to me in the bathroom. We'll take an extra-long shower this morning." Then he chuckles. "Unless she wore you out last night."

I'm a well-trained pet. My cock loves this routine and eagerly twitches. "She didn't wear me out."

"Good boy. Then get moving."

I do. An hour later, we've both had orgasms, I've given him Susa's good-morning kiss, and I'm driving us to campus in my car, because that's what he drove over to Susa's.

But Carter asks me to drop him off closer to the building where his first class is and tells me that I don't need to get his door for him, because we'll just hold up traffic.

"Are you all right, Sir?"

"I'll be okay. The trip took more out of me than I thought. I should have had us walk yesterday—that was not smart for me to do. I'll be okay. I try to push myself too hard." He starts to reach for his door after the car stops but pauses. "Oh, you'll go with Susa again today. Go back to the dorm after your last class and text her."

Then he's out before I can ask him more questions. The car pulling up behind me means I can't throw it into park and go after him, either.

Dammit.

*   *   *

This new, weird routine repeats. The difference is what happens at night between Susa and myself. She experiments with other paddles and floggers and implements they purchased in Las Vegas. She uses the vibrating butt plug on me while she teaches me how to give head to a realistic dildo. The deeper I go, the more enthusiasm I show, then the more pleasure I earn for myself. She feeds me my own cum and manages to make me beg for it by edging me, rewarding me.

It makes me wonder if there's more that will be expected of me in the future.

I find that I don't care, because I'm enjoying everything that we're doing so much it completely drives me back to those sweetest, earliest depths of subspace.

She introduces me to strap-on play.

#loveit

She doesn't, however, have intercourse with me. Not that I'm complaining, because she wrings me dry in many other ways, and I love going down on her.

#everyonesawinner

Every morning, Susa's already awake and up and gone, replaced by Carter, and neither of them will give me a solid answer about when he arrived.

Needless to say, PT is off for the week.

#goodwithit

Friday evening is when everything changes in my world.

Again.

Susa plays with me for about an hour, getting me worked up, edging me, not letting me come and not getting herself off, either. She's put on music instead of the TV, and I'm not blindfolded.

Finally, when I'm begging for relief while she plays with my cock, she sweetly smiles. "What will you do for it?"

"Anything, Ma'am!"

"Anything?"

Uh-oh. I wonder what I'm setting myself up for, but I remember that mindfucks are allowed, and they'll never cross my hard limits, either one of them.

"Anything, Ma'am."

"Good." She buckles my bit gag on me, then sits back and smiles down at me. "Wait here."

She leaves the bedroom.

She's gone for a while, maybe ten minutes or so. I'm watching the doorway. I can't see down the hallway, but I can see the way shadows are cast on the wall when someone walks down it from either direction.

I see a shadow.

Then I freeze as I see a second one. I watch, simultaneously turned on and confused as Carter leads Susa through the bedroom door. I don't know when he arrived because I never heard him.

Susa's wearing a blindfold, leather collar, leather cuffs on her wrists, which are clipped together in front of her with a double-ended snap clip, and matching leather cuffs on her ankles.

And nothing else.

My cock twitches, hard, ready. There's not a damn thing I can do about it, either.

Carter, that bastard, watches, smiling as he sees my reaction.

For *Her*.

He leaves her standing just inside the doorway and climbs onto the bed, where he kneels over me. He holds a finger to his lips, warning me to remain silent. There's an evil gleam in his eyes as he unfastens the bit gag and removes it. Immediately, he claps his right hand over my mouth and smiles down at me for a long moment before leaning in. Not just leaning in, but his body pressing against mine pins my cock between us and I have to force myself to lie still and fight the urge to start rocking my hips against him.

I know over the music she can't hear him whispering in my ear.

"The rules have changed, boy. Susa and I got married in Las Vegas." He holds up his left hand, showing me the wedding band. And when I look, I now see her wearing one.

My heart hammers in my chest as I struggle to process this.

"Susa liked being my pet so much that we decided to make things permanent," he says. "Yes, we've been sleeping together for a couple of weeks now. She wanted to see what being submissive felt like, so now she gets the best of both worlds. She gets to own her boy, and gets to be owned by me."

I stare up into his eyes, wondering if I ever knew this man at all, wondering if this is the mindfuck of all mindfucks.

Wondering if I've just fucked up my life.

But he's not done. "That's *my* wife, and *my* pussy, and *my* ass, and *my* mouth. But I'm a fair man, Owen. I'll make a deal with you. You can have fairly unrestricted access to *my* pussy, but it'll cost you. Taking my pussy means you take *my* cock, too. Your ass becomes *my* ass, and your mouth becomes *my* mouth. When I say, how I say, and where I say. In return, I'll make sure you are kept satisfied, don't worry. Even more than I already have.

"However, I don't share, except with who *I* want to share with. This will only be the three of us, no one else. *Period.* For *life.* That means you don't date anyone else, you don't fuck anyone else. That also means you move in here, immediately, with *us.* The three of us will share a bed every night from this night forward, and you'll completely belong to *me,* in *all* ways. *Both* of you will. In return, I promise I will always take care of you. *Always.* We both will."

I don't know how to feel about this, about any of this. There were never any rules that the two of them couldn't get together, but...

I feel left out.

At war within me, this new knowledge I'm struggling to process, versus the trusted man who held me all the times I cried, who's spent the past months teaching me more about myself than I ever thought I'd know.

The man who's helped my darkest fantasies come true.

"That's the deal, Owen. Take it or leave it. No negotiations about the terms. This means we move from your timeline of asking when you feel like reciprocating, to you *will* be available upon demand for either of us however we wish to use you. And if you don't know me by now, I don't know what to tell you."

He smiles down at me. "So what's it going to be, my friend? Yes, or no? Can you spend the rest of your life with me...and her?" He sits up, his hand still covering my mouth as I stare up into his eyes.

I'm filled with an equal and confusing mix of lust and hatred, except for one problem—I want to say yes.

It's actually my *first* instinct, because I've never been happier than when I am with these two people.

I think about this, though. I want to weigh the consequences of this decision.

Except...other than sex, haven't I already given myself to Carter? One of my biggest fears once we started this journey was losing him and this...*thing* that we have.

He's still watching me.

The hate quickly drains out, leaving no other possible answer. Because I love Susa.

But, more importantly, because I love Carter, and I know he loves me.

I nod.

A slow, evil smile fills his features. "My *very* good boy," he whispers.

Then he reaches down with his other hand and slowly strokes my aching cock.

I can't help it—it's too much, and I'm too damned horny. I now rock my hips in time with his hand. There's no reason for me to feel false indignation or try to fight this. Why lie? My body has already told the truth. Countless times now.

I'd do anything to be Hers, to remain with her.

And if I now have a chance to be *more* to Susa than just a toy and a play partner?

Hell *yeah*, I'll take it.

Every damn time.

If it means I belong to Carter, too, then I'll do it. Whatever it takes.

He releases my cock and my mouth at the same time and I bite back a needy groan when he climbs off me and turns from me. Returning to Her.

I can't help but watch. He leans in and sucks on her right nipple, pulling a needy moan from her. He repeats it with the left and my cock twitches as I watch.

Then he turns and meets my gaze as he pulls his T-shirt off and drops it to the floor. He slowly unfastens his shorts and shoves them down, showing he's gone commando.

His own cock is hard and springs free. Finally, after all this time, I get to see what he looks like fully hard. He's maybe a little larger than I am, but not embarrassingly so. At least in this one way I measure up.

Carter steps behind Susa and wraps his arms around her, cupping her breasts in his hands and offering them up, his thumbs brushing her nipples. I'm biting down on my lower lip to keep from embarrassing myself at this point. To prevent me from begging for more.

To volunteer that I'd do anything at this point for a sample, to join in.

To beg to not be left out, or relegated simply as an observer.

To be allowed to worship her body.

His gaze is still fixed on mine as he nudges her over to the side of the bed, until her thigh is pressed against it. "Up, pet," he orders.

She reaches out with her hands, finds the bed, and carefully climbs up.

His hands slide down her body, settling on her hips.

Her hands brush against my hip, but she has both knees on the bed now.

Carter buries his cock inside her in one hard, fast thrust. The moan that rolls from her nearly makes *me* come, and her shoulders drop to the bed as her head lolls against her arms.

But Carter doesn't do more, still watching me while wearing that triumphant smile that's part smirk. He holds her immobile, his cock deep inside her as his gaze scans my body, down, up again.

Then he pulls out of her and walks around the bed, climbing on it from the other side, straddling my chest and staring down at me. "Open."

I do, automatically. It's nearly an ingrained response at this point.

He orders—I obey.

He circles the base of his cock with his other hand and feeds me just the tip. My lips close around it, my tongue flicking along the slit as Susa's taught me on the dildos—and that's when it hits me.

This was his plan.

All the knowing looks shared between them throughout this experience make perfect sense now.

When he smiles, this time warm and loving, his next two words chase all other thoughts out of my head.

"Good boy." He reaches down with his free hand and strokes my hair.

I'm eager to suck on him now, tasting his pre-cum and her juices mixed together and rolling over my tongue. I have no trouble taking all of him, relaxing my throat as he presses deep and holds there for a long moment.

I've been well-trained.

I understand now.

He slowly fucks my mouth. I feel the tension building in his body, the strain in his thighs and the way his breathing changes. His gaze never leaves me, though, and I'm unable to close my eyes.

I'm his good boy.

Of course I watch, just like I've been trained.

He lets out a hiss and pulls back and I realize my head's come up off the bed, trying to maintain contact, trying to follow.

This pleases him. He releases his cock and cups my cheek, his thumb brushing against my flesh. "Good boy," he whispers. "My *very* good boy."

Desperation and need fill me as I try to reach his cock again. In Carter's world, reward has always followed eagerness. But he smiles and denies me. "Not yet, boy. I have something special in mind."

His hand slides around my neck, cupping my head, and he

leans in again. Slanting his lips over mine, he takes my mouth in a crushing, brutal kiss I know is only the first of many.

I eagerly return it.

He's like a drug I can't get enough of. I know I'll do anything to earn those two words from him, just like I will for Susa.

Anything.

When he finally sits up again, his lips are slightly swollen and red and I know I must look like that, too.

But he's smiling.

Smiling in that rare way Carter has, the smile that tells me he's *truly* happy right now.

I made him feel like that.

This made him feel like that.

That makes *me* happy in ways I know I might never completely unpack or understand, and that's okay.

He's a bastard extraordinaire, but he's never abused my trust. Not really. I don't even consider this an abuse of my trust. I feel closer to him than anyone else in the world, even though Susa runs a close second.

And now I never have to lose either of them.

CHAPTER THIRTY-FIVE

Carter helps Susa sit up and straddle me. I don't even feel embarrassed when he grabs my cock and holds it, lining it up with her pussy.

"Sit and hold still, pet."

I groan with need as her wet heat envelops my cock.

"Don't you *dare* come yet, boy," Carter says.

He shoves a pillow under my head before he straddles me again. With one hand braced on the headboard, and the other holding the base of his cock, he smiles down at me. "Open."

I do.

"You may come, boy. Pet, you may not. I want you to ride the boy." She whimpers but starts moving, slowly at first, and I groan around Carter's cock.

What little is left of my rational brain sees what he's doing—I will forever associate the first time she fucks me with sucking his cock. It's a variation of the same theme.

Operant conditioning.

He slowly pushes into my mouth, the new taste not objectionable, just different. He holds still with my nose brushing against the dark nest of hair at the base before he pulls out all the way to the head and repeats it. Again, and again, slowly, savoring it.

"I expect you to swallow like a good boy," Carter grits through a tensed jaw as he fucks my mouth.

He lets go of his cock and cups that hand around the back of my head, fisting my hair as he picks up the tempo and really starts using me. My own cock is a happy camper with Susa grinding on me, but having to focus on breathing and looking up at him and all of that help me hold back my orgasm to make it last longer.

I want it to last forever, but I'm damn sure not that good.

"Take it all the way, boy," Carter growls before deep-throating me. I swallow, trying not to gag on how big he is, and tasting his juices filling my mouth as he pulses and makes that familiar groan I've heard before in the shower. He then pulls back a little so I can breathe and swallow, his cock softening in my mouth.

He strokes my hair. "Good boy. Come for me, boy. Be a good boy and enjoy your reward."

I'm glad I have his cock in my mouth to muffle me, because it's embarrassing how loud I am when my climax hits and I fill Susa.

I'm not sure if it's more embarrassing that I can definitively say it's only the fourth time I've ever done exactly this particular thing.

Definitely the best time, though.

I mean, sure, we've done a bunch of other things together, the three of us, so it's almost ironically anti-climactic in some ways.

He turns a little. "Lean forward, pet." She does, and from the sound of it I realize he's unclipped her hands. "Blindfold off, and get off him. Use your mouth and get him hard again." He's smiling down at me. "Now, you get *me* hard again."

I do. Susa's going down on me again, and I'm moaning around his cock. I never knew it was possible to feel this horny.

Horny is good, because it allows me to defer the conversation about this new *thing* between us.

Oh, and what the *fuck*, they got *married*?

Once he's hard I figured he'd start fucking my face, but he climbs off me. Susa keeps sucking on my cock, though, so that's nice.

I mean, basically my brain's fried at this point, so I'm just going with everything.

Carter climbs out of bed, retrieves something from the bathroom, and returns. A towel, and lube.

Fuck.

I know what this means even before he makes her move so she's to my side and not kneeling between my thighs now.

"The only reason I'm not letting her sixty-nine you right now, boy, is because I want to see the look on your face when you feel my cock fucking you for the first time." He smiles. "First, last, only cock you ever take, boy. Gotta tell you, that makes me proud to know."

He pushes my thighs apart and shoves the towel under me. "Susa told me you begged for her to fuck you harder when she used the strap-on the first time. You have no idea how happy that made me." His smile widens. "And that was just with a reach-around. Imagine how good it's going to feel having her suck another load out of you while I fuck you."

The lube feels cool as one finger, then two breach me. I moan as my cock twitches in her mouth. "Don't make him come yet, pet. Get him hard and hold him there. I want to feel him coming with my cock in his ass."

His fingers twist and sweep across the spot he already knows very well inside me and I moan again.

"See, you called me a bastard that first time not knowing how much of one I am. I guess I really *am* a bastard extraordinaire." He grins as he scissors his fingers inside me, stretching me. "I'm the bastard who's going to fuck your brains out."

He works me up to three fingers before slathering lube on

himself and pressing the head against me. I'm waiting for it, for the intrusion, to give the last bit of myself to him that I have for him to take, when his expression gentles.

"Ask me, Owen," he softly says.

I know a rational person would have safeworded.

Then, there's me.

So what do I do? Do I stop this insanity and demand we talk? Or at least demand an apology for them planning this behind my back?

No.

What does *this* dumbass do when presented with a clear opportunity to end this madness?

I stare into his eyes. "Carter, I want you to fuck me."

Triumph fills his face, easing his lines and shadows and giving him that rarest of smiles that I long to be the one to cause. "My very good boy."

He's gentle, tender, even. He takes his time working it into me, gives me time to adjust to him, and slowly fills me a little more with every thrust. When his thighs are pressed against mine, he pauses and lets Susa work me close to the edge again before he resumes fucking me.

He also reaches up and unclips my wrists, drawing my left hand up to his mouth so he can kiss it, suck on my fingers. My right ends up stroking Susa's head, and I'm working my hips in time with her, with him.

Nothing's ever felt so right. Every nerve ending rakes fiery pleasure through my soul as he slowly thrusts and builds himself up. "I'm close, pet," he says. "Hurry up." He laces his fingers with mine, and I squeeze.

Susa works magic with her mouth. From the first squeeze of my ass around his cock when I start to come, until the very last throb as he starts coming, it's nothing but pure, sweet pleasure rolling through my system. He doesn't pull out, either. He grabs

Susa by the hair and pulls her off me, kissing her deeply before pushing her onto her back next to me. He leans in and buries his face in her pussy, and she tips her head back to receive a kiss from me.

With my free hand I reach over and play with her right nipple as I kiss her, and that apparently does it for her. She moans into my mouth and keeps moaning until she finally pats him on the head and he sits up with a smile on his face.

I'm totally brain-fried at this point. None of us speak as we untangle ourselves. Carter holds his hands out to us and leads us into the shower in the master bathroom, where we silently hold each other for a few minutes before he takes the soap and washes me, then her with a reverence I've never seen in the man.

A thousand questions I should ask, but I don't want to disturb this spell.

He dries us off and we all return to the bedroom. When I start to drop into Devotion, he won't release my hand and tugs on me, urging me into the bed, in the middle, where I fall asleep immediately.

*　×　*

The next morning, there are a thousand questions still circling my brain, and none of them will come out except one.

He's awake and watching me when I open my eyes.

"Why?"

He smiles, the mischievous Master smirk, and shrugs. "Because."

Then he nuzzles his nose against mine and I realize either he slept through the night or I was so deeply asleep I didn't hear if he had a nightmare. On my other side, Susa snuggles tightly against me.

"I don't want to get up yet, Sir," she grumbles. "It's Saturday."

He drapes an arm over me, his hand ending up splayed over her tummy. "Nope. Not yet. Later."

I choose trust and drift back to sleep.

While we're cooking breakfast together later, another bout of terror fills me as I contemplate moving into Susa's.

Wondering what my mother is going to say.

How I'm going to break this news to her.

Old habits die hard, what can I say? I know it doesn't matter, and I also feel the rage swirl through me that I felt in Las Vegas after learning the truth about what she did, but…

Yeah.

#mommyissuessuckballs

Carter and Susa see me fretting and Carter steps in, dropping me into *At Ease* right there in the middle of the kitchen floor to talk.

"What's wrong, boy?"

This has felt like a game, in some ways, until now.

Now, this is…*real*.

Terrifyingly real. "What if Mom cuts me off?"

"*Breathe*, Owen. That's your anxiety talking. You have your scholarship, the car is in your name, and you have us."

"What if I can't afford to pay for any of that?"

Carter stands in front of me and cups my face in his hands. This isn't the bastard extraordinaire—this is Carter my best friend, my big brother.

My Master. "What did I tell you when we talked that Saturday after your birthday?"

I stare at him and try to remember. We've talked so much, about so many things, since that morning. It feels more like years instead of weeks ago.

He leans in and presses his forehead to mine. "What promise did I make you when I asked about what would happen if you stopped texting your mother?"

I'm struggling to draw in full breaths now because anxiety has a stranglehold on my chest, my lungs. "That I'd always have a place to live, Sir."

"And what did I promise you last night when I asked you to choose this and us?"

Breathing is tricky right now. I feel like I'm not getting enough air. "That you'll always take care of me."

"That I will *always* take care of you," he says. "*We* will take care of you. You belong to *us*. To *me*. We'll put you on my car insurance if I have to, and I'll take up the slack for you in your budget. So will Susa. This is something else I wanted to talk about today. I guess this is as good a time as any. You will give me all your bills so I can go through them. Your first job is to keep your grades up for your scholarship. Your second job is to take care of us. In *that* order, boy. Nowhere on that list is worrying about money. You need my permission to buy things, anyway. Do you understand me?"

"Yes, Sir." Tears roll down my cheeks but I make no move to wipe them away, per his orders.

I want to be their good boy.

"Our first priority is to take care of *you*," he continues. "As long as you belong to us, we will *always* take care of our boy." He gently wipes away my tears with his thumbs before he slants his lips over mine and kisses me. There is so much emotion in that simple gesture that it makes me cry even harder. These are good tears, though. Cleansing tears.

I want this. As fucked up as it might seem, I want it.

I *need* it.

I need *them*.

"The other part of this," he finally continues, "is if there is something you need, then you tell us. I'll decide if it's what you really need. Whether it's something big, like a transmission for your car, or something small, like a pack of breath mints. I will loosen those restrictions as we go, but for now, unless it specifically relates to your schoolwork or keeping yourself safe, you will default in everything to asking permission or asking for it. The only exception is when you're out alone, obviously, you don't need permission to go to the bathroom, or get food with your meal plan, things like that."

"Yes, Sir."

"Do you want to know why?"

"Do I need to?"

He pulls back enough I can see his smile. "I want you to understand you can trust me to take care of you. The more I see that you do trust me, the more I'll relax restrictions. I need you to internalize the fact that I control your life now. I need to know you completely understand and believe that I *will* take care of you."

"Yes, Sir." I get it, I guess. Except I already trust him.

I trust him, and Susa, a hell of a lot more than I've ever trusted my mother—which is not at all.

Especially after talking to Dad.

"You realize Daddy's going to want to murder you, Sir, right?" Susa playfully asks.

Carter laughs. "Your daddy's going to have to accept you married me without a prenup, pet. Not a damn thing he can do about it, either. The trust owns the house, car, and fund, which I legally can't touch because they're pre-marital assets. He doesn't have to worry about that. By the time he's figured out a way to murder me without it being traced back to him, we'll all have passed the bar and be working. Hopefully, by that point, he'll see that I'm not going anywhere and accept this."

"He holds grudges forever."

"He's never met *me*," Carter growls back. "I guarantee you, I can and will give him a run for his money there."

CHAPTER THIRTY-SIX

We don't move us in completely right then. We're so close to finals and we need to study, plus the end of the semester is coming up soon, anyway. We stay there every night now, but the moving is easier to do in stages, to grab what we need immediately and bring more over every day.

We start running the sidewalks through Susa's neighborhood every morning. And morning shower time usually means Carter bending me over and fucking me instead of just jerking me off. Sometimes Susa joins us, but usually she's already up and moving and out of the house by then.

Every night we study, and before bed I usually get a spanking, then he makes love to us. Or we make love to him. Not sure how that should be phrased, but the three of us are usually sated and exhausted when we fall asleep every night. Sometimes it's hard and vicious and sadistic and exactly what we all need, and sometimes it's playful and tender with only a little bit of bite to it.

It's all fantastic.

Susa has to drive up to Tallahassee to visit her folks the following weekend, meaning Carter and I will be alone together at the house from Friday afternoon until late Sunday night. Her father has tickets to an expensive fundraiser, a thousand dollars a plate, and it was an event already on Susa's calendar before all of this happened.

Thursday night, we're in the kitchen preparing dinner. "Before you reach Tallahassee, pet," Carter says, "I want you to put your wedding rings on a necklace."

She frowns. "Sir?"

"It'll be hard to explain them away, obviously, and I don't want you delivering that news alone. When we have that conversation with them, I want it to be together. All *three* of us."

Her eyebrows arch. "Three?"

"I want Owen there for 'emotional support.'" He makes finger quotes around it. "No, we can't tell them that truth about us, as much as I'd like to, but *I* want him there, even if only as a silent observer. Isn't there an event during the break you wanted us all to attend?"

"Yes, Sir." She looks nervous. "Two weeks from now. A weekend get-together for college students. The state GOP is putting it on, specifically geared for those in pre-law or in law school. Seminars, networking. I already have the tickets and the hotel suite reserved."

"Perfect." He looks at me. "Coordinate with Susa, and make sure you and I have appropriate clothes to take before then."

"Yes, Sir."

This means the clock is ticking. In two weeks, all hell's going to break loose, and don't think I don't know it.

I'm not sure if Benchley will hunt down Mom and Austin and bitch to them to make my life hell, but I trust Carter and Susa.

If they say this will be okay and that they'll take care of me, then that's what I'll count on unless they prove me wrong and screw me over.

Which will destroy me in ways I don't even want to contemplate, so I shove all worries like that off to the side.

Going to bed that evening, Carter lifts all restrictions, and we're three lovers. Susa ends up in the middle of us, riding me while Carter takes her from behind at the same time, his cock up her ass.

Her joyful abandon as she climaxes around our cocks reminds me why I'm doing this with them.

Because it *feels* right like this. Even as Carter smiles at me over her shoulder as he starts fucking her harder to find his own joy, I'm struggling to hold back my release as long as possible. To prolong this moment and bask in knowing that I have a home.

I have love.

I have more than I ever dreamed possible, even though I also understand that it could all be ripped from me.

For now, I'll pray I can keep feeling this happy.

*   *   *

Despite the fact that Carter and I have shared a dorm room for the past couple of months, and a bed for the past week—well, not counting the platonic times we slept together—this upcoming time alone with him feels…different.

I feel vulnerable in a way I never have before. What does it say about me that, despite my initial unease, I *don't* want to stop this?

I don't know exactly what Carter has planned for us this weekend. We both need study time with exams coming up. Except I suspect that he is going to put my body to good use without Susa there to slake some of his urges.

When I arrive home from classes the next afternoon, the Snot Box is parked in the driveway. I park next to it and sit there for a moment with the engine running to think.

I take deep breaths and try not to let my mind spin out a whirlwind of possibilities that all make my pulse race in simultaneously good and nerve-wracking ways.

It's like I didn't know Carter at all, and now I have to get to know him all over again.

Of course, it turns out I didn't really know myself, either, so I suppose that's fair.

The sweat covering my body as I shut the car off and get out has nothing to do with the warm, humid air swirling around me. I make my way up to the front door and take a deep breath before letting myself in.

The first thing that strikes me is the aroma. Carter's already got something in the oven, and it smells delicious.

I lock the front door behind me and set my messenger bag on the floor so I can start undressing. I've agreed to this new world order. Even without Susa here, I'll obey.

I'll still be her good boy.

And Carter's.

Carter appears at the end of the hall that leads from the entryway. He's wearing an unreadable expression. I've toed off my sneakers already. I'm reaching for the hem of my T-shirt, and while I'm temporarily blinded by pulling it up and over my head, his hands are suddenly on me, all over me, warm against my bare flesh, sliding around to my back, pulling me against him.

The T-shirt ends up on the floor and he's already slanting his lips over mine in a crushing kiss I need a breath or two to process before getting into it.

He grinds against me through our clothes, my cock responding on auto-pilot to the sensation.

What the *hell* am I supposed to do with my hands?

I opt to drape my arms around him, holding him, my thoughts dissolving as I *really* start to get into this kiss.

His tongue presses for entry and my lips part for him, his soft groan in reply making my cock twitch.

The air stills around us, like time freezing, the world disappearing.

Carter and me.

This kiss.

By the time he lifts his mouth from mine, I realize I've dipped a little at the knees, bringing me down to his height. Even so, he still felt taller than me.

It's at that moment I realize he always has.

His brown gaze narrows as he stares at me for a long moment. Then he grabs me by the hand and practically drags me through the house without another word.

The master bedroom.

He's been preparing. I'm starting to wonder if maybe he cut his last class of the afternoon or something. The covers are on the floor, and he's laid out a couple of beach towels over the bed. His gaze bores into mine as his hands reach for my shorts and he unfastens them, shoving them down my legs.

Planting a hand in the center of my chest, he shoves, hard, and I tumble back onto the bed. Volcanic-worthy fires burn in his brown gaze as he stares down at me.

After he hooks fingers in my socks and yanks them off, dropping them to the floor as well, he climbs up the bed, kneeling over me with his hands caging my head.

"I don't need to tie you up to fuck you right now, do I?" he softly asks.

I swallow, trying to find the strength to speak. "No, Sir."

"Good." A slow smile spreads across his face. "Because I want to fuck you in about twenty different positions before that chicken is ready, and tying you up for every damn one of them will get tedious after a while."

He sits up and rips his T-shirt off, then easily slides out of his shorts, too. He's gone commando, and his cock is rigid, dark with the blood engorging it. I wonder if he's going to get right to the fucking portion of the activities and make me endure it, except then he does something that surprises me.

He stretches out on top of me, settling his weight along my body and forcing my thighs apart with his legs. Propped up on his elbows, he stares down at me. Not like I'd had a lot of sexual experiences before all this exploded between the three of us, but it's odd having the hard planes of his muscles pressed against me. Feeling the coarse rub of hair brushing against my flesh.

The hot, thick cock alongside mine.

With his gaze sweeping over my face, down, up again, a smile fills his face. "Wrap your arms around me," he says.

I do, trying to swallow back my nerves. My cock lays hard and throbbing between us, twitching unbidden. I can't help it.

He slowly grinds against me, just a little, and I try to bite back a needy moan over the friction my now desperate cock is being subjected to.

"That's it," he whispers. "I *want* you to enjoy it, Owen. This is all us this weekend. You might belong to me, but I want you to understand all the good that's in it for you. All you have to do is be my good boy and I'm going to show you things you never dreamed possible. Okay?"

This is Carter. This is the bastard extraordinaire.

This is my best friend, my roommate.

The brother I never had.

He's now my owner and lover and the husband of the woman I wish was mine.

As if reading my mind, he arches an eyebrow at me. "She might be mine in name, but she's yours, too. I meant that."

"How do you do that?"

"Do what?"

"Know what I'm thinking?"

Another slow smile curves those handsome lips that are now a little fuller from the earlier kiss he gave me. "I took the time to study and learn you, Owen. You're absolutely right about that. Susa and I are twins when it comes to getting what we want."

"How long does this last?"

His gaze narrows and the smile doesn't leave his lips. "There is no expiration date on this."

"But…people are going to talk."

"Why?"

"I mean…the three of us."

"My best friend lives with me and my wife. We're all college students. Later, we're best friends from college and we work together. Don't complicate this, Owen. It's not a big deal unless we make it a big deal."

"Work together?"

"Do you honestly think I'm going to work somewhere if the two of you aren't there, too? I'm married to Senator Benchley's daughter. There are law firms who will kill to have that kind of juice. I simply make it a point to tell them when we talk to them that it's all of us or none of us."

Bitterness creeps into my mind despite trying to tamp it back. "Great. So I don't get a job on my merits."

"Fuck merits, Owen. Honestly? Look what happened when our country elected a reality TV star as president. You think he was elected for his merits? Merits mean shit. The three of us are going to make a name for ourselves, and fuck merits in the process. All that matters is our integrity and our results. Throwing Benchley's name around greases the way. I'm good with that. Why do you want to be an attorney?"

He knows this, but I also know he expects an answer. "To help people."

"To *help* people. That's right. You saying you can't help people better as the bestie to Susa Evans and her husband, over trying to scratch a name for yourself alone?"

He's right.

Damn him.

Double-damn him that he'd stopped moving, and now my impatient cock is twitching again. My hips almost involuntarily try to rock against him to resume that sexy, hungry grind.

"You're right," I admit.

"Of course I'm right. The three of us are a team. Susa's brains and contacts, my tactical skills and bastardism, and your face and moral compass."

"My face?"

He sits up, and I think it amuses him that I whine to lose that contact against him. "*Dude*. Do you *seriously* not understand how hot you are?"

I honestly don't know how to process that and stare at him like he just spouted ancient Egyptian or something.

He props his hands on his hips. "*Really*? Those light green eyes, that blond hair—you're a fucking poster boy for pretty. Women will be creaming themselves over you in election ads one day."

"You sound like you already have it planned." The thought of running for office, no matter what I've said or how we've all talked, fucking terrifies me.

"Maybe I do." He reaches down and wraps his fingers around both of our cocks, pressing them together. "Maybe I already have a long-term plan mapped out in my head. Contingent upon us all graduating law school and passing the bar, of course."

He slowly pumps both of our cocks and it feels like all the oxygen in the room disappears. "No one left behind, Owen. It's all of us or none of us, in *everything* we do. So let me remove any lingering doubts in your mind—this is for *life*. I'm *not* letting you go. I'll never order you to leave, unless you were to do something heinous like cheat on us. As long as you want to stay with us, you are *mine*.

"I can't force you to stay, but if you ever feel a reason to leave, I'd appreciate you giving me a chance to fix whatever it is that's broken between us first before you do. I'll even put it in fucking writing for you, if you need it. I'm not saying I'm always going to be easy to live with, or that I won't have fun inflicting some pretty wicked sadism on you, but I know you're in love with Susa. I *want* you to be in love with her, just like I want her to be in love with you."

"What if she ever wants me to leave?"

"She won't."

"How can you be sure?"

He squeezes our cocks and it takes everything I have to keep my eyes open. "Because she's my good girl and she's in love with *both* of us. Best of both worlds for her."

I finally have to ask it before it burns a hole in me and starts to rot whatever this is from the inside out. "Why didn't you tell me you married her? Why didn't you tell me you guys were sleeping together?"

His expression softens and he releases our cocks. Leaning in, he kisses me again. "Because she was worried it'd hurt your feelings. When I told her my idea, she loved it. She didn't know if she fell for you over me if you would have been open to this in the reverse."

He teases me by lowering his mouth close to mine, pulling back before making contact. He does it several times until I realize I'm lifting my head to meet him for the kiss he still withholds.

The smile returns to his lips. "And because I'm kind of a bastard, as you yourself noted." He lowers his lips to just over mine. "I *always* get what I want." His tongue flicks out, tracing my lips. "I wanted *you*."

CHAPTER THIRTY-SEVEN

With Carter staring down into my eyes, I'm not going to deny how nervous I feel with a weekend alone looming ahead of us.

No Susa between me and Carter as a buffer between us, or as an excuse for me.

No way for me to try to deny what's going on.

I'll be forced to face this head-on, instead of being able to lie to myself.

I'm going to be *alone* with Carter.

I realize I'm not opposed to the idea, either.

This confuses me on a number of levels, but then again, most things about this whole situation confuse me.

That means I'll do what I've done to survive throughout most of my life and go along with everything. If I really get to hating this, and what we're doing, then I can always…leave.

But the thought of that, of leaving Susa—and, yeah, okay, leaving Carter, too—fills me with something akin to dread. Like some weird inverse, and yet still negative feeling, of the foreboding that flooded me at the thought of having to return to my mother's home at the end of every semester.

Besides, if I leave, who will take care of Carter if Susa isn't around? Who will Susa have to own?

Who will soothe Carter's nightmares if she's not there?

Who will take care of Susa?

I realize I don't *want* to leave. Not even when I know that the price I pay for staying is belonging to Carter. Because let's be honest—I've always belonged to Carter, *not* Susa. Carter lets Susa play with me, but he's in control of both of us.

Didn't say I minded.

I'm just still trying to figure it all out.

Does this make me gay? Bi? Not that it matters, I suppose. I'm not going to be dating anyone anytime soon.

I'm not going to be dating, *period*. It doesn't even surprise me to realize I don't mind that, either. Not like I'm lacking for love and affection now. From that first day in the dorm, Carter basically adopted me. Adding Susa made what we have perfect.

Weren't we already a family even before this development? Other than the time Susa went to Tallahassee for my birthday weekend, or the evening Carter and I went to Mom's for dinner, I *literally* cannot remember the last time we weren't together for at least part of the day.

Dinners together.

Studying together.

Time off together.

We're blessed by the scholarships Carter and I have, and Susa's blessed by her trust fund. Otherwise, we'd all be scrabbling to find time to sleep, much less curl up on the couch together to watch TV, because we'd all be working one or two jobs to pay our bills.

With Carter's body stretched out over mine again I try to breathe, to relax. It's difficult with my cock screaming for attention, though.

Carter starts kissing his way down my jaw, my throat, pauses to nip and suck my nipples. I had no clue before all this how sensitive they were.

It's obvious where his eventual destination is, and he takes his time to tease me even more. His warm breath washes over the tip of my cock, but he doesn't lick or kiss it yet.

"Watch me, Owen," he says. "Eyes open."

I grab a pillow and pull it under my head so I can do just that.

He works down my cock to the root, just *breathing* on it. *Fuck,* I'm so damn hard it's literally painful.

Back up, his lips so close to the tip of my cock.

"Ask me," he whispers, breath once again blowing over the head of my cock. "I know you want it."

"Please, Sir," I beg. I'm pretty good at begging now.

He smiles. "Please, what?"

"Please suck my cock, Sir."

"Ahh, good boy." He presses a tender kiss to the head and his lips feel scorchingly hot against my tender flesh. "For tonight, it's Owen and Carter." He slowly licks up the frenulum, making me moan. A sexy smile curves his lips. "But I still want to hear you beg me for it."

I...*beg.*

Shamelessly, repetitively—loudly.

Desperately.

I beg and moan, and as he gives me literally *the* best blow job of my life—not that I'd had many to compare it to before now—I realize there are plenty of up-sides to this arrangement.

Point the first—Carter's oral skills. He's damn sure better than Susa, who I thought was amazing, but I expect he has plans to improve her talents there.

He pulls noises out of me I didn't even know I could make as he slowly teases me. Even when I reach down and grab his head and start trying to fuck his mouth, he resists my efforts to rush.

I'm so horny I'm nearly in tears. "Please make me come," I beg. "I'll do anything."

That smile.

Ohhhh, I'm soooo fucked.

That smile of his screams victory. He knows how horny I am. He knows how badly I need relief.

"I'm going to spend *all* weekend making you come, Owen," he promises between licks and sucks. "By the end of this weekend, the only regret you're going to have is that I didn't seduce you the first night we met."

His gaze meets mine again. "I'm not going to lie and say there won't be plenty of times you hate my guts, because you will. As you yourself noted, I'm a bastard extraordinaire. But I *will* promise you that for every one of those times, there will be countless times *just...like...this*." Between each of the last three words, he lightly swirls his tongue around the head of my cock.

Considering I've had more orgasms over the past couple of weeks than I think I've had during the rest of my life combined, I'm not exactly unhappy about that.

Point the second—for the first time in my life, I truly feel *loved*.

Like I'm not an inconvenience.

I feel...

Wanted.

Even before all this other stuff developed.

Which leads me to point the third—after the initial shock of all this wears off, I have to admit I am, overall, happier than I can ever remember feeling in my life.

I miss Susa, sure, but I know I'm not going to be alone or feel lonely this weekend.

Hell, if Carter gives me more than five waking minutes where he isn't climbing all over me or we're studying, I'll be shocked.

Again, didn't say I minded.

Could I have stopped all this, said fuck this shit, and walked away?

Yeah, but *why*? *Why* would I?

He is stubble and muscles and pure need.

I need Him.

I need *this*, all of it.

I need the bite, the edge, the sweet, hot pain.

I need to be owned.

Loved.

I need *Him*, and I'd be lying if I said otherwise.

He goes deep and sucks, triggering my orgasm—and yes, he swallows. My hips buck and I fuck his mouth as pleasure spirals through me. This is unbelievable.

This is the kind of pleasure I never realized existed before.

This is the kind of happiness I never thought was within my grasp.

This is everything I thought I wanted swept away by the reality of what I have.

I have them—*Him*.

Carter crawls back up the bed and draws me into his arms. It's the only place I want to be right now.

"What about you?" I ask.

"What about me?"

My turn to smirk at him. "You said you wanted to fuck me in about twenty different positions before the chicken finished cooking."

"Then I guess we'd better get started." He laces his fingers behind his head and smiles up at me.

I know what he wants. As weird as it sounds, one thing I've been reluctant to do is ride him. I feel self-conscious when Susa's there. I know once I've done it a few times it'll be like every other step of this journey and become no big deal. But the first time he was going to have me do it, he seemed to sense my hesitation and made it look like he'd changed his mind and wanted me on my back. At the time, I thought maybe it was just a coincidence.

But as he smiles up at me, I'm certain now that it wasn't.

"Bastard," I playfully mutter as I reach for the nightstand, where we keep condoms and lube on hand in the drawer there. That first time he fucked me, he did it bare. Later, he admitted it was because he wanted to mark me like that. Usually, he uses condoms with me or Susa when he fucks our asses, as a matter of logistics.

When I belatedly realized I wasn't using condoms with Susa, they calmed me by telling me she's on the pill.

"Bastard *extraordinaire*," he reminds me as I grab a condom pouch and the lube.

"Got that right."

I sheathe him and use plenty of lube, because that's for my benefit. He finally moves his hands, skimming them down my thighs as I straddle him. His gaze on me nearly has physical weight and substance, intense, and I pause.

He *wants* me.

This isn't just a game to him, or fun, or even sex.

He's never pushed me away.

Maybe he can be a bastard, but truth be told, that's one of his charms.

The more we do this, the more I realize that when he looks at me like *that*, it's pure hunger in his gaze.

"What's wrong?" he asks.

I shake my head. "Nothing. Not a damn thing."

Fuck my mother, fuck what people think, fuck everyone.

I never wanted to live my life in a miserable closet, pretending I was someone I'm not.

I never counted on Carter and Susa. It also means I only need to pretend some of the time. When I'm alone with them, I can be exactly who I am, and it's all they expect me to be.

I don't have to pretend for them or around them.

His hands glide up, over my abs, back down to my cock which, of course, is already twitching again with renewed interest.

I suppose there will be a day when we're not going after each other every time we turn around, but today is not that day.

Leaning in, I kiss him and love the feel of his hand tangling in my hair and holding me in place. I reach behind me and find his cock, taking my time as I savor the kiss and line things up. When I press back, he swallows every groan I make, adding a few of his own to the mix. His fingers dig into my head while the sharp intake of breath from him tells me he's mine in this moment.

Not Susa's—*mine*.

This moment seems to freeze as we kiss. Meanwhile, I cage his head with my hands braced on the bed and slowly take him in.

"Fuck yeah, baby," he breathes against me. "Fuck me."

Somewhere in my head and heart, everything got mixed up and turned around and perfection fell into my lap. He gave me what I never really knew I needed, much less thought I could even have in the first place.

He took away what I thought I needed in my life and showed me the truth behind the lies.

Taking my time, I ride him slowly, wanting this to last. "Number one," I joke as I sit up.

His fingers clamp around my hips as he arches up into me, his gaze sharp and piercing. "I think I like this position the most," he says.

"Why?"

"Because I can look up and watch you." He plays with my cock before his hand returns to my hip. "And that." He smiles.

He lets me ride him like this for a few minutes, until my cock completely recovers and is ready for more.

That's apparently the key point for him. He gives me a squeeze, then urges me up and off him, spooning me against him for position number two. On our sides, he can kiss me while he fucks me and strokes my cock for me.

We only make it as far as number six, with me on my back and my ankles over his shoulder as he plows me, when he gasps. "I can't hold it any longer." He finishes, buried inside me, his forehead resting on mine for a moment as he catches his breath. "Stay," he says.

I'm a good boy, so I do.

He gets out of bed and I hear him cleaning up in the bathroom. I haven't come yet, but that's not up to me anymore.

When he returns, he grabs another condom from the drawer and is smiling down at me when he straddles me. As he rips the pouch open and rolls it down me, it finally dawns on me what's going to happen.

I smile. "This can be number seven. I say it still counts."

He takes his time, his gaze never leaving me as he slowly sinks my cock inside him. He's tight, and hot, and I'm not going to last long at this rate.

"Hands over your head," he says.

I comply, already close to coming.

He reaches down and pins my wrists with one hand and cups my face with the other when he leans in to kiss me.

Mental vapor lock kicks in. Pure pleasure, need, hunger engulf me.

Carter nibbles on my lower lip. "Give it to me."

We find a rhythm. Before long, I'm cresting and falling, unable to keep my eyes open as my cock throbs inside him and fills the condom.

His lips slant over mine, nibbling, exploring. "How's that?"

"Thank you, Sir. Much better."

He chuckles. "Let's see if you're still feeling like that by the time Susa gets back."

CHAPTER THIRTY-EIGHT

We end up wearing each other out before the chicken is finished cooking. He helps me clean up the kitchen after we eat. Both of us sleep great, and the next morning when I check my phone, I have a deposit alert.

Mom hasn't cut me off yet.

I don't know what Carter's been saying to my mom, but the allowances continue to appear in my bank account despite my reduced texting schedule.

Whatever he's saying is working, so I don't rock the boat. I follow his orders and let him tell me what to do in terms of dealing with her. Then again, after what I've found out about her, part of me is hoping for a chance to confront her.

When I wake up Saturday morning, Carter is spooned along my back, his arm and a leg draped over me, the warmth of his skin against mine an addictive sensation.

Skin hunger. It *is* a thing—I looked it up. It sadly helps explain why, even early on, I responded so well to Carter's attention. *One* of the reasons, another being, obviously, that I was an unowned and adrift submissive and Carter was the perfect Master to draw me in and draw me out of my shell.

I pull his arm a little tighter around me, hoping I don't wake him up.

I don't understand why I'm not panicked, why I'm not frantic, why there aren't a million thoughts and recriminations racing through my brain at this moment.

Before all this, I couldn't enjoy simply lying in bed and slowly waking up on a weekend morning, because my brain pecked at me, hard and painfully.

It shocks me to realize that's not been happening anymore.

Sure, there are still thoughts in my head, but they're calmer, more rational.

Wondering what's up Carter's sleeve.

Wondering what Susa and I will do today. Well, not *today*, but in general, you get the idea.

Thinking about my upcoming tests.

Reminding myself to do laundry.

It wasn't uncommon, before, for the top three or five thoughts out of ten to include something about my mom.

"You're thinking too loudly, boy," Carter rasps as he nuzzles his mouth against the nape of my neck and kisses me there.

I'm surprised he's awake. "What do you mean, Sir?"

"You tense up. Your whole body. Your breathing gets fast and shallow." He feathers his lips across the nape of my neck and a delicious shiver races through me. "When you're relaxed, your body is relaxed, and you breathe more deeply."

I turn so I can look him in the eyes. This man truly knows me better than I know myself. I don't know why that surprises me after all these months, but it does.

"How do you *do* that?" I ask.

He smiles, but it's sleepy. "If I tell you, will you promise to relax so we can keep cuddling, and let me go back to sleep for a little while?"

"Yes, Sir."

He closes his eyes and snuggles against me again, his face now pressed against my shoulder. "I pay attention to you, boy. That's how. You were raised by a narcissist you always had to pay attention to, which taught you to pay attention to everyone else. You never learned how to pay attention to yourself."

I lie there, wide awake now as I ponder that, while Carter, the bastard, drifts back to sleep.

Sonofabitch.

He's absolutely right.

* * *

The next weekend, we're all together again. While I'm expecting Carter's really going to put me through my paces when we're not moving stuff from the dorm, he does something Friday afternoon after we're all home that catches me off-guard—he orders the two of us to get dressed in shorts and be ready to go in five minutes.

Susa and I don't have time to argue or question the order. She looks as confused as I feel, so I know asking her for info won't prove fruitful. We get into Susa's car, with me driving and Carter riding shotgun. He gives me directions as I drive. Twenty minutes later, we're pulling into the parking lot of an upscale shopping center in New Tampa.

One of the businesses is a tattoo studio, and it's that storefront he directs me to park in front of.

"Don't shut it off yet," he says, so I shift into park and leave it running.

He removes his sunglasses, unfastens his seat belt, and turns so he can talk to both of us. "What we have, for me, is for life," he says. "Boy?"

I nod. "Yes, Sir."

He looks at Susa. "Pet?"

She nods. "Yes, Sir."

It's like he needs a moment to gather his thoughts. "These are our easy years," he says. "I know law school won't be a cakewalk, but once we've graduated and pass the bar and start working, especially once we get involved in politics, things will get intense. All three of us are pretty driven, right?"

Susa and I both nod. I mean, Carter and Susa drive me, so I guess that counts, doesn't it?

"Once the two of you start running for office," he continues, "we might find there are days at a time we aren't even together." He meets my gaze, then Susa's. "I want all three of us to have a subtle, matching reminder of what we have, so that even when we're apart, you know that we're always together in heart and spirit."

He unlocks his phone and shows us a picture, an infinity loop. "The symbol for poly is a lemniscate inside a heart. I don't want something that obvious, and which might make people ask questions. A small one of these, on the inside of my left wrist, and on the inside of your right wrists. Unless you'd prefer it inside your right ankle. If anyone asks, you can always tell them it reminds you that your opportunities are unlimited. If anyone notices we all have them, then we can tell them that the three of us have them because we are friends, and tell the truth, that we got them in college."

I nod. "Thank you, Sir. On my wrist, please." This is *big*. This is permanent. That he's willing to put a mark on himself like that, matching ours...

It's even better than a wedding ring. And I want it where I can easily look at it no matter where I am.

"Pet?"

She's blinking back tears and nodding. "Yes, Sir. Thank you. I want it on my wrist, too, please."

"Then we're good with this? This is a case where I'm giving you the opportunity to say no, if you want, and it won't be held against you. Pet?"

She nods. "Yes, Sir."

His gaze focuses on me. "Boy?"

I nod. "Yes, Sir."

The rare beauty of the smile he gives me warms my heart and threatens to make me hard. It's not a playful smirk, or a sexytime smile, or any number of smiles he has. It's a sweet, fragile smile I rarely see him wear.

He's *happy*.

We've made him happy.

I don't remember Carter smiling as often or as freely as he has since we started all of this. I like being the reason someone is happy. Two someones, because Susa sure as heck seems to enjoy this, too.

Maybe it's not the family I envisioned myself one day having. Maybe it means I'll never have children.

Maybe it's better that I *don't* have kids, especially considering how I was raised. Maybe I'd only be damning a child to being as fucked up as I am. I'd always wanted kids before, but if I have to trade the idea of children not yet born for these two people who, for some crazy reason, want me?

Yeah. I'm not an idiot.

Besides, why would I subjugate a child to being raised always in the spotlight? And with Susa, they will be, once she starts running for office. It won't surprise me in the slightest if we one day find ourselves living in the DC area because she's been elected as a US representative or senator, or is even a cabinet member. She insists she doesn't want to run for POTUS, but if she decided she does, I'd support her.

I'll follow her, and Carter, for the rest of my life and give thanks for it. Because I know that my life is infinitely better for them being in my life.

That makes Carter's choice of symbolism even more appropriate.

We go inside, Carter talks to the tattoo artist, and we fill out paperwork. Carter pays, and we all go back to watch while he goes first.

The tattoo artist prints out the template and examines Carter's inner left arm. "Wow, you've got some fairly fresh scarring."

"Will that be a problem?"

"It means I can't put it any higher than here without risking issues." He holds the template sheet in place to show Carter and get his approval. "There's no scar tissue there. But if we put it there, it might be visible, even with a long-sleeved shirt. I know you mentioned wanting to be able to hide it."

"That's fine." Carter's gaze locks onto mine. "It's more important Owen can hide his."

The man soaps and shaves Carter's inner left wrist, then places the template and gets final approval before he starts inking. It's drawn as a 3D design, maybe an inch or so long, and runs from side to side on his wrist. The interior is shaded with grey and black, and the entire process from start to finish takes less than thirty minutes.

I volunteer to go next. Carter holds my left hand as he approves where the artist places the design on my right wrist, not releasing my left hand until I'm finished and sport a matching design.

Carter remains in place while Susa gets hers, also holding her left hand and approving of the placement.

Once we finish, before leaving the studio, Carter has us hold out our wrists next to his, and he takes a picture of the three of them together. It's impossible to identify who we are, not even catching his wedding band in the picture.

The smile that sweeps across his face as he studies that picture will forever be embedded in my heart and my memory.

Carter—joyful.

Our phones buzz seconds later after he texts the picture to our ongoing group text thread, so we can both save it to our phones.

He kisses her, then me. "Thank you." His voice sounds…well, choked up.

Group hug time.

I'm reminded that this isn't all about me. That Carter and Susa both get things they need out of this arrangement, too. Personal, emotional things.

Maybe I'll never know everything that happened to Carter in Germany, when he was introduced to things that helped make him the bastard extraordinaire he is now. I suspect I probably don't want to, because there's not a damn thing I can do about what happened.

Maybe it's better I simply accept the man *now*, the *way* he is, for *who* he is, and give thanks he walked into my dorm room and my life.

Because he damn sure accepts me for who I am.

* * *

In the weeks following our return from Las Vegas, once we take our finals and get moved out of the dorm, Susa goes from living a borderline spartan life to wanting to completely furnish the house, full-on nesting mode—engaged.

Since neither Carter nor I bring furniture with us, we don't have anything to contribute. Carter doesn't want her blowing a small mint on furniture, even if she can afford it.

He also knows if I don't contribute at least a little, I'll feel like a mooch.

The man knows me damn well, what can I say?

So some of our afternoons are spent at thrift stores, and some of our weekend mornings are spent at yard sales, in addition to more IKEA trips. The house that already felt like a home starts to come together in a way that I feel like I'm an integral part of.

Both of them ask my opinions, want me to make decisions.

It's actually a tough thing for me to do, at first, but it gets easier with time and experience. I gain confidence I never realized I lacked.

Turns out I don't have to have a "conversation" with Mom. She unfriends me on Facebook after I move in with Susa and Carter and belatedly post pictures from the Vegas trip, including making my profile picture a smiling selfie taken with Dad.

The allowances stop then, too, but I don't freak out, because Carter has already switched my banking alerts to his phone. So I don't even know they've stopped until months later, when he tells me.

I still get a small allowance, enough to put gas in my car and little incidentals I might need, but now it comes as a weekly direct deposit from Carter. I don't need to know my bank balance, because I okay purchases through Carter first.

I realize my stress levels are the lowest I can ever remember them being.

Three weeks after I move in with Susa and Carter, he has me send my last text to Mom.

I love you, and if you want to text me, you have my number.

She never replies.

I hate the almost-lie, because at this point I'm pretty sure I do not love my mother. But Carter wants to handle it professionally, his thoughts always on the future and potential weaponization of anything by her against me.

"You're done trying to force her to love you when she's not capable of it," Carter says as he takes the phone from my hand and sets it on the counter after I send the text

Susa wraps her arms around me from behind. "You've got family," she says. "Us, your dad and Katie, my mom and dad, and Carter's family."

"I haven't even met Carter's family," I remind her. "Neither have you."

"They'll adopt you," Carter says. "I wouldn't put you through something traumatic with them."

"No," I snark. "Just with Benchley."

He grins. "Hey, I needed your emotional support."

"No, you wanted a witness in case he tried to kill you."

Susa giggles. "True story."

Benchley Evans is *not* happy with Carter.

As in, at *all*.

He's even less happy that Susa eloped without a prenup, and that she refuses to put a postnup in place.

To add insult to injury, Carter tells Benchley that Susa plans to run for office eventually...and all three of us have changed our voter affiliation to Independent.

I'm honestly shocked the man didn't stroke out right there.

When Benchley tries to bribe me to give him dirt on Carter, I'm not sure if I earn his respect when I politely decline the six-figure cash amount, or if Benchley's more aggravated than ever that he won't be able to pry Susa from Carter.

But life settles down, and I'm happy.

We are happy.

Carter's absolutely right that this is the best time of our lives right now, and I plan on enjoying it to the fullest.

CHAPTER THIRTY-NINE

Time passes...

On the wall of the New Tampa house, prominently displayed in the living room, hangs an eight-by-ten picture, which is surrounded by a mosaic of smaller framed pictures also taken on that day. The featured picture is three of us, in our green caps and gowns, grinning as we throw the USF Bulls horns at the camera, which is being held by Dad.

There are other pictures from that day, of Dad, Katie, and their kids with me and us. Katie is very pregnant with their fourth child, and my little sister Dawn is only two. There are also pictures with Benchley and Michelle Evans, and with Parker and Charlotte Wilson. Plus a few of the Wilson brothers and their significant others who made it, too.

Another series of pictures, set in a collage frame, with us in black caps and gowns, taken three years later upon our graduation from Stetson.

A picture of the three of us, taken for us by a waitress, of us all grinning and happily drunk at the tap house the evening after we received our notices that we'd all passed the bar exam on our first try.

Yes, we took an Uber that night, duh.

My heavy day collar was replaced by a stainless steel necklace that simply looks like a slightly heavier patterned chain. Susa has a matching one she wears, or a bracelet she wears on her right wrist, if her outfit would make the necklace look out of place.

Carter wears a bracelet of the same patterned chain on his left wrist.

Even if we weren't doing that, I'd still feel connected to both of them by the tattoos we all wear.

Our families have accepted that we're inseparable. Any family function invitations automatically include all three of us. Juggling three family holidays—because I've missed enough holidays with Dad and Carter and Susa refuse to allow me to miss any more—is tricky, but we manage it with Susa usually doing that task because she's the most diplomatic.

Benchley still hates Carter. More than once, Benchley has privately told me he wishes I'd married Susa, but it's not like that's a state secret or anything. Although the fact that he openly told me he'd foot the bill for Susa's divorce if I could steal her from Carter shocked me.

Of course I immediately reported that to Carter, who laughed his ass off at it.

So did Susa.

Finding jobs isn't a problem, either. We let Susa take point on that, because Senator Benchley's daughter is a hot commodity. We pretty much end up the subject of a desperate bidding war between four of the state's top firms to hire the three of us.

I leave that final decision up to Carter and Susa. I don't care where we work, as long as we're together.

As Carter himself said, fuck merits. I want a job, financial security. I never want to return to those feelings of desperation where I had to crawl on my belly over broken glass to appease Mom so my pittance of an allowance would continue.

Over the next year, we settle into our jobs at the law firm we chose to work for. We work out of their main office in a high-rise building in downtown Tampa. None of us mind that we have three smaller, windowless offices tucked away in the bowels of the floor, situated right next to each other, because we're together.

Carter, no shocker, is amazing in depositions and trials. Civil, not criminal, because Carter is a mastermind when it comes to seeing the big picture and has easily proven himself many times over. Juries love him, opposing counsel loathes him. Add in the man's memory, and he's practically lethal when it comes to thinking on his feet.

Susa is quickly making a name for herself tackling state-level cases that involve complicated political wrangling.

Me? I'm amassing respectable billable hours with some big-issue cases, like class-action environmental lawsuits. I can digest dry statistics and paint human pictures with the numbers, which my co-counsels envy.

I know that, eventually, Susa is going to put the house in New Tampa on the market and we'll be moving. I don't know when that's going to happen, or where, exactly, we'll be moving to in the area. It's up to Carter, and Susa's leaving it in his hands. I know he has specific criteria for when and where we move, but he hasn't yet shared that with either of us.

That means it doesn't matter, to me. Carter will handle it.

I've made more money in this year than I ever imagined possible, as have Carter and Susa. We're the envy of our associates. There are already whispers that we might be eyed for junior partner status by the end of next year, if we keep this up.

Katie had her baby, and my two youngest siblings are a joy to visit. Dawn is six, Paul is four. The three of us fly out to Vegas several times a year, and Dad's working on getting transferred to Tampa.

I post family pictures of me with them every time we visit.

Out of curiosity, I look up Mom's Facebook profile, just to realize she's blocked me at some point.

Oh, well.

Thirteen months after we start working for the Tampa firm, Carter sends me a text one morning to see if I have a couple of hours free around lunchtime, which I do. He asks me to reserve the time for him. I mark myself as unavailable on my calendar and I'm ready to go when he stops inside my doorway just before eleven that morning.

We always play things cool in the office, even between Carter and Susa. No PDAs, not even innocent kisses. People know we live together, that we're all friends, and that Carter and Susa are married, but we don't want rumors flying. I follow him down to the parking garage and we climb into his car. Carter doesn't tell me where we're going today, which doesn't surprise me.

He only tells me a destination when he wants to.

Or when he wants to mindfuck me.

Again, didn't say I objected.

Honestly? Doesn't matter to me where we're going. It's nice to spend some time alone with him, just like it's nice to spend time alone with Susa. Once we're in the car, he reaches over and holds my hand as he drives, and I can unplug for a little while and just be his boy.

Carter's pain isn't nearly as bad as it once was, even though he still has bad days from time to time. His nightmares have also eased up, although when he has one, it's a doozy, and usually when I'm not in bed with him because one of us is out of town for work.

While Carter and I still work out together nearly every morning, we're frequently discussing work while we do. We've become workaholics, wanting to build a name for ourselves. Susa doesn't join us because she's not a morning person and prefers to work out in the evening, in air-conditioning, usually in our office building's gym. She normally drives herself to work in the morning, while Carter and I frequently ride together. It's not uncommon for us to swap cars so that two who didn't ride in together ride home while the third drives.

This arrangement works for us, and I love everything about it. We spend every night in bed together, except for the rare nights one of us needs to travel for work.

They haven't brought up me running for office in a while, so part of me is starting to relax and think maybe they've put that aside, that we'll be focusing on Susa running in several years, once she's ready.

I'm fine with that, even if there's still a tiny little pang inside me that will always wonder *what if*.

Right now, Carter's wearing sunglasses, so I can't really read his eyes. And he's driving—of course, #controlfreak—and, well, I'm along for the ride.

Maybe literally, maybe metaphorically.

This *is* Carter the bastard extraordinaire, so maybe some of both, in this case.

If I'm lucky.

We take the Crosstown and head east, away from downtown and toward Brandon. Once there, we leave the highway and slow a few minutes later, turning in at a gated community, stopping for the kiosk at the front gate where a touchpad is located. He rolls down his window and, without even looking at the directory, punches in a number he's apparently memorized.

Did I mention it's annoying as hell to me that the man is blessed with an eidetic memory?

The gate swings open. It's not *just* a gate, but a damn *gate*. Like it belongs on one of those houses in a Hallmark movie about a woman marrying a prince or something. Framed by rough-hewn rock walls that look impressively fancy, not faux-natural, like the stonemasons were too lazy to do much about them, and ornate iron scrollwork I could imagine a blacksmith laboring over for weeks, probably.

It's a motherfucking *gate*.

Carter flashes me a sneaky smile as we pull forward, through this *gate* and into the bowels of this obviously ritzy enclave. I'm not sure if we're still technically in Brandon or one of the nearby zip codes, but we are still inside Hillsborough County.

It's yet another Florida subdivision carved out of what had been orange groves, or cattle pasture, or Florida prairie, who knows? Quiet, well-manicured lawns front fairly expensive homes. Not exactly McMansions, but definitely not your average retirement condo community, either. Sedate money that goes out of its way to pretend it's not waving a freshly printed stack of Ben Franklins in your face as a fan against the warm humidity.

Carter obviously knows his way without needing Waze—#ratbastard, #yesiamenvious—and we make several turns down streets with custom-made wood signs identifying them and designating the speed at a frolicking 15mph. It's far fancier than where Mom and Austin live. I've never lived in a place like this before and wonder about the people conducting their lives behind the luxury blinds perfectly crafted to fit in front windows.

Who are we here to talk to?

I've played this game enough times to know asking Carter that very question won't get me answers and will only prolong the reveal. Best to play it cool, put on my courtroom face, and let Carter be…Carter.

Besides, he has fun. It makes him happy.

Can't say that's a bad thing, or that I object to that, either.

He turns down one last street. I see it ends in a cul-de-sac holding a center island with lush oak trees and azaleas. He parks in the driveway of a one-story house where a discreet FOR SALE sign is planted in the front yard next to a custom stone mailbox probably worth more than the Snot Box.

The house directly to the left of it is also for sale with the same high-end real estate agency.

I realize Carter is watching me, that playful little almost-smirk on his face, and my knitted brows have probably revealed my curiosity.

"Questions, boy?"

"No, Sir."

I'm no dummy.

He reaches for his door handle. "Out."

I follow him to the front door, which sits recessed on a beautiful porch. A real estate lock box hangs from the door handle, and he thumbs the dials to the correct combination to open it and remove the key.

Hmm.

He unlocks the front door and we walk in. Carter immediately heads to an alarm panel to the left of the door and punches in a code.

A happy beep that silences the warning chirrup, accompanied by a blinking green light, must mean success.

Yes, I look around. It's empty, our footsteps echoing off laminate floors and tile and tall, vaulted ceilings. It has a gorgeous screened lanai with a large pool and a hot tub. Behind both properties sit thick cypress wetlands so dense it's impossible to see if they end thirty yards or thirty miles away.

It's a beautiful house.

Probably the house he wants to buy for Susa, I assume.

He leads me into the kitchen and there lays a leather portfolio on the granite breakfast counter. Flipping it open, he launches into what basically sounds like a sales pitch.

Finally, I break, ashamed that I'm feeling annoyed over being put through this. "Are you practicing on me?"

"What?"

"To give the pitch to Ma'am. Are you practicing on me?"

He turns to face me, a rare look of confusion flitting across his features before his own courtroom mask reappears. "No."

"Then what are we doing here, Sir?"

"Do you like it?" he asks in a quiet voice I only remember hearing when Carter is dropping all his walls, all his guards, and is being…him.

Authentic.

Vulnerable.

I gentle my voice. "It's a beautiful house and a gorgeous neighborhood."

Fire lights deep within his eyes and I don't have the heart to interrupt him as he once again launches into an animated sales pitch about all the house and housing development have to offer.

Including leading me into the master bedroom to show me the spacious room. It sits on the opposite end of the house from the other bedrooms and is located on the left side of the house. It has a sitting room on the other side of a full bathroom suite, which comes equipped with a large shower and a soaking tub. Sliding glass doors open directly onto the lanai, and I can picture Susa sipping her morning coffee out there and enjoying the quiet.

Standing there, he takes my hands and gives them a squeeze. "The house next door is almost identical, except reversed. The master bedroom faces this one. It'd be perfect for you.

A twinge of pain, or maybe fear, rolls through me. "I know we can afford it, but why can't we live together?"

"We can, and will, but it'll look really weird and you'll have a hard time explaining why we live together. Two addresses solves it all."

I still don't understand. "*Why?*"

He grins, the grin I know means I'm along for the ride regardless. "We talked about you running for governor. Have to start somewhere, duh. County commissioner."

We haven't discussed those plans in a long time, though. Not since we passed the bar and started working. We've all been too busy with work to even think about that.

I study him. "Isn't there a residency requirement?"

"That's why we're buying now. We start living here. By the time we have your campaign structure in place, you'll meet residency requirements, and just in time to file. No one ever runs against this fucker so he treats it like a cakewalk. Except now, his poll numbers suck, and he's at his lowest popularity ever. Susa and I already crunched the numbers. You're going to run for his seat, win, and pick him off like a gimpy gopher tortoise in the middle of I-4 at rush hour."

"How can you be so sure?"

He cups his hand around the back of my neck and my body wants to respond automatically.

Well-trained.

"Why did you become an attorney?" he softly asks.

He knows this, but I answer anyway. "To help people."

"Why'd you say you wanted to run for governor?"

"To help people." Helping Susa become governor is helping people, too.

Right?

"To *help* people." He meets my gaze. "You *really* want to be governor and help people? Make a difference?"

I nod, a little, not enough to dislodge his hand.

"We start *here*. County commissioner, one term. State rep one or two terms, or maybe state senator. We'll decide that closer to the time, when we look and see who's most vulnerable in this district. Run poll numbers and see where we focus. Then we run for governor. I *will* get you elected, but that won't happen without a little political experience under your belt first."

I meet his gaze and know it's already decided. By him, by my body.

By my heart. Because this is what I wanted, even if I thought there was no way in hell it'd ever happen.

"Are you in?" Carter asks.

"Yes, Sir."

"*No*. This is Carter and Owen time. I need to hear you say it, if you really are in. If this is what *you* want. You need to ask me for it."

This all terrifies me for a variety of reasons, some I can verbalize, and some which remain lodged deep inside me. "I can't do this without you."

He grips my head in both hands, his expression fierce and hard. "I will *never* leave you, Owen. You are *mine*, and like *hell* will I ever give you up. But you *have* to tell me what you want. If you want it, ask me for it. Otherwise, we don't do it. We'll just go into practice and forget buying the second house, and we'll all live here together. Then, when Susa's ready to run, you and I will run her campaign. But if *you* want to run for governor, we *have* to have separate houses on paper, staring *now*. So tell me what you want, Owen. *Ask* me for it."

I want it. Almost as much as I want Carter.

Almost as much as I want Susa.

But I want *us* more. "We'll still live together?"

"Of course. Your house will only be for show and basically an investment property, once we don't need it any longer."

I stare at him, shaky breaths rattling in my now-dry throat as I force the words out. "I want to run for governor."

He grins and kisses me. "Then you will. Meanwhile, you're going to get on the HOA board here. They just had two members die, and we're buying in time to get you on the ballot. You're going to practice your election skills by door-knocking and shaking hands and charming the pants off these people. When it comes time for you to run for county commission, you'll already have a loyal volunteer pool to call upon."

Damn, he's tricky. Smart, but tricky.

I don't know why I'm surprised. I shouldn't be.

"Okay."

He's still holding my head in his hands. "So…do you *like* it?"

"Like what?"

He actually rolls his eyes. "This *house*. Do. You. Fucking. Like. It. Owen?"

"It's beautiful. Yes, I love it."

Then he pulls me in again for another kiss. This one is soft, tender. It lasts not nearly long enough, even though it feels like a sweet forever as he holds me there and reminds me why I'll never tell him to go fuck himself, even when he's at his most bastardly.

Because of the times like *this*.

"Good," he softly says as he releases me. "Because I only want to buy it if you like it."

"Can I ask why here?"

"Besides the county commission seat?"

I nod.

He drapes an arm around me and pulls me close, pointing through the sliders to the backyard. "Privacy. On the other side of those wetlands is an eight-foot concrete wall. Far enough away for privacy. The bedroom locations means neighbors on either side won't hear us playing. We'll put a gate between the back yards. When we need to use your house for appearances sake, it's easy to move back and forth."

Something hits me. "Wait…isn't this district Benchley's old county commission district?"

Carter laughs. "Adds a little bit of poetry to the whole situation, doesn't it?"

"Fuck me," I mutter. "I wonder if we can get his endorsement?"

"We will." He smiles at me. "Besides, Susa has so much crap now, we need two fucking houses for it."

I laugh. "True story."

Carter draws me tightly against his side and kisses the top of my head. "Don't you dare tell her I said that, either."

"Your secret is safe with me, Sir." Of course it is.

#notanidiot

"You want to see the other house?"

"Sir's choice."

And, because right now he's like a kid with a new toy, he finishes giving me the tour of this house and then shows me the other one. Different flooring, the kitchen's a little different, but basically yes, the same house, only reversed.

In the kitchen of that house he draws me into his arms again, his expression serious. "This is *only* for appearances," he softly assures me. "*Nothing* changes between us. I swear."

The remaining tightness in my chest finally dissolves. "I trust you, Sir."

He kisses me again, one hand cupping the back of my neck, not forcing me, almost as if he's assuring himself this time that I really want to be here.

Of course I do. Maybe he's a bastard extraordinaire, but, honestly? I'm kind of used to the guy.

And I'd never leave Susa even if I was tired of Carter.

Life wouldn't feel right without both of them in my bed every night. We've lived like this for so long now that in my head they are both my spouses, even if all we can tell people is that we're close friends.

Even if I look like a pitiful professional third-wheel at this point.

I don't care.

Because Carter and Susa know the truth. That's good enough for me.

He locks up that house and we return to his car. He points at the privacy fence both houses share. "No one can see someone coming and going. You park there, or even in the garage, and walk over. We'll put a gate in. If anyone is here or there for a party and they ask about it, well, *duh*. We're friends. Why wouldn't we have a gate?"

"Not sick of me yet?" I was only teasing, and had broken from his side to round the car.

With those spooky-fast reflexes of his, he grabs my hand and jerks me back, all business when he stares into my eyes again. "What part of *mine* didn't I make clear?" he softly asks.

I swallow hard. "Sorry, Sir."

His gaze softens again and he squeezes my hand, pulls me in one last time to brush his lips over mine before donning his sunglasses. It's an incredibly rare PDA that proves to me how deadly serious he is. "Let's get back to the office. We'll grab something to eat on the way."

"Has Susa seen these?"

"Nope." He reaches for his door.

"Are you showing them to her?"

"Why?"

Okay, *now* I'm going to be stubborn. "Uh, so she can give her opinion."

He opens his door, one hand on the top of it, one on the roof. "Why?"

"Seriously, Carter?"

Behind his sunglasses, I see an eyebrow arch.

Bastard mode: engaged.

"Sorry, Sir," I mumble and head for my side of the car.

He smirks. "That's better, *boy*. I'll let that one slide because I'm in a good mood."

But as we head back west to find food and return to work, I'm left confused about why *I'm* the one who gets to basically sign off on our new home.

I also know better than to question Sir about it.

CHAPTER FORTY

Part of me is sad to leave the New Tampa house, but I know Carter is right.

Plus the move makes Susa happy. She loves the new houses, loves the idea of the ready-made cover story.

Loves that it's one step closer to her own run for office.

Loves that it means she gets to help me with my campaign.

I give her free rein—or maybe that would be reign, considering who she is to me—in "my" house. I honestly don't care what it looks like. It shouldn't look like a clone of "their" house, and the decor should look like something I might pick for myself. That's Carter's only two stipulations. Well, and the budget. He sets one for her despite knowing she can easily afford to get whatever she wants.

I, however, would be limited in some ways. We don't want uncomfortable questions asked, and it does need to be "my" money that's spent. There are future financial disclosure statements to be kept in mind.

We get moved in, Susa has a blast picking paint colors and furnishings for me, and life continues.

I run for the HOA and easily win.

It shocks me, but apparently comes as no surprise to Carter and Susa.

So between work and the HOA, I'm pretty busy. The three of us settle into life in the new house—hous*es*, plural—and we become friends with our neighbors. We're completely open that we're good friends, and Carter is like a brother to me. I'm sure some of our older neighbors are wondering if I'm gay or something, but it's none of their business, so I don't give a shit what they think.

I do have to suffer through an annoying number of matchmaking attempts, some of which Carter makes me accept just to get them over with and appear neighborly. We mostly handle those by having the woman meet me for dinner at Susa and Carter's, to make it seem like I want her to be comfortable by not being alone with me.

I then proceed to let Susa take over being a helpful bestie and sharing all sorts of stories about what a workaholic I am, and how I refuse to take time off, and other such charming personality quirks.

If that doesn't scare them off, then I talk about not being ready to settle down, and put off making any additional dates with them. I don't act like a jerk to them, because Carter and Susa don't want me doing anything that might get brought up later by our opponents when they do deep background on me.

I just…act boring.

Thankfully, it works.

Carter and Susa help me prepare all the financial affidavits and do all the groundwork to file to run for a seat on the county commission board, and they go with me to the county elections office to file it.

Surprisingly, Benchley is going to support me, even against GOP candidates.

I don't know how Carter manages this.

I don't think I *want* to know.

But Benchley is also in the last year of his second Florida Senate term, and he's term-limited out. We know his plan is to run for governor in two years.

Things are looking great for me as we make it through the primaries and into the general election.

Three weeks before the general election is when the first true test of our triad hits us out of nowhere.

* * *

Carter is my campaign manager. He's stepped back some of his work for the firm so anything he's working on can't be considered a conflict of interest. There really isn't a position for him at the county once I'm elected—*if* I'm elected—but as they advance me through higher offices, he'll not only be my campaign manager then, he'll transition into my chief of staff.

I can't do this without him, and don't want to.

It's the middle of October when I get a frantic call from Susa a little after one in the afternoon. I'd just finished appearing at a Tiger Bay candidate's forum and was almost home. Carter is in Orlando today, in depositions on a big case until late this evening, and is basically unreachable. I struggle against my own panic as I try to calm her enough to find out what's wrong.

Because maybe this is about Carter.

She's in traffic, her phone in speaker mode, and from the sound of her tearful swearing she's also speeding on the Crosstown, heading home.

"Pet, *calm down*," I order, channeling Carter. "Deep breaths, honey. Slow down your car, and *talk* to me."

She's sobbing. "Daddy. Momma said Daddy's in surgery. He collapsed in his office thirty minutes ago, and they rushed him to the hospital. Massive heart attack."

Fuck.

"I'm almost home. I'll pack for us. You slow down and get here *safely*, understand?"

"Yes, Sir."

I know it's a reflex, and I can't blame her, given the circumstances, but it still makes me feel…weird.

By the time she arrives, I already have our bags sitting inside the front door, including one for Carter. He's in his car and will most likely leave directly from Orlando.

When he's in depositions like this, he usually turns his personal phone off and leaves it in his laptop case. He'll have his work phone on him, but even that will be on silent mode.

So I call his personal cell and leave a voice mail about what's going on, then text his work cell and tell him to check his voice mail as soon as possible.

I'm already walking out the front door with our bags when she pulls into the driveway, throws it into park, and jumps out to hug me. She's still crying.

Benchley might be an asshole of stratospheric proportions, but unlike my mother, he was a good father, and Susa loves him.

"Go inside, use the bathroom, then set the alarm and lock up on your way back out." I've left my keys in the deadbolt outside, so she can use them.

She runs to do it.

I stow our things in the backseat and have to readjust the driver's seat so I can get behind the wheel without kneecapping myself. By the time I'm ready, she emerges, locks the door, and is in the passenger seat seconds later. She's changed into jeans and a blouse, and has scrubbed the makeup off her face and pulled her hair back into a messy bun.

"Deep breaths, sweetie." She nods, but I don't know if she's really processing anything beyond the need to get to Tallahassee, right now, to be with her father.

We're north of Ocala on I-75 when Carter calls my phone from his work phone. "Where are you?"

"In the car."

"Okay, is Susa there with you?"

"Yeah, um, did you check your voice mail?"

"No. Someone just walked in at the depo and passed me a note. It's all over the news, apparently. I just asked for a ten minute recess, and you were my first call. How is she?"

I glance over at Susa, who's on the phone with one of the paralegals at the office, going over stuff with them that they'll need to handle in her absence. She's barely holding it together.

I drop my voice. "She called me Sir without thinking."

"Oh, shit. Okay, buddy. Hang in there. Did you grab me clothes?"

"Yes, Sir."

"I'll go talk to my co-counsel and opposing counsel and see if I can leave. We had to move mountains to get the schedules aligned for counsel and witnesses to do this today."

That's when I know what I need to do. "No. Stay there and try to finish the day and leave from there. We don't know anything yet. They're doing emergency bypass surgery, so there's nothing we can do anyway."

He pauses, and it sounds like he's moving into another room, maybe closed a door behind him. "You sure, Owen?"

"I'm sure, Carter. Keep your work phone on you. I'll text you a 911 if something changes."

This is where three is better than two, because if Susa was alone without me, she'd absolutely tell him to stay and finish the deposition, because I know her.

And Carter would feel like utter shit for doing it, hating himself that he didn't nuke a work situation for her.

We've been lucky. Damned lucky. They did the emotional heavy lifting for me when I needed them. It's time for me to shoulder this load for them.

When we reach Tallahassee, we go straight to the hospital and have to actually get a hospital administrator to approve us coming in, because they had to remove press and now have a very limited list of people who will be allowed to join Michelle in the surgical waiting room.

"Her husband will be coming later," I tell them while they're taking Susa's picture for the temporary visitor's pass.

"You're not her husband?" the administrator asks.

"I'm her—"

"Brother-in-law," Susa says, her voice sounding dull and brittle. "He's my husband's brother."

Okay, then. I was going to default to friend, but maybe she wants to list me as family to help smooth the way.

I get my picture taken, and we hurry down corridors to find Michelle.

Susa bursts into tears again when we find her mom, and they hug, both of them crying as I get them sitting and Michelle tells us the latest update. He's still in surgery, and listed as critical, but stable, but he's not out of the woods yet.

"Where's Carter?" Michelle finally asks.

"Deposition in Orlando," Susa says before I can answer. "I told him to come later. Nothing he can do right now."

Benchley is out of surgery and in the ICU, still unconscious, by the time Carter arrives around eight that evening. Susa's spent the afternoon either in my arms or her mom's, and I went in with the two of them when they allowed a brief visit after moving him from recovery into the ICU.

But when Susa sees Carter, she goes to him and I watch as he whispers to her, Susa tearfully nodding over words I can't hear.

Frankly, I'm relieved he's here.

Michelle leans in. "Must suck, huh?"

"What?"

"The woman you love, married to him?"

I'm emotionally frayed around the edges, worried on Susa's behalf, and in no mood for games. "Who says it's not the other way around?"

I mentally kick myself for saying it, but it was reflexive. Or maybe I've channeled too much of the bastard.

But Michelle looks at me, at them, then seems to not know how to process my statement. Which is fine by me.

When they join us I stand and, once Susa retakes her seat, I hug Carter long and hard.

"My good boy," he whispers. "Thank you. You were perfect."

Everything else melts away except *Him*. "Thank you, Sir."

* * *

Benchley pulls through, thankfully. Carter and I stay two days. Susa stays behind in Tallahassee through that weekend, because her father is a crappy patient and has no patience for Carter's presence. Carter and I are slammed with work and the campaign anyway. Benchley warns us if we don't get our asses back to the campaign trail, he'll pull his endorsement.

So we ride back to Tampa together, leaving Susa's car there for her.

Carter's driving. The Snot Box gave way to a Mercedes a model newer than Susa's two months after we started working at the law firm.

They'd already replaced my Subaru with a gently used Mercedes SUV our first Christmas together, while we were still in college.

And it wasn't a disgusting shade of green, either.

I tearfully and gratefully accepted it, knowing it wasn't merely a present from them.

It was the last tangible reminder of my mother's former hold on me erased from my life.

We ride mostly in comfortable silence. We're almost to Brooksville when Carter speaks. "Michelle asked me an interesting question that first night we were there, when I walked back into the ICU with you."

"Yeah?"

"Yeah. Did she say anything to you?"

I think back and remember my comment to her and tell him.

He smiles.

"Why?" I ask. "What'd she say?"

"She asked me if I trusted you."

I can tell he's going to draw this out, so I go with it. "And?"

"I told her I trust you with our lives, our hearts, and our secrets." He glances my way.

"How'd she take that?"

"Like you said, she didn't seem to know how to process that. I think she was trying to figure out a way to drive a wedge between you and me, to sow distrust."

"I wouldn't put it past Benchley to ratfuck us with the truth, if he had proof. Even to Susa's detriment."

"He wouldn't." Carter sighs. "He'll have to get over it, though."

"Good luck with *that*."

Carter shrugs, and his next comment catches me off-balance. "Oh, he knows not to fuck with me, or you. Doesn't matter how much he hates me. I've got him on a short damn leash, and he knows it."

Then he smiles *that* smile.

Bastard extraordinaire, FTW.

I decide I don't want clarification on that comment. It's better I don't know. If I should know, Carter would have already told me, and that was one of the guidelines he laid out for me early on—that there would be things he deliberately does not tell me so I have plausible deniability.

So I default to what's always worked for me ever since I first met Carter—I trust.

CHAPTER FORTY-ONE

Ten Years Later

I spend four years as a county commissioner, then four years as a state senator.

Benchley's old seat.

Benchley never gets his chance to run for governor. Michelle puts her foot down and forces him to retire from public life after his Senate term ends. Oh, he's still an attorney and does some work for his firm, and is still heavily active in the state GOP, but he's more behind-the-scenes now than actually leading the charge.

It surprises me when he endorses me for the state Senate seat from the primaries on, even over all the GOP candidates.

It downright shocks me when he manages to swing other important GOP lawmakers to support me from the primaries on, too.

When I confront Carter about this one morning during our run, he smiles, but doesn't answer.

Meaning the whole situation gets filed in the "don't ask again" folder.

Meanwhile, Carter has put both myself and Susa through a concealed carry course to get our permits, and we all own handguns. I don't get many credible threats, but Carter has instituted a rule that if we are out and about and not in a government space where we're prohibited from carrying, we're required to carry.

It's a minor shadow on what I otherwise consider to be a

perfect life. Susa and Carter are far more comfortable with firearms than I am, but because I am above all else Sir's good boy, I comply with his wishes.

When I'm elected to the state senate, we end up buying two townhouses that sit side-by-side in a three-unit building in Tallahassee, just blocks from the governor's mansion. Benchley owns the third unit, but he and Michelle rarely spend time there now. They're once again living in their house in Brandon.

We hire a contractor to put a door between our two units, and life goes on. Carter is my chief of staff in Tallahassee, and is usually with me. We're home in Tampa every weekend, and there are times Susa's in Tallahassee, too, especially after she easily gets elected to the state House of Representatives two years into my Senate term. Then, all three of us commute back and forth from Tampa together, sharing the same bed nearly every night.

Susa has really helped me navigate this new job of mine.

When I file to run as governor, the three of us go to Tallahassee to hand-deliver the documentation an hour before the registration deadline closes for the August primary election.

That's the only way this magic works—the three of us.

We'll already have a bit of a boost for the primaries because none of the other candidates who've filed have named lieutenant governor candidates yet. By state law, they're not required to name one until after the primary, and then they have nine days to do it. It's an extra paperwork hassle to go through if someone doesn't win the primary for their party anyway, but it also means it gives them time to juggle people around to see who to appoint to the spot.

Usually based on who grovels and brown-noses the best for them during the primary election cycle, cutting out anyone who supported one of their opponents.

Once again, Carter's proven correct. Fuck merits—it's nothing more than a goddamned popularity contest that's more petty than my freshman year of high school. Mutual cock-jerking aplenty.

In our case, having Susannah Joleen Evans listed on the ballot with me is name recognition. Especially since we're already running ads with Benchley endorsing his daughter's running mate for governor.

It's going to catch people by surprise in both parties, but by the time they realize what we've done, it'll be too late for them to add their lieutenant governor pick for the primaries to make it on the ballot.

That was actually Benchley's idea, and it's genius.

I don't know how Carter twisted Benchley's arm to back us, and I don't even care. It seems that, over the years, Carter and Benchley have forged a strong mutual working relationship centered around Susa and her political aspirations.

I'd say maybe Benchley's brush with death mellowed him, but that'd be utter bullshit. All I know is there will be a lot of former and current GOP lawmakers and party leaders on our side for this primary, leaving a mad scramble among the ranks as the GOP candidates rip each other to bloody shreds trying to win their primary nomination.

We'll be taking notes on how they attempt to wound each other, too. Both for points to hit the front-runner with during the general election, and to prepare for what subjects they might try to attack me on.

The rest of the pack will be focused on winning their party's primary, at first, and not on me. There are two other Independent candidates, but neither are expected to garner more than a few thousand votes each. They're not our competition. The candidates from the two major parties won't be able to divide their efforts between winning their primary and attacking me at the same time. It will make people wonder why they're so worried about me that they're going after me this soon.

It'll make *them* look bad, not me.

Ah, the double-edged sword of closed primaries.

Meanwhile, our ads will start out on the high-road, focusing on my history, on Susa's, on our endorsement from Benchley, on our platform issues. Once we know who our final opponents will be, and we see what tone their ads take, only then will we start going dark and low.

By then, Benchley will have dug up enough dirt on them for his PACs to start running attack ads.

I'm sure there will be ratfucks aplenty.

All we have to do is be careful. It's harder than I thought it'd be to pretend Susa and Carter are nothing more than good friends and adopted family. It's hard not to want to reach out when we're in public and hold their hands, or lay my head on their shoulders.

Touch them.

Unfortunately, it's a skill I get used to, because I used to be pretty good at it while growing up.

*   ×   *

As June fades into July, the campaign shifts into a higher gear. Campaigning never gets easier for me, no matter how often I do it or what office it's for.

Days turn into weeks as I leave free time behind and increasingly throw myself into this new aspect of my life. I'm still a state senator. Traveling back and forth from Tallahassee to Tampa, and then around to other parts of the state to campaign, is wearing on me.

All I have to do is see one of Susa's encouraging smiles on our nightly FaceTime conversations when we can't be together to remember why I'm doing this.

I'm doing it for *Her*.

Even Benchley's grudgingly admitted Carter's strategy is solid and will likely work. Every new set of polling numbers he and Carter dissect keep proving the bastard extraordinaire's right.

Of course he is.

Doesn't mean I enjoy doing this. It means I keep the bigger picture in mind.

It's all for *Her*. I mean, yes, this is kind of what I wanted, but without Carter and Susa, I never would have done this. I likely never would have progressed past county commissioner. That had been a grind I wasn't prepared for, all things considered. It was damned hard work. Sure, I could have phoned it in the way some of my fellows on the board were prone to do, but that's not me.

I was getting paid by the citizens to do the job they elected me to, and I took it seriously.

Just like I take my role as a state senator seriously.

"Senator Taylor" is a very weary man right now, no matter what face I put forth to the public. I get to spend more time with Carter than I do Susa, but...

I'm tired.

On that August primary election Tuesday, we're in the same Tampa hotel where we always rent space to hold our election night parties. We haven't rented the ballroom, but we took over a decent-sized banquet area and are watching the returns roll in with our campaign staff and volunteers. We only have a few paid campaign staffers right now besides Carter, but will be adding more as we gear up for the general election.

We've also rented a suite upstairs for ourselves for later, just like we have for every election night.

Our private celebration.

As the polls close at seven in most of the state—the western panhandle is in a different time zone and closes at eight Eastern time—I stand in front of the computer monitor where Carter's deputy campaign manager, Draymond, sits at his laptop and refreshes the state election results page every few minutes. He hasn't told Dray or Susa yet, just me, but Carter plans on tapping Dray to be Susa's chief of staff if we win the general election.

While Carter is reasonably certain of our chances, he doesn't want to jinx us, either.

By eleven o'clock, it's obvious that come tomorrow morning, my polling numbers for this primary election will be shocking a lot of professional campaign wonks who weren't paying close enough attention before. We also had heavier than normal turn-out for a primary. Provisional, absentee, military, and overseas ballots remain to be counted, but as it stands now, I drew in more votes than any single GOP candidate.

Far more.

In fact, discounting the voters who voted for the other Independent and third-party candidates, I could very well have won last night, if it was a general election.

The two GOP frontrunners will be locked in a recount, but their votes combined don't equal what I pulled in. Since we're a closed primary state, it's impossible to know exactly how many people would have crossed party lines to vote for me in a general election. Looking back at my numbers when I ran for the state senate, we have reason to believe those numbers will be considerable.

Carter nods as he stares at the screen while people all around us are congratulating me. He and I had a private deal—if my numbers were grossly disappointing, I would drop out and make a run for state rep, then revisit a gubernatorial run at a later time.

Now…I can't.

We're too damn close.

Susa wears a beaming smile, full dimple, as she talks with her father.

That seals my fate.

We're doing this.

We're *really* doing this.

All I have to do is not fuck this up between now and November.

CHAPTER FORTY-TWO

As August bleeds into September and my two main opponents start taking aim at me as well as each other, my work load doubles. I'm trying to help ram a bill through committee to increase STEM program funding for our high schools, and my campaigning is two-fold—trying to put pressure on my fellow lawmakers via stoking support with parents and teachers, as well as trying to campaign for governor.

Late on a Friday morning, Senator Taylor has a scheduled televised appearance at a high school in Brandon. Gubernatorial Candidate Taylor will be holding a town hall immediately after just three blocks away, where we've invited teachers and parents and students to attend. It's a magnificent bit of schedule juggling on Carter's part, because it means we'll be home, in Tampa, for the entire weekend. Susa will be joining us later tonight, when she drives in from Tallahassee.

We've just finished the first part of the school appearance, a Q&A session with students in the auditorium, and Carter and I duck into a bathroom on our way to the school's office.

I need a minute to breathe.

It's between classes and just before lunch, and the hallways are almost completely empty as we head to the office area where we're supposed to meet up with the principal. The school is newer, and the office is situated across the large main entry hall from the lunchroom area. We've just stepped inside the glass-walled main office when I hear something I think is a firecracker go off nearby.

Next thing I know, I'm on the floor with Carter on top of me. He's screaming for everyone to get down and literally drags me around the end of the desk and behind it as I hear more of the sounds and belatedly realize it's not firecrackers.

It's gunfire.

The office workers are screaming, and the school resource officer, an armed deputy, comes running out of an office down the hall behind the desk.

"What the hell's going—"

I am not too ashamed to admit I am one of the ones screaming when another shot rings out and takes the back of the deputy's head off. He slumps to the floor with a sickening, wet thud.

Carter climbs off me, checks the deputy's carotid pulse, and then crawls to another woman writhing and moaning on the floor. He drags her completely behind the desk and rips her blouse open to expose a belly wound.

Carter looks around and points me at the hallway. "Go! Stay down! Get in an office."

I go, following three other women, ducking into the first office to the left, which doesn't have any windows. Then Carter, who's carrying the injured woman. He sets her down, yanks off his blazer, and rips one sleeve off it. He tightly balls it up, presses it to her wound, and then grabs my hands and presses them to it.

"Keep pressure on it," he orders, then looks like he's going to go back out there.

"What are you doing?"

"Stay *here*, Owen." He disappears, but reappears seconds later, dragging the deputy's body through the door with him.

Carter unholsters the man's sidearm, checks the safety, and sets it down next to him. I notice he keeps glancing out the door, down the hallway and toward the office lobby area.

After searching, he finds spare ammo mags in the man's utility belt and puts them in his own pockets. Then he rips the man's shirt open to expose his bulletproof tactical vest, and starts removing it from him.

"What are you *doing?*" I'm panicking and probably feel like I'm repeating myself, because I am.

One of the women is on a cell phone. "The 911 operator says for us to stay here. We can't put the school on lockdown. The controls are out in the office." We all flinch as we hear two more shots, close together.

"Where are they?" Carter asks. "The lockdown controls?"

"On the wall on the far end, in the corner, with the PA system controls. It's a button. It's marked."

He's removed the tactical vest from the deputy and is putting it on himself now. "Tell them there's an armed civilian wearing body armor who's going to confront and engage the shooter. Describe me to them so they don't shoot *me*. Tell them I think the shooter is using a handgun. It's not automatic fire, and it doesn't sound like a carbine."

More fear rolls through me. "Carter, you can't *do* that!" I scream.

"If I don't," he says, "no telling how many people will die." He looks back at the office worker. "CCTV cameras?"

"Same corner where the PA controls are." She points.

"Close and lock this door after me." He glances my way, but before I can say anything else, he's gone, with the deputy's sidearm in his right hand and his own in his left, because the tactical vest covers the rear waistband holster he normally carries his in.

I'm still trying to figure out how the hell he got the weapon into the school, then remembered that the resource officer met us outside earlier today, and Carter talked with him in private for a moment before the deputy personally ushered us inside the school.

Shit.

One of the other women closes and locks the door, then props a chair under the knob.

Seconds later, an alarm sounds, and I hear muffled thuds of fire doors releasing and swinging shut nearby. Carter's voice comes over the PA system.

"Active shooter on campus. This is *not* a drill. Teachers, institute lockdown procedures immediately."

The woman with the belly wound is moaning, and I don't feel like I'm helping much, but I decide I need to focus on her and not my debilitating fear. I realize that this is probably the closest I will ever come to knowing what Carter went through that day in the desert.

I also wonder what kind of nightmares this will resurrect within him.

Hell, I wonder what kind of nightmares this will trigger in *me*.

My gaze falls on my tattoo on my right wrist, and I stare at it for a moment before I see the fallen deputy again, where he's lying just feet away, and I realize this situation could get infinitely worse.

Please, let us both live to have nightmares after this is over.

* * *

We can hear gunfire.

I know I'm crying, wiping my cheeks on my shoulders because I don't dare let go of the makeshift dressing under my hands.

At least I'm not the only one crying.

When it goes silent, we all look up at each other, holding our breaths as we listen.

I don't know how many minutes pass, but then there's a knock on the door.

"It's Carter. Open up."

I…okay, I fucking *sob* with relief while one of the women remove the barricade and unlock the door for him.

He leans against the wall and points at the woman with the phone. "Are you still on with 911?"

She nods, and he motions for the phone and starts speaking to the operator.

We have deputies pointing weapons at us just minutes later, until they realize we're the good guys. Carter is led out first so he can show them where the shooter's body is in the nearby kitchen, and apparently where there are three other deceased victims that Carter knows about between the teacher's lunchroom and the kitchen.

It feels like forever before they get EMTs into the office. I don't let go of the woman's dressing until an EMT takes over from me. Then I scramble to my feet to try to find where they took Carter, even though I'm covered with the woman's blood now. Officers want to get my statement, but I refuse to speak with them until I put eyes on Carter myself.

One of the deputies leads me outside to a mobile command center, a repurposed RV with the sheriff's office logo emblazoned across its side. Carter's sitting on the step of the open side door, the tactical vest on the ground next to him, and an EMT checking him out. His sleeves are rolled up, top button of his shirt unfastened, and his tie is loosened.

I run up, fully intending to pull Carter into my arms and kiss him, but Carter stays me with an upraised hand and a stern look. "Owen, I'm *okay*. Let them clean you up first."

We remain locked in a silent battle of wills for probably fifteen seconds before I let another EMT take me over to a nearby ambulance to rinse the blood off my hands. Then there's statements to be given, frantic calls from Susa to answer—and I miss the fucking town hall, obviously. Carter calls Dray to go speak to them for us and explain what happened, although even more people apparently show up to the event after hearing the news reports.

We have to stand in a press conference, where I watch while Carter gives an abbreviated and censored version of events, deferring to law enforcement for details he isn't sure should be publicized or not.

The man Carter killed was the estranged husband of a teacher. Somehow, he'd managed to sneak onto the campus, and then in through a side door, catching it as a student slipped out to go to their car and sneak a smoke.

Having been on the property before, he knew his way around and knew his wife would be heading to the teacher's lunchroom, which was located almost directly across from the office. He shot and killed his ex-wife and another teacher before emerging from the teacher's lunchroom. That's how he saw the resource officer and shot him. Then he ran for the kitchen area, but ended up cornered in there when the staff locked themselves in the office, which was the only way through to the outside door.

That's where Carter cornered, shot, and killed the guy, but not before the man killed another lunch worker, a woman who'd gone after him with a butcher's knife. Fortunately, no students were injured.

It's close to six that night before we finally walk through our front door.

When Susa flies through our front door and is screaming our names a little after seven, she finds us naked in the big soaking tub in the master bathroom, which is overflowing with bubbles. Both of us are drunk off our asses and already fucked each other silly on the bathroom floor after desperately ripping the ruined clothes off each other. And, according to her, there are over a dozen news trucks parked outside the front gate of our community.

We hand our cell phones off to her for the rest of the evening. She gets to work with Draymond, who also shows up at the house, to put together a press release that she goes and delivers herself in time for it to make the eleven o'clock news shows. She also does a few short interviews, Dray accompanying her in case she needs help.

Meanwhile, as Carter and I—still drunk, because we feel we earned it—sit in bed and eat leftovers while watching the newscasts, he nods.

"She's good," he says, pride in his tone.

"Are you okay, Sir?"

After a moment, he slowly shakes his head.

I open my arms to him, and when he tucks himself against me, I hold him tightly and don't let go.

* * *

Anyway, that's how I found myself being interviewed live Sunday morning at our campaign headquarters by Kevin Markos of FNB—Full News Broadcasting—for their morning show. Carter refuses to do any interviews and releases a statement through our campaign office. We are going to attend all the funerals, though, including the full-honors funeral for the fallen deputy.

The woman who was wounded, Cass Pressley, will pull through. We visited her in the hospital one evening, without any press around, so I could see for myself that she was okay.

Carter assures me the phantom feeling of her slick, warm blood between my fingers will go away, one day.

Today is not yet that day. I find myself washing my hands dozens of times a day in hopes that will help.

I wanted to do *Meet the Press*, but Benchley, Carter, and Susa all agree that having the conservative FNB on our side is worth more than all our TV and print ads combined, because we'll win over the "stand your ground" crowd despite our *F-minus* rating from the NRA. I personally despise FNB and everything they stand for—drumming up fake right-wing hand-wringing crises to generate outrage, and skirting the lucrative edge between ultra-conservatism and conspiracy-theory lunacy. It had once been a

well-respected moderately conservative news source, but its sale and acquisition by a global media company quickly led it down a more lucrative and lurid tabloid path.

When you can make Fox News look like PBS, you know you're doing something wrong.

Kevin Markos was once what I considered a respected journalist, but in the three years he's been with FNB, I realize he's just another shill trying to make a buck. He obviously has no personal ethics to be doing what he's doing. Some people thought him joining the network meant it was shifting back to center, more mainstream, and his presence would help restore a modicum of dignity to their programming.

Nope.

Kevin Markos has blond hair just a little too perfect, and eyes so blue that I can't help but wonder if the color is due more to contacts than DNA. He dances around a few bland pleasantries and introduces me to the public before he dives into the deep end.

After recounting the basics of what happened at the school, and showing some B-roll footage from local stations of the aftermath, including a shot of Carter and I at the press conference, he pounces.

"Some people might say this was a publicity stunt to help your gubernatorial campaign, Senator Taylor."

Remember, this is *live*.

I glare at him, unable to disguise my disgust at his question. I don't pull any punches or tone back my sharp anger. I want to deck the guy. He's lucky I'm not putting hands on him, but I want people to understand how ludicrous this asshat is, and what a stupid fucking network he shills for.

How *dare* they question Carter! I don't give a shit what they say about me, but I will *not* stand for anyone disparaging Carter or his motives and actions.

"Yes, orchestrating a violent domestic dispute in a school, by a man with a firearm, getting an armed school resource officer and three others killed, and then ordering my best friend to disobey law enforcement and run into a live-fire situation and risk *dying*, all for our campaign—that was a *very* cunning plan, wasn't it?"

He starts to stammer a reply but I cut him off, steamroll him in Carter fashion, my anger blowing hotter, into a full, rolling boil.

"I don't know where you get your ideas, but Carter Wilson isn't just my campaign manager. He is my best friend. We consider each other *brothers*. I would *never* do something so stupid and selfish as ask him to risk his safety—much less his *life*—for a publicity stunt. I would *never* endanger *anyone's* safety, or their lives. I *seriously* wonder about your lack of ethics if you are honestly asking me an outrageously and blatantly stupid question like that and mean it literally and not as some really lame attempt at sarcasm."

"I'm sorry, I—"

I keep going. "In case you weren't aware, Carter is former military, a decorated combat veteran, and was awarded a Purple Heart and medical discharge for injuries he received from a car bomb in the line of duty. He *literally* threw himself over three wounded men in an attempt to protect them from further injury and nearly died as a result. Tell me, are those the actions of a man interested in publicity?"

"I didn't mean—"

"You *did* mean it, Kevin. Don't lie and say otherwise. Attack my policy positions, my experience, my politics. Question *my* motives, my methods—hell, even make fun of me personally, if you want. But don't you *dare* insinuate I would *ever* put someone, *especially* my best friend, in harm's way over a publicity stunt. Maybe *you* might do that, because everyone knows what publicity whores you and your network are, but *I* have a conscience. You owe that man an apology for impugning his character. He served our country with honor and distinction and nearly died as a result.

He risked his life in a situation he didn't have to in an attempt to save lives. You also have insulted the other victims of this, by your ludicrous statement. What, they volunteered to die to help me get elected? Is that what you're saying? What's *your* military service record look like, huh?"

It's tempting to stand, rip off the mic and IFB I'm wearing, and storm off in a flounce that will lead broadcasts on all the other networks.

But I don't.

Because I'm a professional, and because I know Carter's standing right there, not twenty feet away, his stoic, stony mask in place, his arms crossed over his chest, and creating his own gravity, like a black hole.

I also know Carter would rip me a new one if I storm off.

Nothing else will happen, though, unless or until Kevin Markos apologizes. I'll keep circling back to that point until he does. Carter might punish me for it later, and I'll unapologetically accept every cane stroke he gives me.

But in this one stand that I take, I shall not be moved.

I've never seen the guy look so rattled, but I'll take the win. "My apologies, Senator Taylor. Of-of course I-I didn't mean I thought you orchestrated this—"

"I'm sure the playback will contradict you, Kevin, but apology accepted."

He swallows hard. "Now, if w-we can move on, I-I'd like to talk about your education plan…"

And there we go. I risk a glance at Carter. Maybe no one else would notice, but I see the way the left corner of his mouth turns up ever so slightly in a smirk.

I might get a spanking later, but I'll also get a *good boy* for standing up to Markos.

Carter's proud of me.

That's all I care about.

CHAPTER FORTY-THREE

Election Night

Polls close at seven in most of the state, eight in the western Panhandle, but those votes are negligible at best and tend to trend GOP, anyway. We already have solid guesstimates based on existing voter rolls and past voting trends.

I know we can't just lock ourselves in the hotel room and watch the election returns spin out on our laptops and on TV, but I *really* don't want to be around people right now. I've hit my limit, and I'm feeling more than a little overwhelmed.

That means I do what I always do—I turn it over to Carter and trust him.

He's talking to some former GOP bigwig when I catch his eye from across the room. His gaze starts to dip from mine, then darts back and locks on me again as if re-evaluating. He immediately pats the guy on the shoulder, makes his excuse to break away from their conversation, and crosses the room. His gaze never leaves mine until he catches up with me and heads toward the room that everyone has been told was mine.

I wait until he passes me and fall into step behind him. He opens the door, ushering me inside and glancing around behind us before closing the door and locking it.

He holds up a hand to keep me silent and in place as he first walks over to the windows, pulling the curtains securely shut. Then he glances in the closet, in the bathroom, insuring we're alone.

Only then does he turn to me, hands on his hips.

"*Loyalty.*"

My knees unhinge and I gratefully drop into the pose as he walks over to stand in front of me. With my head bowed, all I can see are his shoes and the cuffs of his trousers. I want to drop into a full formal bow and nuzzle his feet, but that's not what's been asked of me.

Then he kneels in front of me, one hand coming to rest on the back of my head, his nails lightly raking through my hair and scratching my scalp.

My eyes drop closed, a shiver rippling through me as my brain downshifts and falls still. He's close enough the warmth from his body washes through me, enveloping me.

I can smell him, traces of deodorant, of our body wash— everything he does to keep us connected so my senses are filled with him when we're not together.

Even the noises of the people out in the other room drift away, leaving me to focus on the sound of his breathing, the rustle of fabric as he shifts position again, now sitting in front of me.

"Breathe, boy," he whispers, and I do.

I listen to him, because he's leaned in close, his face next to mine now. It's all I can do not to press hard against him, nuzzle him, seek comfort from him. I can hear him breathing, slowly, deeply. I match mine to his and it's not long before the outside world has completely disappeared.

It's just *Him.*

He closes the distance between us, pressing his cheek against mine. "It's almost over, boy, and I'm so proud of you," he whispers, warm breath caressing my flesh like his words caress my soul. "Win or lose, I'm proud of what you've done."

I don't know if I'm allowed to speak, so I don't. I continue to nuzzle him, wishing I could strip and curl up in his lap right now.

How did we get here? To this point? Not only the governor's race, but *here*, the *two* of us?

That very first night in the dorm room, I never suspected how he would come to feel about me.

Never saw myself…here.

I am only here because of him and what he's accomplished. I was his clay and he molded me in the image he wanted.

I happily complied, because it made him happy.

Don't think that's something that doesn't consume my every spare thought. I will *never* forget I am where I am, and I am *who* I am, because of *Him*. Sure, Susa's connections helped pave the way, but Susa is lit by her own inner furnace and guided by the light it casts.

I envy her that sometimes.

My inner furnace is stoked by Carter, kept well-tended and burning by him.

Him.

"You may speak," he says.

"Thank you, Sir. I'm here because of you. And Susa."

His low chuckle warms me, hardens my cock. His lips trace the shell of my ear. "You don't give yourself enough credit, boy. You're the magic sauce. The face, the voice. Panties get wet and drop when you speak."

He drapes an arm around my shoulders, pulling me in, making me lie on my back, and I willingly go. He tucks my head in his lap and I can look up into his face, where now he appears upside-down.

But that brown gaze of his weighs me down, pins me to the present, keeps me grounded.

He strokes my forehead. "My very good boy. You can do this.

Win or lose, you've got this. I'll be right there beside you the whole time, I swear. I won't leave you alone. Deep breath."

I take one, hold it, blow it out.

He lets me lie there for a couple of minutes before he pats me on the shoulder. "Sit up."

All too short a time together, but we can't risk more. Especially not right now. I sit up, putting our faces at the same height.

He cups my face in his hands and presses his forehead against mine. "I want to kiss you so fucking hard right now, Owen, but I can't risk someone spotting it." He's right—I'll look like we've been making out.

We apparently can't do subtle when it comes to that. Us kissing—*really* kissing—always ends up with both of us sporting red and swollen lips, our cheeks pink from stubble rubbing, and our trousers tented from hard cocks.

There is nothing subtle about the way Carter and I *kiss*.

Frankly, I kind of prefer it like that.

His thumbs gently caress my lips and I kiss them instead.

Then he lightly presses his lips to mine, all too briefly, controlling it and barely controlling himself. "You've made me proud, boy. Just a few more hours, regardless, and then the three of us will have time alone together. Okay?"

"Yes, Sir."

He motions for me to stand. I rise, then take his hands and help him up off the floor. He's tried to hide his pain from me today, but the soft grunt he makes lets me know he's really hurting and doing a damn good job of hiding it from most everyone else. The campaign has been a grind for him, too. His pain isn't nearly as bad as it used to be when I first met him, but he's a man, not a machine. The incident at the school, however, marked the start of a pain cycle for him that he's having trouble climbing out of. We've scaled back our morning runs to shorter, slower walks, doing more gentle reps on machines in our spare bedroom, either in Tampa or in Tallahassee.

He had to go back on one of the anti-anxiety meds he'd been able to discontinue our second year of law school because the nightmares resumed with a frequency and fury that scared even Carter. They're only just now starting to decrease in frequency and intensity, even a couple of months later.

It's another reason Susa tries to make sure Carter is with me as many nights as possible, because she knows he does better with me sleeping in bed with him.

He straightens my clothes, and I straighten his, and he pulls me in for a tight, strong hug. "You're *my* boy," he whispers in my ear. "No matter what. Nothing tonight changes that."

"Yes, Sir." As he releases me and heads for the door, despite all our hard work, part of me prays I lose tonight.

Because if I do, it means we can go back to being who we were without worrying about the press or rumors.

I know it's selfish of me, but I've never claimed to be perfect.

I've only claimed to be *His*.

* * *

I awoke that Tuesday morning in the arms of the two people in this world I truly love most, just a guy, an attorney, a lawmaker. Florida Senator Owen Taylor.

A loved and owned boy.

I will eventually go to sleep tonight as Governor-Elect Taylor.

Even before MSNBC and WFLA in Tampa calls the race in my favor, the energy in the suite has amped up, grown electric, frenetic. Everyone's smiling, including Carter and Susa, and I'm hoping the smile I've plastered on my face looks real enough.

But it's pretty obvious how it's going to shake out by ten p.m. I have taken enough of a lead over the other candidates that there aren't enough ballots remaining to be tallied to help them close that gap.

The minority party candidates all call and concede by ten fifteen.

Jack Coffield, the Democrat, concedes at ten thirty-seven, once the last ballots in Miami-Dade are reported. I took the county by ten points, something unheard of.

Only Steven Shallows, the Republican, hangs in there until the guy with the massive electronic whiteboard on MSNBC explains the math and why they're calling it in my favor at ten fifty-eight.

The phone Carter's holding rings at ten fifty-nine.

We're all heading downstairs, a bunch of us crowding into the service elevator at two minutes past eleven. I've rolled down my sleeves and donned my jacket. Susa's straightened my tie with a wink. We're surrounded by campaign staff, including the FHP officer who will now be one of my constant shadows.

I've just lost my freedom.

Ironic, I know.

In the elevator, someone squeezes my right hand, hard, before the doors slide open. I don't have to look to see it's Carter, who's standing directly behind me and to my right. I'm carried forward out of the elevator with the swell of people. There are Hillsborough County deputies awaiting us downstairs and escorting us all to the ballroom's back entrance. Carter takes his position on my left, Susa on my right and staying just a step behind me as we walk out onto the stage to the crowd's cheers literally vibrating the building.

I don't even know what the fuck I'm going to say. I pray Carter prepared something and will shove cards or a cell phone into my hand to read off of before I embarrass the hell out of myself and the people who've put their faith and trust in me to fix this state and run it the right way.

I slowly walk along the front of the stage, waving, leaning in and shaking hands, saying *thank you* a thousand times, it feels like.

Then I catch Carter's eye and he glances at the podium.

There is his tablet, sitting there, ready.

Waiting.

Of course it is.

Except I turn and walk back to the two of them, then face the crowd. I grab Carter's and Susa's hands and march them up there with me, raising our hands together, the only time like this I'll be able to publicly show everyone the truth, and they can't even see it despite us standing *right* there in front of them.

See US.

See these two people.

I love *them.*

They are my life.

They *are the reason I'm here, not any of you.*

All that remains unsaid, though, while I stand there listening to the applause and cheers thunder around us, lifting us up.

Carter squeezes my left hand and I look over and smile. He gives me a tiny, slow nod.

My boy, that nod says.

Reading each other's silent cues, the way we have ever since the beginning.

I finally lower our hands and reluctantly release them. But then I hug Susa, long and hard, and turn and hug Carter.

I don't risk saying anything, knowing there are cell phones all around us shooting video, not to mention the TV cameras. I cannot risk anyone trying to read my lips.

Carter claps me on the back and releases me and I finally turn to the podium, aware that, behind me, Carter has held out his right arm to Susa and she's stepped across the void to tuck herself against his side.

Of course she has. She's his wife and has every right to stand there with him.

Out of the corner of my eye I watch him kiss the top of her head.

I know he'd do it to me, too, if not for the roomful of people who've just elected me.

Long-term plan.

I start the ball rolling, don't fuck up too badly, get re-elected, and then Susa can bring it home during her eight years in office.

Long-term goals. Carter's plan.

He hasn't failed us yet, and even Benchley says it's a good, solid plan. *This* was the hardest part—convincing an electorate to vote for a third-party candidate. They've done it once now, they'll do it again.

Especially if we don't fuck it up.

People forget how many Democrats held the high office in our state before a series of GOP governors were elected and fucked it all up. Having a third-party candidate who's socially liberal and fiscally conservative isn't actually that much of a stretch.

Overwhelmed, I take a moment to clear my throat and stare out at the crowd. The lights from the cameras make it hard to distinguish any one person from another out there. Behind me on stage are our core campaign staff—Comms, Volunteers, Finances—all of them, and their immediate families. Dad and Katie and their four kids.

I take a deep breath and think about the quiet moment I shared upstairs with Carter.

Loyalty.

The crowd finally quiets, waiting.

"I just got off the phone with Steven Shallows a few minutes ago, and he's the last of my opponents to concede the race to us."

If I thought the crowd thundered before, they are positively howling now, deafening. I reach out and tap the home button on Carter's tablet to unlock it and punch in the familiar code. It's already queued to my acceptance speech, in a large enough font I can read it without picking it up or having to lean over it or squint.

Carter thinks of everything.

I smile, nodding, not waiting for the crowd to quiet this time, and hoping they settle themselves when I start to speak into the microphone.

"I'd like to congratulate my opponents on their races, and hope that we can all put that past us now and work together for *our* state. I'm not a governor for any one party—I'm a governor for the great state of Florida, and I represent *all* of its residents, even if they didn't vote for me."

I can tell this speech is going to take a while by how they're cheering. I let them have this time, because I don't want to appear ungrateful.

But I'm tired.

Oh, so tired, and I know I can't go to sleep yet. I also know Carter probably has a whole morning's worth of TV interviews, state and national, already scheduled for me for tomorrow.

"It's time to put partisan politics behind us. The time is now for us to put our state first. To put the citizens of our state first. To put its schoolchildren first. To put its environment first. We have a lot of hard work ahead of us, and I'm eager to get busy. We have teachers who should be paid far more than they are, and not just to make sure kids can take tests. They need the freedom to actually educate. I want to pay our teachers what they're worth, and draw even more of the best teachers to our state to teach our kids. I want Florida to be known as the best state to educate your child in, and the best state to be a teacher in. I want to eliminate all the useless testing and return our focus to educating our children.

"Our kids deserve clean air and clean water. Our health depends on it. Our tourism dollars depend on it. Our wildlife and agriculture and aquaculture depends on it. And I've made no secret that I'm coming after pork projects. No more eighty-thousand-dollar office renovations on the taxpayers' dime. You have spoken loud and clear and sent a message to both major parties that we are *done* messing around. We are *done* listening to the same-old same-old, we are *done* with their excuses as to why things can't get done, and we are *done* doing business as usual, with a wink and a nod behind closed doors.

"We have a lot of work to do. We can't immediately achieve everything we want to do. Changing our education system is going to take time. I want to focus immediately on working with utilities to harden our infrastructure against natural disasters. We can do a lot, but I need every one of you to put pressure on your local lawmakers. I need each and every one of you to get to know your local lawmakers by name. If they walk up to you in a grocery store, I want you to know who they are. I want you to show up at their offices and demand town halls and push them to work *with* me, with *all* of us, and not let partisan politics grind us to a halt. I want you to know their voting records and hold them accountable for their actions. Don't let them get away with business as usual.

"We've proven that both parties are imperfect. I'm not saying I'm perfect. I'm not saying I won't screw up. But I'm saying that you have spoken, and I'm listening. I'll keep listening. I won't turn a deaf ear to you just because the conversations are difficult or things I don't want to hear. But the only way we can move forward is if you make your voices loudly known to everyone who goes to Tallahassee. To everyone sitting in a county commission chamber. To everyone who sits on city commissions and councils, our local school boards, and even down to your HOA boards.

"We all have a voice. We all deserve to be heard. I'm a gun owner. I don't want to take your guns, but I think we can all agree we don't want kids getting mowed down at school, and there *has* to be a better way. The NRA and its foreign dollars are no longer welcomed in our state capitol."

Of all the points I brought up, that one get the loudest applause, and I twist off the cap from the bottle of water Carter puts in my hand and use the natural pause to take a drink. I let the cheers and applause spin out, which turns into raucous chants of *TAY-LOR! TAY-LOR!*

Let the network cameras eat *that* up. Of everything I say, that's the lightning rod that will draw press coverage, and I welcome it. I know we're live in at least Tampa, Orlando, Tallahassee, Jacksonville, and Miami. And MSNBC and CNN are likely carrying this live, too.

Fuck FNB, I don't care if they're showing it. Them or Fox.

No one thought I'd do it, but we did.

The underdog.

The third-party nobody.

The next governor of the great state of Florida.

I still have another paragraph to get through. "There are too many people for me to thank to remember them all." I glance to either side of me and list the major people who are there, list a few who aren't. I specifically call out Dad, Katie, and the kids.

Fuck you, Mom.

"I also want to thank all of you who voted for me, who knocked on doors, who called people, who drove people to polling places, who helped register voters. *You* did this. *You* are every bit as responsible for this, and don't think we're going to forget it. We ran a campaign without dark money. We ran a campaign without the NRA's help—in *opposition* to the NRA. I'm proud to be an *F-minus* candidate in the eyes of the NRA. We ran a campaign listening to *you*. We ran a campaign *for* you. *You* made this possible, and you have every right to celebrate this victory as *your* victory."

I go off-script here. "Last but not least, I want to thank Benchley Evans, for all his hard work behind the scenes, for believing in us and in our campaign, and for believing enough in our goals to support us. Also, because he's the father of your new Lieutenant Governor-Elect. And, of course, I want to thank your Lieutenant Governor-Elect, Susannah Evans."

I turn, clapping, and she's smiling, pink high in her cheeks as she steps forward and nods, waves.

"I also want to thank her husband, Carter Wilson, for letting me borrow her for the next four years—and hopefully four more after that." That gets me some laughs. "Oh, and for putting up with me all these years. Ever since we were roommates in college. He's my best friend, my adopted big brother, my chief of staff, and the first person who ever told me he believed in me and would vote for me. Thank you, Sir."

I turn and applaud. Carter's gaze is on me as he steps forward, holding his hand up, smiling and waving to the crowd. Only the three of us know I said *Sir* with a capital *S*.

"I'm going to turn the podium over to your lieutenant governor-elect, now. I know y'all would rather talk to her than me, anyway." That earns me another, slightly louder round of laughs.

I turn, giving her a little half bow from the waist. "Ma'am," I softly say as I wave her in.

I step back to stand at Carter's right side. When he slings his arm around me, like a casual bro hug, I drape mine over his shoulders and unfasten the button on my blazer so it doesn't pull weird.

Like that, we stand there and listen to *Her* speak.

I don't even care what she says.

All I care about is that, for this exact moment in time, we're here, *together*. The three of us. I care about making sure I get a copy of a picture of me and Carter standing there and listening to *Her* speak.

And I know that we are seriously going to kick some motherfucking ass.

CHAPTER FORTY-FOUR

It feels like forever before we can finally head upstairs again and everyone leaves. I'm exhausted, and not just physically.

I stand at the windows in our suite, looking out over downtown Tampa, and hope to hell I didn't make the biggest mistake of my life doing this. That it won't ruin *us*.

Susa walks up behind me and wraps her arms around my waist, resting her chin on my shoulder. I've shed the jacket again, and my shirt sleeves are rolled up, my tie loosened and the top button unfastened on my shirt.

"We did it," she says. She sounds so happy and contented in this moment that all my fears evaporate.

This.

Her.

She is why I did this, the *only* reason I did this. Yes, in the back of my mind I wanted this, but had it been up to me we wouldn't be standing here right now. The plan we have to follow so she can get elected on an Independent ticket. Otherwise, I'd be a mildly successful attorney in private practice leaving work at the office every Friday afternoon before heading home to jump in the pool or do…whatever.

Unless Carter and I had hooked up anyway, I'd also probably

be alone and miserable. Maybe not openly miserable, but definitely not happy.

Satisfied.

Content.

Only by giving up control to Her and Carter got us here, and don't think I don't know that.

"What time is it?" I ask, knowing we can't spend the whole night celebrating. There will be early morning news shows to prep for, interviews to give, and I need sleep so my first official statements don't make me look like a tool.

"Almost one," Carter says. I hear him walk over and feel him drape his arms around Susa and me from behind, pressing her firmly between us.

I reach back, around her, my fingers hooking through Carter's belt loops.

We stand like that for a couple of minutes, them knowing I need this time to breathe and reflect and compose myself.

They know me like no one else knows me.

It also hits me that I don't want to be anywhere else *but* right here, with these two people. It means I'll do whatever they ask of me, because they've proven over the years that they have my back and will do anything for me. They are ruthlessly on my side, and that's no exaggeration.

They love me, and I love them. I can't imagine life without them.

"What's tomorrow?" I finally ask.

"Wake-up call at five thirty," Carter says. "Need to have you over to WFLA by six thirty to prep for their interview, the Today interview, and the MSNBC appearance. I got them to agree to film the morning one and the afternoon one on top of each other instead of making you come back to sit for a live shot later. Then to WTSP at eight for them and theirs. Fox affiliate at ten, and then back here for CNN and FNB at noon. Lunch up here, a nap for you, then a shorter round of afternoon interviews, including another live NBC Evening News spot."

I grumble at that second-to-last one. "Can't cut those bastards at FNB from the list, huh?"

"We're not playing that game," Carter says. "We're not running a banana republic, and I don't give a shit how crappy they are, they're still getting press credentials. Pet, you need to prepare, too. You'll be with Dray tomorrow, and he'll be knocking at six. He's got your schedule and will take care of you, along with Elise.

"Kevin Markos can go fuck himself sideways," I mutter. "That fucking bastard."

I still haven't forgiven the guy for that interview. I don't give a rat's ass how well-respected the guy supposedly is—or was. His network is a shit-show, I think the man's a garbage fire, and I hope one day he has an epic on-air meltdown like Steve Carell's character in that movie, *Bruce Almighty.*

If he ever does, I'm buying it on DVD to watch on loop and show at parties.

If I thought Carter wouldn't kill me himself, I'd love to buy www.kevinmarkosisanasshole.com, .net, and .org.

Yes, I absolutely would.

No, I'm not petty at *allll.*

I'm pissed off, is what I am, that the man still has a fucking *job.*

Rationally, I know Carter is completely right.

Doesn't mean I can't hold on to revenge fantasies. Like maybe the guy being bound and gagged on his knees while I cane his ass and then piss all over him.

Then again, for all I know, the guy might get off on that kind of humiliation. Why else would he whore himself out to a network like Full News Broadcasting if he wasn't a goddamned emotional masochist?

Hell, when you can make Fox News look rational and

moderate, you're doing something wrong.

"Come to bed, boy," Carter playfully says.

It's that tone that finally draws all my attention. I let go of Carter's belt loops and turn around. Susa's looking up at me, and behind her, Carter's smoky gaze holds mine. "Does Sir have something in mind for tonight?" I ask.

"Sir wants to make a pet sandwich before we collapse for the night." He smiles. "I'll even let you choose which position you want, boy."

"Top." I smile back. "I know how much you love watching me."

The edges of his eyes crinkle in amusement. "I do love watching you fuck." He grabs Susa by the hair and tips her head back, so he can look her in the eyes. "I would suggest you go get ready, pet."

"Yes, Sir." She sounds like she's already dropping into subspace. He releases her and she hurries over to the bathroom.

Carter steps in close, pressing me against the window, his hands against it and caging my body. "Unless, of course, you'd rather have *me* in the middle tonight."

"Mmm." I grab his ass and pull him against me. Fucking Carter is a privilege I have to earn, not counting the night we frantic-fucked each other after the shooting. When it's offered as an option, I usually don't turn it down.

"But then how will you watch me fuck you, Sir?"

He nibbles on my lower lip. "Boy's choice tonight."

I grab his tie and hold him in place as I kiss him. "Then you know where I want you, Sir." Although from personal experience, I can tell you being in the middle is no hardship.

I release him and he smiles as he starts stripping on his way to the bathroom. "Change of plans, pet," he says as he disappears inside with her.

I quickly strip and throw the covers off the bed. As I'm sliding my cock inside Carter's ass a few minutes later, I'm staring at the old scars covering his back, scars that no longer look as fresh as they did that first night in the dorm, but scars that always remind me who this man is.

He wears his soul in his flesh.

I've never doubted Carter's loyalty to us because I've seen it in action in ways big and small.

I have the personal nightmares from that day in the school.

I have the memories of all the times he held me over the years as I cried, and all the things he's done for me.

Loyalty.

Devotion.

Carter is a bastard extraordinaire, yes, but he is a loyally devoted one to the two of us. I know he'd be a great father if that option wasn't closed to him, to us.

Part of me aches over that, but I lock it away, because I hate what-if rhetoricals that are meaningless. They're a waste of time, and we have precious little time to accomplish big things.

I'm waiting, sitting on the edge of the bed when Carter and Susa emerge from the bathroom. They're both naked. He walks over to me and I draw him into my arms, looking up at him. Susa stands behind him and wraps her arms around him. Like this, we take a quiet moment.

I can still remember those early days when I was starved for affection and physical contact of any kind. Skin hunger.

It's not a problem I have anymore.

"I want Christmas," I say. "We warned everyone Christmas would be iffy anyway, if I won. I want Christmas alone with both of you. Just lock ourselves in and not go anywhere or answer the phone or anything."

He plays with my hair and nods. "Done. Christmas Eve *and* Christmas."

Relief fills me and I lay my head against his chest, listening to his heart beating there. "Thank you, Sir."

We climb into bed and I take a moment to enjoy watching Carter fuck Susa, getting her primed before falling still so I can get into position. It's sexy to watch them fuck, just like I understand why Carter likes watching us fuck. We're not machines. Some nights, despite how Carter owns us, he knows one of us might not be in the mood. He's a bastard, not an asshole. On those nights, a show is sometimes put on for the third.

Sometimes, that show is for Carter, especially if his pain is bad.

And to be certain, with the campaign and stress, sometimes it's more a matter of we're falling into bed, whoever's together that particular night, and doing some power cuddling without any sex being involved. Carter's almost forty-five now, I'm thirty-seven, and Susa's thirty-five. We're not exactly old farts, but we're not horny college kids any longer.

We're reasonably responsible adults who were just given the keys to one of the largest states in our nation.

Oh, shit.

I must have frozen, because Carter looks back at me. "What's wrong, Owen?"

"I..." I swallow. "I'm the *governor*...of *Florida*."

He smiles. "You're just now realizing that?"

Susa giggles.

"No, I mean, seriously, I'm the fucking *governor* of *Florida*! Who the *hell* thought this was a good idea?"

He tips his head back enough he can kiss me, and that starts distracting me. "There's a motion on the floor, Senator Taylor. How about you fuck me—sorry, I mean, *Governor* Taylor, not Senator—and we can discuss this further after you, Representative Evans, and myself have had some orgasms?"

Susa's giggle lasts longer this time. "The representative at the bottom of the dogpile votes *aye*." she says.

I grab his hips and start fucking him, feeling a little sadistic satisfaction of my own when his eyes practically roll back in his head. Somehow, he starts moving, and we find a rhythm that also has Susa happily moaning below us.

By the time we've collapsed in a happy heap, I'm done for the night. We clean up and curl up in bed, tonight with me in the middle.

"I can't believe people voted for me," I mumble against his shoulder.

He chuckles. "That's because you're hot as fuck, *Governor*."

I groan.

Susa giggles.

God help us all, I'm now the governor of Florida.

CHAPTER FORTY-FIVE

Now

All of that was a really long and roundabout way of bringing us to today, here, right now, in my new office.

A new office we are in the process of breaking in the right way, if I do say so myself.

By "right way" I mean Carter's way.

The only way that matters to me, and to Susa.

I needed you to understand the path I took over the past sixteen years to get here, to understand the man—Carter, not me.

To understand none of this would have happened without *Him*. Susa helped a lot, to be sure, but she couldn't have gotten me elected without Carter's help, the force of nature that he is, to drive me across the finish line.

I am thirty-seven years old, and I am now the governor of the great state of Florida.

I still can't believe it.

Governor Owen Taylor.

Fuck you, Mom.

I haven't spoken to her in over ten years, haven't texted her. I'm sure eventually something will crop up about that, now that

I've won the election. Her whining to some willing ear that her ungrateful son has abandoned her.

I'll let Carter take care of that, if and when it does happen.

I was happy to have Dad, Katie, Susan, Danny, Dawn, and Paul there with me on stage on election night. They moved to Tampa eight years ago, and Dad was a volunteer for my campaigns for the state Senate and for governor. Katie and Dad know the three of us are close, but we sort of have a don't ask, don't tell vibe going on. Susan, Danny, Dawn, and Paul know Carter and Susa as Uncle Carter and Aunt Susa.

I was kind of hoping seeing them with me on TV would give my mother a stroke or something, but I'm not that lucky, I guess.

Maybe that can be our squad goal for the re-election.

I'll ask Carter. Something tells me he'll approve.

Some of Carter's sadism, and Susa's ruthlessness, have worn off on me over the years, I suppose. I've had to learn them as political survival skills.

Right now, my first term as Florida's governor is starting out on a sexy note.

My chief of staff has my gorgeous lieutenant governor bent over my new desk, her skirt rucked up around her waist, her torn panties stuffed in the front pocket of his slacks. He's just pinched and bitten the insides of her thighs since he can't risk spanking her in here right now. We don't need people hearing that, or, worse, capturing the audio on a cell phone.

Now I'm being waved in by Carter like a hockey line change.

He moves to the side, to make room for me. He keeps a fist in her hair to pin her to the desktop. "Arms, pet."

She dutifully moves them behind her back, and he uses his other hand to pin her wrists together.

He tips his head to receive a kiss from me. "This is your reward, boy," he softly says. "You worked your ass off and I'm so proud of you." He drops me a sexy wink. "Take what you want and don't worry about getting her off. I'll take care of her later tonight. She can wait."

Part of me is tempted to fuck her silly, and part of me wishes I could spend hours teasing and tormenting her.

Reality calling—there are people in the outer office, and we're on a very tight schedule today.

So I slowly swipe the head of my cock up and down through her folds, where she's wet and slick and more than ready for me thanks to Carter having conditioned her body every bit as well as he's conditioned mine, before I slowly sink inside her all the way to the root.

I have to bite back a needy moan. I want to savor this, remember it.

I know I'll be getting hard every time I sit here at my desk and think about this moment, right here.

I'm also sure Carter's dying to fuck me over this desk, too, but that will have to wait for another time.

Maybe tomorrow. Who knows?

Carter leans in and whispers in my ear. "Also, until further notice, you have unrestricted permission to fuck her whenever and however you safely can."

My hands caress her ass before settling on her hips, and I catch sight of the tattoo on the inside of my right wrist, the matching ones on Susa and Carter's wrists. "Thank you, Sir," I whisper.

"You're very welcome. In fact, I encourage you to find or make those kinds of opportunities as frequently as possible. Don't worry about making her come when you do. Grab her and fuck her."

"Yes, Sir." I don't even feel guilty about that. It's life with Carter, and he always balances the scales, in his own way.

He bends down and whispers something in her ear that results in a barely muffled moan from her in the affirmative.

Carter returns to me, kissing me. "She's under orders to submit to you, boy." He nips my lower lip, which is risky, because if we get going, we'll both look like we've barely survived a twelve-hour orgy. "Enjoy. That's my gift to you for all your hard work."

"For how long, Sir?" I'm struggling to take my time, but with her feeling so good, I know it won't take me long to blow.

"Until I say so." He grins. "I know it'll be difficult to safely find time. I don't want you to lose any opportunities just because I was on a conference call or something. At least for the next few months."

That was said loudly enough for her to hear, and another soft, needy moan rolls from her.

My strokes take on more force, faster. "Thank you, Sir. And Ma'am."

He nuzzles my ear. "Thank *you*, boy. Love you."

"Love you, too, Sir." I kiss him this time, my lips slanted over his as I quickly chase my orgasm and find it. Carter swallows my whines as I tighten and spill and fill her with me.

Just me, this time. Not second place, not having to clean her up later and taste him and me together inside her. Not having to pull out and painting her body with it because Carter wants to test my control or torture me for funsies.

All me, only me, completely inside her. It's a special treat he knows damn well how much I cherish. The man fucking *knows* me. He couldn't have given me a better gift if he'd tried.

I stay where I am, my cock softening inside her, my hands caressing her ass. I squeeze, enjoying the way she whimpers and rocks against me, and I love the way her flesh looks white before pink fills in my fingerprints on her flesh.

He'll get her later tonight, I'm sure. Especially considering the panty infraction. She'll be lucky if he doesn't tie her up, cane her, and then do orgasm torture on her for about an hour.

He doesn't break our kiss but he releases her wrists and hair and grabs my head, holding on as he deepens our kiss, controlling it now.

Always in control.

Finally, he lets me up for air and pulls her up and into our arms so we can both kiss her.

He pats her ass and then points at my bathroom. "Go straighten your hair and your clothes. Leave the bathroom door open. Don't you dare wipe up until you're back at your office, though, pet. Let's see how fast you can make it back there before Owen's dripping down your legs."

He grins.

The ire that flashes through her gaze as she starts to pull her skirt down says "fucking bastard," but she's more than smart enough not to add strokes to the panty punishment.

I love the glisten of moisture I see along the inside of the backs of her upper thighs when she turns, before her skirt comes down and blocks my view.

Marking my territory? Absolutely.

Nothing less than Carter has done to both of us throughout the years.

That's part of the fun.

He arches an eyebrow at her. "Hey, if *someone* hadn't worn panties without permission today, *someone* would have been allowed to come, and *someone* would be allowed to clean up now like a good girl. Bad girls get treated as such. Now get moving, pet, before I shove you out that office door looking like the governor just fucked you over his new desk."

A soft *meep* escapes her and she hurries over to my bathroom to straighten herself in the mirror there. Carter sends me to kneel where I was, back to *Primed.* My knees aren't happy about this, but I'm not going to argue.

We can't waste time right now. I'll get what I get from him in these few precious minutes the three of us have alone together. It's doubtful Susa will be able to sneak out to spend time with me tonight after the inauguration ball. I know Carter plans to ride back to the mansion with me after having the limo drop Susa off first. He'll explain he needs to go through tomorrow's schedule with me and will walk himself home later.

No one will question that.

Unfortunately, even with my townhouse so close, I can't justify living there, either. I'm supposed to be living in the mansion, and I'll do it. It'd look more suspicious if I went home all the time.

Carter already told us he'll arrange occasional rendezvous for us at the townhouse, but we'll have to be careful when and how we do them. It's too risky right now, when so much media attention is on us.

Patience. This has been a long-game, and will continue to be for a while.

We won't risk fooling around in the limo tonight, either. You never know where someone might have planted a camera, and we can't afford any self-inflicted scandals this early in our term.

Make no doubt about it—it's *our* term, not just mine. Susa and Carter are steering this ship. I'm merely trimming the sails when and how they tell me. It's obviously a successful formula, and I'm not about to do something stupid and fuck it all up now.

When Susa emerges from the bathroom, she brushes a kiss across my lips and one across Carter's before he lets her out and locks the door behind her, leaving us alone once again.

Carter picks up my office phone and dials someone.

"Dray? Carter. Listen…"

I kneel there and struggle not to burst out laughing as he gives Susa's COS very specific orders regarding her future wardrobe choices.

She is *not* going to be a happy camper when she returns to her office and learns about that.

Then again, she wouldn't be here either, if she minded the bastard extraordinaire's ways.

CHAPTER FORTY-SIX

I maintain my kneeling position on the floor of my new office despite my feet practically going numb, my knees screaming at me, the muscles of my back burning with the strain.

Primed.

Hence the name.

Carter lounges against the end of my desk and studies me.

Eventually, he speaks. "Why, exactly, do you think I've done all of this, Owen?"

I blink, surprised he's used my name while we're alone.

That means we're talking as equals.

I still don't break my position, although I allow myself to look up into his dark brown gaze.

"What do you mean, Sir?" I ask.

He sweeps his arms apart, indicating the office. "All of this. Us. *Her*. Getting you elected over the years, especially to *this* office. Why, exactly, do you think I've done all of this?"

Confusion fills me. I am not a stupid man, but this kind of circumspect talk when alone with me is not normal for him.

Usually when—especially lately—we're either working or fucking. Or sleeping.

More sleeping than fucking, as of late. I guess we're getting old.

"I don't know, Sir. I'm not even sure I'm following you."

He holds his hands out to me, palms up and wiggling his fingers, the meaning clear.

I unclasp my hands and reach for his. His fingers close around mine and he gently tugs, indicating for me to stand and come to him.

He apparently doesn't care I'm naked and that, despite the fact that I just fucked a load into Susa, my well-trained body has once again been anticipating...something. Anything. That it might mean suspicious stains on the front of his slacks when he spreads his legs and has me stand between them, my body comfortably pressed against his.

I drape my arms around his neck as Carter's hands skim down my back, to my ass—*his* ass—cupping it, pulling and holding me tightly against him when I don't immediately close the remaining distance between our hips.

I can feel his hard cock straining inside his boxers through the material of his slacks.

His tone remains soft, patient. "Why, Owen, do you think I married Susannah and put myself all-in, not just with the three of us as a relationship, but to get you elected, especially as governor?"

We've never really discussed this. I'd always assumed it was because he wanted to. That was Carter—what he wanted, he got. If he didn't want to do something, he had no problem saying no.

Nothing stood in his way when he wanted something.

Ever.

The way he'd married Susa. The way he'd gotten me elected, and, as a result, was himself now one of the most powerful men in Florida politics.

The way he'd got *me*.

"I-I don't know, Sir."

He smiles, and something in my heart tightly squeezes, but in a good way. This isn't the smile of my friend, or the bastard extraordinaire, or the sadist, or the adept politician, or even my COS handling official business.

This is the gentle smile of the loving husband, the smile he reserves for Susa in their most tender and private of moments when they're not Master and slave but two people in love with each other.

The same smile he also reserves for me in private.

His gaze searches mine for a long moment before he speaks again. "Because I knew from the day we met that the only way I'd ever get *you* was to make sure I took whatever it was that you loved and wanted most and held it so close to *me* that you couldn't help but come with it." He tips his head forward, the way he does with Susa, only I'm taller in this pairing.

His forehead presses against mine, warm, firm, and the look in his eyes takes my breath away. "Because I love you, dummy. I've been in love with you from the day we met. Somewhere between showing you how to fold your clothes and make your damn rack properly, I knew I was in love with you. That's not to say I don't love Susa, because you know I do. But I fell in love with her because *you* fell in love with her first. I knew if I'd just come right out and told you how I felt about you early on, even though I sensed then that you had a slave's heart, you probably would have bolted."

I don't know what to say, except…

He's absolutely right.

I nod a little, just enough to convey it but not enough to lose contact with him.

I like it when we stand like this, little pockets of private time where I feel like our souls are plugged in to each other.

"I did all this, Owen, because I have always loved *you*. I'm *in* love with you. I needed to climb inside your soul and find out what

393

made you tick so I could match you there and keep time with your heartbeat. Weave myself into your life in such a way that I knew you'd never make me leave."

Some people might feel played.

But I'm not some people, and this man has proven to me time and again that, yeah, ever since we first met he's always put me first in his life. Even to his own detriment.

The prickle of tears in my eyes catches me by surprise. Because like this, open and honest and bared to each other, one thing hits me hard and deep and, surprisingly enough, for the very first time.

Of course I love him—he's my friend. That I've known and admitted for years.

But he's more than that, really. *Much* more.

My *best* friend.

My right-hand man.

My lover.

My Master.

But...

We have said those three words to each other many times, but not exactly in this way. I'm an idiot that it took me this long to realize it.

I finally say it. "I'm *in* love with you, too." I don't know when, exactly, lust turned into love, and turned into being *in* love with him, but it's there, before me, in stark truth.

I'm *in* love with Carter, and have been for years. For sixteen years now.

On my ass, his thumbs slowly stroke up and down just behind my hips, and he's still looking into my eyes.

A soft, relieved sigh escapes him. "You don't hate me?"

"Carter, how could I ever hate a bastard extraordinaire like you?"

The left corner of his mouth quirks in a sexy smirk. Between us, I feel him grow harder. "You weren't bi when we met."

"I'm not bi now. You're absolutely right that this wouldn't have happened any other way."

His gaze softens. "I wish I could legally marry you, too."

This time, *I* kiss *him*. "Me, too. But this is okay."

"She's really happy, you know. She gets the two men she loves. She didn't have to choose between us, in the end. I can give her the Dominant stuff that you can't, and she can give you the things I can't."

He grinds against me a little, his meaning crystal clear what "things" Susa can give me that he can't, and I have to swallow back my needy moan as my well-conditioned body responds.

"Does she know?" I manage to ask. "That it was your plan the whole time?"

He shrugs. "I was open and honest with her in the beginning that I was bi and I thought you were hot. When discussing fantasies, I told her it'd be even hotter with the two of you together. Suggested it would actually make some things easier for all of us. She might have let it slip that she'd be more than a little okay with that. She was adorable, her face beet red as she blushed when she admitted it."

"Before or after you married her?"

"Before. Wouldn't have married her if she couldn't love you and have both of us." He grins. "Getting her hooked on dominating you once I saw how service-oriented you were took a little trial and error. Had to play armchair psychologist to find out how to coax her inner sadist into the light and convince her you actually enjoyed that. I knew she was capable of it. Just had to let her figure it out."

"How'd you know? That I would enjoy that?" We've been together for so long that it feels like we've always been together. It's difficult to remember there was a time in my life when I didn't even know them, much less have them in my life.

He gently squeezes my ass. "You open up when you get really drunk. On your twenty-first birthday, I showed you some gay BDSM porn and FemDom porn, and knew I'd hit the jackpot."

I wince, groaning. How could I ever forget that night? Although, to be honest, much of that night is an alcohol-induced black hole, and I really don't remember everything that happened. What lives in my memory are the days and weeks in the immediate aftermath. "That was *not* one of my finer moments."

He chokes back a roar of laughter. "You will *never* know how badly I wanted to go down on you that night when you whipped it out and started jerking off. Well, you know *now*. I actually considered doing it, except that wasn't consent and I might be a bastard, but I need consent to be one."

"So what if I'd said no to you that first night the three of us were together?"

"I didn't think you would. I was hoping I'd read you correctly and had you so horned up you didn't want to say no. Would have *really* fucked up my plans if you had, though." He smiles again. "I would have found a way to convince you. Eventually."

He leans in and nips my lower lip. "You're like a goddamned drug, Owen. I can't get enough of you. Even all these years later."

"Her father despises you. He told me he wishes she'd married me."

Now he grins. "I know. Ask me if I fucking *care*." He kisses me again, hard, deep, nothing gentle about it.

Possessive.

His fingers knead my ass and I have to fight the urge to grind hard against him and get myself off without permission.

Would *totally* be worth the sore ass later from the punishment caning I'd get, but I don't want to spooge his slacks and create questions if someone sees him before he can change.

We're well past the days of being able to take risks like that. This is serious, the big leagues, and I have a serious job to do.

We all do.

"I'm going to get his daughter elected governor," Carter continues when he ends that kiss. "*We* are. You and I. That's something he never could have done. He fucking tolerates me for that reason alone, if nothing else. Because he's a greedy sonofabitch and I have the political cachet now that he *wishes* he'd had in his heyday."

His smile fades. "She hates her daddy about as much as he hates me. She's better at hiding it, though. I mean, don't get me wrong, she loves Benchley, but she hates the politician he is. I might have tapped into that hatred to get her to enjoy giving you what you needed."

I frown. "She doesn't enjoy topping me?"

"Oh, she absolutely does *now*. She was uncertain, at first. The more you enjoyed it, the more she enjoyed it. A self-perpetuating cycle. I give her what she needs and wants as her Master, and you give her what she needs and wants as her slave." Another of those sexy, slow smiles curls his lips. "And you get to fuck the hottest lieutenant governor in the whole United States whenever you want."

"And you get the best of both worlds."

"Almost." He nibbles down the side of my throat, over my heart, and bites, hard. It won't show there. Ever since the campaign started, he's always been careful about my neck or leaving marks anywhere that might show. I'm supposed to be single.

Visible marks might trigger questions we don't want asked.

It makes my pulse race and my cock throb with need.

I miss the days when he'd bite down on my neck and mark me there, just at my collar line, a boner-inducing game where I always wondered if my collar was hiding marks and watching Carter evilly smile as he watched me do it. Especially if we were in court.

"Almost?" I gasp, barely able to think when he does that to me.

He releases his bite and kisses the mark. "Almost." He lifts his head and stares at me. "We *won*. We have this time to try to do what we talked about. I will work my fucking ass off to pull every string I can to make this happen for us. But there's something I need you to do for me now, and only you can do it."

"Sir?" It's instinctive and I can't help it.

He releases my ass and cups my face in his hands. "I need Owen right now, not boy."

I nod.

"You're in this for life, right? With me and with Susa?"

That's a silly question, but I nod again.

"I need you to *say* it, Owen. I need to *hear* you say it, right now."

Now I'm a little confused. He sounds intense in a different way than I'm used to hearing from him. "I'm in this for life, Sir. You know I am."

He arches an eyebrow at me.

"*Carter*, I'm in this for life, *with* you and Susa. Seriously. I wouldn't be here if I wasn't. Just try getting rid of me."

He releases my face and his right hand dips into the front pocket of his slacks. He pulls something out, then he takes my right hand and I feel him slip it onto my ring finger. It's warm from being close to his body. He brings my hand up to his lips and kisses the ring before his lips travel lower, settling over the tattoo on my right wrist.

When I am finally allowed to see the ring, my eyes blur with tears. "I ordered it the next day," he quietly says. "I couldn't find the nerve to give it to you, because I was afraid you'd tell me no. So I put it away to keep it safe. I decided I'd give it to you either the day I could marry you, or the day I got you sworn in as governor, whichever came first."

The blue and grey Doctor Who rings he'd shown me back in college, the night we'd celebrated my twenty-first birthday. That was one of the things I do remember from that night.

Gallifreyan writing scrolls through the center part and appears etched in grey against the dark blue ring.

Carter strokes my finger, where the band now sits, before looking up at me. "Inside it says, 'Mine in all lives.'"

I stare at the band, blinking, stunned.

It's perfect.

I look up again to meet his gaze. "I don't have one for you."

"You can pick whatever you want later. For me, and one for Susa to wear. For now, I'll tell you what I *really* want from you."

"What?"

The deep amber flecks in his brown eyes pick up the light, making it appear like tiny fires burn brightly there. "Susa wants to have a baby."

I frown. "You had a vasectomy. She knows that."

"I know that, and you know that, and *she* knows that. She started beating around the bush a couple of nights ago, wondering if my vasectomy could be reversed, or would I be open to talking to a doctor about IVF or...something. I told her we could discuss that in a few months, once we're all settled in our new jobs. I also told her that, for now, if she's serious about wanting a baby, she needs to stop taking her birth control pills because it can take a few months to fully leave the system. And I told her to take a couple of days to think about it."

Carter lets a beat pass before his next words. "She tossed the packages in the trash before we went to bed last night."

He lets that information sit and settle in my brain for a moment.

I gasp as I recall the sight of *my* semen coating the insides of her thighs before she'd left my office.

Carter said fucking her was my reward, his gift to me.

How he leaned in and whispered in my ear that I was such a good boy for him. That, until further notice, I could grab her, bend her over, and fuck her whenever I wanted and we had a safe opportunity to do so.

Encouraging me to find such opportunities as often as possible. No restrictions.

How he told me she is under orders to submit to me like that because I've been such a good boy for them.

He knows I wanted children, but one of the compromises I accepted by agreeing to be his was knowing that would no longer be in the stars for me.

When his true implication finally hits me, it literally takes my breath away.

I kiss him again, my hand threading through his hair to hold him in place and my lips crushing his.

"You *are* a fucking bastard extraordinaire," I mumble against his mouth.

He chuckles as we kiss. When his hands settle on my ass once more he squeezes, tightly and nearly painfully, and I *love* it. I lift my mouth from his so I can stare down into his sweet brown eyes.

His playful smile looks gorgeous, sexy. "I know. Ain't I, though?"

He is.

And I love him.

Really, *truly* love him.

THE END

The Governor Trilogy continues in *Lieutenant* (Book 2), *Chief* (Book 3), *Yes, Governor* (Book 4) and *Pet* (Book 5).

ABOUT THE AUTHOR

Author Lesli Richardson, who is better-known by her more prolific wild-child Tymber Dalton pen name, lives in the Tampa Bay region of Florida with her husband (aka "The World's Best Husband™") and too many pets. She writes a wide variety of heat levels and genres, from mainstream sci-fi all the way to scorching ménage.

The USA Today Bestselling Author (as Tymber), two-time EPIC award winner, and part-time Viking shield-maiden in training loves to shoot skeet and play D&D with her friends. She's also the bestselling author of over two hundred books and counting, including *The Reluctant Dom*, *The Great Turning*, *Cross Country Chaos*, the Bleacke Shifters series, The Great Turning series, the Suncoast Society series, the Love Slave for Two series, the Triple Trouble series, the Coffeeshop Coven series, the Good Will Ghost Hunting series, the Drunk Monkeys series, and many others.

She lives in her own little world, but it's okay—they all know her there.

She loves to hear from readers! Please feel free to drop by her website and sign up for her newsletter to keep abreast of the latest news, snarkage, and releases.

Honest reviews are always welcomed. They help with a book's visibility and can boost its placement on book retailer sites. Even a few lines about what you felt reading the book will help. Thank you so much, it's greatly appreciated!

Visit my website to sign up for my newsletter, find out what's coming soon, and more!

http://www.tymberdalton.com

Made in the USA
Columbia, SC
15 October 2021